CHAPTER 1

Breck Sanderson lay dying. There was no doubt. He'd never done it before, but it was obvious. His skin had taken on the furniture's dusty veneer, his eyes the ghostly drear. His breathing did little to fill his lungs, as the locked windows and drawn velvet drapes did little to dispel the room's dank, stale air. Even his voice, once booming and angry, was difficult to distinguish from rasps of air entering and leaving his crusted lips.

Yes, he thought, *soon all their prayers will be answered.*

But I'm not dead yet.

His home was the largest of eight along the perimeter of Sanderson Island—a fusion of granite resting in the northern reaches of Lake Champlain a mile off the Grand Isles shore across from St. Albans. On the second floor, lying on forest green silk sheets, he continued doing what he'd always done—dominate, control, and dispense a warped justice—two more people to bully, and one more person to bring into line—the latter, he would do from the grave.

"Get me Hank and leave the room again," he hissed to his sister, Bilba, the only other person in the room.

A shallow nod.

Hank Petrelli, a burly figure, entered and stood near the bed respectfully, meaty hands fidgeting.

Breck's eyes turned toward him. "Would a million bucks help you open that car repair garage you've wanted?"

Hank wanted to volley something snappy back, like usual, but he couldn't think of anything. The garage meant too much. Besides, no one was casual with Breck Sanderson, dying or not. "How?" he finally managed.

"Kill Bray Sanderson and the million's yours."

"Your nephew? The one in the newspapers? He's never been anything to us."

"Throw him off a cliff, drown him—stuff green olives up his nose."

"The garlic ones?"

"I'm dying here. No jokes. I want Bray Sanderson in hell right beside me. And you're gonna do it. Then you're off this rock. Thumbin' yer nose at them like they thumbed their nose at you. How's that for a joke?"

"How will I get the money?"

"Insurance. So it's got to look like an accident."

"Like always."

"With that garage you can swim in grease all day long. Never have to wash Sylvia's stockings again."

Hank chuckled. "Oh, you know about that. It's a code. Couples have codes."

"Code? Enough of your games. Do we have a deal or not?"

After another moment's thought, he grabbed Breck's dying hand. "Deal."

"Good. Tell no one about this. When Bray takes that long whiff of green olives you want no witnesses—and no one protecting him." Breck wheezed a breath. "Send Teri in. After her, I die in peace."

"Can I say something, boss?"

"It better be goodbye."

Hank stammered slightly but recovered. "You're a gruff old weed, but you always been good to me. Thanks."

"You did your job—for nearly twenty-five years." Breck's granite features softened slightly. "You picked up where your dad left off—when he died."

"I was only fourteen. Little more than a kid."

"Your dad was like a son. Quick—with a knife and most everything else."

"He trained me to be quick, too. To go into the family business since I could walk."

"But you were just too good to be freelance. You've been family, what, six years?"

"Marrying that idiot niece of yours was a small price to pay to join *your* business."

"And you're going to pay 'til you die if you don't earn this million now."

To my wife whom I love more than breath.

BLOOD MONEY

WILLIAM KRITLOW

THOMAS NELSON PUBLISHERS
Nashville • Atlanta • London • Vancouver
Printed in the United States of America

Published in Nashville, Tennessee, by Thomas Nelson, Inc., Publishers, and distributed in Canada by Word Communications, Ltd., Richmond, British Columbia.

Library of Congress Cataloging-in-Publication Data

Blood money : a novel / William Kritlow.
    p. cm.
ISBN 0-7852-8027-8
I. Title. II. Series: Kritlow, William. Lake Champlain mysteries ; bk. 3.
PS3561.R567B57 1997
813'.54—dc21   96–399758
                                                                                CIP

Printed in the United States of America.

1 2 3 4 5 6 — 02 01 00 99 98 97

BLOOD MONEY

Hank licked his lips as if already savoring the payoff. "I'll get Teri."

Breck went on to savor the moment or two alone. Alone was best. But it ended abruptly when his grandniece stepped in. Though on the lowest rung of the ladder, at thirty-one she walked with purpose, her deep green eyes gathering a sparkle from stray light in the dreary room, her ancestral black hair glistening from it.

"You want me, Uncle Breck?"

"Close the door—tightly."

"Yes, Uncle Breck." Only after she'd heard the latch click firmly did she turn back to him.

Breck's voice was little more than a snake's hiss. "You're not to breathe a word of what I'm about to tell you to do. Is that clear?"

"Not a word. Yes, Uncle Breck." Her heart both thundered and whimpered within her.

"How'd you like to buy all the guns you want?"

"I can do that now."

"How'd you like to do that from a house off the island?"

Her eyes became intense.

"There's more. How'd you like to show the rest of them that you're as good as they are—maybe even better? Especially that bean-counter brother of yours. You beat him good on the SATs, and he's got the bigger house. And how would you like to do all that with a million in the bank and from somewhere off this rock?"

"How?" she asked.

"I want you to kill Bray Sanderson."

She gasped.

Although his expression remained a death mask, he enjoyed the sound of it.

Less than five minutes later it was done. Breck's set up for revenge was complete. Every member of Bray's immediate family—including his brother—would be out to kill him. Breck was certain that at least one of them would succeed. Feebly, as if with his last breath, Breck laughed. And then he laughed again. If only he could be there when the family member who actually did kill

Bray found out that the promised million dollars would be going into a continuing trust to maintain his, Breck Sanderson's, grave.

Bray Sanderson, rooted deeply in his midforties, black hair dusted lightly at the temples with gray, sat in his back garden, his right leg propped up on a pillow. Having been released from the medical center the afternoon before, his tripod cane leaned against the wrought-iron chair. And a few cottages down, the midmorning sun glistened off the rippling blue of Lake Champlain. His eyes had every reason to be weary, but, instead, they sparkled with life. He was studying a check. One for over eight thousand dollars.

It was the first, and he'd be getting one every month for the rest of his life.

He was rich. But more importantly, he was as free as money could make him.

Had his leg not hurt so badly he would have jumped up and cheered. But it did hurt, so he merely smiled and allowed a restful sense of well-being to take root.

Bray heard the back gate squeal open behind him.

"Hi," came a familiar greeting. "Being a man of leisure obviously agrees with you. How's the leg?"

Win Brady held the springloaded gate for Ginger, his fiancée, and stepped in. Win, in his early thirties, was tall and athletic-looking with handsome, angular features. His only compromise to age was his thinning, sandy hair. Ginger Glasgow followed him in. A tall, Nordic beauty with piercing blue eyes and short, naturally blonde hair, she, like Bray, was a cop. "No matter how it feels, you look relaxed," she said cheerfully.

"It hurts," Bray called back stiffly over his shoulder, "Doctor said I was lucky it wasn't blown off altogether."

"The Lord just wanted you on two feet," Win smiled, "so when he catches you, you wouldn't be able to cry foul. When do you start therapy?"

"Tomorrow. I needed rest today."

They were both alongside of him now, and Ginger looked down at the check. "Where'd that come from?"

"I'm rich."

"Insurance settlement?"

"This what you were telling me about in the hospital?" Win asked.

Ginger sat on a nearby chair. "That inheritance? Couple more of these and you'll be able to buy this lake. How does the inheritance work again?"

"It's actually kind of interesting," Win began. "When Bray's uncle—Breck, wasn't it?—died, the proceeds from a million-dollar life insurance policy went into an interest-bearing trust. Bray gets the interest in monthly payments for the rest of his life."

"Not bad," Ginger cooed. "You could retire. Or—maybe start your own detective agency and hire me as your first detective."

"Maybe I'd just like to go to Florida," Bray said.

"You'd miss the winters," Win inserted.

"Like I'd miss a hangnail."

"You'd miss Pam," Ginger stated.

"I'd miss Pam," Bray said gravely. "She came by this morning and made me breakfast—so I wouldn't have to move around. Why'd you guys have to go and screw that up."

"There's a simple solution," Win told him.

In the middle of their budding relationship, Pamela had come to know Jesus Christ as her personal Lord and Savior. Since Bray hadn't, the relationship had slipped into limbo. But Pam still loved him and with him laid up like this she had to help out.

"Yeah, right," Bray groaned, massaging his leg in response to a fresh stab of pain.

Ginger's brows furled as if she'd just thought of something. "But who gets the million when you die?"

Bray sighed frustratedly. "You're not going to start that, too."

"Did somebody start something?" Ginger asked, befuddled.

"Your buddy, Win, there."

Ginger eyed Win. "Our minds work alike."

"Win's mind doesn't work like anybody's," Bray said. "And yours hardly works at all. You guys are playing good idiot, bad idiot."

"Us?"

"Win's got this theory—"

"You do?" Ginger gasped.

"Oh, stop it. Both of you." Then he turned to Win. "You're talking about my family."

"What theory?" Ginger asked, bewildered.

"I said stop it," Bray told her.

"Really, I don't know about any theory," Ginger said.

"It's a good theory," Win defended.

"It's a sick theory. They're my family, Win. My family."

"But," Win began, "you don't get along with your family."

"Only Breck—there were the usual family battles with the others—and I parted company with my folks—but it was mostly Breck. He hated me and, just to balance the scales, I hated him back."

Ginger's brows dipped even further. "Somebody who hates you makes it possible for someone else to get rich when you die?" she said. "And you're not suspicious? Bray, you don't trust anybody."

"All families feud," Bray said. "Darn few hire hitmen."

"Bray's right," Win said. "We've just been around too many murderers and druggies lately. We're the ones being too suspicious."

Bray studied Win for a long moment. "Talking to you is like playing chess. You just made a move—you want me off guard. Then you're going to try to convince me that a member of my own family wants to knock me off—just for money."

"It's possible."

"Anything's possible. But not this—not this."

"Bray," Ginger said with warm concern, "we just want you to be cautious."

"I don't have to be cautious," Bray stated, flatly. Then an even darker cloud seemed to settle over him. "You'll never know how much I've blamed them for over the years. But it wasn't them. It was me. Granted, Breck was domineering, and nobody could hold a grudge like he could. But I was no prize." He took a deep breath as if to prop himself up. "I was about three months from coming home from Vietnam when my mom and dad died. Their boat exploded—just like mine." His eyes came up to Win's and Win caught a glimpse of the pain. "I got the usual notification, and with it orders to go back for the funeral," Bray went on. "There was even some talk about getting me an early out since

I was probably so devastated. I refused to go back. I was so angry at them, I even refused to come back for their funeral. *From Vietnam*. No wonder they hated me. What kind of son is that? Breck was bad—but I was worse."

"Call them," Ginger said. "Explain."

"No—not yet," said their friend, his eyes off toward the lake.

"When he's ready," Win said.

"I may never be that ready. I did what I did. There are prices to be paid."

"Maybe they'll contact you," Ginger suggested gently.

"We'll see," said Bray, his tone resolute.

Win studied his friend. Only a month ago Win would have described the Burlington detective as an energetic, smart, but crusty curmudgeon. Not now. Bray had softened. Probably the explosion had accomplished some of it. Bray had risked his life over a month ago to save a boatload of party-goers and in doing so had been caught in a horrendous blast. He'd survived severe internal injury and was still shackled by a bad leg. Lying in a sterile hospital bed contemplating his guilt undoubtedly had softened him, too. But Win knew there was more. Everybody needs family—the emotional support they give, that sense of belonging, that sense of value and worth that being connected to others provides. It's difficult to find it anywhere else. Even in church. Family seems somehow obligated to provide it even at the worst of times.

Win was ten when his mother died. His family died with her; his wealthy father, even though a strong Christian, all but abandoned him emotionally. Overnight, Win found himself on his own. He couldn't deny that one of the reasons he wanted to marry Ginger and adopt Chad, Ginger's son, was to recapture that sense of family again.

Bray knew what Win knew, probably missed what he missed. Up until now, a man he hated stood in the way of reclaiming it. Now it was his own guilt. No wonder that crusty exterior was dissolving right before Win's eyes.

Bray suddenly smiled as if tucking all the dark clouds on some other horizon. "I can't dwell on all that. Things are really looking up for me," Bray said, waving the check.

"And after a few months of therapy on that leg you'll even be able to get rid of this," Win said, patting the cane.

"I think I'll keep that around for a while. Pam fixing me break-fast is too much to just give up."

"Well, we have some errands to run," Ginger said, laughing. "There's a wedding coming up, you know."

A few minutes later Win and Ginger were back in Win's sky blue 1954 Chevy. "More to pray for," Win said as he fired up the ignition.

"I know what I'm praying for."

"And what's that?"

"That all Bray's talk about getting together with those people just fades away—just heads for the bottom of the lake like a rock."

Win just shook his head. "You can't deny God's brought Bray right here, and it seems like the next step—"

"You have no idea what God will do next."

Win had to nod. "You're right there."

"Those people could have contacted him over the years. No uncle is that much in control. It's not all Bray."

"Phones do go both ways."

"When you first suggested Bray might be in danger I thought you were nuts—now I'm not so sure. The island's up north?"

"Between the Isles and St. Albans. They live and work on it. Bray and I had long conversations about that."

"For how long? Forty, fifty years?"

"No. Couple hours—in the hospital."

"No," Ginger's groaned. "Seriously, how long have they lived on the island?"

"Forty, fifty years."

Win pulled the Chevy out onto the road and headed toward the village.

"What kind of people live like that? What do they do, any-way?"

"Bray doesn't know. Nobody does. To them secrecy really matters. I know—I can't believe it either. Bray thinks it's invest-ments and Breck came up with some kind of mysterious for-mula."

"I bet they're all bonkers."

"You do?"

"Of course. Wouldn't you be? I know I'd be. All that time holed up on an island keeping some huge secret under some megalomaniac's thumb. It'd make me crazier'n a loon." She pointed toward the approaching bank. "I need to deposit my check."

Win eased the Chevy in that direction.

"You talk about the next step," Ginger continued. "The next step should be cutting his phone line and screening his mail."

"You think that would do it?"

"I just don't like it. The more I think about it the more I think you're right. That inheritance was set up that way to throw Bray off guard and to pay off a killer. I know it as sure as I'm sitting here."

Win pulled up in front of the bank, set the emergency brake, and killed the engine. Then he eyed Ginger for a long moment. "Well," he finally said, "I have this feeling we're going to find out one way or another pretty soon."

CHAPTER 2

It had been nearly a month since Teri had seen that ashen face, those eyes with death radiating from deep within them—black suns. A week since she'd agreed to murder her Uncle Bray. But Breck was dying. He couldn't hold her responsible for agreeing—couldn't come back from the grave to punish her if she didn't do it. And what would be the result if she didn't? Bray would stay alive—not a bad thing. She'd be out a million dollars. But she'd already made at least that and would again. But having to stay on the island? That was a bad thing. A horrible thing. But was avoiding a horrible thing worth killing someone?

It was a curious question. To be responsible for someone's death. She never thought she could be—voluntarily. And yet the idea wasn't as repugnant as she thought it should be. Shouldn't she be running from it? Cringing when thinking about it?

Instead she found herself planning it. She considered the cliffs and the deep lake. She wondered what a body might look like impaled on a sharp boulder after a long fall. Yuck! But, again, she didn't recoil from within.

That scared her.

Maybe she could use her guns. No. Not her. She was too good with them—no one would ever believe it was an accident.

She had gone so far as to begin writing down possible alternatives when she stopped and realized what she was doing. She was planning to murder someone.

Compromising herself for a dead patriarch she had despised, a million dollars she didn't need—and a ticket off the rock. That last one caused her to keep the notion alive. She decided to seek help.

"Dad?" She found him on the little island in his office, a room whose walnut paneling hid the chiseled rock walls. The little island was just that. It was about thirty yards from the big island on which the family lived and was where the Sandersons conducted business.

"Teri," he smiled. Walnut hair, salted at the temples, no one could smile like Bray Sanderson's brother, Phil—as if his teeth were coated with phosphorus. "I was hoping you'd stop by."

"You were?" she asked suspiciously. "Why?"

"Oh," he stumbled. "No reason. Now, sit," he said, offering a chair with a sweep of an executive hand, "we'll talk."

After sitting with expectant eyes, she finally spoke. "Can you imagine what it would be like to kill someone—on purpose?"

"Nope. Can't." He shook his head. "I *can* imagine what it would be like to want to." He laughed at this. "How's your work coming? You're project manager on that new piece of equipment Bilba ordered. Someday she'll learn to go through me when she spends that kind of money. But how's it going anyway?"

"Okay," she said, standing.

"Good, good," he said brusquely. "Well, I'm a little busy now, but you stop by anytime." Then, with an executive flurry he ushered her out of his office.

Unsatisfied and feeling very much alone—a feeling so common she had trouble discerning it, Teri returned to her house, picked up a pencil and began planning again.

☎ ₒ

Randy Michelson felt terribly lost. A soul thing. Nearing thirty, good-looking. Having spent four years in the Marines, he thought he should be on the road to some kind of career by now. But he wasn't. He'd gotten the guard job on Sanderson Island nearly six months ago through a Marine buddy and at first was excited. The money was incredible, the hours okay, and he lived on the island, so he saved even more. He didn't know what they did there. Only a few knew. But they were so secretive it couldn't be legal. At first that didn't bother him, but lately he'd begun feeling uneasy about it.

So, although he hadn't planned on visiting the church on his afternoon off, he wasn't surprised to find himself knocking on the office door in back.

Seconds later the door opened. An older man with smiling eyes, maybe in his sixties, greeted him. "Hello, young man, can I help you?"

"I don't know," he said, his feeling of need dissolving as the door opened.

"Sure you do. Come in. I'm Laz Spreckles, pastor here. This is Mel Flowers. Mel's church is on the Grand Isles too. A bit south of here."

"I'm interrupting."

"Naw. Just figure you're meeting with two pastors instead of one. A two-fer sale."

Randy chuckled uncomfortably but stepped inside.

A man in his forties, Mel Flowers, stepped up. He too smiled like a preacher. Dark-headed, a little thick around the middle, the man thrust out a hand to Randy. "Very glad you came."

"Randy Michelson."

"Well, Randy, what can we do for you?" Laz asked, leading him into the small sanctuary.

An hour later Randy left more troubled than when he arrived. Flowers did most of the talking to him. A penetrating guy, Randy thought. Said some important things. But Randy knew he'd never return. They wanted too much from him.

"I hate these meetings," Teri Sanderson groaned, the clear summer morning shining in her midnight hair and green eyes. Her brother, Tommy, was a year older, also black-headed and a good six inches taller. They walked across the island's well-manicured common area, just missing Uncle Breck's grave. "And I hate where they put that grave most of all."

The grave lay at the center of the commons, surrounded by pink and crimson impatiens, shaded by a palm tree whose spreading fronds twenty feet above their heads reminded everyone of a bad haircut. Teri and Tommy avoided looking at it.

"And that vase of fresh flowers—Bilba's going overboard," she said. "How did she find something to like about him and we never could?"

"She's just grateful."

"To him? She's never grateful to me."

"But you never do anything for her."

"Because she's a witch."

Tommy shook his head frustratedly. Computers never displayed logic as fuzzy as that. "You just hate losing."

"And you like it?"

"I don't lose. I know the system."

"Know it or not, this meeting might actually accomplish something positive. It might get us off this rock."

"Doubtful."

"Everybody wants it."

"Not enough," Tommy smiled smugly.

After a long silence, Teri asked, "You get your stuff moved?"

"Yesterday—took the whole day just to move next door. The guys were sweating like pigs. Technology can be heavy. And delicate."

"Movin' on up," Teri sang. "I'll move tomorrow. The guns I'll move myself."

"Well," he said, the smug smile getting more so, "you're the last one, then."

They entered Breck's house—or mansion, as they called it. Now, the mansion was Bilba's, Breck's younger sister. At seventy-three, since her energy was waning, she'd done no redecorating in the two weeks since Breck's death. The place still resembled, as it had since it was built, a dreary medieval chateau—lots of wood, more leather, dark wall art everywhere, many coats of arms and medieval weaponry. A tapestry of St. George killing the dragon hung in the rec room—the only place one might consider laughing. Breck had always identified himself with St. George. Others often identified him with the dragon. No lights illuminated it.

"Her stuff still downstairs?" Teri asked idly.

"She didn't have much. All that lace—Bilba's fairyland—butterflies and fairies—fluttering outside and inside her head."

"And it's all cheap. She's got to be saving for something big," Teri said, as if imparting important information. "That's another reason why they'll vote to get us out of here."

"You'll see."

They went to the pantry in the kitchen. After closing the door behind them, they pushed a can of tomato paste. A can of olives above the door lit and dinged. A moment later the door unlatched and swung open onto the lower level—a cavern. Hank met them. "You're the last."

"Like always," Teri said.

The conference room was just an extension of the cavern. Unpaneled, the rocks still showed drill and chisel marks. But it wasn't all rock. High on the walls ringing the room were monitors revealing every important spot on the island, above and below the surface.

Bilba, a thin crow of a woman, sat in Breck's old chair at the head of the mahogany table. As Teri and Tommy entered, she slammed a cherry wood gavel on the table.

Phil Sanderson, Teri and Tommy's father, jumped, startled. "Don't do that," he retorted. "Why don't you let me chair this thing?"

Bilba only frowned.

Sylvia Sanderson-Petrelli, Hank's much older wife, leaned far back in her leather chair. A woman of large middle and bosom, she used her girth to rest folded arms. Her eyes narrowed. "Let's get on with it. We all know the agenda."

"Breck," Bilba said, pointing the gavel at Sylvia, "God rest his soul, did things right and I will too. That way everything happens as it should. Which is why this change may not be good."

"Sure it's good," Sylvia fired back. "And Breck was no saint."

"Not by a long shot," Teri muttered.

"Well, okay," Bilba said, thoughtfully. "As we're all aware—"

"Painfully aware," Sylvia echoed.

"I have to admit," Bilba said, "I, too, would like to see change. But I have no quarrel with Breck—never with Breck."

"I do on this anyway," Phil said flatly.

Bilba went on. "The way Breck set up the distribution of—well—proceeds from our little enterprise is that they can only be spent from a central account that is overseen by Tommy, our accountant."

Tommy nodded.

Teri groaned.

"And if we're living off the island, nothing, not even gas, is paid."

"We're prisoners," Sylvia stated. "He's got a headlock on us from that grave."

Hank laughed. "It'd take more'n a headlock to hold you down."

"Shut up," Sylvia told him.

"So," Bilba went on. "Phil, Sylvia, and I are now the ruling council, and the time's come to make some changes." She turned to Phil. "I've pretty much decided to vote for it."

"Good," Phil said.

Tommy raised a respectful finger. Bilba nodded toward him. "I know we all want to make the island just a workplace. We'd have freedom to live, and I mean *live*, other places."

"So let's get on with it," Phil said curtly.

"I have more, Dad."

"Then say it," Phil snapped. "Time's an enemy."

Tommy's expression remained steady. "Just remember, Breck set up that payment method for security."

"He always thought of everything," Bilba said admiringly.

"He was a megalomaniac," Hank said tempering it with a laugh. "He loved symbolism, and that palm tree's a symbol of us still in the palms of his hands."

"Or havin' em crushing our Adam's apples," Teri whispered.

"You don't have one," her father snapped.

"Shut up," Sylvia fired at Hank. "Symbolism. What do you know?"

Tommy continued. "It's not that he enjoyed power, he was just a good businessman. He knew that if we displayed our wealth, neighbors, friends, and particularly the authorities, would want to know how much money we had and how we made it. We could be the subject of a crusade."

"I don't plan to live lavishly—a little elbow room would be nice," Bilba said.

"You? Lavish? That'd be somethin' to see," Hank laughed.

"Hubby, dear," Sylvia hissed, "you're not listening to me."

"Have I ever?" Hank laughed again.

"You wouldn't live lavishly, Aunt Bilba," Tommy said. "None of us would—at first—not until we really wanted something expensive and knew we had the money to get it." His eyes touched everyone's for emphasis. "Look. We enjoy spending the money we have. Our homes are small but crammed with the things we love. Do we trust each other not to spend?"

Faces studied faces.

Sylvia straightened, doom etched all over hers. "So we stay prisoners? I'll go nuts. Absolutely nuts."

Hank patted his wife's hand. "Then nothing'll change."

Sylvia turned fiery eyes on her husband and slapped his hand away. "I've just about had it with . . ."

Bilba clapped the gavel. "That's enough, you two."

Sylvia turned to Bilba and recrossed her arms over her bosom. "But he's really being nasty. You heard it. Nasty."

"You're not a child," Bilba responded. "Don't whine."

"But he's not being nice to me," Sylvia continued. "Breck would always make him be nice to me. Make him, Bilba."

"Be nice to her," Bilba admonished dryly.

"He won't. I know he won't," whined Sylvia.

"Then—just leave. Divorce him. Leave the island." Phil told Sylvia.

"You'd like that. Then you could divide up all I have. Boy, would you like that."

"Sounds good to me," Teri quipped.

"And why should I leave?" Sylvia barked. "I'm the one who's family."

"But he's the one who works," Phil snarled back.

"I gotta be honest," Hank said, ignoring the fight. "Tommy's right. I want to spend what I make. And out there I could have my high-tech repair garage."

Sylvia retorted, "With neon signs—'*Look, I'm rich—I'm rich.*'"

"I am."

"Because of me—only because of me."

The gavel came down even harder. "Breck wouldn't tolerate bickering and neither will I," Bilba told them.

Hank backed off. "Phil would spend his. Who wouldn't? It might as well be taxes—and who wants to pay those."

"But I *can't* be a prisoner anymore, and I won't," Sylvia said, slamming her hand flat on the table—a rifle shot. No one paid any attention. They were studying one another—assessing their options.

Hank turned toward Tommy, "Tommy'd buy every computer he could get a hand on, wouldn't ya there, hacker."

"I'm not a hacker," Tommy said, his voice calm. "I play by the rules. But there's no denying I couldn't help myself. This island's my only refuge." A contradictory thought rose from somewhere deep within Tommy. A secret longing that took him back to a college acquaintance—Carlos. Carlos' graduation hopes rested on passing a particular computer class. If he didn't graduate he'd disgrace his father, the governor, nearly king, of Aguilar, a small island country off the coast of Venezuela. Tommy helped, and Carlos treated him to a week in Aguilar. Tommy found it a tropical paradise. The beaches and people were wonderful, and, if they had to, they could live entirely off what the island and sea provided. Now that he was committing his life to the family island, the fact that he preferred to spend his life on Aguilar came rushing up.

Tommy was yanked back to reality by Hank thrusting an angry finger at Phil. "And you'd buy a stretch limo and a newspaper and an office building and make every office your own—just to look like you were somebody. Power mad—just give me power."

"I resent that," Phil declared.

"You're just an Iacocca-wannabe—"

"John Gotti, more like it," Sylvia muttered, but Phil heard her and fired a disdainful look her way. Sylvia wasn't deterred. She grabbed Hank by the arm and pulled him back, "Now just shut up."

Hank yanked his arm away. "If you tell me to shut up one more time . . ."

"I just want to live a normal life," Teri said, her voice somehow rising above Hank's.

"Normal's what happens," Tommy stated flatly. "And right now all this is happening."

"No. Normal is where I'm not the last one in line for everything. I scored so much higher than you on the SATs—I've got you beat intellectually six ways from Sunday and because you're a stinking year older—"

Phil straightened. "I think we need to revisit this issue."

"We're still prisoners!" Sylvia exploded. "You know how long I've lived on this island? I don't even know how long."

"And they were wonderful years under Breck," Bilba said.

"And you're going to live here a whole lot longer," Hank said.

That did it. Sylvia launched her massive girth to her feet, her chair slamming into the rock wall. Whipping Hank away from the table, she clapped her fat hands around his throat.

Instantly his eyes bulged and his feet kicked. But Sylvia was a woman possessed. "I can't take it. I can't. I won't. I can't." She chanted with arms locked and her hands closing more and more tightly around Hank's neck.

Phil leaped onto the table and grabbed Sylvia by the shoulders and pulled her back. But Sylvia outweighed Phil and wouldn't be physically coerced into releasing Hank.

Bilba pounded the gavel—hard, then harder, the surface of the table taking a beating. "Stop this. You can't kill him here. Not in front of the children."

"Sylvia—please," Phil said, using all the muscle he had.

Hank managed a few intelligible syllables. "Shtop. I'm schoking. I'll wash shyer shtockings."

That obviously mattered to Sylvia for she released him. Phil fell backwards, actually rolling off the table, while Hank fell back into his chair gasping for breath. Sylvia sat down. "I'll expect you to do it right after the meeting."

His breathing coarse, much like a leaky bellows, Hank nodded.

Bilba stopped banging the gavel and just stared at Hank and Sylvia both. "Can't you argue on your own time? Now, there's been a motion made to turn the underground shooting range into a bowling alley."

Teri stiffened. "But that's my range. I paid for that."

"You'd be compensated," Bilba said maternally. "At used prices, of course."

"But I use that range every day," Teri persisted. "I shoot."

Tommy faced her. "But no one else does."

"But a bowling alley?" Teri whined. "You going to import a lounge singer, hire some guys who smell bad?"

"You were lookin' at me when you said that," Hank exploded, his throat recovering. "She was looking at me."

"I'll do it again, Hank," Sylvia raged. "I really will. Shut up!"

Phil, having regained his chair, his hair pushed back in a semblance of order, told his daughter in condescending calm, "Space is a premium, so we're going to make it something we can all enjoy."

"But no one bowls."

"We'll learn," Tommy said, keenly aware of an impending triumph.

"You're going to take away the only thing I enjoy—"

"It's not the only thing," her father said. "You swim, boat—"

"The *only* thing I enjoy—" she reiterated forcefully. "And on the same day you're also dooming me to stay on this rock the rest of my life?"

"And what's wrong with that?" Her father injected.

"You can go anytime," Tommy said icily.

"And leave everything I've worked for?" she screamed.

Bilba slammed the gavel. "Calm yourself, child."

"How can you do this?" Teri cried.

"We want to," said Sylvia, "and majority rules."

"But I'm a person, too."

Hank laughed. "Getting a little dramatic there."

"I have a right to at least enjoy something."

"No more than the rest of us," Tommy said, eyes icy again.

Teri suddenly stopped. She took a deep breath. Something she hadn't thought about in nearly a week had occurred to her. "There's a way off this rock," Teri said. "There's a way."

"What's that mean?" Bilba asked. "What did she mean by that? She meant something. What?"

"Ask *her*," Sylvia told her.

"What did you mean by that? If I were Breck you wouldn't dare not tell me. Tell me."

Teri said no more. She merely folded her arms across her chest and fell back in her chair.

"What do you mean by that?" Bilba asked, her voice flustered. "That sounded ominously rebellious. We'll have no rebellion here. No mutiny. Nothing like that."

Teri looked at her with steel eyes.

"Phillip," Bilba said, her gavel pointing at her nephew. "She's your daughter. Your responsibility—"

"I am not his responsibility," Teri insisted. "I am my own responsibility. I am way over twenty-one. I am an adult. I think. I am a person. I'm not the whipping girl here. And I'll do what I please."

"You'll do only what is allowed," Bilba said, her voice sounding more like Breck's with each word—threatening, savage, unyielding, capable of immense violence. The voice must not have been hereditary because it couldn't have been born in that frail wire of a woman who loved lace and butterflies.

"There's a way," Teri whispered, just loud enough for everyone to hear.

Bilba lost it. "You would have obeyed Breck and you will obey—" The gavel came down with an incredible impact and when it hit, the handle broke. The head bounced into the air, spun a few times and came down on Sylvia's head. She leaped up, having been watching Teri at the time. "It broke," Bilba said, eyes focused on the jagged end. "It's not supposed to do that. It never broke for Breck. Why did it break like that? Defective, that's what it is. SuperGlue. I bet that would hold it. SuperGlue. Anybody have any?"

"I got some," Hank said, taking the gavel's head from Sylvia, who was staring at everyone at the table in turn.

"We'll need this fixed," Bilba said. "We can't hold a meeting without a gavel. It would be no meeting at all. We do need the gavel."

"I'll fix it with SuperGlue," Hank said.

"Then it'll work fine. SuperGlue. Good. I think SuperGlue would be best."

"Can we go on with the meeting now—hopefully end it?" Phil asked.

"We had to get this gavel thing taken care of," Bilba said. "We have to be flexible. Flexibility is the hallmark of a vital organization. Hmmmm. I rather like that. Flexibility is the—what did I say—oh, yes—hallmark—like the card. I'll have to remember that."

"Can we go now?" Phil pressed.

"We haven't voted on the bowling alley thing. Your daughter got rebellious on us. Okay, let's vote." The vote was five to one.

"Okay, now we can go."

"Not just yet," Bilba said, then cleared her throat, a clue she was about to say something hard for her. "Now, what about Bray Sanderson? Don't you think we should invite him here and make amends?"

At the mention of Bray's name, the five others at the table straightened, some imperceptibly, others definitely. But however they did it, their attention was now alive and focused again.

"Something I was going to suggest myself," Teri said, her face actually aglow. "I've been wanting to spend some quality time with my uncle."

CHAPTER 3

There weren't many things Win wanted to change about his Chevy, but right now he wished it was a convertible. It was a Friday afternoon in August. A huge forest fire on the New York side of the lake had been blazing for a couple of days, casting tons of ash in the air, but a luscious afternoon rain had cleaned it all out. Lake Champlain's deep blue sprawled on his right, while the emerald green of the Grand Isles did the same on his left. Wonderful. Having the top down would make it perfect. The invigorating wind still hit him through the open windows—but it wasn't as romantic. Of course, having Bray in the seat next to him instead of Ginger had killed the romance anyway.

Bray had been faithfully going to therapy for his leg, and, though he still had to use the tripod cane, the stiffness had lessened considerably and, with it, the pain. This was his first trip of any length since the explosion and, although Win thought under any other circumstances Bray would be reveling in the outdoors, he now appeared anxious.

He'd gotten the invitation from his family the day before, and, after some long discussion with Win, decided to go. Win was now driving him up. So far it had been a quiet drive, neither had said much. Win didn't want to push Bray—it wasn't wise. But they had only about twenty minutes to go. If Win was going to help his friend, he'd have to get something going soon.

He peered into the yellow-smudged sky. "The ash is coming back," Win groaned. "Had to hose the car off this morning. Even starting to smell like smoke again. They say it's playin' havoc with the weather. Dry as a bone there—wet here." In the six months he'd been in the area, he'd never seen a color like that—pale yellow, like a cat's eye, the sun reflecting through a growing haze—eerie. "Even the cows are turning yellow." Since picking

Bray up, Win had tried to appear cheerful, however those curious colors more accurately reflected his true feelings—concern. He still had a hard time justifying it, but that didn't seem to matter—the feeling persisted.

"Things change so fast," Bray mused, voicing a thought that had been rattling inside his head for a while.

Win nodded. "Six months ago I was safe at the seminary and didn't even know this place existed. Now I'm the assistant pastor in a growing church, going to marry Ginger, the most beautiful woman in the world, in two months, and gain a ten-year-old son. Must be something in the water. You *will* be back by October 8th. You're my best man."

Bray groaned. "Organizing, advising, rings. A friendship with you has nothing but downsides."

Win pointed his chin toward the side of the road. "Cows. Aren't there laws about letting them graze unfenced? Look, there's another one with Mickey Mouse on his side."

"Her side. Cows are *hers*." Bray sighed. "I'm opening up here and you're talking cows?"

"But this is Vermont. Bovine literacy is crucial."

"Not to me. Not now. I was a poor, depressed loner. Now I'm an independently wealthy gimp who is, for the first time in twenty-five years, about see what's left of my family."

"And whose fault is that? They were only an hour away."

"They could have been across the street—it would still be twenty-five years. And then there's Pam."

"Hey, look! George Washington."

"What?"

"On the side of that cow—the spots—looks just like that painting of George Washington. Why don't we put together a presidential herd? Find cows with various presidents on 'em. Of course, they'd have to be pretty exact—differentiating between Washington and Millard Fillmore might be tricky—"

Bray sighed. Win could be a bit much. "Stop. This is my conversation. From now on we talk about my stuff."

"Sure—but you're missing a sure thing. A herd like that could be big."

"Pamela Wisdom's big."

"She wouldn't want to hear you say that."

"I'm talking emotionally—to me. Leaving her is difficult. She likes me," Bray's voice became a bit lighter. "She comes over every couple of days. Makes breakfast, cleans up the cottage, helps me with my exercises." Eyes went up and he sighed. "She still won't talk about anything permanent until I belong to that cult of yours. But a little is better than nothing. What in heaven's name does she see in me?"

"She's relationally blind," Win stated.

"There is a downside. She reads to me from that Bible of yours. After every sentence or two she looks up to see if I've changed. Grown wings or something." Another frustrated shake of the head. "If an explosion didn't do it, why would words? But she'd leave if I didn't listen. She even holds my hand sometimes. Her *touch* is exciting."

"She's an attractive woman."

"She's *spectacular*. Diane would approve." He stopped to survey the landscape. "You'll see the island in another five miles or so," Bray said, glancing at his watch.

"When we talked a couple of weeks ago you mentioned some guilt you were feeling."

Bray's expression darkened. "When I first got the invitation I nearly tore it up. I didn't think I could face them. But my mom raised me better than that. I decided I had some apologizing to do."

"What about them? They could have called you."

"But why? Not coming back for my parents' funeral—it was like slapping them in the face. I have to apologize."

"You were young. Angry. Probably at the whole situation—probably at your parents for dying on you."

"They were my parents—I could have come, and I didn't." As if to end the discussion, Bray glanced down at his watch. "Slow down a little. If we get there too early, the launch won't be there."

The launch *was* there. Teri had tied it off at the dock a half hour before.

The reason she was early had its roots in a wave of anxiety that broke over her a few days before and woke her in the middle of the night.

Riding the crest of it was the uncontrollable urge to pray.

But she'd never prayed before. How to do it? An idea came. Rising from bed, she found a stash of birthday candles in the kitchen. Lighting one after another, using their wax as little stands, she placed them around the bathroom sink. With the glow dancing off the enameled walls, she found a corner of her heart where *the god of her* lived. She prayed to it for calm.

To her surprise, not only did calm come sweetly, but so did strength—an iron resolve.

In the days that followed she scavenged the family's candles, so when she went to her bathroom shrine a few hours before she was to pick up Bray Sanderson, the room was ablaze with them—on the sink, on the toilet tank cover, on the toilet seat, inside the open medicine cabinet, and on the edge of the tub. Several hundred eyes glowed white, watching her kneel. Beside her was her best friend—her Churchill double 470. Much like a side-by-side shotgun, it was a high-powered, double-shot weapon capable of downing a thick-pelted wild beast at 250 yards. Something she'd never done. Now her only hope was to obliterate a few bowling pins—which she looked forward to, of course.

Gripping the rifle she got down on one knee before the commode and prayed for success.

Having reached the dock, she'd carefully extracted from a hatch the long, narrow box in which the weapon was concealed and had stepped quickly to a place across the road she'd found the day before. When Bray's car came along, she'd be ready for it.

"Twenty-five years," Win said. "I was seven."

"I was eighteen when I left. That'd make it twenty-seven years ago. A lot happens in twenty-seven years."

"It's neat they want to get reacquainted."

"Now that Uncle Breck's shuffled off to the happy hunting ground—which won't be quite so happy now that he's there—they probably feel like they can."

"The way you describe him even I'd have trouble loving Breck," Win admitted.

Bray laughed. "Like you love everybody."

"I try."

"Trying and doing are two different things."

"At least I don't hate anyone. Except that guy at the gas station who keeps ogling Ginger. But I'll be perfect one day—well, after I die. So you'll never see it. Actually, no one will."

"So we have to take your word for it."

"Yeah."

"Perfection sounds dull," Bray said. "What you call *sin* keeps me alive." He went on. "But whether you think you could love him or not, Uncle Breck truly hated me. With every fiber of his being. I know that because he once said, 'I hate you with every fiber of my being.' I have to agree with you. His leaving his inheritance to me is confusing."

"Any theories?"

"Maybe his reason was guilt too. I was the only one he drove away. He made the others rich, so he paid 'em back for all the trouble he caused. Never me. And he drove me away from my family—my folks. He felt guilty. So, he's making me rich."

"Has he shown a lot of guilt in the past?"

"None. No, he's not known for his guilt. But neither am I, right?"

"I guess, but I'd hate being worth a million bucks to someone dead. My least favorite thing."

"Then you ought to be the poster boy for happy. You're worth nothing alive or dead. Anyway, maybe a kid'll get the money in twenty or thirty years. Someone else he feels guilty about. But by then I won't care."

"So you don't know who gets the mil?" Win asked.

"They won't say. Breck's terms won't let them. It doesn't matter. When I'm dead I won't need it. If you think about it, this is the only way he could have set it up so I'd have a steady income. If I got a lump sum, I'd buy the lake and be broke again."

"You going back on the force?"

Bray shrugged. "I gotta work. Florida was a good idea once—but no more. Not the way Pam feels about me. She really likes me. You think eight thou a month might lure her back to me?"

"Doubt it," Win said flatly. "Were the rest of your relatives anything like Breck?"

"No—Breck was quite unique, and he had them all by the short hairs. When I left, my parents didn't even come after me—I waited on shore a full 24 hours before cutting a trail to the Army recruiter's. You mentioned being angry with them. I was. For that. Then they died in a boating accident. Had that boat I was on blown up a second earlier, I could have gone the same way. Spooky."

"But it didn't. Praise God."

"And now they've invited me—my brother Phil, and his kids, Tommy and Teri, my cousin Sylvia and her husband, Hank, and Breck's sister, Bilba."

"And they all live on the island? All that togetherness would kill me."

"Not them. They love it."

Sylvia peered out her bedroom window. Living two houses from the mansion, her bedroom window faced the Grand Isles. She watched the launch resting at the distant dock. Of course, she couldn't bring herself to pilot it, or any other boat for that matter. But a guard could. As he'd prepared the launch for Teri, he could have been preparing one for her. To get off this island.

She hated Teri.

Hated them all.

How dare they keep her a prisoner? How dare they keep all her money in trust? How dare they not just make an exception in her case and let her off the island so that she could breathe?

But the million for knocking Bray off would do it. She studied the thick travel brochure she'd had one of the guards get in St. Albans. A cruise ship standing tall and sparkling white in the tropical port of Antigua, small boats darting about, the crisp blues, reds and whites of their sails glistening in the sun.

Soon, she thought, *so very soon.*

But could she actually do it? Kill Bray—kill anyone?

She dropped the brochure on her dressing table and stared out the window again. The wind pushed through the maple leaves nearby.

She preferred not to ask herself the question. Rather, she preferred just to think it already done. "Not long," she thought, "and I'll be off this rock. Then Hank can take care of himself. It'll serve him right."

"Did you have a good relationship with your brother and the others?" Win asked.

"I don't have a good relationship with anybody. You're the best relationship I got and you know what a zero that is. Uncle Breck hated me because I wouldn't bow down to him. What Breck hated—left." Some silence. "I told you they hired me a personal physical therapist. That was nice of them, huh? They can't be all that upset with me."

"Oh, a fruit stand," Win pointed to a small shack by the road, plastered with signs. "Ginger wanted me to bring back some tomatoes and corn. Love tomatoes and fresh corn on the cob."

Bray grunted. "How can you love corn? You have it, what, once a week, then for only one meal? That's not love—it's like. You *like* corn."

"But I *love* tomatoes. If this car were filled with tomatoes, I'd eat my way out."

"Okay. There's another fruit stand by the dock. Five bucks if you can start at one end of their tomato bin and eat your way to the other. And I'll pay for the tomatoes."

"You're on," Win parried. "Well—"

"There it is," Bray said, his arm going up, pointing across the lake.

Win slowed, then pulled onto the shoulder. Opening the door he slid out and, resting his arms on the roof, peered over the top of his car. He'd been this way several times in the past few months but had never seen the island. But now, bathed in that eerie yellow ash, there it was. Maybe a mile offshore, as if floating on a mirror, was a knuckle of rock. Clustered on that rock were several large houses. Trees, like out-of-control hedges, separated the houses. Of course he could only see one side of the island and only two of the houses, but there was every reason to believe the other side looked the same. One of the houses blinked a watchful eye as the yellow sky glinted off a window. Then it blinked again—the window closing? Phil? One of the others checking on the launch? It looked so foreboding. How could anyone even go there, let alone live there? Win slid back behind the wheel, and they were soon back on the road. "What's on that other island? That little one near it?"

"Don't know," Bray replied. "Breck kept everyone off but the inner circle—his team. My dad said it was where Breck made his money." Bray went silent and just stared at the island. Words were forming. "I don't believe in good and evil," Bray began. "'Things are just the way they are, some better than others.' Remember that speech?"

Win nodded.

"Breck was the exception. He was evil."

Win believed in good and evil. Believed in the absolute purity and goodness of God—Father, Son and Holy Spirit—and the absolute evil personified in Satan and his horde. For Bray to acknowledge that, Breck's heart must have been truly black.

"Breck was the most wonderful man," Bilba said to Ron Gunn, a green-clad guard. They were in her darkly decorated drawing room and he stood nearly at attention, while she sat at Breck's roughly hewn desk. "If he wasn't," she continued, "I'd never be doing this."

She wouldn't be. The money meant nothing to her. But what Breck wanted she did and, since it was Breck who'd asked, she felt duty bound to comply.

Gunn nodded. He didn't care about mission or motives. It was extra cash and cash gave him freedom. "If it's supposed to look like an accident, I'd better only loosen one of the railings."

"The most likely one."

"I should do it before he gets here."

"You have about an hour."

Ron nodded again. "Anything else?"

"Why would there be?"

"Just asking."

"Well don't. Go do it. And only see me if I call for you."

She leaned forward, her eyes animal intense. "And tell no one about this."

"Sure." Ron Gunn left her drawing room. She was such a stupid old bat. He'd bring up the money later.

"The invitation said they want to be friends again. When I RSVPed I talked to Phil. He'd been drinking a little, and I didn't get a really good feeling. But he said that I'm the last of the family not with them and they want to patch things up—and no matter how messed up, family's family. They want me there until I lose the cane. Could be a month." Bray pointed forward. "See that circus tent?"

Win nodded. Partially hidden by the trees stood a red-and-white-striped canvas roof held up by a rigid center pole. An American flag waved proudly on top. It reminded him of the tent Pastor Mel Flowers and he had used to start their little church a few months before.

Bray glanced at his watch. "Right on time. You have at least one talent."

"What if you just can't take it there?" Win pressed his point. "Or what if there's trouble?"

"Trouble? I'm a cop. I smell trouble—a mile off."

Hank whistled cheerfully. It was something he did when his mind was focused on cheerful things. Like a million bucks and his high-tech auto repair *salon*—the word *salon* dripped with class. He whistled as he walked down a long cement staircase to the hidden dock—a natural cavern eaten into the St. Albans side of the big island.

Years before, when they needed additional dock capacity, they'd taken the natural cavern, enlarged it, and placed protective boulders in front for security, leaving a ten-foot passage to the lake. Behind the boulders, moored to a floating dock, were several bullet-shaped Sea-Doo boats, their hulls nonreflective black—their aft sections extended to add a secure storage compartment. The powerful inboards were in a constant state of prep and repair. As he stepped through the small walkway at the cavern's edge, two of the boats were on hoists, being prepped for the night run.

Hank stopped whistling and stepped over to a workman who smelled of grease and gasoline, a scent Hank preferred to cologne. "They have to be ready on time, Foster?"

"Always."

"I want to work on one of them myself."

"Which?" the man asked, taking a dirty rag and wiping the sweat from his brow. He left a black smudge. Hank almost grabbed the rag and wiped his hands and the back of his neck with it just to feel the oil and grit.

"One we've had trouble with."

"Eight," he said quickly. "I was going to take it out and scuttle it."

"Eight, then." Hank took a few more steps down the dock feeling it dip and sway beneath him. Turning back to Foster, "You got some cousins in St. Albans, don't ya? Been in an' out o' the can?"

"Never the state pen."

"Same last name as yours?"

Foster shook his head. "Brightstar," he said, wiping the back of his neck. "Not the name you'd expect."

"Where?"

"Their second home's Clancy's Bar—east, near the hills."

Hank's eyes narrowed like a snake's. "I never talked to you about this."

"About what?" the mechanic said, looking dramatically dumbfounded. It was the eternal kinship of mechanics—it knit them together with greasy iron threads.

A few miles from Sanderson Island was another island. Over thirty years before, one of the guards, suddenly caught by a savage storm when returning from his midnight run, found that it had an important feature. Having often passed the island, when terrorized by the turbulence, he'd aimed his outboard toward it. When he was twenty yards away, a wave picked him up and plastered him against a rim of boulders, while the surf tore his skiff apart, bending it around the boulders like braces on teeth. Thrown into the waves the guard knew he'd perish. But mercifully, the god of all storms lifted him over the boulders and deposited him, bruised but alive, at the mouth of a strange geologic phenomenon—a cave that descended below the island at nearly forty-five degrees. The boulders at its mouth concealed it and acted as a dam, keeping the lake at bay. Since rescue would be a while, the guard explored. The cave, shaped like the result of a giant's finger poking into clay, descended in convenient steps about a hundred yards.

Uncle Breck, when told about it, quickly devised a use. Storage for *sensitive stuff*—stuff they wanted to keep an eye on, perhaps use again, but should be destroyed if discovered.

They laced the cave's ceiling with explosives and planted more below the boulders at the entrance. The blast would bring down the roof, and when the boulders at the entrance were blown, the lake would bury what was left. Nothing would ever be detected or retrieved.

A few years ago, fuses had been replaced by a coded radio-controlled detonator.

Standing at the cave's entrance, Tommy toyed with the detonator controls as he stood peering between boulders into the shadows. The afternoon sun cast everything in that eerie yellow hue. He felt the ash settling in his hair.

Tommy smiled.

Over the week he'd made a study of the cave's inventory, a sheet with which he, as auditor, had been entrusted. Nothing on it mattered if lost, and a few things should have been destroyed long ago.

"And some of 'em," he chuckled darkly, "you'll just die to see, Uncle Bray."

A rock tumbled from the cliff above and struck the inside curve of a boulder near him. It bounced to the cave floor and began its descent. Tommy studied the sound of it. The rattle of a single rock dancing down the incline, knocking others loose, then still others until the sound resembled rain.

He slapped the control mechanism on his palm a couple times. A plan began to emerge; a trail took shape—stepping-stone by stepping-stone, twist by turn—like that stone rolling downhill.

Tommy smiled. "And it'll end with a real bang."

Bray sniffed out the window. "Nope—no trouble out there." He chuckled softly. "Well, if trouble knocks, I'll call, and you can pick me up. I'm actually starting to look forward to this—clearing the family air."

Win was about to say something about all the ash in it when both heard the loud pop. The car pulled hard left. Win compensated by cranking the wheel hard right—toward the lake, ragged rocks and thick tree trunks and the water beyond. A blowout—Win's side. He slammed on the brakes and worked the wheel trying to keep the car on the road. He failed. The rear fishtailed and skidded onto the grassy shoulder. The locked rear wheels slid helplessly on crushed, wet grass.

"The fruit stand!" Bray cried.

Win had already seen it, and it was coming up fast. He pushed even harder on the brakes, but the pedal was already to the floor. "Lord, what's happening?" The car left the grass and plowed into the thin, gravel parking strip between grass and tent. Win gulped. Bray cried out.

The car burst through the first tier of fruit—apples and splintered wood broke in a scattering wave over the hood—ripe peaches bounced and splattered against the window. In seconds he would hit the center tent pole and the young boy who worked the cash register in front of it. The kid's eyes popped.

The rear of the car must have been riding on a sea of pulp for it suddenly swung around, snowplowing through the next tier of bins. Corn and avocados leaped up as if vainly trying to escape. Though some scrambled over the roof, armfuls plunged through Win's window, burying his legs. "Tomatoes!" Win cried as the car plowed into a wall of them. As tender red skins broke and a crimson wave erupted and burst over the roof and flooded through the window, the car smashed through the counter behind them.

Realizing this was his last chance to escape, the kid jumped for it, giving Win a view of a frantic set of legs just as the car slammed into the center pole. Win was thrown unmercifully against his door and Bray against him as the door caved in.

An excruciating pain blazed from wrist to shoulder. Win could actually feel the shattered bone digging into the flesh around it. He cried out and tried to move his arm, but it wouldn't move. So, buried to his neck in tomatoes, he lay back, shutting his eyes as if to close out the pain. But the pain wouldn't be denied. It worsened, burrowing its way to his heart.

"And me without ranch dressing." Bray groaned, pushing fruits and vegetables aside. Then he stiffened. "Good grief—a cow!"

Through searing pain, Win saw what Bray saw. A crazed Holstein, eyes savagely aflame—something unusual for a cow—ran, head down, toward Bray's door. Though still stunned, Bray pushed the tomatoes, corn, avocados, and peaches away from the door but against Win. Win whimpered.

The cow hit. Twelve hundred pounds of black-and-white spots slammed into Bray's door. The door caved in and the car rocked savagely. Over his own cry, Win heard the tent pole creak and splinter. But it held.

Leaving its deep imprint in the door, the cow dropped like a sack of beef.

"Couldn't be a concussion," Bray said. "There's nothing to concuss."

The kid with the wide eyes said it first, "It's dead. Wow. Look at that udder. Like a blimp—good milker. Farmer Kellogg's gonna be ticked. His fruit stand—now his cow. You guys insured?"

Bray turned to Win. "You insured?"

A voice strained, "Probably for everything but fruit stands and charging bovine." His face screwed into a painful wince, so tightly that it took several seconds to see the five-dollar bill Bray held up. "What's that for?"

"The tomatoes. Plowing through 'em this way's as good as any."

"For the Chevy fix-it fund," Win said, feeling the blood drain from his face.

"You okay?"

"Arm's broken. It hurts—I mean *hurts*."

Before Bray could react, a white Chevy Caprice pulled up and parked on the gravel, its red and blue bubbles pulsing. As the officer stepped out, a woman in her early thirties, dressed in a cheerfully flowered blouse and blue Bermudas ran by him, streams of raven hair flagging behind. "Uncle Bray? You all right?" she cried.

"Uncle? You're Teri?" Bray asked.

"I've seen so many pictures of you lately. You're a hero. How come a hero's flattening fruit stands?"

"It's not me," Bray said, "it's my injured buddy here—Win Brady." Bray's eyes shifted to the approaching cop. He called to him. "My friend's got a broken arm. He's going into shock. Call an ambulance."

The cop kept up his slow, deliberate pace toward the car.

Teri stepped between the cow's legs, glanced at the full udder and placed well-manicured fingers on the window sill. "Broken arm? The poor dear," she cooed sympathetically. "I'm sort of the nurse on the island. Can I help?"

Having been examining his arm, Win now turned to her. Through a painful haze, he saw a beautiful woman leaning through the window, her eyes large, her lips soft and deeply worried. He didn't see her mouth suddenly drop, nor her eyes widen. Nor did he see her take a deep, calming breath, her overwhelmed heart having lodged in her throat. *He's wonderful,* her heart whispered to itself, *wonderful.*

"I hate pain," Win told her.

"At least you're normal," she managed, regaining herself.

"I can't move it. I better just wait for the ambulance."

"He a friend?" Teri asked, trying to behave as if her world hadn't abruptly changed. Could it have? Truly? She took another breath, trying desperately to get her heart beating again. She heard the cop's thick boots coming up from behind. "You got good-looking friends, Uncle Bray," she smiled, achieving a certain offhandedness.

"Move it, lady," the cop growled.

Still emotionally off balance, she stepped aside.

The cop pushed his large moon face toward the open window. "Ambulance was called before I got here." He pushed a head in. "Hang in there, buck," he said. Then he looked at Bray. "You're with BPD, right? Sanderson. The guy that nearly bought it saving the St. Albans."

"Bray Sanderson."

"Sanderson—" the cop repeated. Then, as if finally making the connection, he turned toward the distant island. "Tom Flagg," the cop introduced himself, without extending a hand.

Amenities over, Bray prevailed upon Flagg to drag the cow out of the way, which he did using his car and a nylon cord the kid provided. The cow extracted, Teri opened the door. Grabbing his cane, Bray hobbled out. With Bray out, Teri could get to Win. "Can you lie down?" she asked, the sense of weakness returning because of the very nearness of him.

"Don't know," he managed, taking a deep breath to muffle the pain. His breath took her in—a heady whiff of wildflowers and the musk of rain and a telltale hint of sour smoke. Gentle hands caressed his back and shoulder and then tugged as she tried to ease him over. But he'd hardly moved before the pain became unbearable. Bones separated in at least two places, jagged edges scraped adjacent flesh. He whimpered.

She stopped. "We need to secure that arm," she said, eager to ease his pain.

"No," Win whispered, "Wait for—ambulance."

"You might faint—you look pale." Without hesitation, she leaped from the car and found two splintered boards, each about two feet long, each thin but sturdy. She called to the cop. "You got tape—first-aid kit?"

Slats and tape in hand, she returned to Win and found his face even more ashen, his lips colorless, his eyes glazed.

Putting all teenagy, breathless feelings aside, Teri went to work. She tenderly placed one of the boards behind his arm, then the other on top, and applied just a hint of pressure to straighten the arm. Win cried out. Then, as gently as she could, she worked the tape. First she secured it to his hand, then she gently worked it around the boards, tying them firmly in place.

Although the pain was volcanic, he steadied himself by leaning against her.

If she'd only been Ginger he could have snuggled into her neck and kissed her ear and lost his pain in just being near the woman he loved.

But she wasn't, so he remained still, breathing in her freshness and feeling her warmth. And praying—always praying. For strength—lots of strength and endurance—bushels of endurance. His prayers must have been answered. Before he knew it, she said:

"Now let's try it."

"Move it? Are you sure?"

She didn't bother a reply. Although the bones in the arm weren't completely immobilized, at least they didn't separate as he eased over on his side, a pile of corn husks gathered for a pillow. When his head hit the husks he felt stronger.

Bray's head appeared over Teri's shoulder. "The ambulance is only a few minutes away."

"Good," Win managed. "Never broken a bone in my life. I'm a wimp."

"No," Teri protested. "It took guts to let me put that splint on that way." Teri's eyes were floating with admiration. *Such courage.* Her heart kept missing one beat after another.

Seconds later the paramedics arrived, and a few minutes after that, his arm resecured in a formfitting plastic splint, Win was removed from the car. After treating him for shock, they strapped him to a gurney and slid it into the ambulance. Bray and Teri remained close throughout.

Bray called to one of the attendants, "Help me up in there. I'm going to the hospital with him."

"No," Teri said, a slight sense of panic in her tone. Then she calmed. "It's just a broken arm."

"I'll be okay," Win told him.

"You'll be okay," she reiterated. Then she gently pulled her uncle back. "Take good care of him, guys," she said, as if her instructions mattered. "He's special."

"I'll call Ginger," Bray told him.

"And find out where they're taking the car."

"It'll be at the wrecking yard, St. Albans," Flagg sang out.

"Great," Win groaned. "The bill goes up. But what about you, Bray? You going to be all right?"

Teri patted her uncle's arm. "We'll take good care of him. And come by the island when you can. I'll show you around—personally."

They closed the ambulance doors and as the ambulance pulled out onto the road, its siren blaring, Teri turned to Bray. "Who's Ginger?" she asked.

"His fiancée. Beautiful gal."

Teri only nodded. But in the nod was the memory of his closeness. The smell of him, the sense of his power. It had happened so quickly. If only she could just buy him. Write a requisition to Tommy and wait for him to be delivered. Ah, more to pray for.

A few minutes later, Bray stepped carefully onto the sixteen-foot crystal-blue Bayliner and sat expectantly. Teri backed it away from the short dock, eased it around, and headed under half power toward the island, her eyes toward the ambulance and its pulsing lights as it hugged the lake on its way to St. Albans and the small hospital there.

Lying in the back of the ambulance, Win's arm a ferociously dull ache, he said another prayer and longed for Ginger to be at his side. Over the past few months he and Ginger had grown even closer—planning the wedding, unplugging drug runners. Now he lay injured, and she was miles away.

And Bray was heading off to an island where he might, literally, be a large, limping target.

CHAPTER 4

Teri Sanderson guided the Bayliner over glassy water, her attention divided. Fortunately she could work the controls instinctively, seeing the island's dark outline approaching in the back of her head. In front was Win Brady's smiling image—without pain—laughing occasionally, caressing her with sparkling eyes. Suddenly another image subverted it. Breck's. Lying in bed, his skin chalk, his eyes dying, his lips speaking of murder. She shuddered.

Bray sat surprised at how calm he was. He'd imagined, while lying in the hospital, that it would be years before he'd enjoy the growl of an outboard again. Surely the sound would force him to relive that night with its horrific explosion.

But it didn't. The instant Teri fired up the powerful engine, the thrill of being on the lake returned. Plus, there was another thrill. Seeing Teri. If others in his family resented his past action, Teri didn't seem to. But she was also lovely—and she was being gracious to him. Since few of his family ever had, Bray appreciated her that much more.

Bray's brother, Phil, had always been ruggedly handsome. Teri, though all woman, reflected Phil's classic features, high cheekbones, clear, vibrant eyes. But she'd also received a soft, girlish charm from her mother, who had died when Teri was quite young. Bray's looks came from his mother, Marsha Sanderson, Henry's second wife, a woman with pronounced, European features.

"Everybody there?" Bray asked, the boat jarring awake some of the injuries he'd thought had healed.

"Dad, Tommy, Sylvia, Hank, and Bilba. The whole clan."

"It's been a long while. What are they all like now?"

Teri shrugged. "Dad wants to run everything. When Bilba croaks he will, if he can wait that long."

"He's got a choice?"

"I know I don't. I take over when Bilba, Dad, Sylvia, Hank, and Tommy die. Then there won't be anyone left to boss around."

"Tommy still a bit sullen?"

"You left when we were just kids—"

"September 1969. Long time ago. You were five or so."

"I remember—I think."

"I traded a life with you guys for the rice paddies of Vietnam. Shows how bad I wanted to get off that island."

"Been there—haven't done that." Teri smiled.

The same girlish quality Pam has, Bray thought. And for an instant he sensed Pam's presence, even felt her touch. But no. Not today. Today was a homecoming, a day for welcoming people back into his life, not for missing people who refused to become part of it.

He heard Teri. "Maybe we could invite your friend back there to visit you."

"Win? I'd have to invite Ginger, too."

"It'd be great to have them both," she said, her voice strained. "You asked about Tommy. After mom died, Uncle Breck took Tommy under his wing, and Tommy turned from sullen to intensely brainy—very intense. Of course, I beat him—I *slaughtered* him on the SATs."

"Then Breck did something good for Tommy?"

She shrugged. "Maybe not. Tommy had a personality when he was sullen."

"Your mom died on Christmas Day. You were a little more than a year old, then your dad never remarried. A tough break for you kids."

"Hardly think about it anymore. Aunt Sylvia—"

"*Aunt* Sylvia?"

"Yeah. Even though she's Dad's cousin, Tommy and I always thought she was built more like an aunt. She and Hank will be there, of course. The blimp and her mechanic."

"That's not too charitable."

"I'm a little mad at all of 'em. They took away one of my toys."

"Toys?"

"I like shooting—they replaced my range with a bowling alley, and nobody uses it."

"Families can be families," Bray muttered. The island was still a ways off, distance casting it in a yellow tint.

"Bilba's old. A walking skeleton. The only time she looks even remotely human is after she spends an hour or so in the butterfly house."

"She still doing that?"

"Yeah. Some insect lover comes up from one of the colleges a couple times a month to keep it stocked. In return he does research."

"Have they talked at all about me over the years?"

"Gotta be honest. Not much. But when your picture showed up in the paper—then when Uncle Breck died. Well, we wanted you to come up, but we were afraid to ask you because we were embarrassed, having not contacted you before. We finally decided to take the bull by the horns—so to speak."

Bray felt his guilt begin to wane. Maybe there'd been mistakes on both sides. And, now that Breck was gone, perhaps those mistakes could be rectified. "I'm glad you did," he said. "This is a nice boat."

"It's mine. We mostly have those two-seater Sea-Doos," she said, "waverunners, too. The lake's our sandbox. We're pretty self-contained. That's why we have the butterfly house, I guess. Bilba'd spend her whole life in there if she could."

He smiled, and Teri smiled back. There'd been a connection made with this young beauty, the first he'd ever made with a member of his own family. It felt wonderfully right—like sunlight breaking through a gray morning.

"Hank's younger than Sylvia?"

"Twelve years."

"She always seemed to straddle the fence between hysteria and coma. What about you? I figure you're over thirty, right?"

"Thirty-one."

"Why no guy in your life?"

"Who says there isn't?"

"Because of your reaction to Win back there."

"Win's a neat name. Short for anything?"

"Winsome. His folks were sixties people. Long hair, beards, peace signs and strange names—probably."

"Winsome," she said, savoring the sound. "Neat eyes. Muscles. He work out?"

"Not with that arm."

She turned. "Okay, you're not getting into this thing."

"He's engaged, and they're both my friends."

She decided to hold her list of questions until later. Instead she feasted on Win's image for a moment—one she imagined to be excited at her nearness.

"So, what's the family business?" Bray slipped in.

She only smiled. "Success equals secrecy."

"Drugs?"

She laughed. "Not quite that secret. If someone broke silence we'd have to break both legs, but that's about all." She laughed again. But her laughter ended as she brushed her arm off. "Ash— it's been falling all day."

Bray noticed a dull sheen on his jacket. He slapped his sleeve, the ash billowed and blew away—gnats in a yellow sun. "Better the ash than the fire," Bray said. "Everything still happening on the little island? I remember everybody headed for it during the day. In shifts. Then they'd each take turns trying to recruit me."

"I started just out of high school."

"What keeps you here?"

She took no time to think. "Money. I can buy things—just about anything I want. What woman my age can say that?"

"Rich ones."

"And I'm rich; rich is good."

"Smart's good, too. And on this island you're probably one of the smart ones."

Teri smiled at her uncle as if he'd broken the code. "Smart's even better."

"Being on top's better than that—right?"

Another smile. "You know me pretty well."

"My job. You on top there?"

The smile vanished. "I'm the lowest banana in the bunch."

"Maybe it's time to find another bunch. But, that takes nerve."

Teri grunted. "So now I don't have nerve? Is Win as sensitive as you are?"

"As me? Naw." He hesitated. "His fiancée's a cop. Carries a gun."

"I got guns. Lots of guns. And it's a long walk to the altar—relationships slip."

"That's true," Bray said, resigned to changing no minds here.

Teri said nothing. She neither wanted to hear about Ginger nor about keeping her hands off Win. She *couldn't* keep her hands off him. Being near him had affected her too deeply. Why? She didn't know. It didn't matter. She *did* know that if she ever felt his hot breath on her expectant lips, her heart would melt. You don't just give up feelings like that.

Suddenly experiencing the vision of those expectant lips in her mind, her breath caught. Her toes clenched.

She had to snap out of it.

Surprising even herself, she laughed—as if everything everywhere were some kind of joke. She laughed loudly—extravagantly—throwing her head back and letting the wind blow her midnight hair around. Just as unexpectedly, Bray found himself laughing with her. There was something enchanting and unafraid in her laugh. Something that offered no challenge, but merely relished in what was; the laugh of a free spirit—like the wind might laugh.

"I feel so free on the lake," she finally said.

Bray wanted to tell her that Win felt the same way. Where Bray used the lake for recreation and transport, Win used it to feed his need for autonomy. But mentioning that she and Win had something in common would only stoke a fire that needed no stoking.

"You were married once?"

"Diane died three years ago. Cancer. I've a new friend now. Pam Wisdom."

"Why marry anybody?" Teri shrugged. "I can't figure it."

Bray didn't reply. Diane's memory refused to yield. Why *had* he married her? They were so different. She was a ship in a storm—stalwart, taking the wrenching blows and remaining afloat. Only the mightiest of waves, cancer, took her down. He'd never loved anyone more. Now Pam. She seemed a woman to fight the storms—a spine of iron. He was probably more like Pam. Active—meeting life on its own terms. As he had with Diane, he wanted to spend eternity with her even though she didn't want the same. But why? Why marry? Why not just live together—play house?

Bray seldom thought too deeply about these things. As he did in action, he also did emotionally—shot from the hip. Quick, without study. But in his hospital bed, trying desperately to break the Pam-habit, he studied the ties that bound him to her. If he could identify them, he could cut them or stretch them so thin they would break on their own.

An image had come to mind.

A thousand threads—strands reaching between them, connecting every sinew, emotion, thought—binding him to her as nothing else—total understanding, total acceptance. Those threads compelled marriage; there was no other alternative. They required the intimacy that only marriage brought. *They were the intimacy.* They had existed with Diane, and now he sensed them connecting to Pam. Not all of them, but enough to know that the others were coming and only needed the emotional and physical contact to complete the attachment. Oh, how he longed for that contact. And yet he knew she'd never allow it—*being lousy with religion like she was.* There was really only one alternative. Lying in that dark hospital room he had tried to sever the threads—tear them, rend them.

But as she began visiting him, helping him, even reading that confounded Bible to him, the threads had become stronger, demanding that she be in his life.

"You okay?" he heard.

Eyes glued to the approaching island—now only twenty yards away. "Oh, just thinking," he said. "Looks like we're about there."

Several muscular guys in forest green *Star Trek* jumpsuits were waiting for them on the dock. The instant the boat touched, one of them tied it off.

"Weren't as many before," Bray said as one helped him from the boat. As he stepped onto the dock, he wondered how much had changed. And how much was for the better?

Ginger Glasgow stepped agitatedly down Northwestern Medical Center's carpeted hallway. Pushing an anxious hand through short blonde hair, she took long strides, ones her ten-year-old son, Chad, scrambled to match. "Most go to fruit stands to buy fruit." Ginger grumbled, "Only Win Brady goes to break his arm."

"I guess that's what they mean by *tough bananas*."

"If I want cleverness—"

The one-story, seventy-seven-bed medical center spread out amid the oak and maple trees and seemed larger than it really was. At night the shadowy halls meandered forever.

"Where is he?" Ginger asked, confusedly. "And he's in pain."

"It's just a broken arm. I had one."

"You had a sprain—a wrist—that's nothing like a break."

"It hurt."

"Not like a break."

They followed the corridor to the left and saw the emergency room sign. Chad pointed. "In there? And mine *was* nearly broken."

Ginger softened. "I'm sorry. Sure it hurt—a lot. And you were brave getting through it. I'm just upset."

"Sure. Who wants a groom who lost a fight with *tough bananas*," Chad laughed.

Ginger just groaned and pushed through the double doors to the emergency waiting room. They were alone in it except for the receptionist, an incredibly beautiful brunette. She looked up with large, liquid brown eyes. Her desk nameplate read Candi Silver.

"Win Brady, please."

"Mr. Brady's having his arm set."

"I'm his fiancée," Ginger said.

"That's a shame," Candi said. "He's cute. Most men around here smell like moose droppings. Not him. Not even close."

"High praise," Ginger said dryly.

Candi smiled. "I'm glad he broke it around here."

Jealousy. When was the last time she'd felt it? Chad was six. He'd told her he wanted to trade her for one of his teachers. That shook her up a little. But this was the first time she'd felt jealous of Win. Well, not the first time. Actually, she'd been feeling it quite often lately. And he'd done nothing. "Can I see him?"

"Sure you can take it?" the brunette challenged. "Setting an arm can be brutal."

"I'm a cop." She dropped her purse on the counter. The gun inside hit hard. "Where is he?"

Not all that intimidated, Candi grabbed the phone and punched in two digits. "The hunk's main squeeze wants to come back." Silence for a moment, then she looked up at Ginger. "He's being brave. Maybe I should show you the way."

"I'll find him." Ginger glanced at a nearby door. "Through there?"

"Selfish, selfish, selfish," Candi clucked.

Chad placed an elbow on the counter, his chin on his fist. "You ever date younger men?" he cooed.

"Chad, get over here." Ginger gave him a slap on the behind as he scooted by. "I guess I need to talk to him," Ginger fired back at her. "He needs to learn to recognize the right kind of woman."

"The talk would do him good," Candi Silver said, her pen tapping her unnaturally white teeth. "I'm sure he hasn't had the opportunity to see one at home."

Had the door not had a piston hinge, Ginger would have slammed it.

She found Win in a curtained cubicle. The doctor, an Iranian fellow with intense, dark eyes, was wrapping the cast. He kept focused as Ginger and Chad entered.

Win couldn't have been happier to see her. He needed her smile. *The Lord is so good.* "Wow! You're beautiful," Win said.

"Really? Still?"

"Forever. How long you been here?" he asked, giving her his own smile.

"A minute. You've got quite a fan club out there."

"Fan club?"

"She's beautiful," Chad cooed.

The doctor's eyes came up. "Our receptionist," he said flatly.

"A fruit stand?" Ginger scolded.

"Better than an eighteen-wheeler."

"When I heard about it—" She stopped and leaned against the steel railing on Win's bed. "I didn't want to lose you to an auto accident."

"How did you want to lose him, Mom?"

"Chad," Win admonished. Ginger's first husband, after drinking himself into a blur, had killed himself on the road. "The Lord brought a boatload of bananas for a cushion."

"You broke it? How many places?" Chad asked, staring at the thickening cast.

"Three," said the doctor. "This will be on for a long time."

"Oh, no," Ginger groaned. "The wedding. I knew it."

"You know what?" Win asked.

A vision of Win in a full body cast being pushed down the aisle on a gurney, Chad guiding the intravenous stand and bottle alongside, flashed on the IMAX screen of her mind. "Nothing," she said, wincing. "I know nothing. Not a thing."

"Did it hurt?" Chad pressed.

"Do honeybees buzz?" Win countered.

"Not around me they don't," Chad winced.

"How long will he be here?" Ginger asked the doctor.

"Not much longer. Maybe you could get a Coke. Come back in a half hour. Not only do I have to finish up this thing, but I must tell him how to take care of it."

"Can I use your arm as a bat?" Chad laughed.

"Pray he doesn't use it as a paddle," the doctor replied dryly.

Forty-five minutes later Win, Ginger, and Chad stepped through the waiting room.

Ginger was relieved to find Candi gone. She wrapped both arms around Win's right arm on their way to the parking lot. The moment they pushed through the double doors, though, a police car pulled up. Tom Flagg, the cop at the fruit stand, stepped from the white Caprice, his expression emotionless. "Got a minute?" he called.

"Can it wait?" Win asked. "My arm still hurts."

"I bet," the cop said. "But there's something you need to see."

Working his tripod cane, Bray stepped between age-stained wooden houses, following Teri who continued to the commons. Everything on the island was now bathed in afternoon shadows.

A lot had changed in twenty-seven years. He remembered a wilder place. Now cement and stone paths connected the houses and crisscrossed between rolling lawns, flower beds, and shrubs.

Trees were meticulously placed to provide shade and shelter. At the center stood a palm tree, its fronds noticeably ragged. Behind it stood a wooden structure a couple of stories tall, its eight sides glass—the butterfly house. He remembered it and the glistening white gazebo sitting to the southern edge.

The eight houses seemed inexplicably larger. Built around the commons, they went from smallest to largest, the largest being the only two-story. And since they were arranged in a circle, the largest was next to the smallest. Breck's subtle way of rubbing it in.

"That's my old place—Phil's and mine," he said, pointing to the third from the smallest.

"That's mine now."

"Really? Oh, sure." He counted. "It would be."

It hadn't changed much. The trees were larger, the plants accenting it were different, their reds and yellows more brilliant than what he recalled.

"Your things are probably still in the attic. We just stuff everything up there. See the palm tree? That's—" her voice turned low and ominous, "the grave."

"I'm surprised he didn't have himself stuffed—like Trigger."

"We'd have to ride him. And where would Bilba put those stupid flowers—?" Teri suddenly laughed. "I can think of a place."

"Okay, we're getting a little carried away here."

They both laughed.

"We're going to the mansion," Teri said, her hand sweeping toward the Brick's old place.

"Where else? It's Bilba's now."

The mansion had the widest path leading to it, the most windows, and the widest door. Even the fir trees were decidedly larger. Two green-clad guards eyed them impassively as they approached.

"Who do they work for?" Bray asked.

"Uncle Breck fingered Bilba, but my dad raised a stink, and now they report to a council."

"Let me guess—Bilba, Phil, and Sylvia?"

"The girls have taken over," Teri forced a laugh.

"Think so?"

Teri shook her head. "Dad wouldn't allow it."

Before Bray could reply, the front door flew open, and Phil stood there, muscular arms outstretched, every bit as handsome as Bray remembered—dark hair and eyes, firm, square jaw, just a hint of white at the temples. Bray couldn't help envying Phil's good looks. If Bray had them, maybe Pam couldn't resist him. "Bray, you son-of-a-. . . . Hurt so others might live. A hero! Welcome back to your island." Two strong arms wrapped around him squeezing. Pain radiated everywhere. Bray swallowed a scream—it returned as a groan.

"Oh," Phil exclaimed, pulling away, "Sorry. Just so excited to see you. It's been, what? Twenty years?"

"Twenty-seven," Bray managed, unfolding his chest and leaning heavily on the cane. "Good to see you, too."

"Come on inside," Phil gushed. "The others can hardly wait."

"How many of these guards do you need?" Bray asked as Phil opened the door.

"Me? None," Phil commented, opening the door. "Everybody else? Too many."

Later, Bray would notice that little had changed inside. A few more things standing about, a few more coats of arms on the wall, but it was just as dark, just as dreary. A medieval castle that Uncle Breck ruled as king—the perfect role for him.

But now he noticed none of it. The family he'd waited nearly thirty years to see stood brightly in a greeting line, their hands ready to grab his when offered, the resentment he had anticipated nowhere evident.

Tommy's hand was first. Like his father, Tommy was handsome, the same squared jaw and black hair. Unlike his father, whose eyes were cheerful with solid laugh lines, Tom's were intensely green and drilled Bray like a hunter's would a deer.

"Good to see you again, Tom."

"You're an inspiration, Uncle Bray," Tommy said, pumping Bray's hand. "I'd make a good detective," he went on, his tone as penetrating as his eyes. "I like to figure things out."

Bray chuckled softly. "I'm finding that just about anybody would make a better detective than me—from preachers to pretty blonde traffic cops." Bray stepped to the next hand.

Hank Petrelli resembled a brick wall: broad, hard, like an NFL tackle. But his playful eyes resembled a child's. He didn't look forty. Thirty-five maybe, even with the graying temples. His hand was meaty and handshake firm, a man's grip, used to tools, ready to wrestle a torque wrench. "It's good to finally meet you," Hank greeted. "We saw your picture."

Bray liked Hank immediately. He was real, a working man. Good to have a brew with.

"What went through your mind when you were heading toward that burning boat?" Hank asked.

"Here I go—flunking another I.Q. test."

Hank laughed. "I'm bravest when I'm being dumb too." Then he slapped Bray good-naturedly on the shoulder.

Bray winced.

Sylvia came next. She offered her hand with a gushing smile. "It's good to see you again."

"And you," Bray said.

"You've stayed away a long time."

"But not anymore."

"Good." Then she took a deep breath, her bosom rising like a tide. "What's it like living out there?"

Bray gave a shallow shrug. "Somewhere between *Leave it to Beaver* and *Miami Vice*."

Sylvia nodded vacantly. "Here it's *Birdman of Alcatraz* meets *Village of the Damned*."

Bray smiled, "I'll have to remember that." Glancing about, then turning to Phil, he asked, "Where's Bilba?"

Before the sound of his voice died away the grande dame appeared. A plushly carpeted stairway hugged the wall on the right side of the room and Bilba, draped in a brilliant sun-yellow gown, stood at the top of it. Tall, slender, her face as angular as a greyhound's, she surveyed everyone with predator's eyes. Then, as if her body were invaded by a younger, more cheerful spirit, her rigid mouth relaxed and formed a smile. Then, after her first couple of steps, a welcoming hand went out. Bilba became the picture of a loving aunt.

"Bray Sanderson—my Bray," she began. "I can't tell you how pleased I am that you accepted our invitation. We've treated you abominably over the years. Please enjoy your time here as we will enjoy spending it with you." She'd learned and recited the speech perfectly. And, as it turned out, with far more warmth than was in her hand. When Bray finally took it, he found it cold and bloodless. But that was okay. This was Bilba, and Bray felt that any warmth from her at all was like a bonfire from anyone else.

She kissed him on the cheek. Her lips were ice.

Icy lips or not, Bray had never felt so accepted, so included.

"Thank you," Bray said to Bilba, then turned to the others. "Thank you all. This is great. Wonderful. Part of a family. For the first time."

They all clapped, then Tommy led them in a cheer. The warmth of the moment rushed through Bray's veins. He wanted to embrace them all.

Dinner was joyous. A lot of talking and laughing, memories volleying from one side of the table to the other. Quiet prevailed only when he told them of Breck's legacy.

"He put a million dollars in trust, and I'm being given the interest for the rest of my life."

Phil splashed more chardonnay in his glass. "In cash? An income?"

"How unselfish of him," Hank said, his tone flat. Now he took a long drink of beer. "The guy was a prince."

"Are you sure it was Breck?" Tommy asked.

"That's what the attorney said."

"Maybe guilt," Phil offered, and Bray nodded agreement.

"Breck?" Tommy said, his brows canting. He took a long swig of grapefruit juice.

"Who gets the million?" Hank asked, with a good-natured smile.

Bray didn't notice the others tighten when the question was asked. "Someone when I die. But who cares, right? That'll be a hundred years from now."

"Certainly a lifetime," Tommy said.

They all laughed again, a forced, calculated laugh.

Ginger followed the police car in her Ford Escort while Win tried to make his arm comfortable. Impossible. He'd never broken a bone before, and he wasn't prepared for the profound ache. Chad, in the back seat, placed a hand on Win's shoulder. Now and then he'd pat his father-to-be.

"I hurt my wrist once," he finally said. "I know what you're going through."

"I appreciate your empathy."

"Is that what I'm showing?"

"Right. Empathy."

Chad smiled, immensely satisfied.

Ginger saw the wrecking yard coming up. "You ready to see your car like that?"

"My car," Win groaned. "I loved that car."

Reflecting their headlights, the police car pulled into Max Helper's wrecking yard and they followed. Well-lit, probably for the Doberman, the wrecking yard was smothered in grease and strewn with battered cars. No surprises there. They followed the police car down a long lane and parked not far from a tin-sided shack.

Ginger pulled up behind him, and everyone got out of the car.

Officer Tom Flagg, moving at a slow, deliberate pace walked up to them. "It's over here."

Win nearly broke down and cried as they walked toward what remained of his Chevy. "Max, this here's the owners," Flagg called to a man emerging from a tin shack. The guy had a bloom of white whiskers and a shock of ink-black hair and leathery skin in between. "I want to show 'em what you showed me."

"Show us what?" Win asked. Both he and Ginger walked beside Flagg, while Chad trailed behind, peering into random wreckage.

They reached his car. A traumatic moment for Win. "The frame's gotta be bent," Win groaned, running a hand over the deep, rounded dent where it had hit the pole. Then he brushed some of the rotting fruit away.

Chad stepped up, mouth wide in shock. "Wow! You did it up good."

"It may not be his fault," Flagg said.

"A blowout? My fault?" Win exclaimed. "But what do you mean?"

They all heard an engine growl to life and seconds later the forklift ground across the gravel toward them.

"Any reason for someone to shoot at you?"

Win grimaced. "A bad sermon, maybe. Someone shot at me?"

Flagg reached into his pocket and pulled out a plastic bag.

"Looks like somebody's filling," Win commented.

Ginger stepped up and took a good look. "A large bullet. There hasn't been time for lab work. Where'd you get it?"

"Farmer dug it from the brain of that cow you hit."

"*It* hit me."

"You hit a cow?" Chad laughed.

"It charged the car. Crazed cow. Frightening." He turned back to Flagg. "You sure that's a bullet?"

"Seems logical. Seems like lead—still hard—and in a cow's brain."

"How'd it get all banged up?" Ginger asked.

"Hitting things before it hit the cow."

"Why shoot at me?" Win asked the real question.

"Well," said Flagg, "the farmer dug it out of the cow while I was still there. Puttin' two and two together I checked the tire that blew. The tread looked pretty good—the rest of it was pretty ripped up. Couldn't tell much. But when Max here pulled it to the yard, I checked underneath."

The forklift lifted the edge of the Chevy, exposing the undercarriage. Flagg knelt down and aimed the beam of his flashlight toward the oil pan.

Win felt obligated to get down on all fours and study the illuminated area. He quickly found a crease in the oil pan, one about four inches long that deepened then stopped. "You're talking about this?"

"Then it ricocheted to here," Flagg said, pointing to the long nick on the chassis.

"Maybe a rock. I plowed through a lot of 'em."

"This isn't a rock we pulled from that cow's brain."

"True," Win said, back on his feet as Ginger took his place.

"If a stone did it," Ginger said, "you'd think the nick would go from front to back—not sideways. And it would need to go pretty fast to dent steel." After another few minutes she backed out from beneath the car and got to her feet. A stern brushing did nothing to shake the dirt from her jeans. Giving up she stepped over to Win. "That could be the path of a bullet."

"To hit the tire and the oil pan both, it would have had to bounce off an asphalt road," Win pointed out.

"Could have hit a rock," Flagg speculated.

Win took a deep breath. "Maybe."

"You want the bullet to leave a note?" Ginger offered.

"Sure," Win offered, "'I did this. signed, Bullet.' That would work."

"So, anyone want to shoot at you?" Flagg asked.

"I had a passenger," Win said.

"They were shootin' at him?"

Win only shrugged. "I'm not convinced anyone was shooting at anyone. This is Vermont. There are guys everywhere who can't tell Bambi from Bossy from a BF Goodrich. A stray bullet could have downed Bossy and the creases could be from just about anything."

"Someone shooting at you guys is the least likely possibility," Ginger said. "You check for any lead wipe on the creases?"

Flagg nodded. "Took scrapings. Should know by Monday or Tuesday."

Win eyed the policeman. "Maybe I can look around a little. I know about where the tire blew—maybe I can find something."

"We can both look," Ginger offered.

Flagg motioned to Max to let the car down. Then he turned to Win. "You gonna fix that car?" he asked.

"I don't know. The insurance company will probably call it totaled and fair market value won't fix it. I'd have to come up with the rest and assistant pastors don't make much."

"And," Ginger inserted, "you have a wedding to budget for."

"You two getting hitched?" Flagg asked, smiling for the first time.

"We'll invite you," Ginger told him.

That pleased him.

A few minutes later they were back in the Ford Escort.

"We'll look around in the morning," Win commented. "It's just all so strange."

"If there's anything to find, we'll find it," Ginger said.

"I just hope Bray's in no trouble tonight," Win said, looking off toward the island. Then, studying his cast, he added, "Of course, he'll probably sleep a whole lot better tonight than I will."

With after-dinner drinks in hand, the Sanderson clan retired to the sitting room, a darkly masculine room with thick, soft leather chairs and battle murals covering the walls.

"Before you sit," Bilba said, holding a glass of grapefruit juice, "I'm sure you'd like to extend your last respects to your Uncle Breck."

"He'll have time to do that later," Phil protested.

"Now," said Bilba.

And now it was. Leaving the others behind, Bilba walked Bray out to the grave. Lit dimly by perimeter garden lamps, the setting was deeply reverent.

"I designed it myself," Bilba told him proudly. "He left instructions and I followed them to the letter as I always did. But there were a few discretionary things."

One of those things was the heart-shaped border of impatiens. "A nice touch, don't you think? The palm tree over his head, the flowers around?"

"That vase of flowers—also a nice touch."

"I replenish it every morning."

"He must have done something wonderful for you."

"He comforted me when I needed comfort. Took me under his wing when I was lost. I flourished there." As she spoke her eyes never left the base of the palm. But then she woke from her reverie. "Enough," she said, "we're all alive and must carry on."

Bray took a deep breath. There was something he wanted to say. "Aunt Bilba, I need to apologize to the family for not coming back for my mom and dad's funeral. That was bad of me."

"You were overseas, weren't you? We thought nothing of it. We're the ones who should apologize—not calling you sooner. You had an excuse. We didn't."

Again Bray felt cleansed as they walked back to the main house. When they reached the others, Bilba said to Bray, "Your bags are in your room upstairs." Then she addressed the gathering. "Has anyone shown Bray his room?"

"I will," Teri volunteered. "I got him here, I can at least finish the job."

"The party's over?" Bray said disappointedly.

"We don't want to overtire you, Bray," Bilba said sympathetically. "You're still convalescing."

She was right. He was tired.

"And we want you rested for your therapist in the morning," Phil said, grinning.

"I'd break my own leg to get that therapist." Hank laughed, "Well, time to go to work."

"Tonight?" Bray exclaimed.

"Every night," Hank groaned, "or at least five of 'em."

Phil, who'd been all but buried in one of the more comfortable leather chairs, stood. "I'll take you up."

"But I was going to take him up," Teri protested.

"Bray and I need to talk."

"Not business," Bray pretended. "Please don't let it be business."

Phil grinned, "With you having been properly prepared by the visit to our dearly departed—and having had three splashes of excellent brandy—now is the perfect time for business."

Taking another sip from the snifter, Bray said, "When I say no, you're not going to throw me off a cliff or anything, are you?"

Phil laughed. Really laughed. The others chuckled politely.

CHAPTER 5

Bray," Phil began, his movements exaggerated from drink, "you've been working for ingrates all your life—the army, the police. It's time to work for yourself. Expand your world. Stretch those horizons in both directions farther than dreams can dream."

Bray's room, though it looked recently dusted and the linens appeared fresh, was musty and airless. For Bray, talking business made it more so. But before he shut Phil off completely, he had his question to ask to clear his conscience. He raised a hand and gestured Phil to put what he was saying on hold. "Before you go further, I've got an apology to make."

"Apology? For what? Apologize to family? Nonsense."

"For not coming back for Mom and Dad's funeral. I should have."

"You were off defending your country—probably savagely fighting from bordello to brothel—drawing the battle lines anywhere you had to." Phil loved this monologue and laughed heartily.

"No. I'm serious. I should have—they were my mother and father, and they were killed—horribly killed. I should have come back."

"We always figured we had driven you away. We owed *you* the apology. In a way we are apologizing by inviting you up here now."

Bray looked at his brother deeply, then finally nodded. "Okay. You accept mine, and I'll accept yours."

"Done," said Phil.

"Good," said Bray. "Now, back to what you were saying. I'm really not interested in the family business. With Breck's insurance I'm making more money than I need."

Phil's finger raised. "Don't think *need*—think *want*. You could buy your own police force—own your own army."

"I'm a little bombed, Phil," Bray confided the obvious.

"That means we think more clearly."

"It does? Maybe for you—"

Teri appeared at the door smiling, and everything for Bray brightened.

Bray said to Phil, "Bugger off, Phil."

"We'll talk again," he promised. "But I, too, have an engagement. A personal wine tasting."

Bray nodded and graciously ushered him out—and Teri in.

When the phone rang about midnight, Win was actually relieved. Sleeping with the heavy cast and severe bruises on his left side was like curling up in a punching bag. Lying in the confines of a '57 Corvette bed with sides level with the mattress didn't help much either. Searching for comfortable, he'd twice tossed the cast over the top of him, smacking it on the bed's fiberglass edge—each time shock waves rifled to his heart.

He caught the phone before the second ring.

"Hhhiii," Bray slurred, a feat with one syllable.

"Hi, yourself," Win greeted, "sounds like paradise agrees with you."

"Paradise." Three syllables become six. "You should shee it. A bottle of great wine in my room. My very own balcony overlooking Breck's very own grave and the lake beyond—shounds like an ad for a Hawaiian Cemetery—don't it?"

Teri had thrown open the velvet drapes, opened the balcony French doors, and let the cleansing lake breezes in. Even the distant smells of fire couldn't mute the lake's sweetness.

"Everybody good to you?"

"Everybody's great. And I have noshing to be guilty about. They're apologizing to *moi*. Phil's a little disappointed. He put the full-court presh on me to join their little group here. But when you're independently wealthy, you can make career choices. I'm short o' wondering why I left in the first place."

"What blurred your memory?"

"The brandy—the monster meal. They made me everything I like. And the hero's welcome. And the wine waiting for me in my room. And the beautiful chick here with me—right now."

"Careful—"

Bray laughed. "It's Teri. She helped you."

"Teri." The memory brought with it a whiff of wildflowers.

"She likes wine, too, and getting bombed with your niece is shafe, right? Wanna say hi?"

"It's past midnight, Bray, I couldn't be clever on a bet."

"Saying hi doesn't require clever."

"Come on, Bray, give me a break here."

"I heard that," Teri's voice came on. "Just wanted to ask about your arm."

"Feels like a one-ton butterfly is going to break out of it any second."

"You should be here," she said after a soft laugh. "That butterfly could carry *us* off and we wouldn't care."

"Naw, I'd be an extreme wet blanket. I'm engaged."

"And she carries a gun."

Win smiled. "Thank you for the arm. The doctor said you prevented major damage. I appreciate that."

"That's okay. Believe me, my treat."

Win blushed. "Well, thank you. Maybe I'll see you when I pick Bray up."

"That long?"

Win found himself thinking about the scratches on the Chevy's undercarriage. "Maybe sooner," he said. "Let me talk to the drunk again."

After some phone juggling Bray came on. "Guess what? The therapist is something."

"You sound a little *too* excited about that."

That's when Win heard some curiously anxious sounds. A gasp, a few quick words—frightened, even panicked. A muffled shout, nearly a scream, then what sounded like the phone bouncing on the floor.

"Bray—you there? Bray?"

What caused the sounds had happened quickly.

Phone in hand and feeling loose, Bray had leaned against the balcony railing.

Wood creaked then cracked. The railing moved. He gasped and tried to pull himself upright. But his weight wouldn't shift. The railing creaked again, then cracked again. He cried out. Grabbing for anything, he found nothing but the cordless phone in his hand. Vertigo swept over him as every muscle tightened. His injured leg collapsed. He sensed himself falling.

The railing broke free, his body dropped and began its crushing descent. That instant, adrenalin replacing alcohol, Teri wrapped her arms around her uncle's waist, spun and threw him back into the room. The phone bounced on the floor. Teri, in turn, spun again and landed against another section of the railing. It held. Still experiencing the panic, she collapsed against the building wall hyperventilating, her hand pressing her chest.

Bray's heart raced. His lungs pumped. He lay still for several seconds, then he worked himself onto one arm. That's when he heard Win's muted voice calling through the receiver. Regaining what he could of himself, he grabbed the receiver. "I'm okay," he said.

"What happened?"

"An accident," Bray said now feeling immensely tired and weighed down, the alcohol submerging his system.

"What kind of accident?"

"I'm okay. Really. A balcony railing gave way. Teri pulled me away from it. Threw me on the floor."

"Well stay there for a while. How'd it give way?"

"I leaned on it. Listen, Win, I'm suddenly pretty tired. I think I'm going to call it a night."

"You want me to come up?"

"It's an old house. You know how things rot on the lake. I'm the prime example. It just gave way. I need sleep. I'll call tomorrow."

Win hesitated, trying to keep him on the line. Maybe he was right. But the blowout, now this—"Why don't I come on up and—"

"I'll call you tomorrow—or I guess today. Listen, Win, I'm fine, really."

Win heard the dial tone. Hanging up the phone he fell back into his bed wide awake—his arm throbbing just a little less insistently than his head.

Bray looked up at Teri. Still against the wall, her breathing was nearly normal. "You okay?" he asked.

"More to the point, are you?"

"You saved my life. They'd be scraping me up from the sidewalk." He started to get up, but Teri was quickly on the floor beside him.

"Win's worried?"

"Well," he stammered, "he thinks I'm in danger up here."

"Danger?"

"Like someone's trying to—"

"Hurt you?"

"I probably laid it on a little thick about Breck, and then the tire, and now the railing. He'll get over it."

"Sure," she said, but she couldn't hide the strain in her voice. "So, you got any jacks? We could play right here."

Bray laughed gently, placing a paternal hand on hers. A curious, fatherly feeling was breaking over him. Though undoubtedly the result of the wine and circumstance, there was no denying it.

"You okay, Uncle Bray?" Teri asked.

"Sure. Fine. Just thinking."

"About what?"

"Nothing, really."

"What?" she asked again, more insistent.

"Diane and I could never have children. Her uterus or something. But I always envied your father that he'd had you—and Tommy. But mostly you."

"Me? Really? I'm no prize."

"I'd want a daughter just like you."

"Really? Your daughter?" Teri said, wonderfully stunned. And though her expression didn't change—the hint of questioning in her eyes and mouth remained—a lonely tear slipped down her cheek, disappearing in a quick swipe of her hand. "Thank you, Uncle Bray." Her heart fluttered, not only from a sense of longing fulfilled, but from a sudden hammer blow of guilt.

"I really have to go," she said quickly. "I'm light-headed. I think I'm getting sick."

"I didn't offend you, did I?"

"Oh, no," she said, so sincerely it was nearly a gasp. "But I have to go. You'll be able to get up all right, won't you?"

"Sure. I—"

And she was gone.

"Well," Bray said to the door, "thanks for saving my life."

Teri ran all the way to her house—maybe even over the grave. But graves didn't matter. She grabbed the butane fireplace lighter and took it to the bathroom. Except for those on the commode, all the candles were still intact. Using the lighter like a blowtorch, Teri fired up those candles. Within seconds the bathroom blazed. Collapsing on her knees before the toilet, she clasped her hands together and began praying. "Oh god of stupid women, help this one. He's so nice. He's like the dad I wish I had. And I tried to kill him. I can't believe I did that—" she prayed for at least ten minutes, so long that the little candles began dissolving to pools of wax. Her final plea was for Win—"I have to have him—I really do. Just hearing his voice tonight—But that's for another time. Right now I have to make it right with Uncle Bray. His daughter. I haven't been anybody's daughter—ever. I've been an employee. Been tucked in at night by a dental plan." She said "amen" because it seemed right, then blew out the candles wondering if she should make a wish.

Spent, she fell into bed.

But she didn't sleep. She relived Bray toppling over that balcony.

She *had* saved his life. Maybe the god of stupid women had given her a chance to atone for her sin. Sure—that was it. Maybe the god of stupid women pushed Bray just so she could save him. And she had.

Feeling immensely better, she lapsed into sleep.

Using the cane, Bray stood and expected to go to his bed. But he didn't. Drawn by a hauntingly beautiful moon glistening off the obsidian lake, he hobbled to the balcony. After testing each railing with the cane's tripod, he leaned against one.

The little island, separated from him by a glistening ribbon of water, lay tomb dark.

Do I really care what goes on over there? he thought.

A dim patch of reflected light appeared on the little island revealing a tangle of trees and shrubs bordering a trail. The light remained for a few seconds then died. Moments later Bray heard an inboard's insistent buzz. He scanned the lake and found a moving shadow—black on black—a dull finish on a reflective lake. A small boat, maybe one of those Sea-Doos, buzzing toward Burlington. After only a couple of minutes, though, darkness swallowed the boat. The buzzing remained, but it, too, died eventually. *Must be something urgent,* Bray thought. *World markets never sleep.*

Ginger was still on disability leave from the Burlington Police Department. She'd been severely injured when her patrol car was forced off the road not long after the boat explosion that injured Bray. She'd hoped to be well by now, but painful complications with her knee required another operation. Although she could walk on it reasonably well, if she ran or sat for a long time, the pain became excruciating. So home she went, and what a blessing that turned out to be. With the wedding in a couple months, there were a million things to do. And now that Win had been hurt, a million and one.

Of course, at five in the morning when Lake Champlain was still black, she considered none of this. In fact, she was surprised to be considering anything at all. Why was she awake? The alarm couldn't have gone off.

Then she heard someone rattling around in the kitchen.

"Win? That you?"

"Yeah," Win said, a voice both cheerful and guilty. "I thought I'd surprise you with breakfast. Came over by boat."

Flopping down the hallway in her slappy-slippers, she tied the knot on her summer robe. "At five?"

"It'll be dawn by the time we get there."

"Get where?"

"To where I had the blowout."

"That couldn't wait a few hours?"

"It could. But we don't want traffic spoiling things, which it would if we waited. Anyway, I couldn't sleep after Bray called last night. He nearly fell over a balcony while I was talking to him."

"He what?"

Win described his conversation with Bray and Teri.

"So, you talked to Teri."

Win's head cocked. "Sure. I wanted to thank her for . . . Didn't you hear the part about Bray and the railing?"

"Of course. What did Teri have to say?"

Win just sighed. "Eggs okay?"

"How 'bout pancakes?" Chad called from his bedroom.

With the fire still raging somewhere in northeastern New York, dawn broke as it had before—tinged yellow, sometimes brown. But even for that feeling of dirtiness, dawn was painted in long, crimson strokes. They arrived just as it was dissolving into something hotter and far less breathtaking.

When Win pulled over onto the shoulder and stopped, Ginger stretched, yawned deeply, and wrapped warm arms around Win's neck. After giving him a warm kiss on the ear and taking just the tiniest nibble from his lobe, she said, "So, astounding preacher-slash-detective from the great northeast, you think the blowout and the railing are just too coincidental?" She nibbled his lobe just once more. "What do you think God's up to?" She blew in his ear this time.

Win's toes curled. "October 8th," he muttered. "Uh—God—yes. What he's doing."

She nibbled his neck this time.

"This is not how God designed theology to be discussed."

"Sure he did. This makes it palatable. Puts it all in perspective." She nibbled his neck again then pulled away, her eyes liquid with a rosy contentment.

Still affected, he spoke slowly, the words traveling a long distance before tumbling out. "Don't know—but he's doing something."

"And if all things work together for good, it all has to do with your broken arm—my knee—and a dead cow."

"Right. If the bullet had hit a tree—no bullet."

"Right," Ginger said, studying his neck again. "Even if I never find a wedding dress—I still get that neck to nibble on."

"You get it all."

"All?" She gave a breathy gasp. "Wow! All." Then she smiled coyly and straightened. After clearing her throat like a professor, she said, "So, we're looking for what the bullet hit to bounce up and nick the oil pan."

"Right."

"Which should be in the middle of the road."

"Exactly."

Ginger nodded. Then she looked to the west along the embankment. "If the perp did shoot at your tire, he'd have to do it from up there."

"Probably."

"So, what's your plan, man?"

"From that little bend south of here you slow the cars down so I can look over here." He pointed north.

She looked to where the road curved. "I'll scream very loud. I don't want to marry a hood ornament."

Stationing herself where she could see both Win and oncoming traffic, she sat on an ancient tree stump and waited.

Win began his search. He had remembered the spot pretty accurately. Only about ten yards north of Ginger's Escort, he spotted signs of road trauma. A deep scar in the asphalt caused by his wheel rim digging in, slivers of rubber evident in the tar. Then a little further up, more scars where he'd tried to straighten himself out and had overcompensated.

The fruit stand still stood precariously, the smashed fruits and vegetables laying around gathering flies. The good produce had long since been removed to other markets.

What he hoped to find was probably back from those scars in the asphalt. Astride the center line, Win studied the roadway.

"Car!" he heard Ginger call.

He stopped until the car passed, then he continued, pebble by pebble, gouge by gouge, bent close to the road's surface.

"See anything?" Ginger called to him.

Eyes remaining on the road. "Just tar—lots of tar."

"I'm getting bored here. Maybe I should look on the embankment."

"Just a little while long—" he stopped. Something caught his eye. A rock, a pebble really, once doused in tar, was now chipped, its white core exposed. It hadn't had time to blacken again. And it looked like something was embedded in the remaining piece—something that glinted—lead? Straightening, he fished out a pocket knife to dig it out when he heard Ginger. "Hey, slow down—slow down—SLOW DOWN!"

Win turned to see Ginger spin out of the way of a red Dodge Viper careening around the curve. The driver probably figured he'd have the road to himself this early, and to see some gal trying to slow him down when he had a Viper to drive—well, guys set their priorities. By the time Win stood, the guy behind the wheel had seen him. The Viper swerved toward the lake as Win dove for the embankment. Landing on all fours, Win watched the crimson flash skid on the road's gravel shoulder. An instant later, the Viper regained traction on the blacktop, then disappeared as the road bent around the damaged fruit stand. "Now that's a car," Win muttered.

"You okay?" Ginger cried.

His arm complained but otherwise he was fine. "I found something. I'll dig it out."

"Ah," Ginger said relieved. "Then we can search the bushes."

Win returned to where he'd found the rock. "It's gone." He pushed a frustrated hand over his eyes. "That guy must have knocked it loose."

"Look along the side of the road—it can't be that far away."

But it was. Five minutes of careful examination turned up nothing. "I can't believe it. It looked like a piece of the bullet might still be in it. What's God up to here?"

Ginger abandoned her post and ran to where Win stood. For a minute the two of them stared down at the small hole in the pavement as if the rock might reappear. It didn't.

"Maybe it's time to take a look at the embankment?" Ginger suggested.

Win nodded and they began searching west of the road—an ancient apple orchard, the land between the gnarled trees layered in weeds, brush, and pink and yellow wildflowers. They searched slowly, step by step, foot by foot, keeping to the high places near the road.

"What if he climbed a tree?" Ginger said.

Win stopped and looked up. "He'd take the chance of being seen—unlikely."

"I think I see something," Ginger said, eyes focused several yards ahead. Getting there, she stopped and immediately began studying the earth.

Win didn't see it until he got there. "A depression—"

"The weeds are pressed down. Someone's been lying here."

Although most of the weeds were recovering, there were spots where an elbow, a hip and toes could have dug in.

"Over here," Ginger pointed. If a person had lain in the weeds and fired at the road below, the tip of the rifle barrel would have touched a small bush. "Look—it's burned. The flash started a little fire. Maybe he had to put it out."

"It rained a little beforehand. Maybe that small area stayed dry, and before the flames really got going, it hit wet greenery."

Ginger pushed a hand into the bush. "Cigarette butt," she said, holding an old Marlboro between thumb and forefinger.

"You think the cigarette did this?" Win asked.

"If there were powder burns they went up in flames. No way to know."

"We get so close, then—smells so pretty here in the morning—wildflowers, spicy apple." His nose caught the aroma of something else. A hint of sour smoke—he'd smelled it before. But where? Maybe it was just the ash from the New York fire—*only God knows*. "Any casings around? Footprints? Anything?"

A quick survey found nothing.

"We know nothing more," Ginger finally articulated it.

"Not so. We know there was a bullet in that cow, and we haven't refuted my tire being shot out."

"Nor have we refuted your imagination."

Win draped his right arm over Ginger's shoulder. "But Bray's my buddy—and this isn't a court of law."

"So suspicions matter."

"Sure—especially when the stakes are high."

"In that case," Ginger said, slipping an arm around Win's waist, "what *did* Teri talk to you about last night?"

Bray woke early, light spearing him from a break between the thick tapestry-like curtains. Surprisingly he'd slept well. At home he could never get his leg comfortable. Here, of course, he'd sedated himself pretty well before lying down.

After a quick shower in the adjoining bathroom, he dressed in khakis and a brightly flowered shirt and hobbled over to the window. He threw the curtains open and let the sunlight hit him squarely in the face. What a morning! The rich blue sky, a few cotton-puff clouds off toward New Hampshire, the lake deep and velvety—a glass calm—all reflected his soul like the lake reflected emerald green trees.

Where is the ash from the distant fire? he wondered. Maybe a wind with a free and indomitable spirit had washed it away.

He filled his lungs—the air smelled freer, directionless but ripe and enthusiastic—a vagabond with worlds cheering him on.

Was this how the independently wealthy christened the day? How it would be from now on? Letting the senses drink in the morning? Taking breaths that actually tasted the air? If it was, he'd get used to it in no time.

Hmmm. The railing's fixed. In the middle of the night? He hadn't heard a thing. Of course, he had been pretty drunk.

A light tap at the door and Teri stepped in carrying a glistening silver tray. On it was a steaming mug of coffee, a thick cheese Danish, and a newspaper folded open to the comics. "I think I got it all."

She placed the tray on a small walnut table not far from the balcony doors. "It's a special French Roast. My dad likes it. He insisted."

"Sounds good," he smiled congenially. The surroundings compelled it. At home he would have just grunted. "They fixed the railing."

"Really?" She verified it for herself. "I didn't tell anyone," she said, puzzled. "Someone must have stumbled over it below."

"Me," came Bilba's penetrating voice from behind her. Teri turned as Bilba slipped into the room. She wore a bright, cheery blouse and baggy black slacks. Except for her hair pulled back in a severe bun and her hollow black eyes, she looked remarkably stylish. She moved stiff-legged, as a crow might. "You slept well?"

"Fine, Aunt Bilba," Bray said. "Wonderful. Thank you for sharing a room in your home with me."

"I'm still not used to it being mine. Breck lived here since he laid the foundation. Redecorating will be like killing his memory. But don't you just hate all this medieval stuff?"

Bray heard Teri say, "Bray nearly fell when that railing gave way last night."

Bilba gasped. "Were you hurt?"

"Teri pulled me away just in time," Bray told her.

"Oh, my goodness," Bilba exclaimed, her hand to her throat. "It was close then. I got up early this morning and nearly tripped over it. Had a workman take care of it."

"I slept right through it."

"I told him to be quiet."

"He could have done it later," Teri said, as if thinking aloud.

"A missing railing is a hazard." Then Bilba looked at Bray as if seeing more than there was to see. "Seems you've cheated death again." Then she brightened, but the brightness seemed behind a dark veil. "And Teri's brought your morning things? Prefer oatmeal myself. And the news. They can't seem to put that fire out—but the winds have shifted so at least its not bothering us for the time being."

"Good coffee," he said, taking a long sip. "Danish looks great."

"Sweet," Bilba said, disdainfully, moving toward the door. "I need to spend time at the office. Weekends mean little around here."

"Thank you again, Bilba," Bray said and received a stiff smile in return. She left. "I thought she'd loosened up last night," Bray said.

"That *was* loose," Teri said, staring at the empty hole Bilba had once occupied. After a long moment she turned back. "Have your breakfast then we'll take a walk."

"Let's hope you don't have to save me from any cliffs."

Teri laughed graciously, but, to her surprise, a small voice deep within her wondered the same thing.

Win and Ginger searched a little bit more and found nothing. On their way back, they stopped for coffee at Judy's, a restaurant in a restored Victorian home. They were greeted by Judy herself.

They had coffee near the window that looked out over the lake, if you craned your neck just right. "I wonder how that farmer's making out. No more fruit stand—and that cow had to have been a good milker. Had an udder like the Goodyear Blimp. I'll call him later."

"Good. So," began Ginger. "you still think Bray's in danger?"

"It's not like God's waving a neon sign."

"It's his family, Win."

Win sighed. "I missed reading my Bible this morning. Don't like that."

"Read twice as much tomorrow."

"Doesn't work that way." He returned to his original subject. "Two coincidences—nothing to refute the worst—"

"And nothing to confirm the positive." She stiffened. "I have been around crime too long. I'd actually feel better if one family member were out to kill another."

"Sleuthing's habit-forming. Crime gives a reason for more sleuthing. Sniffing clues is as addictive as sniffing—"

"Stop that," Ginger said firmly. "We're also Christians, and you're a pastor. How can we actually want Bray to be in danger? We're supposed to *want* his family to embrace him."

"But danger might bring him closer to the Lord."

"So we're to want all the unsaved people in the world to be stalked by killers."

"It's accurate to say that they already are." A chill rifled through him. More profoundly than just the result of a thought.

"You okay?" Ginger finally asked when his eyes hadn't blinked.

"I felt something again. Not as deeply, but something."

"I hate this about you. It's just too spooky."

"I'm not too fond of it either, but it was another heads-up. Something's going on—something."

On the island, Tommy pulled his drapes slightly apart and spied Bray and Teri as they strolled by his house. Moments later, a briefcase in hand, he stepped across the common, avoided the grave, and crossed quickly to Bilba's mansion. After silently climbing the stairs, he disappeared into Bray's room.

CHAPTER 6

The butterfly house stood two stories. Its octagonal structure was made predominantly of wood columns, trusses and thick, double-paned thermal glass. This allowed the desired warmth and humidity to be maintained with the help of an atomized warm-water spray that circulated continually to keep the hot summer sun at bay. A nylon screen rose and fell as needed for shade. Except for a circular walk with wooden benches in every quadrant, the floor was a large flower bed supporting a host of tropical greenery and vines. A gentle brook meandered through with a burbling fountain at one end and a small pool at the other. In the center of the structure, like a rotting native god, stood a flowing cement sculpture. It vaguely resembled a ten-foot hunchback holding an egg.

As she often did before "work," Bilba sat on the bench facing the entrance. As before, she saw none of the vegetation, none of the cement sculpture; her attention belonged to the butterflies.

Dancing, bobbing, flitting about, lighting here and there, in bunches and alone. They darted everywhere, light glistening magically off their wings—black, white, orange, pink, delicate, wild. She sat dazzled by them, mesmerized and captivated—a seventy-three-year-old child. Sometimes she'd call to them, or find herself whispering. Sometimes she'd leap up excitedly on ancient legs. Other times she'd sit transfixed watching just one the whole time.

This morning she sat, a smile wandering about her face, her eyes large, her heart fluttering like the wings around her. She was so enraptured with her little charges that she didn't notice the green-clad guard enter until he stood before her. Finally she left her trance and peered up into his face. Like Bilba, Ron Gunn was angular and severe, taller than average with muscular shoulders. He didn't speak.

She finally did. "I was sure that railing would have been the end of it."

"Ms. Sanderson pulled him back."

"I know," Bilba said, marveling at the butterflies as they flitted about. Waves of them hovered and turned in unison then suddenly broke apart in sparkling arrays.

She looked up. "Teri? Yes. She's formed an attachment to Bray—very fast. I've only had one attachment in seventy-three years—well two. She'll learn."

A monarch landed on the top of her ear. Bilba stiffened. The butterfly flexed its wings.

"What next, then?" Ron asked, wanting desperately to brush the butterfly from her ear.

"Set another trap," Bilba said, several butterflies bobbing on invisible springs before her face. "Those cliffs give you any ideas?"

"I have to know where he's going."

"Find out," Bilba told him, her head rigid, her eyes trying desperately to turn far enough to see her ear and the butterfly perched there.

"I deserve something extra for doing this."

"Extra?"

"More money."

"Like a tip?"

"Like payment."

Bilba looked up at him as if lost. "For taking out a couple of screws? Or loosening a boulder? You do those things anyway."

"But now someone's going to die."

"Hopefully, yes, but people die and you do nothing."

"But now if I do nothing, someone won't."

"If you do nothing you'll be fired."

"Then I'll go to the police."

"And tell them you did nothing?"

"I'll tell them you wanted me—"

"In fact you've already done something. But I'm not following you. Do you want to work here and earn large sums of money for doing very little, or do you want to return to the mainland and earn smaller sums of money for working much harder?"

"But I deserve more money for this."

"Is the butterfly still there? I can't feel him anymore."

"He's there."

"I wonder why I can't feel him anymore. You'd think I could feel a butterfly clutching my ear. Don't you think?"

Ron didn't reply.

"Are you sure he's there? I dare not try to feel him."

"I'll figure it out and let you know."

"Don't tell me. Then I'm not involved."

"But what if you fall into the trap?"

"Me?" Bilba laughed. "I never go anywhere. Someone could lay a trap for me, and I'd be years falling into it. More than years. Decades."

"Okay. I'll do what I can."

"Thank you, Ron. I'll be eternally grateful."

Ron nodded and left. *That and a dollar-six will get me a cup of coffee*, he thought as the door closed behind him.

Teri's tours were thorough. As they walked the perimeter of the island, often in back of the houses, Bray peered over every cliff surveying every rusty boulder and shale cove that hugged its base. He saw every outbuilding, every house, every back garden, every gardener and every lookout point, some with glorious views of the lake and the distant shoreline.

"I remember it as wilder," Bray commented, "more weeds. And there used to be boats shuttling people to and from the small island."

"We've gone underground," Teri said, offhandedly.

"A tunnel?"

"A secret," said Teri in a low tone.

"You guys got the crown jewels over there?"

"And we all wish we were the head on which the crown is placed." Teri said, walking idly to land's end. Two waverunners burst from below her and headed off toward St. Albans. They roared only a couple hundred yards then crossed. One spun on its tail, then joined the other in a race for another couple hundred yards. "Couple of guards on break," Teri commented. "You ever done that?"

"I'd be willing to try." Bray watched as a fisherman near the action shook a fist at them. "When the leg's better. How many of those guys are there?"

"Thirty or so."

"They bunk here?"

"Some."

"Big payroll," Bray commented.

Teri said nothing. She kept an evaluative eye on Bray. What was it about him? Ah. He was so relaxed. Unusual for this island. Everyone else was tense, even anxious. And small wonder. Arrows could come from anywhere. Bray didn't even know there were any. "You know about the memorial trees?" she heard herself ask.

"Breck's little way of making believe he cared."

"The Charlotte tree is over there," she pointed. "My grandma—never knew her."

The oak's witchy limbs reached beyond the cliff—the image of someone vainly trying to escape. Reaching it, Bray read the brass plaque on its trunk. *Charlotte Sanderson, born August 12, 1919, died July 4, 1942.* "My dad's first wife," Bray said. "Your dad was a year old when she died."

"I was one when my mom died, too. Funny somehow, Dad and I have something that important in common, and I only realized it now."

"Where's your mom's tree? The Shelly Oak."

"There." Teri pointed ten yards away, another oak grew out from the cliff's edge, twisting its way toward the sun. It wasn't as spectacular as Charlotte's, its growth stunted, perhaps from the weather—or maybe just a bad acorn.

Reaching it, Bray read the plaque aloud. "Shelly Sanderson, Died December 25, 1965."

"Quite a Christmas present."

"Quite," Bray whispered.

"Tommy says he remembers her. I think he's dreaming. He was two."

"I certainly remember her," Bray said, thinking back to that Christmas. "I was fifteen when she died. Ice fishing accident. A neat lady."

"In what way?" Teri asked, her tone eager.

"She was moving all the time. Couldn't sit still. Talking. Bubbling. She had a sense of humor, too. I see some of her in you. You've got her brains."

"I do? So she would have beaten Tommy in the SATs, too."

"Obliterated him." Bray's brows dipped. "Aren't you a little old to be quoting SATs?"

"Around here it's all I got. Do I look like her?"

"You look like your dad. Tommy looks like her. His eyes, chin."

"You liked her then."

"Very much. I couldn't believe it when she disappeared under the ice like that. On Christmas Day. Charlotte on the Fourth of July. Holidays are tough around here."

"Every day is. Want to see your folk's tree? Actually two trees twisted together."

"Symbolic."

"Sweet," she said.

The trees stood in back of the house in which Bray's parents and their two sons had lived—the one Teri now occupied. Like the other memorials, the twisted pair clung precariously to the cliff and reached up then out over the water at a shallow angle. Unlike the others, they were located on a hollowed-out ledge just below the cliff, accessible by a short cement staircase—no railing. Any fall would end on a garden of boulders and a surging surf. It was not a memorial to be enjoyed.

"What's the plaque say?" Bray asked, unable to read it from where he stood.

Teri shrugged. "Don't think anyone's ever gone down there." Then she asked. "You never saw them again after you left?"

"Had lots o' guilt about that. Maybe still do."

"I didn't know my mom," Teri mused sympathetically, "and my dad—well—our relationship isn't really father and daughter."

"What then?"

"Employer/employee—teacher/pupil—hammer/nail." Then she asked, "Did you hate them?"

"I have the feeling I just wanted them to choose me over Breck. They didn't."

"Same here. And Breck's dead. Makes it hard to believe in yourself. You believe in yourself?"

"Only myself," Bray said, his eyes up and scanning the distant horizon. The waverunning guards were hardly noticeable. "I depend on me."

"You can depend on me—for some things."

"Certainly for coffee and Danish—"

"And the comics." Keeping her eyes on the lake, and after a couple of false starts, she asked, "Do you believe there's a God, Uncle Bray?"

Bray laughed and shook his head, "Not you, too."

Offended and slightly hurt, Teri recoiled, "What's that mean?"

Seeing he'd done some damage, he backpedaled, "I didn't mean it that way. Really."

"It just that I've been praying lately for someone to talk to. And you came along. Now I'm not sure who to thank."

"Thank yourself," Bray said. "You're the one who's easy to talk to."

"Seems weird to pray to yourself."

"You're your own god," Bray said with conviction. "I've regretted depending on others." He looked down at the trees again. "Supply your own needs. It's much easier than relying on someone else."

"I do that," Teri affirmed. "Want to see how?"

"Sure."

Teri smiled eagerly and walked toward the back of her house.

Something moved. She glanced up and saw a fleeting shadow on Hank's roof. A guard? They've got their own observation spots, why up there?

Thinking no more about it she led Bray into her home.

The instant he stepped across the back threshhold, Bray's jaw dropped. On every wall, above every door, within every bookcase, hung guns—rifles, shotguns (over/under and side-by-side), pistols, Uzis—everything and anything that would fire a bullet. One whole wall supported historical weapons—blunderbuss, Revolutionary War muskets and powder horns, Civil War rifles and pistols, western rifles, six-shooters and single shots. A tommy gun hung surrounded by prohibition-era weaponry.

"You shoot all this stuff?"

"Someday."

"Planning your own war?"

"Never thought that far ahead," she said, stepping toward one of the more exotic pieces—a double-barreled, over/under flint-lock pistol. "The bullet's huge."

"No rifling—not much accuracy."

"But if you're close—" A smile crept across her face. "I wonder if I could take out a couple of these bowling pins with this." An idea struck. "Wanna try? It's all electronic—pin setters and scoring, a spiffy ball return, those neat chairs. We could put a whole bunch of holes in all that stuff."

Popping off a couple bowling pins actually sounded like fun. "That downstairs?"

"Sure. Nobody'd care. You're family, right?"

But, for Bray at least, good sense bubbled up. "Naw. Better not." He glanced at his watch. "Anyway, I've got a beautiful therapist on the way."

"Lecher. What's your duty gun?"

"A .357."

"I have a Churchill double .470. Really sweet—" But her voice dissolved as she remembered what she'd used it for last and the old orchard in which it was now hidden. She'd considered retrieving it, but she'd been stopped by the fear of being detected. "But—well—I left it somewhere."

"How? Something like that?"

"Getting it worked on—never went back—got busy." She knew how unconvincing she sounded. She normally lied without flinching. Not this time. She felt incredibly uncomfortable lying to Bray. Maybe truth was tied to respect—to love. She cocked her head questioningly. "But would you have done something like that? Blown up bowling pins?" Teri asked, still subdued.

"Sure. It'd be fun to see their heads explode." Then he chuckled. "They'd be all the guys I'd proved guilty but the courts released."

"Ah, perfect justice. Would Win do it?"

Bray reflected. "Sure—but then he'd pay you for the headless pins—patch up and repaint the backstop, and insist on being contacted if he missed anything. Otherwise, he's as spontaneous as the next guy. With me, I just figure—who'll know?"

Teri smiled. "Right. Who'll know?"

Somewhere in her brain she saw Win Brady's steady eye aiming at a bowling pin, the butt firmly against his powerful shoulder, the weapon steadied by muscular arms. She felt the gun kick as he popped off a round. What a man.

Bray tapped his watch. "Beautiful therapy. Maybe later we could go boating or something."

"Sure. Neat."

Teri watched as her uncle hobbled across the commons, around the grave, and on to the main house. As she did, her mind revisited Win and the gun he held. "Magnificent," she whispered.

Still at Judy's, Win and Ginger downed their third cups of coffee. "Did I tell Judy I wanted decaf?" Win asked. "I'm starting to buzz." Then he said with a strong note of finality, "We can't tell Pamela."

"I love you and have a lot of respect for this—gift—of yours. But there's nothing to tell her."

"She'd want to know."

"What? We know nothing."

"We have intuition—strong feelings. All that's valid here, but we still don't want to tell her. It'd upset her for no reason."

"Maybe we should," Ginger offered, making a reluctant shift. "If Bray were hurt, or worse, killed, and we hadn't told her, she'd hate us—and for good reason."

"But there's nothing she can do."

"She can pray," Ginger pointed out.

"She's doing that anyway."

"I just don't like believing this about Bray and not telling her."

"There's got to be some rank I can pull here. I'm not your husband, but I am your pastor."

"Assistant pastor."

"Assistant carries weight."

"You're not going to order me to do something, are you?"

"Does seem a little risky, doesn't it?"

Brandiwyne Hortentia, the therapist, had been working to help Bray walk without a cane for a half hour before she finally suggested he strip down to his shorts and get up on the massage table she'd brought.

She *was* beautiful.

Too beautiful. Her blonde hair was too full, her hazel eyes too fetching, her full lips too ruby, and when she smiled, the effect was almost too warm. Brandiwyne Hortentia was simply too much of a good thing. Bray definitely preferred Pam.

But—Brandi might grow on him.

She didn't. After only a few minutes of massage, he decided he didn't like being poked, prodded, and rubbed—warm oil or not. He was actually thankful when he heard Phil's voice.

"How you doing?"

"I'm the only guy in the world who doesn't like back rubs."

"You don't?" Brandi exclaimed, startled. "But your aura—"

"Two things," Phil began, "We're looking for your stuff, should have it by this afternoon. And, have you thought about my offer? I want you up to your neck in money."

"But I don't know what you guys do."

"Did you know everything a cop did before you signed on?"

"You have a point."

"And family won't steer you wrong."

"They won't?"

"Not intentionally."

Bray sighed. He didn't like being sold. Nor did he like being pressured to buy a pig in a poke. And he still didn't trust family—not completely—though he'd never admit that right now. "I gotta think about it."

"It's easy work, Bray; the money's great, and you'll be with the family."

Brandi found a particularly tight muscle in his neck and decided to dig it out and take a look at it. Bray screamed.

"Before you know it," Phil went on, "you'll be running this place."

"After the ladies—and you—retire."

Phil eyed Brandi. "Turn your ears off."

"They're seldom on," Brandi stated.

Without hesitation Phil went on. "I run this place now. I call all the shots. Have for a couple years now, and believe me, I can make your life paradise here. And with Breck gone, we've got a vacancy. What I used to do."

"And that would be?"

"Ops management. Hank's doing it, but it should be family. But the big thing is you'll be working with us. Me and you—dynamite. Brothers. Real brothers."

"We weren't before," Bray said.

"We were kids. Petty jealousies. Now we're adults, and with your guts and my—what shall we call it—winningness, we'd be more than dynamite. We'd be, uh, lots of dynamite."

Brothers.

The notion appealed to him. Probably appealed to all men. Someone to mess around with, someone who's known you from birth (or near enough), who's been on the same train and made all the same stops you have. Who deep down inside loves you like no other guy your own age ever will. Someone you can hug without worrying about what kind of bar you're in. A brother is a guy's emotional safe haven.

He'd been close to a couple guys in Vietnam—and to Win—probably closer to Win. Of course, there hadn't even been Christmas cards to the guys in 'Nam. They were close at the time—sometimes more than close. But that was then. Win was like a brother now, but they had different values sometimes. Still, he could count on Win. Win would have written to him in 'Nam. Phil hadn't. Of course, Phil making him rich and powerful now might make up for that.

"So you'll think about it?"

Bray's eyes remained somewhere else.

"Great," Phil exclaimed. "Great. Can hardly wait. This'll be great. Really great."

Bray watched Phil leave his room. After the door was closed, he heard Brandiwyne mutter, "Oily aura—oily. Don't you think?"

Bray said nothing but had to admit it was a reasonable assessment.

Bray found the note after a quick shower. He'd hobbled from the bathroom and saw it on the floor near the open balcony door.

There was no telling how long it had been there. It must have been on the table and blown off.

He picked it up and then noticed a silver chain lying near it. Hanging from the chain was a quarter-sized, stylized stone bear. He'd seen it before. But where? Maybe it would come to him later. He considered the note. Handwritten on both sides, there was a date at the center of one side—June 3rd. No year. A diary page?

He sat on the chair and began reading.

"... *telling me that there's nothing to worry about but I'm not so sure. He keeps wanting us to join. I don't want to. Everyone's stuck here, and I don't want to be stuck here. One of the guards seems to be watching us. I told Hank about it. He says that I'm imagining things.*"

Hank. Sylvia?

The handwriting seemed familiar.

"*We watch the news every night. The body counts—the news people making us look like barbarians. Nardo's last letter only talked about some whore that got murdered—*"

His mother. His name was Braynard so everyone called him Bray. His mother, exercising her passion for uniqueness, called him Nardo. She also called his father Hank instead of Henry. Both were codes to her—and June 3rd must have been 1970. He'd left September 13, 1969. While an MP he'd worked on a prostitute's murder. His mother seldom minced words. When were they killed?

His heart made an actual *thud*. A feeling had broken free from a whole prison of suppressed feelings—a rogue emotion that surged through him.

His mother had touched this page, had deposited her thoughts here. He'd never missed his parents. They were there when he grew up, disappointed him the prescribed number of times, and then were just gone. But he'd lied to himself—particularly about his mother. A woman younger than her years, more cute than motherly, who laughed more than scolded—even when he desperately needed it, wanted to hug him more than discipline—he missed her. A tide of emotion lodged in his throat.

"*It's too hard to picture my little boy dealing with such things. Only yesterday he had such little toes and those sweet little fingers and that smile. There are nights when I feel so far from what's real that I go to sleep with that sweet, sweet little smile. He was such a wonderful little guy. Even as he grew. Like me in so many ways. Doesn't like to be part of the crowd. A loner. I wish I were alone again. That guard's still around."*

That feeling choked him. He'd never heard those things before. He loved his mother, but at times he wondered if she'd ever really existed, if his memories of her were only wishful thinking. These words turned wish to reality. If he hadn't left, maybe they'd still be alive. The feeling in his throat went dry with guilt and took root. He coughed to dislodge it.

"Hank thinks I'm nuts. Just because he's older. At first it was neat, but now I'm just a kid who needs to be tolerated. But I know what I see. The guy's always there. I see him the first thing when I go out in the morning, and he's hiding in the brush when we go to sleep. I want to talk to Breck about it, but Hank says to forget it. Breck wouldn't listen to me anyway. I always thought Breck liked me. Nobody likes me after they get to know me. I'm so stupid sometimes. But I know what I know. We need to get out of here. But they're family. Course it's not my family. It's Hank's family. They're weird. Mine's no prize either. This whole thing is weird. At least with Nardo here it was bearable."

Bray read that last sentence twice.

"We just have to get off this island. All Hank does is play cards, and I keep wanting to take all the aces and eights out of the deck. I've even told him to sit with his back . . ."

Finished, Bray set the page down. His mother was worried. They were killed in the summer—early summer. June?

Thinking, he looked away from the page, but then turned back to read the last few lines again. They died in either June or early July. He'd been on duty with the MPs in Saigon for only a few months when it happened—the investigation of the prostitute's death had happened early in his assignment there.

His mother was worried, and then they died. Murder?

Bray sighed. He hated games, and he was being toyed with. If they wanted him to know something, why didn't they come right out and tell him? Why the innuendos?

He examined the page again. Nothing more.

Maybe if he hobbled around looking profoundly perplexed whoever sent this page would come up and explain. He actually practiced looking profoundly perplexed in a mirror—did a pretty good job of it until he realized: "That's how I always look."

Of course, maybe he knew enough for now. His mother had been worried for her life, and then had been killed.

He picked up the necklace and allowed the bear to hang. Navajo. A green stone with a stab of chocolate. The rogue feeling broke from his heart again. The necklace belonged to his mother. She didn't wear it often—only when she went on a trip. She wore it like some wear a St. Christopher—a travel charm. She wouldn't have worn it for a casual trip to town.

He picked up the phone in his room. "Phil somewhere?—Oh, Phil. I didn't think it would be this easy. Are there any of my mom and dad's things around somewhere? In an attic maybe? Right, maybe next to my stuff. Great. Talk to you later."

Hanging up the phone he placed the bear in his palm to get a closer look and noticed that something came off on his hand. Soot? He studied it more closely. Then, moving as quickly as his bum leg would let him, he went to the bathroom. Taking some toilet tissue, he rubbed the bear gently along the edges. The tissue blackened. The charm had been singed. He continued rubbing until it was clean.

She would have definitely worn it that night if she had been escaping.

CHAPTER 7

Win tucked Chad in, a pleasant ritual made less so by the cast.

"Arm hurt?" Chad asked, the summer sheet pulled up to his chest.

"Aches."

"Did God or Satan do that to you?"

"The fruit stand," Win smiled. Chad loved to ask him questions that tended to plague mankind. A kind of rebellion—instead of a physical pummeling, Chad got him intellectually. But as rebellions go, it seemed healthy enough. "I'm sorry. You deserve a better answer."

"I do."

"I told you once that to see God working you have to look back and see what he's done."

"You say that lots. That and 'If all your friends ate worms, would you?'"

"That's your mother."

"I get confused."

"Well, it's like this, everything that happens to his people—us—is God working—"

"So God did it?"

"Satan destroyed Job's family."

"So Satan was working for God."

"Doing only what God allows him to do."

"So who broke your arm?"

"I don't know, Chad. But I do know this. Good will come of it."

"Is pain good?"

"It just hurts. Pain isn't necessarily bad, and pleasure isn't necessarily good. Some things just gotta be. Like saying goodnight, Chad." Win kissed him on the forehead.

Dave Brubeck whispered *Take Five* on Ginger's favorite jazz station while she sat on the sofa massaging her aching knee, her bare feet resting on the coffee table. The music ended and the news followed: "What's come to be known as the Sacred Valley fire has blackened more than fifty thousand acres and destroyed over a hundred homes. Experts say that with the drought and the scorching summer winds, the fire is likely to cause considerably more damage. In the Lake Champlain area, the weather forecast is pretty normal—warm, maybe rain later tonight. But with all the ash in the upper atmosphere, we may be in for some surprises."

Win slipped onto the sofa next to her and gave her a gentle hug. "We're a great pair—broken arm, strained knee. If we didn't have God on our side the world would run right over us."

"It has. At least the fire's keeping its distance." She looked up, more on her mind than knees and arms and weather. "I've been thinking. The stakes are pretty high if you're right about Bray. I shouldn't talk you out of doing something. And, if what you felt at Judy's was more than indigestion, God's telling us something too."

"Well, I've been doing some thinking too."

"I can see it coming, we've switched positions again."

"I guess the effect's the same. If God wanted us to do something radical, there'd be no doubt."

"Like a neon sign flashing: 'Rescue Bray—Rescue Bray.'"

"Or maybe just a clear indication that something's wrong."

"Let's call him. See if anyone's flipped the neon sign on."

Win grabbed the cordless, and after what seemed like forever, Bray came on.

"Just touching base," Win said to him.

"Touch away," Bray said. He sat in the gazebo in the light of a single bulb hanging above him.

"Today go okay?"

Taking the bear necklace from his shirt pocket, he let it swing before his eyes. "Yeah. Just looking at some stuff I left behind," he glanced down at a spread of comic books. "Phil found the box of it." Then he remembered. "The therapist is beautiful. Blonde—ditsy—just my type." He dropped the necklace back into his pocket.

"We'll be sure to tell Pam," he said.

"You do that. Jealousy's good."

"Well," Win said, trying to sound upbeat. "I'll call tomorrow."

"Do that. Maybe I'll have been bounced off a cliff by then."

"There's always hope."

Win hung up. "He's fine," he said, disappointedly. "The physical therapist is beautiful, blonde, his type. I'm doing it again, aren't I?"

"Why don't we just snuggle up, listen to some good jazz, and *pretend* your best friend is being stalked by a mad killer."

"Well, when reality lets you down—" He kissed her lightly on the lips. "You know what his question was tonight?"

"Chad?"

"Did God or Satan break my arm."

"Well?"

"You want an answer, too?"

"He's entitled, and I'm not?"

The white gazebo stood in the northeastern quadrant of the commons. A primitive structure—octagonal, ten feet across, even the latticework relatively plain—still it held a special place in Bray's heart. Built when he was ten, it became his salvation its very first night. That day's sweltering heat had only grown hotter when the sun died, as if the winds continued to blow over glowing coals. But for some reason, Bray found the breezes that washed the gazebo cool and incredibly refreshing. He'd slept there all night that first night with neither blanket nor pillow and had never slept better.

Now, thirty-five years later, the day not as hot, the breezes not as refreshing, Bray parked there beneath the stark bulb. It lit the pile of his old comic books he'd spread on the center table.

But since Win's call, he hadn't thought about them. He'd thought about his mother and the bear necklace in his shirt pocket.

Who'd sent it to him? And why?

One of the family? Or a guard? Obviously someone who wanted him to ponder his parents' deaths. Why didn't they just talk to him? Or, if they wanted anonymity, written things down. Why give him just enough information to make him curious?

The diary page and the necklace. And if his mother had been wearing the necklace when the boat blew up, how did *whoever* get it? Maybe that was the point—her body hadn't just disappeared to the bottom of the lake. More likely, though, *whoever* got the necklace from his parents' personal effects. But what about the soot? It was either real or a convincing touch.

He clutched the necklace through his shirt.

He loved his mother. They hadn't used that word much then. All his relationships had a subdued nature to them. His father paid little attention to either Phil or him, and his mother, though young and bubbly, always seemed a little preoccupied. But looking back on his relationship with her, he'd always loved her and she'd loved him.

Holding the little bear brought back the warmth.

Hank slipped up unnoticed. "I hear you have some Spiderman, there, bucko."

"A few." Bray looked up.

"Spiderman's the man. Used to live for the next issue." Hank quickly sorted through several comic books lying on the table. When he found a Spiderman he stopped and studied the cover. "I remember this one."

"Don't you think you're a little old to be getting so excited?"

"For Spiderman?" He picked up the comic and thumbed through it. "Not hardly. Maybe with you here, there'll be some time again." A thumb came up and gestured to the center of the commons. "Of course, there's no relaxing with that grave being so close. Graves belong in graveyards. And graves of strong-willed people belong in graveyards with tall brick fences so you never have to think about 'em again."

Bray laughed. "So, you're glad you married into the family?"

Hank studied Bray for a long time, then confided, "Some of 'em are a piece o' work." He peered up at the half moon. With so little earthen light, the moon usually glowed like a beacon, but with ash from the New York fires, it appeared anemic.

"What do you do?"

"Everything. Mostly operations. The stuff that gets done, I do it. Me and the guys—the workers. They all belong to me."

"So you're the 'Spiderman' around here—you're the man."

Hank grinned. "Hank, the man—sounds good." He laughed, filled with the thought. "Funny how some bosses just aren't as powerful as they think."

"That's always true. How long you been here?"

"Six years. Look at this one." Hank pushed Spiderman in front of Bray. "The artwork's incredible."

"How'd you meet Sylvia?" Bray asked.

"She brought her car in for repair one night. I had a garage in St. Albans—open late."

"Swept away by her beauty?"

"The light played tricks."

"Must have been Houdini."

Hank laughed. "Didn't pull no rabbit out of that hat—pulled a troll." He laughed some more.

"You guys have cars?" Bray asked casually.

"Sure. In a garage in St. Albans. We take trips now and again."

That's when the troll strolled up. Bray was always amazed how a woman the size of a refrigerator could glide up so light-footedly. "Hi, Bray. Studying for a test?"

"Just relaxing with some old loves."

She eyed one of the Archie comics. "Don't the plot twists lose you?"

Hank peered up. "Speaking of getting lost."

Looking at his Spiderman comic, she frowned, "You prefer a bug's company to mine?"

"Sometimes."

"It's time to wash some socks," Sylvia said, her eyes firmly on her husband. "I want you to join me."

Hank swallowed as if downing a peach pit. Then metamorphosis. Looking up at her with immense charm, he said, "Sure. Let me read a couple more, and I'll be there by the time you snuggle in."

Sylvia gave a shallow, suspicious nod and glided off.

"So Spiderman will have to wait," Bray observed.

Hank sprang to his feet and scooped up the book. "I'll return it in the morning. When she comes out looking for me, tell her a guard dragged me off."

"What do I get for this?"

"Not dragged off by a guard."

"Sounds fair."

Hank disappeared into a hole in the darkness.

Teri sat in her front room watching Bray through a separation in the drapes. With Hank gone, Bray seemed to be enjoying the old comic books again. At peace with things—in control—while she, after having her discussion with him, felt at odds with herself. She wanted some things very badly. Up until yesterday, she could have named the top two of them easily. She wanted freedom from the rock and independence from everyone she'd grown up with. And she was willing to do something terrible to get them.

But things had changed. Suddenly a perfect life wasn't quite so precisely nor easily defined.

Where had been the operative word yesterday, now it was *who.* She wanted—needed—to connect with someone. She wanted to feel understood and to bestow understanding. Some of that came with Bray. It was wonderful to talk about complex ideas, even God, and be taken seriously. She'd been treated respectfully, caringly. Like a father ought. Suddenly that was important.

But it only whetted her appetite. There was a banquet out there, and she knew precisely where, no—*who* it was. Could the connection have been made with just a single look, with only a few minutes with him? She'd learned so much in those few minutes. Win's bravery as he dealt with the pain. And his gentleness—he could have lashed out like a wounded animal, but he hadn't. Though tormented, he'd been pleasant and restrained.

She had to see him again.

And soon.

But she wouldn't be seeing him again—certainly not soon. No matter how much she wanted it. He had no reason to come, and even if she manufactured one, the family wouldn't let him stay. Hopelessness closed around her like an icy, bleak winter. So tight was its grasp on her that she needed to physically break free of it—generate heat—activity—a walk.

Out the back door, she contemplated the darkness. Silently. Hardly able to breathe. The hopelessness persisting. She wasn't sure what to do with it. Having no hope unnerved her. She wanted to blow up bowling pins. She wanted justice. She wanted Win.

Win.

She said the name. Then, as she said it again, she saw his face. That wounded face begging to be helped, his woeful eyes. She loved helping him. It meant he needed her. He would stay if he needed her. And he was so cute on the phone. *The one-ton butterfly.*

She heard something.

It broke her reverie like an ice pick. It even had the sound of an ice pick.

She listened more intently. It came from somewhere near the cliff.

Such a dark night. Clouds now shrouded the moon and left the lake, the trees, the islands, everything black. Her back windows were curtained, so there was no light from inside. Strangely concerned that she might be detected, she crouched and listened.

Someone was digging.

A guard performing a legitimate job? At this hour? In the dark? No. Someone was up to something out by the cliff, near the trees dedicated to Uncle Bray's parents. She decided to wait and see what happened.

Phil's voice stole up behind Bray. It had a mushy quality to it like Bray's the night before. "Braynard Sanderson, comic book king, perusing his kingdom."

Bray turned. "Cops do that."

Phil laughed a loose kind of laugh crammed with joyfully evil intent. "Want some wine? I've tapped the cellar. Californian. No? I do." And he wrapped his lips around the top of the bottle and took a long swig. "Just a hint of apricot—good legs. Wanna see 'em?" He hiked up his pants.

"Hairy," Bray said. "Sit."

Phil did. Hard. The gazebo shuddered.

As Phil took another swig, Bray heard another set of footsteps—quick and purposeful. "Uncle Bray," Tommy greeted, his voice official. "We finally found your parents' things."

Phil looked up at his son. "Good ol' Sherlock Tommy."

Tommy peered down at his father. His expression marked by a lack of expression—a deadness in the look.

"Thank you, Tommy," Bray said warmly. "But sit. Talk for a minute or two."

"Can't right now, Uncle Bray," Tommy replied, the deadness remaining in his tone. "Things to do. I'm in charge of stuff—money and stuff. And there's a lot of stuff to deal with. Your parents' stuff was in the attic where we found yours, but it was buried beneath some other things. Workers are taking the boxes down now. There are only three. In your room okay? The important things were undoubtedly handled by the will. What's left no one wanted."

"My room's fine."

"Put them in his room." Phil's tone was laced with cold impatience.

The dead expression came alive with contempt. Tommy glared at his father for an instant then came back to Bray. "It'll be about an hour," he said. "You should be able to get through a couple more comics by then."

Bray didn't like his mocking tone but ignored it. "At least three," he said.

"You two make a good pair. You're speed-reading. And he's speed-drinking."

Phil shook his head. "I'm savoring every drop—wine must be savored."

"The drops are about a gallon each. Excuse me, Uncle Bray. I've got things to do."

"Then," Bray pressed, "join me later. I want to get to know you."

"There is nothing to know," he said flatly. "Absolutely nothing. Goodnight, Uncle Bray." Without looking at his father again, he disappeared into the same hole Hank had.

Bray stared at it for several seconds, then his attention was abruptly brought back to Phil, who slammed the bottle down on an Archie comic. "Kids. Can't understand 'em. Gave 'em everything. I couldn't understand you, either. Every week you'd take your dime down to that greasy little drug store in St. Albans and get your comics the day they came out."

"If you hadn't won the dime from me in poker first. Only the odds kept you from winning it all the time."

"But even when you lost, you got your dime back. Mom always replaced it. You always won." Another drink. "Always."

"She was your mother, too."

"She was more a sister than a mother. Or a girlfriend. She was only eight years older than me."

Bray nodded. "Dad should've been jailed. How old was he? Thirty-one? And she was seventeen?"

"He saw her waterskiing. She was cute. Even at nine I could see that." There was a long pause while he stared into the golden bottle. Whatever he saw held his attention for quite a while. Then he woke. "The guy was a dirty old man." He squinted at a frame or two of Archie. Then eyes back to Bray. "You and she grew up together."

Bray shook his head. "She was a good mother. She cared. Worked hard. Didn't take much from anybody. And she taught me right from wrong. I miss her." He realized his hand was rubbing the bear through his pocket. He stopped. Took a deeper than usual breath. Then, putting on his most casual air, he asked, "Did she leave a diary or anything?"

"I 'member you two taking boat rides. I'd head off to school, and you and she would go riding around. I'd be learning algebra, and you'd be, well, being nursed or something." More staring at the bottle. "Diary? Don't know. My mom left one. Big whoop. Talked about flowers mostly. Didn't learn much." His eyes grew large again. He seemed to need large eyes to accomplish what the regular-sized ones did before. "So, have you thought about the offer?"

"All the time."

"A decision?"

"Not yet."

Phil frowned and slammed a drunken hand to the table. "But this is important. You don't know how important. You'd become a gazillionaire in seconds."

Bray had to agree. That was important. Yet he'd not thought about it at all.

"They never found their bodies?"

"Who? Dad's and Marsha's? You got some kinda one-track mind there. No. Never. Gas leak prob'ly. Explosion doused them in it. A horrible thing. A couple guards saw it. She was so beautiful—perky—I needed perky in my life. Truly horrible. Of course," Phil looked at him fully in the face, "you know about things like that—firsthand."

"They didn't find the boat, either. The lake's not all that deep where it happened, is it? Currents aren't all that strong."

"The boat was probably blown to bits, and Dad and Marsha were cinders. They found a few pieces but nothing more."

"Where were they going?"

"To the mainland—movie or something—shopping. They took off after most of us were in bed—then boom!" Phil again looked off somewhere. "Dad was hard on us. Spent his life working."

Bray groaned, "He hardly worked a day."

"He was never home."

"He wasn't working."

"Sure he was working. He nearly ran this place." A hand swept unsteadily around the compound. "We were stuck in that house with your mother while he was—working."

"You're in denial. You saw it. He was playing poker—he and the guards. Day and night. Poker."

Phil stood, nearly fell over, but then with the help of the table, straightened. "Dad worked. He was an executive around here. Like me. Except I make more money." He grabbed his bottle by the neck and took another drink. "California," he said, pushing the bottle at him. "Good legs, wanna—"

"I already did."

"Well," he swayed there for a moment. "Take care, little brother. And give that offer some thought, real thought. Your life might depend on it." And Phil laughed, really laughed, and drank and laughed some more. He found his way back to his house and, when he did, all but fell into the open doorway.

"Always sellin'," Bray finally said.

After sitting there for a while, his third Archie comic reading much like the first, he found himself just staring, using the blackness as a backdrop—seeing the explosion, hearing his mother's screams, feeling the blistering blast of heat—for an instant, reliving his own experience. Who could have done it? Were they still alive? He took the diary page from his shirt pocket and reread it. It had an even more profound effect on him this second time. Was the guard who followed them still working here? Was the person who ordered it? Was it Breck or someone else? There was no denying it, Bray wanted revenge. *How long after June 3rd did they die?* he asked himself. The memorial plaque. On the trees. The date might be on there. Figuring he might need it, he'd taken a small flashlight with him from his room. Now he flipped it on and walked toward the back of the third house.

For Teri, kneeling in the shadows had paid off. After a while, she detected movement, then, when her eyes were fully adjusted to the darkness, she saw what was going on.

Someone stood on the lower ledge where the trees grew and was digging. The ledge was down only three or four feet, and since all she saw was his head bobbing up and down now and again, the guy must have been working on his knees. What could he possibly be doing?

And why?

It couldn't be legitimate work. Should she confront him? Or wait until he stood so she could recognize him later?

Or not confront him at all? Ah—the best option. On this island, anyway, going slowly was always best. If she tread too heavily on someone's sacred soil she could find herself on the mainland, alone and broke.

So, she waited.

But not long.

Uncle Bray limped from between the houses, a small flashlight trained before him, his cane feeling its way. Bray wasn't very good at this. In just a few seconds, he'd nearly tripped over a wheelbarrow and almost tumbled into a bush.

Teri noticed that the digging had stopped. Only silence came from The Henry and Marsha Sanderson Memorial Trees.

Obviously the guy didn't want to be noticed. Maybe a guard engineering a scam of his own. And if Bray interrupted him— deadly trouble.

"Uncle Bray, hi," she called, rising to her feet.

"Hi," he returned, searching for her in the darkness. Finding her, he called, "What are you up to?"

"About five-seven," she laughed, making her way quickly to him through the grass.

She had just about reached him when they both heard the cry. A man's cry. Frightened. Then terrified. Then a sound that one may hear only once, yet identify instantly. The sound like a sack of sand hitting the pavement. Then the telltale shock of air forced from dying lungs. The sharp groan, if life still existed, would be followed by a deep wail of pain. But there was no life, so there was only the crackle of breaking bones.

CHAPTER 8

Bray hobbled quickly to the cliff and peered over it. Teri, right beside him, gasped.

Although the only light seemed to come from the phosphorous white waves slapping the rocks, they made out a body, face up, draped over a large and jagged boulder. "One of your guards," Bray said. "That couldn't have been any fun. He must have been climbing the cliff."

"I don't know," Teri lied, instinctively.

Suddenly a brilliant light illuminated the body in horrifying relief. The blood rushing from the back of his skull glistened red, his face became a tortured sculpture—lifeless, waxy, with a frozen scream.

"Ron Gunn," Teri whispered.

Before Bray could acknowledge the name, the light found them.

"You okay, Teri?" Hank called from a boat about ten yards off shore. "And you, Bray?"

"Better'n him," Bray called. "We heard him hit. No idea where he fell from."

"We'll take care of it."

"Want me to call the police?" Bray called down.

"No," Hank said. "We'll get the area blocked off then get them on the horn."

Bray waved agreement, and they both stepped back.

Within an hour a lake patrol boat arrived carrying a detective Bray knew only as Raif from St. Albans. There were a few questions asked of Hank and a couple others, then the medical examiner appeared, a young doctor with a loud, persistent manner. There wasn't much for him to do since the cause of death was a no-brainer. The body was then removed. The police remained to collect evidence, and before two hours were up, the guards were in the process of cleansing the area. By two in the morning, long after Bray was in bed, the area was back to normal. Gunn's death left no marks.

For Bray it was unnerving. Not the death itself, but that it had occurred when he was supposed to be so distant from it. And not just death, but violent death, unexplained death. What was the kid doing when he fell? He wouldn't have been climbing in the dark. Not if he had a brain. Nor was he on the tall cliff where he and Teri had been.

That only left the tree ledge. But why there? If it hadn't been so late and if there hadn't been the real risk of joining the body at the bottom of that cliff, Bray would've limped out there and checked. Or if he truly cared or if it was any of his business. But neither was true and he probably *would* fall, so he just opened the balcony door to allow the lake breezes in.

That's when he noticed three boxes stacked near the wall.

His parents' boxes. So much had happened he'd forgotten that they were being delivered. Excited, he opened the first box. Twenty minutes later, the contents of the boxes studied and restudied, he closed the lids. Nothing. No diary. Nothing but ash trays, a few books, some old Christmas cards. Nothing.

Not only had he hoped to find something to shed light on what his mother had written, but he'd also hoped to feel a little closer to them. Neither occurred. Cheated, he stripped to his shorts, lay upon his bed uncovered, and fell asleep.

Teri sensed an opportunity.

After leaving Bray, she grabbed a flashlight and returned to the cliff. The medical examiner had just ordered the body taken away, and the police were going over the area once more. She directed the flashlight beam to the ledge a few feet below. There were Gunn's tools, a spade and a handpick. He'd been digging something. It didn't matter what—a tunnel to China for all she cared—it looked suspicious. And it could be interpreted as someone trying to set a trap for Bray. She knew Win thought Bray was in danger—the tire blowing out, the railing giving way—and now this—a trap being set. Win would no longer just think Bray was in danger, he'd know it. To protect his friend he'd just have to come.

To complete the picture there was just one more thing she needed to do.

She called down to the police below, "I've left some gardening equipment, can I step down there and get them?"

"Pretty late for gardening," the cop called up.

"They'll rust if they're out all night."

"If you got the guts, go ahead," the cop called up.

Unable to breathe, she stepped down to the tree ledge. When there, she saw what the dead guard had been doing. And it was just what she'd planned on doing. The god of the candles was still taking care of her.

Below the main ledge, he'd hollowed out a yard-long area below the grass. Exactly what she was going to do. Why he'd done it didn't matter, but now with the digging done, all she had to do was tell Win about the trap—in person.

"What are you doing?" Bilba's accusing voice came from above. "Did you see him fall?"

"Just heard it," she admitted, frightened of Bilba and hesitant to lie. "I saw these tools. Thought they might rust."

"Conscientious. Anything else?" Bilba asked, suspicious.

"Something dangerous. This hole here. I was going to fill it back up."

"Tell the gardeners. They'll do it right."

"Just worried someone might step on it."

Bilba hrumphed. "Leave it and come up or you'll be splattered all over those rocks, as well." Her commands complete, she left.

Alone with her plan again, Teri wasted no time.

"Hank," Teri's voice rang out as she entered the hidden dock below the cliff, the dull black power boats tied up expectantly.

"He's helping the police," came a green-clad voice. Michelson. She didn't know his first name.

"I'm going to take a boat for a little while," she told him. "I saw Ron Gunn die. I need to work the sight of that off."

"That's tough," he said, his voice soft with understanding. "You saw that?"

"Right after. The body broken up, all bloody."

Michelson nodded sympathetically. "I know you're capable, but can I help?"

A nice way to ask, Teri thought. "Sure. Bring one over." Michelson moved eagerly and within seconds a silent-running Sea-Doo throbbed beside her. He helped her in and when she was behind the controls she gave him a friendly wave. Pulling out onto the lake, she was just about to gun it when Hank's boat glided up. "Where you going?" he asked.

"Gonna take a ride."

"You'd better stay around. The cops are calm. Don't need 'em upset again."

"I'll be okay. I know the problem."

"What did Bray say about all this?"

"Thought you were doing a good job."

"Really?" Hank laughed. "New career possibilities." He laughed again. "Okay, have your little jaunt, but there's weather coming. Get back early."

Teri nodded, grateful she was so convincing.

The boats were double-engined and double-mufflered and whispered over the water. With clouds still shrouding the moon leaving only meager light, the going was hazardous, but she had no desire to slow down. She was on a mission.

After forty-five minutes, a dockside phone booth, and a greasy-looking cowboy she'd asked for directions, she pulled up to Win Brady's dock.

Almost eleven, the place was dimly lit, the thin curtains drawn across the large windows. She docked the Sea-Doo noiselessly and clattered onto the dock. Skirting the lawn chair at the end of it, she made her way to the cement patio. She heard music—easy listening. After a deep breath for courage, she knocked.

Voices—a man and a woman speaking in low tones. The curtain parted and Win Brady stood there. Barefoot, he wore black shorts and a white-and-red pullover. He looked wonderful. Even in his cast, he looked so muscular and in command.

He fumbled with the sliding door but finally got it open. "Teri? That you?"

"In the flesh."

"Who is it, Win?" Ginger's voice came from behind.

"Teri. Bray's niece." He turned back to Teri. "Come in. You out for a ride? You came a long way." Then a thought struck. "Is Bray okay?"

"He's fine," she said, still standing on the patio. "For now."

"For now?" Win squeaked.

"Can I come in? I'm a little wet, and it's cold."

"Oh, I'm sorry. My manners turned off."

Ginger stood next to her man. "Come on in," she offered. Once Teri was inside, Ginger pushed out a hand. "Ginger Glasgow, Win's fiancée."

Teri shook the hand with a manufactured smile. She'd hoped to catch Win alone and didn't care who knew it.

"I'm sorry, again," Win said self-consciously. "I should be introducing. We're having herbal tea. Want a cup?"

"I can only stay a sec." Her expression went serious; she'd practiced. "I need to tell you something."

"What?"

"Could we be alone?" she asked Ginger. There was no good reason, but Teri thought she'd take a shot.

"We have no secrets," Ginger said firmly.

Win jumped in. "Unless you feel more comfortable—uh—alone."

Ginger frowned but said nothing.

With no good reason for the request and worrying that she might give herself away, she said, "Just keep this to yourself."

Ginger zipped her lips and locked them behind a distinctively sarcastic smile.

Win noticed and didn't like it. Tucking away a scowl, he turned to Teri. "Sit on the couch, and tell us what it is."

Needing time to think, she walked slowly to the couch. Win planted himself opposite her on the coffee table while Ginger stood behind Win.

Teri looked up at Ginger—*A blonde vulture*, she thought.

"Uh," Teri began. Although she'd just spent an hour with nothing to think about but water, she'd spent no time preparing her story. "I think someone's try to kill your friend—my uncle—Bray," she finally blurted out.

Ginger groaned, and Win stiffened. "I knew it," he said. On his feet he paced frantically. "I knew that million was for a reason.

I'm getting good at this. And Teri's bringing the last piece of the puzzle." Pointing at Teri, "I'll follow you up in the boat."

Now that was easy. Teri grinned involuntarily and said, "All right!"

"You're going to the island?" Ginger protested as Win hurried to his bedroom.

"Bray's in trouble. I need to help." Win grabbed his red, white and blue nylon overnight bag and threw it on his unmade Corvette bed.

Suddenly angry and wanting to lash out, Ginger grimaced, "Don't you ever make this thing?"

"In time." He pulled open his underwear drawer and tossed in a handful of briefs and socks.

Ginger pushed her face into Win's. "Stop and think, just for a second."

"What's to think about? Bray's a target. I have to help."

Since Win wore mostly shorts for summer, he grabbed a handful and chucked them in. "Shaving stuff," he muttered. "I don't have a shaving kit—maybe one of those plastic shopping bag things."

"Win, please wait a minute."

"I've got those bags in the kitchen. In a drawer I think." He started toward the hall. Ginger slowed him down. Grabbing both shoulders, she spun him around then pushed her face into his. "Stop, Win. Think. You don't even know why she thinks that. She might be overreacting."

"I might be," came Teri's voice from the bedroom doorway. "You sleep in a car. How do you guys get in there?"

Ginger turned stoned-faced. This was Win's bedroom. No other woman should ever see it. There were those in Christendom who believed even she should have never seen it. "We're Christians, and we're waiting until we're married."

"So I'm not interrupting anything," Teri said with just a little too much smart aleck in her tone. Ginger turned on her. Win could easily see there was a blowup coming, and though he didn't understand why, he loved Ginger and wanted nothing to go amiss with her.

"I'm getting packed. Maybe you should wait out in the living room."

"Sure," Teri said, eyes drilling Ginger.

"Teri, wait," Ginger heard herself say."What makes you think Bray's in trouble?"

Finally someone asked her. "A guy set a trap for him."

"Who?" Win asked.

"A guard—an employee," she replied. "He's sort of—well—dead."

"Dead?"

"He fell off a cliff. That's how we knew he was setting the trap."

"Was Bray supposed to fall off a cliff?"

"About thirty feet."

"What was the trap?" Ginger asked, sounding like a prosecutor.

"He'd dug out a place just below the cliff. If Bray stepped on it, he would have done a half-gainer onto the rocks."

"This happened tonight?" Ginger asked.

"About two hours ago, maybe a little longer."

"What does Bray think about this?" Ginger asked, again the prosecutor's tone.

"I didn't tell him." *Why? Why didn't I tell him? Win's gonna ask, and Perry Mason-ette will make a big deal out of it. Come on, head, what should I say?*

"Why?" Ginger asked. "Shouldn't he know someone's trying to kill him so he can get off the island or at least protect himself?"

Get off the island. Sure. He could do that. But she didn't want him to. Then Win would never come, and she needed him there. But first things first. Why didn't she tell Bray?

"Because he wouldn't believe me," she told Win, ignoring the fact that it was Ginger's question. *But why won't he believe me?*

"Why?" Ginger asked.

Win answered, "Because he's Bray. If it's not his idea, he just doesn't believe it. I've had the same trouble with him."

"And," Teri continued, "if you tell him not to do something, he does it."

"He's not like that," Ginger protested.

"Sure he is," Win affirmed. "He relishes doing what you've told him not to."

"But the fact remains," Ginger said accusingly, "you don't have absolute proof the trap was for Bray."

"There's no such thing as absolute proof," Win said, turning toward the hall. "Shaving bag."

"Win, can we talk?" She glared at Teri. "Maybe alone *is* better."

Teri glanced at Win, got a nod, then disappeared down the hall.

"What's going on, Ginger?" Win asked, concerned.

"Nothing's going on. I just don't want you going off when there's no need to. You've got church in the morning. A class."

"If Bray's in trouble—"

"You don't know Bray's in trouble. And you don't know what's waiting for you there—and you know nothing about her."

"She's the one who did my arm."

"Splinting an arm isn't a character reference."

"There's no need for a character reference. If there's even a ten percent chance that Bray's in trouble, I need to help."

"There's something wrong with that family. They live on a little island, for crying out loud. How many years? It's been decades—on that little island. Win, use your head here. There could be something dangerous going on."

"That's the point. If there is, I'm needed."

"But just don't go right away—take your time. Investigate a little. Let Breed investigate."

Larin Breed was Commander of the Detective Division of the Burlington Police Department. Ginger hoped one day to work for him, *if* she outlived all the other candidates that were ahead of her on the list.

"There might not be time," Win protested.

"There's time."

"How do you know that?"

Ginger grabbed some air. "Assuming Teri's right, the guy who hired the digger now has to hire someone else," Ginger said. "Then they have to come up with another plan. There's time. Maybe lots of it."

Win studied her. "What going on, Ginger? There's more to this than—this."

"I just don't like you going off with—well—someone we don't know. We're dealing with the Addams family here."

"I'll be fine. Jesus is in this. We keep hoping Bray'll come to know the Lord. Well, the Lord's working on that island, and I want to be there if I'm needed."

"So, you feel left out."

"That's a little simplistic, don't you think?"

"I don't think so."

"Well, it is."

"You're a man—trying hard to be a man. You know your dad's not been there for you—and Bray's your buddy. Now he's off having an adventure, and you want to be a part of it. Get your share of massages—"

"Now that's not fair."

"Sure it's fair. You guys are—guys."

"I'm not sitting here while Bray might be in danger. That's the simple part."

"You're leaving me to have a Hardy Boy adventure. Just because some raven-haired beauty—"

"What's going on? What's all this jealousy? Would you believe it if some guy was telling me? Because it's an attractive woman—"

Ginger said nothing. She looked like she wanted to, but she only kept her eyes level with his, beginning to breathe heavily. Almost like she was on the verge of tears, but there were no tears, only a steady, anxious gaze.

"I'm going," he finally said. "If there's nothing going on I'll leave. If there is, I'll get Breed involved. I'm no hero. You know that."

"But you are a hero," she said joylessly. "You've saved Chad— you saved Bray."

"I don't go looking. I'll be back."

"I don't like it."

"You don't have to," Win said.

Ginger sighed, choking back tears. "I love you, Win."

"I love you, too," Win said. "I'll be fine."

"Listen to me."

"I have. And now I'm making a decision."

Ginger turned her back on Win, but then spun back around. "If you die on that island, I'll never speak to you again."

Win kissed her as sweetly as she would allow, grabbed his bag and joined Teri in the living room. He kissed Ginger again, and this time, with Teri in the room, she wrapped eager arms around his neck and kissed him back.

"Call Mel." Win said. Mel Flowers was Win's boss—the pastor at the Grand Isles Community Church.

So he and Teri could ride together, Win lashed her Sea-Doo behind his Bayliner. Kissing Ginger again on the dock, Win climbed into the Bayliner, took the pilot's seat next to Teri, and fired it up.

A few moments later, Ginger watched the two boats, one bouncing on the growing chop behind the other, head north. The moon was out, the edges of the clouds glistening sharp with it. But Ginger didn't care about the clouds, it was that woman's black hair. The moonlight christened its edges, too, as it billowed wildly in the growing night wind.

Ginger's heart plummeted. Why? Win was right. He should go. But seeing him sitting beside that woman like he belonged there—even though she meant nothing to him—caused something to grip her heart and hold on to it for dear life.

"How do I get on the island?" Win asked, the boat plowing through the growing turbulence.

"I hadn't thought that far ahead."

Win nodded, swallowing some frustration.

"Do they like visitors?" he asked.

"Not particularly."

Win studied her from the corner of his eye. She seemed immensely nervous, her eyes rigidly ahead, her palms flat on her jeans.

"You okay?" he asked.

"Just wondering if this is a good idea."

"Too late now."

"No," she said, calming noticeably. "This is the right thing to do. The right thing."

"Good," he said.

"Definitely a good idea." She smiled and leaned back in her chair relaxing.

"Then, how do we get on the island?"

"Sneak on. I'll hide you in my house. No one would notice."

"Hard to investigate when I'm not supposed to be there."

"Yeah, but I could ask the questions and tell you what people say. It'd be like a vacation for you. We've got a satellite dish. I wish I could have a deal like that."

"I don't think so."

"Why not? Sounds wonderful to me."

Win said nothing and turned his attention back to the lake. And to the Lord. A silent prayer—a few words, a big request. *Lord, help me get on the island. And bring Bray into your kingdom.*

Before the words left his heart, the wind grew and the chop increased. The wind clawed through trees on shore, then, within minutes, waves began pounding them. Then, just as Win adjusted to the new violence, a prize fighter's fist of wind whipped across the water and slammed into the Bayliner, jolting them. Knocked off balance, they scrambled to recover, but before they did, they were hit by another. The wind had found a hole it was savagely trying to fill. As it did, it beheaded the crests of the waves, gashing them white.

"I've never seen anything come up this fast," Win cried out.

"Head for an island," Teri shouted.

Another wave slammed into their side.

"We go any faster, we might lose your boat."

The Bayliner's bow gashed a swell. Lightning split the sky a mile or so ahead, and a thunder exploded.

"I don't like this," Teri said, her voice shuddering.

Her eyes looked lost, her hands gripped her knees as if they could somehow save her. All of her trembled.

"We'll be okay," he comforted.

But the instant he said it, another wave battered the boat's side, the crest spilling in.

Sea-Doo or not, he eased the throttle forward. The engine became a tenor, and they began to skim the tops of the turmoil, the Sea-Doo whipping about behind.

In the six months he'd been there, he'd learned to love the lake, loved boating on it, loved pushing the limits of the boat and himself. He loved the freedom. When the water churned like now, he loved it even more. The challenge—both physical and mental—the combat.

No rain yet, the wind became deep and throbbing, earnestly scouring the lake's surface.

Fifteen, twenty minutes. The boat skipped and slammed, crashing through and smashing the waves, the Sea-Doo on the back bouncing like a cork. Win's eyes searched relentlessly for trouble while Teri sat in her chair, legs set firm apart for stability, hands planted on the dash. When they hit the thirty-minute mark, Win felt confidence returning. He'd taken everything the storm could offer and the island couldn't be more than a few miles ahead.

"We're on the last leg," he called to her.

Teri relaxed perceptively.

"I've seen the lake a whole lot worse. We'll be okay." He actually eased up on the throttle. "We can't get there too soon. We have to figure out what we're doing. How am I going to get on the island so I can stay?"

"I gave you my suggestion."

"I can't haunt your house. I've a God who'd frown, and a fiancée who wouldn't understand—definitely wouldn't understand."

"You won't get on otherwise," she reiterated, her tone obstinate.

Win gnawed on his lower lip for an moment. "There's got to be a way. Some reason why they'd let me on."

"There isn't. No matter what you tell them, they'll find a reason to send you packing. Guaranteed. I know them. You're only hope is to hide out in my house and tell me what to do."

Win was beginning to believe she was right when a swarm of lightning flashes illuminated their world just for an instant, creating a Polaroid in his brain. Teri saw it, too. She rose from her seat and leaned over the top of the windshield, peering disbelievingly into the night.

"Is that what I think it is?" Win muttered.

More lightning.

"Good God in heaven!" she gasped. "A tornado! It's sucking up the water. Oh my G—it's devoured that island!"

"It's going to cut us off," Win cried, his head twisting from side to side. "We have to get someplace safe."

"Safe?!" Teri cried, her desperation crackling. "Where's that?"

CHAPTER 9

"You asleep?" Ginger asked Pam, pressing the phone to her ear.

"Not since the phone rang."

"I have to talk to someone."

"That's what boyfriends are for."

"It's *about* my boyfriend."

"Win?"

Ginger lay on her bed. On the way home the image of Win and Teri fading into the darkness stayed with her like a sunspot.

"I'm jealous," she said, then withered at how juvenile it sounded.

"Of Win?"

"Who else?"

"Well, Chad could be in love with his teacher."

"Fat chance of that. No, it's Win. Twice in two days."

"Two different women?"

"A hospital receptionist and Bray's niece."

"Has he shown interest in them?"

"None. But guys are clever. My husband sure was."

"You're talking Win, here. And I thought your husband was a drunk."

"He was a drunk. But he messed around, too. At least, I think he did. There was evidence."

"What evidence?"

"He told me."

"That's a confession."

"He was drunk when he told me so I was never sure."

Silence for a moment.

"Has Win ever even looked at another woman?"

"You mean like ogled?"

"Sure, ogled. Men sometimes look at women by accident."

"Accident?"

"They see things out of the corner of their eyes and want to see what it is. They're never sure. It could be something else with willowy legs—a sports figure or something."

"He never ogled."

"Then why are you jealous?"

"Don't know," she groaned.

"I bet you know exactly why."

"No, I don't."

"Sure you do."

"I don't."

"Wanna bet?"

"Who'd bet on something like that?"

"You won't because you know."

"I don't know."

"What makes you jealous?"

"That receptionist was obviously after him."

"How obvious?"

"It was obvious, that's all."

"I bet he rejected her."

"I wish."

"He responded?"

"He did nothing—yet."

"What about the other one? The niece."

"They went off together."

"What?"

"In the boat. Just about an hour ago. Together."

"Why?"

"She came and took him away."

"Away?"

"To that Sanderson Island."

"Why?"

"Oh," she said, realizing where this was going. She hesitated, but went on. "Bray. He could be in danger."

"Bray!"

"Oh, don't worry," she said unconvincingly. "Bray's a big boy."

"What danger?"

"Win's got this dumb idea that someone wants to kill Bray for the million dollars. I think that woman just wanted to get Win alone."

A long silence. Finally, "Jealousy is silly," Pam said stiffly.

"Well," Ginger said, "I'm sure cured. Am I glad I called you. You should hang out your shingle. Jealous people everywhere need Pam, the miracle cure."

"I sense sarcasm."

"Jealousy is *not* silly."

"You're right. It's stupid."

"I've learned to respect my feelings, not to consider them stupid."

"Not all. Just that one."

"And why is it stupid?"

"Because you can't win with it. Wanna know why?"

"Like I have a choice."

"Here goes. If you're wrong, there's no reason to be jealous in the first place. And if you're right, don't be jealous, just get rid of him."

"Incredibly pithy. A big bunch of pith. I'm jealous, and that's that."

"Well, then, you're stupid."

"That's a little strong, don't you think?"

"As Balaam's ass."

"Balaam's—" Ginger swallowed hard. That was enough. "They hired a physical therapist for Bray, a beautiful blonde. She rubs his back, his legs. I bet she uses those tasty oils—"

"Blonde? Tasty oils?" There was a long silence. "I'll kill her."

It was coming. Lightning flashed and silhouetted it. Outside of a movie theater he'd never seen anything like it. Black, whirling, a flexible drill cutting the earth. Rooted somewhere in the heavens, it dug into the lake, sucking up water, trees, air, and rocks.

Darkness returned and swallowed it.

The hair on his arms and the back of his neck went electric.

More lightning, jagged fingers of it.

Another snapshot. A vertical snake, its head buried in another island, trees flying every which way. Darkness swallowed them again as the lake reacted. The boat pitched and bucked as never before.

"Win!" Teri screamed.

"We've got to get somewhere."

Eyes glued to where the twister should be, Win punched the throttle. The engine cried, the nose leaped up. Overcoming the Sea-Doo's drag, the Bayliner plunged and threw a fist of water as Win headed for the mainland, the furthest point from the tornado.

Teri gasped, nearly screamed. "Where is it? It has to be coming at us."

Another lightning swarm. This time the tornado's tip rose several hundred yards into the air. For an instant they thought they'd been reprieved. But then another jagged flash, and they saw it had returned—a squirming arrow digging into the water a couple of football fields away. The lake around it lurched up, the white phosphorus glowing in manic fists. They lost it in darkness again, but now there was sound. An insanity of sound—loud beyond loud—piercing, drilling into their brains. But there was no time for sound, for hearing, for seeing, for anything but escape.

Something massive flew within inches of their heads. It clipped the nose of the boat, bored into the waves.

"A tree!" Teri cried.

"Just a limb."

Win pushed on the throttle but the boat had no more to give. Another flash. Win's heart caught. The snake was only yards away now. A thick, twisting black rope, its head carving the earth beneath it. If it kept coming it would nail them any minute.

Where could they go?

There were no islands, no mainland. If they could dive beneath the waves, they might find peace, but the lake didn't go that deep.

"Win, we're going to die!" Teri cried and grabbed his cast.

"Doesn't look good," he said, knowing there was only one place from which salvation came. He looked to heaven. "Get us out of here, Lord."

"Win, we're gonna die."

Another limb slammed into the water near them. Then another tore into the side of the boat, ripping it just above the waterline.

The lake poured in. But there was no in, no out; there was only the lake and them.

Lightning slashed the night's black fabric. The tornado was on them.

"Down!" Win cried. "Down on the floor of the boat!" He didn't wait for her to react. He pushed her to the floor. "Grab onto anything!"

She grabbed onto him. He, in turn, tore open a hatch door, threw his cast around the frame and locked himself there. They waited for the worst.

"So," Ginger said into the phone, sipping a diet 7-Up, "you want to take anything back that you've said about jealousy?"

"She does what?"

"She's a physical therapist. She does physical therapy stuff. I don't know what she does. Works muscles, plays the flute while he puts on a headband and limps around the room—"

"Whose flute?"

"Okay, I've gotten my revenge. He's just trying to make you jealous."

"He's succeeding."

"But jealousy is stupid."

"For everyone else. He's unsaved. He could walk off into the sunset with that bimbo just as easy as he could with anyone else."

"Pam," Ginger said, her tone suddenly serious, "is that the man you want?"

More silence. Then a deep sigh. "I first saw him twenty years ago. His wife came to do dolls, and he picked her up. They were so cute together. No sugary sweet stuff like other couples. They were just cute. They'd banter back and forth, joke, laugh, sometimes chide one another, but there was never any doubt they loved each other. He'd give his life for her. And she'd cook even what she didn't like for him—the equivalent. I envied them. I know we say that there's no love without Christ. But I'm not so sure. Common grace, I guess. But they loved each other, and I want that for me. And I'm no prize. A little crude sometimes, a little critical sometimes, sometimes a little too passionate, but always caring. He's everything I want in a man—except for the Christ part—and sometimes I wonder if I'm just denying myself by waiting."

"What does light have in common with darkness?"

"The fear of spending life alone," she said with passion.

"And you think Bray will opt for the bimbo?"

"She's probably a very nice woman. I hate nice women." More silence, then a deep, fortifying breath. "If he's in danger, we have to do something."

"What? We can't get on the island. Win needed that gal to get on."

"We do know something."

"What?" Ginger asked, puzzled.

"We know they live on that island instead of like normal people. We know that no one knows what they do on that island to make money."

"That's not much."

"You're the cop. You're the one who's supposed to be coming up with this stuff."

"What stuff?"

"The stuff that's going to get my Bray away from that bimbo. I'm not going to watch him die when I'm only an hour or so away."

"And how is a cop supposed to help you?"

"There's something extremely abnormal about that family living alone on that island. It's incestuous, unhealthy. They've traded a normal life for whatever they're doing there. And I bet it's illegal. I bet there are so many skeletons in those closets when the wind blows they rattle."

"Ah, cop stuff."

Pam hesitated for a moment. "You've given up."

"Given up? What?"

"I've just realized," Pam said thoughtfully. "You've already counted Win out."

"No, I haven't."

"But you have. It's in your voice. If you had a wedding dress, you'd be returning it."

"That's not true. I'm getting it any day now."

More realization. "That's why you haven't gotten the dress."

"Why?"

"You don't think the wedding's really going to happen."

"Well," Ginger began, suddenly uncomfortable. "it probably won't."

"And you're looking for reasons."

"No, I'm not. They just keep presenting themselves."

"Win with Teri is just one of them."

A long silence with heavy, thoughtful breathing for accompaniment.

"There are more," Ginger finally said. "His getting bored with me is an element in all of them. Except the one where he gets a call to Ethiopia. I'm not going to Ethiopia. The south of France maybe—or Venice—not Ethiopia."

"Then it's not jealousy, it's a self-fulfilling prophecy."

"And that's psychobabble."

"No—it's true. But we don't have time right now to worry about that—we have to do something about Bray."

"And that would be?"

"You're the cop, you tell me."

Ginger thought for a moment. "So you think what they're doing is illegal?"

"No doubt."

"So we have to stake them out."

"Find out what's going on."

"In Chad's boat." Ginger cringed. "I wouldn't go thirty feet on the lake in Chad's boat."

"You let Chad go out in it."

"He's not so scared he bites his nails down to the first knuckle. We need a better boat."

"Who's got one?"

"Win, but he took off in it with another woman. Oh—" a thought struck. "I know where there's one. And I bet I could get him to let me use it. Oh, why am I doing this? I hate being on the lake—hate it." Then she grunted, a knowing, calculating sort of grunt. "And you know what frosts my shredded wheat? We're going to be lying in the mud while Win's having the time of his life. He's probably having it right now."

Randy Michelson stood near the end of the visitors' dock in the glow of a single light. Since he was on watch, he'd walk the length of it periodically just to turn and walk back. Now he stood peering out onto the boiling water.

Hank wandered up. "How's it going?"

"Okay—a little bored."

"There was a tornado on the other side."

"Really? You saw it?"

"What I could. It did some damage—"

Michelson saw Hank's expression change. Curiosity, narrow eyes peering into the darkness beyond him. Michelson turned. Just where the light from the lamp ended, there floated a boat— a Bayliner—one that had seen far better days.

Tossed by the choppy water, it glided toward the end of the dock. When it was only a few yards off, Michelson's jaw dropped. "There are people lying on the floor—a guy—oh, Lord—Teri!"

CHAPTER 10

Bray, like others on the island, had awakened to screaming wind. Standing on the balcony to get a better look he felt a sensation on his skin like he'd been plugged in, and a current was running through his cells. The air seemed brittle, like he could crack it with a stick. Then he'd seen it. The lightning had exposed the funnel cloud rooted both in sky and earth. After making its mark, it had just left, an alien creature returning to the mother ship.

Even after an hour, the lake still bucked and rocked. And radio news carried eyewitness interviews, some who'd experienced it. Bray listened, fascinated.

Just as they were going into the meteorological reasons for such a thing, this tornado being a small, localized version, he began to hear calls from below. Something about a boat and people on board—unconscious people. Then a name—Teri—and that she wasn't alone.

Still in his robe and shorts, he dressed quickly and ran down to see what was going on. He got to the visitor dock in time to see one of the Sea-Doos towing in a devastated Bayliner—Win's?

Ravaged by the storm, its side had been mutilated by a long angry gash, and its windshield, though shatterproof, had been shattered with only jagged peripheral teeth remaining. In the Sea-Doo, Teri lay cradled in a guard's arms. She had to be out cold. Lying on the floor of the Sea-Doo was another passenger. Wrapped in a plastic blanket, his head resting on a rolled jacket, he was also unconscious.

From the back of Bray's consciousness he heard men calling back and forth. "Where were they?"—"Floated right in"—"That Teri? What she doing out?"—"She had some guy with her," the pilot said to a guard on the dock. "He's pretty far gone."

The guy's face floated beneath the light.

"Win?" Bray gasped. "Win?" a louder, more frightened gasp. To anyone on the dock, "That's my friend. Is he breathing?"

The guy holding Teri answered, "I don't know. I didn't know him. I knew her. She's hurtin'."

The instant the boat hit the dock Bray grabbed a nearby green shirt. "Get him on the dock. Get him over here."

Energized by Bray's insistence, a guard leaped onto the Sea-Doo and pulled Win up by the shoulders. Bray frantically grabbed another guard. "Give him a hand. Come on—give him a hand."

Two others joined in, and the three of them lifted Win to the dock.

Michelson had anxiously watched from the sidelines, but now he got involved. He took Teri from the guard attending to her, laid her on the dock, and checked her vital signs. "She's out cold, but everything seems to be strong," he announced, the relief in his voice more than evident. "We need a first-aid kit—one of those ammonia things."

Teri being watched, Bray dropped beside Win and listened to his heart.

If there was a heartbeat, it was weak. He checked his pulse— a thin thread. Positioning himself, Bray set Win's head back, cleared the airway, then barked into his face, "Win, wake up, breathe. Come on." When Win remained still, Bray began applying CPR.

He felt the chest give way under his stiff-armed pressure, felt the lungs expand when he blew into Win's mouth, hoped the heart was pumping as he pushed it, hoped air was getting in as he blew. How long had he been like this? Would any of it be enough?

Someone ran up with a first-aid kit for Michelson who rummaged through it and found the capsule he was looking for. Snapping it, he waved it beneath Teri's nose. Immediately she jolted—a hand came up and wiped the intense odor away—weak eyes fluttered open. She groaned. Her eyes closed again but before her body could relax, Michelson gave her another whiff. Now she was awake. "How'd I get here," she said breathily. "Win—is Win—?"

"Still out," Michelson said.

More groaning from Teri as she worked herself to a sitting position. Then she saw Bray working on Win. "You wouldn't believe what it was like out there. Oh, no. Is he dead?"

"Not if I can help it," Bray said with an iron tone.

Hank spoke to one of the guards, "Rouse Doc and get him out here. No 911. I can't deal with them right now. The doc'll do more for them anyway."

Bray heard only a little of what had been said. His full attention was on Win, on the rhythm of his movements—four thrusts with clenched hands on his heart, two lungs full of air into his mouth, his nose pinched off. Four thrusts, two blows, four, two. The rhythm. A minute, two minutes, more screaming Win's name. No movement.

Hank was leaning over, his lips inches from Bray's ear. "If you go more'n four minutes there's probably going to be brain damage."

Bray checked his watch. Right at three minutes.

He picked up the rhythm again. "You know that for sure?"

"Read an article. Talked to some paramedics in town just the other day at a bagel shop. Said after four minutes brain damage—and even if they come to, they're usually just revived long enough to get the family around to watch 'em die."

Bray gave Hank a hard look.

"Don't listen to him, Uncle Bray."

As if the mention of his name were a cue, the muscles in his bad leg knotted. The pain of it blazed through his thigh. Instinctively, he lurched back and pushed out his leg to stretch the muscle. Now the pain subsided slightly, but his leg injury burned. "Someone, quick. I can't—my leg. I can't."

Without a moment's hesitation, Michelson jumped in. As if he'd been doing it all his life, he took up the rhythm—muscular arms working deftly.

Leaning on both arms, legs outstretched, Bray watched—feeling impotent, wanting desperately to help his friend. Three-and-a-half minutes. "Come on, Win," Bray urged. "Come on. You can't die. I can't carry that around. Come on."

Michelson blew into his mouth, cried Win's name, and thrust four times then repeated the cycle.

"Best men don't let other best men die," Bray said as he felt Hank's hand on his shoulder.

"Right now he's a carrot. Maybe Michelson should let him go."

"He's my friend—Michelson won't let him go."

"It'd be best."

"Not yet," Michelson said.

"My leg's better. Want me to take over?"

Michelson shook his head.

Phil arrived, still moving slowly, trying to shake off sleep and alcohol. "What happened?" he asked Hank.

"I met him on the lake," Teri said quickly. "We were hit by that tornado thing. I think, anyway. I was hiding in the bottom of the boat. I don't remember much."

Phil only nodded. "How long you going to keep it up?" he asked Bray.

"Until he comes to," Bray said.

Michelson grunted as if to agree.

"It's hopeless," Hank sighed. "I tell you this, I'm not going to wheel him around if he does come to."

Seeing Michelson beginning to sweat, Bray crawled over to him. As he leaned over Win, the bear necklace slipped from Bray's shirt pocket and fell across Win's lips, the bear itself resting on his cheek.

That instant Win coughed. Bray grabbed the necklace as a handful of water belched from Win's mouth. He breathed, took in a gulp of air, then coughed again and again, swollen eyes fluttering open. Red, searching eyes, foggy with cheated death. He must have seen Teri for he asked, "Teri, you okay?" As she nodded, he vomited. Michelson rolled Win onto his side and cleared his mouth to let whatever come out.

Teri groaned. "That's not how I looked."

"Worse," Hank said. Then he asked Win, "What's the capitol of North Dakota?"

Win looked up through red eyes. "This school?"

Bray laughed, relieved. "He thinks there might be brain damage."

"North Dakota?" Win managed. "Fargo or Bismarck or Bear Butte. I didn't know it in the first place. We on the island?"

"You bet," Bray said.

Michelson got to his feet and slipped from the group.

"Any Tylenol?" Win groaned. "I got this headache." He started to get to his feet, but Hank placed a restraining hand on his shoulder.

"Relax," he said. "We've got a doctor coming to take a look at you both."

"I feel okay," Win said, remaining prone, "except for the headache, and my chest—why's my chest hurt like this? Feels like I was hit by a bat—one of those trees must have—"

"CPR," Bray said.

"Uncle Bray kept you alive," Teri told him.

Win smiled up at his friend. "Thanks." Then he rubbed his temple. "I wonder if this is how a hangover feels."

"Probably," Bray said, his smile connecting both ears. "Getting it this way wasn't as much fun, I bet."

Ginger woke to the news about the twister. A curious phenomenon, small as tornadoes go, but still something to see. Even though no one was injured, local residents were hysterical, some wondering if it could reappear. The newscaster finished up by blaming it on global warming. The tons of ash in the air from the New York fire were also mentioned.

But Ginger didn't hear it all. After she heard the time it hit, all that mattered was Win's current state of repair. Although there were no injuries reported, a boat could be sucked up into one of those things and never seen again—who'd know it ever existed?

She made a quick trip to Win's and found Bray's number by his phone and called.

After a brief scuffle with the guard/operator, Ginger was connected to Bray's room. It just rang and rang. When the guard came on again, Ginger insisted on talking to Win. "After they revived him the doctor took over."

"Revived him?"

"Nothin' big. But I bet he saw that white light at the end of that tunnel."

"White light?"

"I'll find somebody. I guess he's still alive."

"Still alive?"

So when Win did come on the phone Ginger was near hysterics. "They said you might be dead."

"That was last night."

"I'm coming up."

"No, you're not. I'm fine. Really. For me CPR works."

"CPR? They had to do CPR?!"

"Just for a few minutes. I'm fine, sort of. A little sore. I'm fine."

"Win, I love you."

"I love you. I won't be here long." That was a lie. He could be a while figuring things out. What little he saw of their operation last night told him it was tightly knit, efficient, and the guys in green were formidable.

"How can I be here while you're hurt there?"

"I'm fine."

"What happened to that girl?"

"Teri? She's okay. We're both fine. When I see you I'll tell you all about it."

"I still want to come up."

"No. I barely survived what God had to engineer to get me on this island. I'd never survive what he'd have to engineer for you. Just stay put. Plan the wedding, and I'll be back as soon as I can."

After a few more *I love yous* they hung up. Ginger immediately got on the phone to Pam.

"You know what we talked about last night?"

"It was late," Pam yawned. "I wasn't myself."

"I'm going to mention just one word—therapist."

"What should we bring?"

Teri woke at six. Her internal clock always rang at six no matter what tornado she'd met the night before. Attesting to the encounter, her insides ached, and her throat seemed tile-coated— singing in the shower she sounded like Kermit. But all that was okay. Win was on the island, and she desperately wanted to see him. That tornado, even though it hurt, gave her just about everything she wanted—it didn't land him in her house, but close enough.

Win was given the room next door to Bray's. But after the doctor gave him the sedative, he didn't care. Fortunately, rest was all he needed—everything else seemed to be working okay.

Ginger's call woke him, but he was ready to awaken anyway. Though rested, he also hurt; his throat and chest ached, and his leg and arm muscles screamed. Although he remembered nothing, his ordeal must have been strenuous.

"You okay?" Bray asked as Win emerged from the bathroom.

"Define okay."

"Alive."

"I'm that." Win hesitated. "Thanks for saving my life."

"Michelson—a guard—helped. Anyway, you owe me money."

"No, I don't."

"You sure? Then I should have let you die."

"Parts of me thinks you did."

Bray smiled. "Hungry?"

"Not sure." He thought. "Yes," he replied, taking a couple more steps, his muscles loosening slightly.

"Teri's been roaming around trying to find a way in here. I told her food was her best bet."

"Keep her at a distance, will you?"

"She's just enthusiastic. But why are you here?"

"Came to visit," he said.

"Why?"

"Teri needed to talk—about someone dying—she ended up at my place."

"Ginger must have been thrilled."

"Premarriage jitters. Who died?"

"A guard took a half-gainer off the cliff—wasn't a pretty sight."

"Dangerous work."

"No one knows what he was doing on the cliff," Bray said. "But enough chitchat. Why are you here?"

"I've been looking for an excuse," Win told him. "Teri gave it to me. You're my buddy. You can't be taking a vacation without me."

"We're not married."

"And don't think I'm not appreciative."

"So, what's the inside of a tornado look like?"

"My memory's a little vague on that point; I think it looks like a deep, dark, flushing toilet." Win took a thoughtful pose. "I'm always amazed at natural things like that—storms, volcanoes—I think God created them so we can get a glimpse of just how powerful he is."

"Well, powerful or not, he took his time bringing you around. Good thing brain damage doesn't matter in your case."

"God was there," Win stated.

"If he was he got preempted. This did it." Bray pulled the little green bear from his shirt pocket. "It fell across your face and you woke up. I'm not superstitious, but this worked. It sure brought you good luck."

Win eyed him incredulously. "God was there."

"This is what touched you."

Win looked at the little stone figurine swinging back and forth. "You're kidding, right? It's stone. Even you've got a higher IQ. God worked through you. Not through some rock."

"It shook me up a little, too. I don't believe in that sort of thing. It touched you, then, bingo, you were alive—coughing and puking—something to see. It was my mother's. And you owe it your life."

"I owe you, the guard, and God. What about you? Any more close calls?"

"It's been smooth sailing."

"Nothing strange happened?"

"To me? Naw."

"Let me see where you nearly fell."

"Nothing to see. The railing was repaired before I woke up. There wouldn't be anything to see anyway—it was an accident. You about ready for breakfast? I'm supposed to call down to the kitchen—Teri's waiting."

"Some coffee maybe," Win said. "You gonna carry that bear everywhere?"

Bray hobbled to the phone. "You didn't see your eyes pop open when it hit you. That God of yours would have to stand right in front of me and turn water into wine—good wine—better still, good whiskey—before I'd believe it was him and not this charm."

"God giving you a case of Wild Turkey—that'll be something to see."

"Wild Turkey's good." He dialed the kitchen and talked to Teri.

"You gonna show me around?"

"Teri's job."

Teri pushed through the door. On the silver tray she carried coffee, a bowl, a box of Reese's Puffs, a banana, and a glass of orange juice. And a Bible!

"Reese's. How did you know? I just started eating Reese's."

"The grocer's daughter keeps your register receipts in her hope chest." She set the tray on the table. "The tour starts in about an hour. During Uncle Bray's therapy session."

An hour later Win stood on the cliff overlooking the Henry and Marsha Sanderson Memorial trees.

"The guard fell from here?" he asked, surveying the boulders below. For an instant he imagined the dying man sprawled across them. *We're never promised tomorrow*, he thought, his heart heavy for the man.

"It was horrible," she said.

"Stairs look risky," he said. "I'll stay up here." Getting down on all fours, then, on his belly, he peered over the cliff to the guard's excavation. All evidence of it had been erased.

Win rolled over, "Hole's patched up."

"It is?"

"But if it was there, that would do it. One step here and over he'd go. He'd be gull bait."

Sitting there for a moment, Win studied the lake. Peaceful, the water like glass. So different from last night. Summer could be so unpredictable. He brushed his hands off on aching legs.

Teri provided Win shade, the sun's aura brilliant around her. "I wonder who patched it up?"

"Same one who repaired the railing. It's new dirt. A little looser. You know the guy who fell?"

She nodded. "He'd worked for us for several years."

"Did you see him talking to any family members beforehand?"
She shook her head.

"Well," he began, looking up at her. "I know why they're doing it," he said. "But who might be doing it?"

"You know why?" Teri asked, concerned that her name might be included in his thinking, like the rifle still hidden in the old orchard was suddenly a part of hers.

"A million buckaroonies."

Teri swallowed hard. "That insurance thing Bray talked about?"

"The question is, who gets it?"

"You think one of the family?" Teri asked, trying to sound the way she ought—curious, a little angry that it was a member of her family trying to kill her favorite uncle.

"It could be a guard. Someone your great-uncle trusted. A million would mean something to a guard. It would to me."

Teri just shook her head. Since he hadn't implicated her, she gained strength. Now she just had a role to play—the innocent, naive niece. And she hoped she'd be playing it for a long while—opposite him. "That's easier to believe than it being one of the family," she said.

Win looked up again. Another shadow appeared just behind her. A tall, thin, crow-shaped shadow with sharp edges.

"So," said the shadow.

Startled, Teri turned. "Bilba," she exclaimed.

"What are you doing there, young man?" the old woman asked moving out from behind Teri.

"I'm on a tour," Win replied.

"On your hands and knees?"

"Just checking something out. With that guy falling last night I was a little reluctant to—"

"Then we are a chicken. Even chickens walk."

Win grinned. "I'll do just that," Win said struggling to his feet.

After giving Teri a withering look, Bilba turned and walked toward the space between the buildings. "Miss Sanderson," Win called out, not wanting her to get away. "May I speak with you?" Under his breath he apologized to Teri for leaving and stepped after Bilba.

Hearing him, Bilba turned with the air of ancient authority.

Taking that for a response, Win moved quickly to her side. "I'm Win Brady," he said pushing a hand into hers. "I'm Bray's friend. The storm brought me."

"Yes, I know. Actually, I was going to find you and ask how you were doing."

They began walking.

"I'm fine. I still hurt a little. But I'm on the mend. I need to thank you, everyone actually, for being so nice to me. One of the guards helped save my life, and the doctor—well—I didn't know they made house calls—island calls."

"You're a friend of the family," she said as if that explained everything. "Is your room satisfactory?"

"Wonderful."

"Food?"

"Excellent."

"Yes. Well," she said as if out of words. "I have duties. I'll see you later, as they say. Perhaps at lunch. I'm sure you'll be well enough in a few days to return home."

"Oh, yes. Home. I was hoping I could stay with Bray for a while. I have a couple of weeks of vacation—"

"We'll be happy to make you a reservation someplace. Now, you rest and recuperate somewhere other than on the edge of a cliff. Having a scrape with death takes a lot out of a person. I know. I've been having a scrape with it for seventy-three years."

Seeing the joke, Win laughed.

Bilba remained effortlessly stone-faced.

"Thank you, again," he said, backpedaling, "for everything."

Bilba nodded. Win thought he saw something of a smile, but it was fleeting and shallow, and it could have been only a muffled burp. Then Bilba excused herself. As she walked away, Win marveled at how she looked—more like a spirit than flesh, so thin, appearing weightless, as if she were hovering over the earth rather than a part of it. *Spooky*, he thought.

But then, that's how this whole place is, Win said to himself.

CHAPTER 11

Win watched Bilba for longer than he thought, for he was startled when Teri showed up beside him.

"She's like a ghost," Teri said, eyes on her as Win's were.

Win only nodded. "Well," he finally suggested, finding some cheer, "why don't we roam the rest of this island while you tell me more about your family."

So, as they walked idly from memorial tree to memorial tree, Teri told him what she wanted him to hear.

"Both died on holidays—hard to believe," he commented along the way. When they stopped at the Madge and Sam Sanderson Memorial Tree, an oak with muscular limbs that pointed toward the small island, Win pushed his face near the plaque. "Where's everybody actually buried?"

"Glory Road Cemetery, St. Albans—family plot. Everybody but Bray's folks are there—they were never found."

"This tree's for your grandparents," he read the plaque. "Killed in a plane crash, midnight, September 10, 1951."

"Heading for a Maine vacation."

"At midnight?"

"They wanted to get someplace early. Anyway, that's what it says."

"They take off from Burlington?"

"I guess. There or somewhere else. It was Grandpa's plane. What were planes like in '51?"

"Slower, I guess. Strange a vacation would start that late." Teri shrugged. She'd never thought about it before and didn't care much about it now. Ancient history was just that. She'd also shrugged when he'd asked her about the business.

"Guards? Were any particularly close to your Uncle Breck?"

"He saw them only when he had to. Hank or my dad handled them."

"So Uncle Breck would go to Hank when he wanted the guards to do something."

"Or my dad."

"Is it still their job?"

"Hank's now. Though Dad will say differently."

"What's your job?"

She only smiled. But as they stood on the cliff closest to the smaller island, she added, "Believe me, they'll destroy the place if anyone finds out what goes on over there."

"Destroy it?"

"Blow it up. And I hear they can."

"They?"

"Bilba, Dad, I guess Sylvia, maybe Hank. Poof! and it's gone. Then they duplicate it somewhere else. Secrecy's that important."

"Then it's illegal?"

"The formula for Coca-Cola's not."

"Okay, your point's made. Back to basics. Everyone's financially comfortable, and no one wants to live anywhere else—that's what you said, right?"

"We're a tight family. We have our squabbles but only squabbles."

"The look Bilba gave you back there—part of a squabble?"

"I guess," Teri said, remembering it. "Sometimes she gets a little strange. Her age."

"All that being true, why would Uncle Breck offer only a million bucks to knock Bray off."

"It wouldn't be enough for me."

"What would be enough?" Win asked, eyes leveled at her like a gun battery.

"Ah, nothing—I mean no amount."

Win holstered his eyes. "But he never had contact with the guards."

"I wouldn't say never."

"But no relationships with them."

"None came to dinner."

"No strangers on the island?"

"Just you and Bray."

"So we have Uncle Breck tempting a member of his family with a sum that clearly wouldn't be enough to tempt him—or her."

"A million's still a lot of money."

"To kill a member of your family?"

"Depends on the person."

"Your uncle knew everyone pretty well. Knew your hot buttons."

"Sure. I guess."

"So he knew how to tempt you."

"I guess."

"How would he tempt you?"

To her surprise, she told the complete, unvarnished truth. Maybe because of his strength—to the point, intelligent—or maybe because of his voice—strong, guileless. But she blurted it out. "He'd wave you in front of me."

Taken completely off guard, Win turned crimson.

She, too, was aghast. Blushing red, she gasped, her hand clapping in front of her open mouth. "I can't believe I said that. I didn't mean it. Really. I didn't."

"It's okay. But," he went on, recovering by chugging ahead, "what else would he tempt you with?"

Breathing hard, forcing herself to think, she finally shrugged. "Don't know. Not sure anything's that tempting." Still wanting to escape from what she'd said, she began moving away. "Listen, I've got to go on duty soon, and I want to do some things first."

"Sure," Win said, empathetically. "I'm tired myself. Last night was really something."

"Incredible," she answered, moving even further away. "I'd better get going."

As she walked to the rear of her house, Win wondered how he could possibly get her to tell what she knew. There just had to be more.

As Teri strolled away from him she suppressed an excited laugh. *He went for it*, she squealed in her head. *He thinks I know something. He'll do anything to find out what it is. Anything.* If she could have done a backflip without it being conspicuous she would have. *I'm in control.*

"You were right," a green-clad guard told Hank. Hank sat where he often did in the summer—in the corner of the cavernous docking area where shadows and water kept things cool. "They were snooping around where Gunn fell."

"I recognized that kid's name right off," Hank spat. "From the papers. He and Bray work together. And now the kid's on to something. Bray was just too quick to accept our invitation. Once a cop always a cop. Now I've got two reasons to do what I gotta do." He looked up at the guard. "Get *Savage*."

Savage was Tommy's Sportster Sea-Doo—an eighty-four horsepower, purple-and-green three-seater that Hank had souped up for him. About once a week, Tommy broke free of the computers and took his boat out. He'd done it just a couple days ago. He wouldn't miss it.

The guard nodded and left Hank alone to work out the rest of his plan.

Win returned to the main house. As he mounted the top of the stairs, he saw Bray and who he assumed was the therapist approaching from the direction of Bray's room. She *was* beautiful.

And when Bray saw him, Win smiled at the transformation. In a single, fluid moment, Bray went from helpless gimp to Mister Cool with an envy-seeking grin. "Hi," he greeted coming to a stop. "Meet Brandiwyne Hortentia."

"Great name," Win offered, shaking the woman's hand.

"Autographs take time," said Brandi. "You okay? You're moving stiffly."

"Muscles. I'm a tornado survivor—need to put that on a T-shirt."

"Maybe I can help."

"She's good," Bray affirmed, the grin even bigger.

"It'll work itself out."

Brandi smiled. "If they all did, I'd be out of business."

"No worries there," Win commented. "I've come to see my buddy here."

"Well," Bray began, "walk with us to the dock."

He did, and while he and Bray watched Miss Hortentia motor toward the Grand Isles shore, Bray asked, "Think Pam would be jealous of that?"

"Think sinners go to hell?"

Bray scowled. "Now why'd you have to go and say a thing like that?"

"My job. She helping your leg?"

"In ways you just wouldn't understand. You have a good tour?"

"Saw all the trees. You had your share of tragedies—a couple on holidays."

"Breck liked to remember these things."

"Or he wanted other people to."

Bray only nodded. "Teri win you away from Ginger?"

"She was pleasant."

"Well, don't turn your back on her," Bray laughed.

"Why?"

"She didn't take you to her house?"

"Just around the island."

"Well," Bray said, wrapping his free hand over Win's shoulder, "you'll see. You'll see. Where are you off to now?"

"Thought I'd rest for a while. Tornadoes suck it out of you."

"Rest—that's the ticket. Let's play some pool."

 。

As Bray racked up the balls, the big-screen TV flashed on a picture of the New York fire's frontline battle. Men scrambling amid the flames, tractors building firebreaks, pregnant planes dropping water and retardant. The commentary went on for quite a while describing the devastation and the sacrifice of those involved. And when it ended, Win felt strangely unaffected and safe. While Bray set up, Win found himself musing about that fire as a metaphor for the Christian in a sinful world. The fire as Satan devouring and destroying, the ash that dirtied the sky and rained down on them were the effects of sin. But for all the falling ash, Christians were forever clean in Christ. And on that last day, when the fire was finally extinguished, the world would be clean again. Win rather liked the metaphor. And so intent was he on it that he didn't notice Teri strolling in.

"Hi, Uncle Bray," she said, slipping an arm in his and kissing him on the cheek. "You beating him?"

"I always beat him," he quipped coolly, unwinding his arm and setting up the next shot—his fourth in a row.

"That true?" Teri challenged Win.

"Since this is our first game ever, we'll see."

Win did.

He never shot again, and when the eight ball dropped, Bray came up from leaning over the cue ball with a maddening grin. "Want another?"

"We're meek, not stupid," Win said.

"The mantra of the defeated," Bray laughed raucously.

Joining in the laugh, Win turned to Teri, "Who invited him here, anyway?"

Not completely realizing what she was replying to, Teri said, "Bilba—another command mistake."

"Bilba?" Bray sound surprised.

"Well, she brought it up at a meeting—we all seconded it."

"See," Bray said, "they *all* invited me. They all love me."

"Anyone particularly excited about him coming?" Win pressed.

Teri wrapped an arm around Bray's waist. "Me—and I was right."

Bray gave her a hug. "Come on, Win, shoot another round. We gotta do something with the rest of the morning."

As it turned out they played pool through lunch—an undisciplined affair. Family appeared in drips and drabs, grabbed a sandwich or salad prepared by a cook/guard then disappeared again. Tommy's stay was the shortest. After stepping in the room he glanced about, saw Bray, snatched a sandwich, and took it back with him. Sylvia stayed the longest. She gave them a shallow wave when she arrived, then she sat and ate in front of the big screen. After a couple of soap operas, she left.

About an hour after lunch, Bray withered. Complaining that his leg ached, he went up to his room to rest.

Win and Teri were left alone with their Diet Cokes. After an uneasy minute, Win asked, "Unanimous votes normal around here?"

"Nope," she said, shaking her head. "They argue over what date it is."

"You'd think someone would object to Bray coming. After all, he might discover the secret. You'd be going against Uncle Breck. That sort of thing."

"Nope. All agreed. No discussion."

"And up he came."

"All the way." Teri took a long drink. "You shoot?"

"A little rotation."

"No. Guns."

"Oh. A pistol once. Hit the lower right corner."

"I shoot. Used to have a rifle range. They turned it into a bowling alley. But no one bowls."

"Your own range?"

"I paid to have it put in, and they tore it out. You like guns?"

"As long as they're pointed somewhere else."

"Wanna see some?"

"You have some?"

Teri grinned. "Come on." Seconds later Teri led the way from the main house. Setting a path across the commons toward the palm tree, she headed for her house. Win wouldn't get there this time.

After Win took only a few steps onto the grass, it began.

First as a faint sensation—discomfort that quickly became dread, the sense of being watched, paranoia. He hardly recognized it. But, after the next couple of steps, the burner was turned up. Paranoia darkened to fear, dread turned specific—snipers behind rocks, someone watching through the crosshairs of a high-powered rifle.

He spun. Studied each house, each tree.

Only then did he know—it was happening again.

The presence.

As before. In the bell tower at Sugar Steeple, in the cove where he'd fought the druggie. A wave of dread washing over him, submerging him, blades of anxiety swirling inside him. True panic, of being in imminent danger, of bony hands reaching for him, ready to drag him into an evil sea. Only after leaving the seminary and coming to Vermont did this curious gift materialize and, frankly, he wished it hadn't.

He stopped.

"You okay?" Teri asked.

"Not particularly," Win said enigmatically. He took another couple steps. It grew stronger.

It's irrational. There are no bony hands, no stalker.

He forced his brain to clear. *It's nothing, it's nothing,* he kept chanting. *It's nothing.*

The palm tree.

Was that it?

The center of the island. Or was that just where the presence lived for the moment? Another few steps. He stood within ten feet of the palm tree now, and the feeling intensified. His taxed muscles began to contract, as if seeking refuge within themselves. His heart tightened into a fist. His breathing became rapid and erratic. Beads of sweat popped from his forehead. He was heading into a black tunnel with rats and bats and snakes and traps and slashing knives.

"What's going on?" Teri asked, standing back, greatly concerned.

"Is there something under that palm tree?" Win asked, his voice strained.

"Breck's grave."

"Grave?" Win stared at her. Another step. "Breck's?"

At the mention of the name, dread swelled to a tidal wave. Suddenly he was facing a Kodiak bear unarmed. Or balanced on the edge of the Grand Canyon. Vertigo clawed at him. A pervasive dizziness strangled balance. He staggered.

"Win, what's happening?"

He didn't reply. He didn't know what to say. Words were a lost art—the facility of another time.

He stood before the heart-shaped flower bed at the base of the palm, unable to go any further. His knees buckled, and he fell to all fours, knocking over a small vase of fresh flowers.

Good God in heaven, he gasped. Bowing. He was bowing. He'd been forced to his knees. Whatever it was had forced him to bow.

He couldn't. He just couldn't. Bowing? No. Never.

He tried to stand. He couldn't. He pulled his feet beneath him and pushed. But there wasn't enough strength in the universe.

"God," he cried audibly, "please—you can't let me do this."

He strained his legs further.

Dread became excruciating terror. It invaded every brain cell, every ganglia, every emotion, every thought. The sensation in the bell tower so many months before had been a pinprick compared to this total invasion. It spoke! Words—not feelings—words that seemed to come from a braying serpent, its teeth sharp for tearing. It spoke clearly—no ethereal whispers here. It drove the words into his skull, one at a time like nails—upon each hung his doom.

"You are mine," it said. Then again. *"You are mine!"*

As pronounced as if audible. Then it hissed every bit as powerfully, "You are mine." It echoed to his core.

"Win, please, what's wrong?" Teri cried.

Bray heard her through the open balcony door. Slipping from his bed, he hobbled there. The instant he saw Win, he knew his friend was in trouble. A seizure? It had to be something like that.

Struggling to get to his feet, Win couldn't even hold his head steady.

Win was about to go down on his belly when a guard grabbed him beneath his arms and dragged him several feet from the tree and the grave below it.

The instant the hands touched him the terror dissolved. Calm returned. But a calm that found Win drained. Now he rested against someone's knee, his muscles rubber.

"You okay?" A familiar voice.

Turning Win found Michelson grinning. "Tornadoes and graves—they can take a lot out of a fellow."

"Oh, Win," Teri cried, now on one knee, her gentle hand stroking his cheek.

"Just need to rest a minute."

"Did you have a seizure or something?"

"Something seized *me*," he said, his heart pounding, his breathing erratic, each slowly returning to normal. He worked himself to his feet. Stretched. So many aches, muscles bent and brittle.

Suddenly there was another. Like a crow dropping from a telephone wire, Bilba appeared. She was at the grave picking up the vase and rearranging the flowers. When finished she turned her attention to Win. "How can you desecrate my brother's grave like that?" she admonished angrily.

"I'm sorry. Really." Win apologized. "I stumbled. My muscles haven't recovered from the beating last night."

"Then you should have stayed in bed."

"I should have."

Bray emerged from the main house and hobbled toward Win. Bilba was still talking when he arrived. "Yes, you should." Bilba's eyes leveled on Teri, but she said nothing. Win sensed that to Bilba, Teri was a lost cause, that no words could help. Then she turned to Bray. "He's your guest. Please keep him off our sacred grounds."

The crow returned to the wire as she moved quickly away. But then she stopped and turned to Michelson, "When you're done here, which better be soon, come to my office."

"Your office," Michelson acknowledged. "Yes, ma'am."

She disappeared into her house.

Bray slipped an arm over Win's shoulder. "There's never a dull moment when you're around."

"You okay now?" Michelson asked, his tone helpful.

"Fine," Win told him. "Thanks. I guess that's two I owe you."

"Then I'll see you folks later," Michelson said, his eyes coming to rest on Teri. They lighted gently there for a moment, then he left.

Win rubbed the back of his neck and glanced at Bray, then Teri. "Give me a few minutes, guys. I need to think—gather myself up a little."

"You sure you're okay?" Teri asked, sincerely concerned.

Bray placed a hand on her shoulder. "Give him a sec."

Heart still rushing, breathing still deep and disturbed, Win walked between houses to where he could see the lake. Six months before, this lake didn't even exist for him. Now it was like the blood in his veins. He couldn't imagine living without it—just like he couldn't imagine living without Ginger or Chad. Or Jesus.

Blessed Jesus.

Where were you? I was on my knees. I was bowing to—

He couldn't bring himself to say it.

I wanted to stand, but you didn't help. I needed your help, and you didn't help. You let him tear the spirit right from me. I was on my hands and knees—

What was it? Satan? Unlikely. Satan was an angel. He could be only in one place at a time. It was unlikely he would waste time and space on him. He, Win Brady, was small potatoes. One of Satan's lieutenants? It didn't matter. Win had been touched again—more than touched. He'd been grabbed, shaken, thrown to the ground. Spiritually battered. Humiliated before his Lord.

Where is this in your Word? You're turning me into a medium. Your Word is all there is. Not this. Why am I groveling in the dirt? Satan battering me. Aren't you supposed to run interference for me, Lord? Am I a spiritual punching bag?

A breeze so soft and cool blew in from the lake. He needed that breeze. Not only did it refresh but it comforted.

And when it left he knew.

Jesus loved him.

He also knew there was evil on the island. No more evidence was needed. Oh, he needed to find out the whys and the whos, but one thing was settled for him. There was evil on this island.

"You are mine," it had said.

It was after him, too.

CHAPTER 12

Still weakened, Win found Bray playing pool by himself.

Bray straightened as Win entered. "You okay?"

"When dealing with an infinite God, the spiritual walk can get confusing."

"That's why I leave it to you." Bray hesitated, a look of solemn resolve. "I want to show you something in my room."

On the way upstairs, Bray asked, "What happened out there?"

Afraid to sound like a lunatic, Win replied, "I just got a little weak. Couldn't get up."

"A seizure? If it was, don't deny it. It's not something to fool with."

"No seizure."

"Good." He patted him warmly on the shoulder, "Good." Then he said, "I need to show you something."

They entered his room and Bray closed the door behind him, then pointed to a book lying on the table near the balcony door.

"Open it," Bray told him.

"It's not going to explode with those long springy things is it?"

"Open it," Bray repeated with a no-nonsense tone.

The book was *Something of Value* by Herman Wouk. Without picking it up, Win opened the cover, then pushed back a couple of pages. The book had been hollowed out. Lying within it was the charred remains of what looked like a copper tube, maybe a half-inch in diameter. The ends had been sawed neatly off and in the center of it was another saw mark, this one cutting the tube nearly in half.

"Someone's trying to tell me something. First there was this—" Bray pulled out the diary page, which Win scanned. "My mom wrote it just before she was killed."

"Your mom was worried. Whoever is doing this is going to a lot of trouble. Hollowing out a book?"

Bray shrugged. "That way they could walk around with it, and no one would notice." He lifted the copper tube out, the charring coming off on his fingers. There were no other fingerprints.

Bray sniffed it. "A gas line," he said.

Win sniffed it too. "Faint—pretty old."

There was a folded note. Win took it out and opened it. "From the *Contusion*."

Win looked up at Bray and saw bloodless eyes looking back. "What's the *Contusion*?"

"My dad's boat—the one that blew up. The one that killed them."

"Because of a gas leak?" Win asked, eyeing the notch in the pipe.

"Don't know—they couldn't find it afterwards."

"Somebody did."

Bray nodded, his intestines knotted.

"Slow this thing down!" Ginger cried over the roar of the powerful twin Mercury inboards. Having enlisted her next-door neighbor, Mrs. Sherman, to take care of Chad, Ginger sat beside Pam on the raised pilot deck of Larin Breed's thirty-four-foot Carver Montego.

This was not the kind of craft a policeman would normally own. However, Breed had given Mike Grogan, a dirty cop destined for many years behind bars, a thousand dollars for his twenty-six-foot cruiser. Mike faced a fiduciary dilemma: give the boat to Breed for a thousand bucks or to the DEA for nothing. Larin then traded up for this slightly used Montego Sports Cruiser.

"You're not going to hurt it, are you?" he'd asked anxiously after Ginger had asked to borrow it. "I've waited all my life for a boat like this. Thank God for drug dealers."

She'd fervently assured him that not only would she keep it safe, but she'd probably never drive it over ten knots. He was walking away when he realized that he'd insured it for the replacement value, far more than he'd paid for it. After doing some quick math and applying the numbers to even larger boats the DEA would soon auction, he turned. "On second, thought, I'd do anything for Bray. What's a boat when weighed against my love for that guy? Do whatever makes sense."

Ginger still promised to keep it under five miles per hour. It wasn't so much a promise to Breed as it was to the terror lurking deep within her. If they went slow, perhaps that terror would remain subdued.

Pam broke that promise about two seconds out of the Burlington marina. Broke it? She shattered it. Ginger's terror leaped to life.

The Montego was a sleek craft built for speed. Though normally the engines topped out at 300 horsepower, they had been replaced somewhere along the line with two 415 horsepower hogs. When cranked up, which Pam liked to do, it literally screamed over the waves.

"We're hardly trolling here," Pam fired back. "I used to date a guy with a boat like this. Half throttle and they fly."

"I hate the water. I really do hate it."

"You live on it. How can you hate it?"

"It's easy. Swimming's okay, but boats . . . "

"Were you scared by one in the womb or something?"

"There were no boats in my mother's womb. Just slow down."

"No," Pam said firmly. "It'll take us all day to get there if I slow down. And every minute out here is another fingerprint on Bray's body."

"We should have driven."

"But we need the boat anyway. You'll be fine."

"You sure aren't very understanding."

"She's a beautiful blonde. I have no understanding." She cranked the throttle up another notch. The inboards roared in immediate response. "Most of the afternoon's already gone."

"Oh, why didn't I go to church," Ginger groaned, watching the wake. "I need everybody on my side. How deep is it here?"

Bray fingered the small brass pipe as he and Win sat at the bedroom table. "Their boat blew up. Neither they, nor the boat, were ever found. They did find pieces of it, but not the heavy stuff— the engine and control mechanisms, the fuel system. Judging from the investigation Raif made last night, I doubt if anyone looked for that stuff very hard."

"The bottom of that lake can swallow things up," Win said, remembering his search for a particular motel key not long ago, one with a drug dealer on the other end of it.

Bray gave a shallow nod. "That page is from my mom's diary. She'd been worried. Implied she and my dad were in danger."

"Someone might kill them?"

"People worry about a lot of things. Murder seems extreme. Of course, they did end up dead."

"So somebody has the diary."

"Looks like it."

"This could be a fuel line from anything. There's nothing here to tie it to the *Contusion*. Funny name for a boat."

"I named it," Bray told him. "Actually there were several *Contusions*."

"It's a bruise or something, isn't it?"

"I mispronounced *Constitution* as a kid. Dad enjoyed immortalizing our mistakes. Once my mom said something was *as easy as falling off a dog*. He put it on a plaque."

"Nice guy."

"A prince. Played cards all day. He had to do something to feel superior."

"So—what's going on?"

"Don't know. But, there's something sick about it."

"Do you think they were actually murdered?"

Bray thought for a moment as if considering that possibility for the first time. "No. These people fear visitors, particularly cops. Cops could figure out their little business. I bet the boat blew up, but instead of coming clean to the authorities, for the sake of secrecy they hid everything. Someone doesn't like that and wants me to look into things."

"You going to?"

"Not on this. This could be from the back of a refrigerator. Hit it with a blowtorch and you've got your fire residue. And it could be anybody. A guard's more likely, someone fed up with the way they do things around here."

"Maybe your parents' remains aren't lost."

"For a while I wondered if they'd been buried. But the more I thought about that—well—"

"You want to find the rest of the stuff—if it is stashed somewhere?"

Bray shrugged, "What good would it do?

Win took a deep breath. "Spooky. Think someone's telling you that you're in danger too? Someone telling you to watch your step?"

"You still reciting that verse?"

"What if I told you the guy who fell from that cliff was making a trap for you?"

Bray's brows tilted inward about forty-five degrees. "Trap?"

"He'd dug out an area just below the cliff. If you'd stepped on it while visiting your parents' memorial trees, you'd've gone over."

"Let's see it," Bray said with a certain eagerness.

"It's been filled in."

"Then how do you know—"

"Teri told me. She saw the guy digging it. That's why I'm here. She was concerned for you and—trusted me."

"She probably dug it out herself just to get you here. You may not have noticed—"

"Come on—"

"She's got you in her sights."

"Dig and repack it?" Win said, as if actually seeing her doing it. "For me?"

Bray smiled triumphantly. "Kids—go figure."

Bilba's eyes came up and met Michelson's staring down. He stood before her desk at attention. Such a handsome young man—well-groomed sandy hair, blue eyes—oh such blue—muscular body. A powerful man. *Much like Gordon. What would Gordon look like now—after nearly fifty years? Probably have a little paunch and the hint of jowls, but his eyes would still be blue. And Little Erika. She's forty-seven now—little Erika forty-seven. Does she know about me? Oh, well, it was all for the best. Breck was so right about that. But how could she miss that kidnapper so?*

"You wanted to see me, Miss Sanderson?"

"I did," Bilba managed, pushing the invading thoughts back where they belonged. "I've been watching you lately."

"Me? Why?"

"You do things very well."

"Thank you."

"You seem eager to please."

"I am," Michelson said, gratified. "I want to do well."

"Good. It's time to do something *well* for me."

"Yes, Miss Sanderson?"

"You know Bray Sanderson, my nephew?"

"The guy with the cane."

"Yes. He needs to meet with a fatal accident."

"Fatal?"

"As in dead."

"Accident?"

"As in, well, accident."

"He does?"

"Soon."

"Can I ask why?"

"Sure. I'll not answer you, of course."

"An accident. What kind of an accident?"

"The kind that would kill him."

"Ah," said Michelson. "Is this part of my regular duties?"

"It is now."

"So I'm to do something that kills him."

"Anything, yes. But it has to look like an accident."

Michelson nodded. "Okay," he said, though the tone was doubtful. "I've never really done anything like that before. Do you have any suggestions?"

"Only one," Bilba's eyes became rock-hard. "If he's still alive in twenty-four hours, you won't be."

"That's more like an order."

"Then I *suggest* you follow it." Then she added, "And don't tell anyone about this. You'll die for that, too."

Michelson, a little dazed, stepped from the room.

Bilba returned to her work satisfied. She'd handled it just like Breck would have. Maybe even better.

Win hadn't seen Teri since his grave ordeal early in the afternoon and, after talking with Bray, wasn't sure he wanted to. Had she really concocted this whole thing about the guy digging the trap just to get him out there? Had she built a fabrication on someone's horrible death? Somehow he couldn't bring himself to believe that.

But why? She obviously had no respect for his feelings for Ginger—or Ginger's feelings for him. But lack of respect and looking at a man's broken, bloodied body and saying, "Wow! Does this give me an idea," are two very different things.

She couldn't have done that.

Win, he said to himself, *time to trust your instincts.*

His ordeal by the grave—

For an instant he relived the intense tightness in his heart. Then shook it away. He wasn't sure exactly how his ordeal related to these thoughts about Teri, but he had the distinct feeling that one of the reasons he'd been taken through that particular *valley of the shadow of death* was for him to know that God was with him in everything—even his instincts.

There was evil on the island and at least some of that evil was after his buddy.

A reminder: It was after *him*, too.

Win shuddered.

He sat in the gazebo with the morning paper. He didn't read the paper much. He left that to Bray. But he'd been troubled by this thing with Teri and grabbed the paper in the rec room and took it out to the gazebo to read in hopes of getting his mind off everything for a while. It hadn't worked until now. Now he wasn't troubled anymore, just anxious—about Bray, about himself, about Teri—curious about what the family was up to and if Bray's parents really had been murdered. But he wasn't troubled. Not of soul anyway.

So he read the paper.

On the front page was the story about the tornado. It was unusual in that it cut across water and the islands—usually they did one or the other. There was no mention of anyone surviving it or of anyone being given CPR. On the third page he found the story about the guy who'd fallen to his death. He'd read the story casually until he saw quotes. One from Phil saying that the guy had been repairing some abutments—had been working under intense floodlights and with safety cords, but the cords must have broken.

Teri said things had been dark. That she could hardly see the guy and that he'd fallen from the tree ledge.

They'd lied.

For an instant he thought it might matter, and then he realized that they were probably trying to avoid being sued.

Or that's what they'd say.

But one of them knew what that guy was really doing.

How could he smoke whoever it was into the light?

The Sanderson family parked their cars in a small garage just off the St. Albans dock. Since they were the only ones who used it, they were the only ones with keys. A suitcase in hand, Hank looked around to see if anyone was watching, then unlocked the door and entered. After donning the suit in the case, he took the keys he'd surreptitiously borrowed from Tommy and, after obscuring the license plate with mud, borrowed Tommy's Mercedes.

Fifteen minutes later Hank pulled up to a ramshackle bar east of St. Albans—the name *Clancy's Bar* chiseled on a wooden sign.

Hank stepped into the musky gloom and up to the bartender. "I'm looking for the Brightstar boys."

"Why you dressed like a monkey?"

"An ape. This is an ape."

It was. A costume he'd always wanted to wear. When this plan took shape he'd had a contact buy it in Montpelier. Although it was hot and it itched, he figured he looked pretty good.

"Okay, why you dressed up like an ape?"

"A fetish. Now where are the Brightstars?"

Laughter erupted from a corner of the room. "If yer looking for bananas, we got some."

Hank turned to see four guys sitting in a corner booth. Foster was right. They looked nothing like Brightstars—sparklers looked like blazing suns in comparison. Their hair was long and scraggly, their faces vacant moons, their eyes wide but only fractionally effective, and teeth that would provide cabins and summer homes for several hygienists, if they had insurance, of course. They wore flannel shirts with the arms torn away and cutoffs. Their tennis shoes were dirty, and a couple of them had huge, ragged holes in the sides. One had a sole that hung loose except for a few strategically placed threads. All arms crawled with tattoos.

"Can I join you?" the ape asked. "Name's Bonzo."

One of them, the bulkiest, the one in the corner with his arms draped over the bench on either side, spoke first. "You a bill collector? 'Cause if you are—"

"No, Wink," another chirped. "He's a singin' telegram. Always wanted to get one."

"Who'd send you a singin' telegram?"

"Ethel Merman?" another croaked. "He wrote her love letters."

"She's my kind o' woman."

"She's dead."

"Okay, who are you?" the bulky one asked.

"Bonzo," Hank repeated. "I've come to make you guys a lot of money."

"Money?" Wink said suspiciously.

The word was repeated by each in turn, by a couple twice.

"One question," Wink exclaimed. "You buyin'?"

"Sure."

Suddenly they straightened, faces eager and alive. "Beer, we want beer."

The ape ordered, and a moment later the four of them were sipping mugs of the golden liquid, the heads thick and making mustaches as the mugs dropped. "Now, I want names."

"Teeter, Skids, Parsnip, and I'm Wink," said Wink, pointing to each as he introduced him. "Why the ape costume?"

"A party."

"And we weren't invited," Teeter groaned, brokenhearted.

"You guys know waverunners?" the ape asked, raising the beer to his huge rubber lips and only then realizing there was no way to drink it.

"Sure," Wink said, "we're good at it, too. Real good."

"I'm the best," said Parsnip, a thumb beating his chest.

"You ain't neither," Teeter protested.

The ape put a hand up to quiet them. "I'm sure you're all good, probably great."

"Right, we're great."

"Olympic types."

"Excellent," the ape said, "because I want you guys to use your talents to do me a big favor."

"A favor?"

"Right."

Wink went somber. "People don't get paid for favors."

"Well, you'll be the exceptions."

"That means we're getting paid," Parsnips pointed out to Wink.

"Right."

All nodded with satisfied grins at one another. They drank more beer.

"You got waverunners?" the ape asked.

"Of our own?"

"Right."

"No."

"Nope."

"Not a one among us. But we're still good at it. Ain't we?"

They all nodded frantically.

"Okay, I'll make a phone call, and tomorrow they'll deliver four waverunners right out front."

"Out front?"

"O' here?"

"And then they'll take 'em to the lake. You'll have all tomorrow to brush up on your skills. Then Tuesday, the day after tomorrow—"

"Today's Sunday?"

"You sure?"

"The day after tomorrow, Tuesday, you'll follow these instructions." The ape reached into a side pocket, took out a folded piece of paper, and placed it on the table. Wink grabbed it, opened it and began reading. The others crowded around. "What's camo-flaig-ee mean?"

"Camouflage—hide. Make sure no one can see you."

"I can do that," Teeter stated.

"Me, too," Parsnip nodded.

"There's some days I think I'm invisible," Skids said, his voice floating.

They finished their beers and looked at the ape who, in turn, waved for another round.

"When the job's done I'll pay you five hundred each."

"Says here we're suppose to hurt somebody."

"Right. I want to teach 'em a lesson."

"Most apes I know do their own dirty work," Parsnips said, a little suspicious.

"How many do you know?" the ape asked.

"Why?" Parsnip asked. "You want to join a support group?"

Wink smacked Parsnip upside his head, then turned his attention back to the ape at hand. "Well, we got a lesson to teach you," said Wink. "We don't work that cheap. We want two hundred now and two hundred later."

"You drive a hard bargain. But okay."

They were all pleased at Wink's negotiating skills.

The ape pulled a wad of bills from his other side pocket. "Half now?"

As if slobbering over fresh roadkill, their eyes devoured the money.

The ape counted out eight bills and handed them to Wink.

"Good," said Wink. "Sorry we had to skin you so bad."

"Good men are worth good money."

"That's true of apes too," Skids laughed.

"Remember. Tomorrow they'll be here. Before ten."

"Then we will be too."

About a half hour later, having made his call about the waverunners, promising to fax additional instructions later, Hank drove back to the garage, parked Tommy's car, removed the ape suit, placed a heavy rock inside the suitcase with the suit, and got back into the *Savage*. About a hundred yards offshore he slipped the suitcase into the water. It sank.

There was a lot of work to do, but with any luck at all he'd take care of both Bray and that Win-kid on Tuesday. Then for one thing, he'd be a million richer. And, if the rest of his plan worked, soon he'd have the rest of the money too—all the money he'd ever want—forever.

Dinner came early. A summer buffet of cold cuts, salads, and a whipped cream dessert laid out in Bilba's dining room. Missing were Sylvia, Hank, and Tommy. Teri seemed to be backing off Win a bit. She kept her distance, only speaking to him casually. After dinner Win overheard Phil corner Bray about the job offer, but Bray gracefully put him off. "Just too much going on today. I don't know how you people take the pace around here."

Phil never asked him what pace he was referring to, but laughed stiltedly—then challenged him to pool.

Hank arrived just as things were breaking up, made himself a quick sandwich, and left for "work."

As the balls were being racked, Bilba swept into the rec room, eyed the television for a moment—more news on the never-ending fire—and announced, "I want to talk to Bray."

Bray stiffened and without a word handed the cue to Win. As Teri settled in an overstuffed chair with a magazine, Win prepared for a beating.

As a child Bray had never been allowed in the butterfly house. As a teen he didn't care about it. Now, as an adult he just couldn't appreciate it. After thirty seconds he wanted to attack the butterflies with a can of Raid, and after a few minutes he wanted to burn the place to the ground.

He couldn't imagine how Bilba could sit there enraptured. The instant she entered her eyes glazed over as she was transported to another world. But this trip lasted for only for a minute or two. She returned and looked up at her nephew.

"You're not in love with this place as I am."

"Different strokes."

"What's that mean?"

"Just that different people like different things."

"And I'm different."

"We're all different. Now, what did you want to talk to me about?"

Bilba took a deep breath. She had been sitting on one of the benches. Now she got up and walked over to the rambling sculpture in the center of the room. "Breck built me this place. As a present."

"I heard that."

"When I was quite young. Twenty-five. Nearly fifty years ago."

"Long time."

"You would never come in here."

"You would never let me."

"Breck never let you. I didn't care as long as you didn't let the butterflies out."

"I don't think I would have enjoyed it like you did. You'd look so content when you came out."

"Content." She mulled over the word. "I owe Breck a great deal."

"I know."

"No, you don't. No one does. Only Breck."

Bray cocked his head. He sensed he was about to be let into a secret world of hers. He wondered why. "What happened?"

"I feel a duty to Breck. I want you to know why."

"It's not important."

"It is to me." Bilba watched a particularly beautiful purple-and-orange butterfly flit before her eyes. When it took residence on a vine nearby she continued. "I made some bad choices when I was a young lady. I fell in love."

"How could that be a bad choice?" A little gnat of a butterfly zipped around his ear, it was all Bray could do to keep from flattening it.

"As it turned out the man was a bad person. Now, what I'm going to tell you no one knows. You must keep it to yourself."

"Sure," Bray said, his skin crawling as he felt a butterfly land on the back of his neck.

"I became pregnant."

Now that was a little tough to believe. Almost as hard as believing that Bray was letting a butterfly walk along the back of his neck. His eyes widened. "These things happen," he said to her. *But how could they have possibly happened to Bilba?*

"The father was a local man, Gordon Fritz. He was the son of a local dairyman. Quite dashing. Sandy hair, blue eyes—wonderful blue eyes. Anyway, I didn't tell him about the baby until I was far along. By then Breck knew about it—I was quite large."

She was so skinny, Bray thought, *Breck could probably tell if she had a pea in her pocket.*

"Gordon and I decided to get married after the baby was born. Breck was so wonderful, he made sure I was completely taken care of. I stayed in my house. Had around-the-clock nurses, and when the baby was born, he paid for everything and made sure we wanted for nothing. I named her Erika, with a *k* for that German touch—in honor of Gordon's nationality." She hesitated, and the sparkle in her eyes faded to gray. "Gordon's parents found out. I don't know how. Gordon must have told them, though he denied it. They forbade him from seeing me or the baby. We were devastated. But Breck was wonderful. Made sure the baby and I had everything we needed. Then one night, while little Erika slept, Gordon came and snatched her away. Took her. Kidnapped her. I never saw either of them again."

Bray was actually touched by the story and found himself watching the woman with empathetic eyes.

"Breck took me in. I cried for months. My child whom I loved. The man I loved. Both gone. Betrayed. Breck never complained. He made sure I was comfortable. He even paid for a psychologist who helped me through that terrible experience. Breck was so selfless, so loving and endearing. I owe him so much."

"I can imagine."

"So if he tells me to do something, no matter what it is, I have a duty to at least try to do it."

"I understand."

"You do?" She beamed elatedly. "I'm so glad. So very glad."

"What is it you have to do?"

"Something difficult. When the time comes you'll know. But all that is unimportant right now. I wanted to make certain you knew my motivations."

"You were courageous then."

"Getting pregnant? No courage required there. No. None at all. I rather liked the 'getting' part." She laughed. "Well, I must return to work. It was a wonderful talk. Wonderful."

As if a great weight had been lifted from the woman, she all but danced from the butterfly house. Bray all but ran, swiping the butterfly from his neck as he did. Outside again in the fading afternoon light, Bray took stock in what he'd been told.

He understood the *what*. It made her more human. Put a little flesh on her emotional bones. Gave him something with which to be empathetic, and it explained some of her hardness.

But he couldn't fathom *why* he'd been told.

Maybe someday he would. Right now he wouldn't worry about it.

Win was in the process of losing his third game when Bray, cane in hand, hobbled back. Without so much as a word to Phil, Win slapped the cue into Bray's free hand, smiled at Phil, and headed toward the door—defeat is always softened with a change of scene and fresh lake air.

Before he made it to the door, Teri intercepted him.

"The gazebo's beautiful. If you crane your neck just right you can see the sunset."

Had it been Ginger asking he wouldn't have hesitated. In fact, he would have been the instigator. But it wasn't Ginger, and craning his neck for Teri somehow didn't seem right. But there was no real reason to put her off—and there was something else beginning to dawn as this sun set that needed exploring. "Sure," Win said, and they made their way to the gazebo.

There had been few comfortable moments for Ginger on the trip up. Fortunately the boat was large and stable, but still, the fact that there was a large, unforgiving body of water beneath her was cause for anxiety. Since keeping danger in sight often softens the unpredictability of it, Ginger spent most of the trip aft, where she could keep a wary eye on the lake. However, now that they'd gotten there and the Montego was trolling in a circle around the island, she was up on the bridge, binoculars firmly on her eyes, surveying the island.

"What do you see?" Pam asked from the pilot's chair.

"There's a row of houses on top and cliffs around the edges," Ginger said, "Not much to see."

"That little island's nothing but rocks and trees. That cove's not much, either."

"Keep going around, and maybe we'll see an opening." Just as she spoke one appeared. An unusually wide walkway between houses presented her with an unfettered looked into the central commons. She gasped and stood. "It's Win. And he's with—everything's true. I can't look at this."

Pam brought her binoculars around and after a moment, she, too, took in a deep breath. "Who is she?"

"The woman he ran off with."

"Ran off?" Pam sighed. "Teri."

"They're talking. I love gazebos. That one I want to burn down."

"People talk."

"He's alone with her."

"People talk alone."

"Is he holding her hand? Can you see if he's holding her hand?"

"They're sitting on opposite sides of a table."

"I used to love his long arms."

Pam sighed. "He's there to find out what's happening to Bray. He'll talk to everyone."

"Doesn't her black hair look good on her?" As the cruiser plowed slowly through the water, easing gently with the chop, Ginger let a hiss of forlorn air escape. Then she brought the binoculars back up. "We'll be history soon. I know it. How could he resist hair like that?"

Pam paid little attention to her as her binoculars swept the island again. No Bray. She brought the binoculars down. "We'll keep circling, then find a spot for the night."

Ginger only nodded. She knew her fears were irrational. Win loved her. She'd seen it in so many ways. But now, with the sun about an hour from the horizon, she couldn't help but think that the sun was setting on her and Win as well.

"I'm so lonely here, Win," Teri said, her hands folded before her, her eyes studying them. "I have to stay because of the job, but I'm so lonely." She leaned toward him. "Life's so much better with you near. So very much."

"I'm glad. But I'm still—"

"I know you care for me a little bit. Or you wouldn't have come."

"Bray was in danger. You couldn't have kept me away."

"Do you find me attractive?"

"You're a beautiful woman."

"Beautiful? I've always thought myself plain. Even dull."

"Not with all that firepower in your house."

Teri smiled, her favorite subject opened. "Guns are exciting, aren't they?"

"Sometimes."

"Want to go shooting? I know a perfect place."

"Sounds like fun."

A standing rule—*No visitors downstairs*. Teri knew it, everyone knew it. But at that moment Teri didn't care. After each chose a powerful target rifle from her wall, Teri took both weapons, placed them in long, leather gun cases and carried them to Bilba's house. With Bray and her father still in the rec room, it was easy to sneak Win into the pantry elevator.

Win took mental notes on everything. The condiments that worked the secret elevator in the pantry, the look of things when they got off, the passage they went down on their way to wherever they were going.

"The bowling alley," Win exclaimed.

With a devilish smile Teri lay the two rifles on the bench seats, unzipped one of them, slammed a round she got from her pocket into the chamber, aimed and fired. The headpin lost its head. The wood erupted and showered the other pins. The bullet must have ricocheted, for two other pins were chipped. "Go ahead. You take a shot."

"But we'll have to patch up all the holes."

"The guards can do that."

"You sure?"

"Absolutely." Teri slammed another round home.

"Like free sin."

"The free-est."

"Well, then." Win extracted his weapon, took the bullet from her, aimed, and hit the metal cage above the pins. The bullet whined and buried itself in a nearby wall.

"My turn," Teri said setting up a trick shot. It worked, the head from the four pin burst as did the seven pin. She admired her work.

Win was in the process of loading when Teri said, "Win, I can't be subtle with you anymore. I just can't."

"You were subtle?" The rifle was at his shoulder, and he was drawing a bead on the surviving pin in the second row.

"Getting you here. Maybe Bray wasn't in as much trouble as I said—"

Win fired. The bullet grazed the pin, and it wobbled slightly. The rifle came down. "He's in danger. I'm probably more convinced of it now than ever."

"You are? But that doesn't matter now. I've wanted you ever since I helped fix your arm."

"Which I truly appreciate."

"You do?" She cooed, eyes liquid and huge.

"Aren't you going to shoot?" Win asked, hoping to distract her from the topic.

"Oh, sure." She aimed quickly and fired. The pin Win had grazed exploded. Wood showered everywhere.

"You were wonderful to help me like that," he said. "There's something I've wanted to talk to you about—"

"I was?" An overwhelmed hand came up to her throat. "Really?" Excited beyond rational thought, Teri wrapped her free arm around Win's neck and kissed him.

Shocked, Win pulled away. "I can't, Teri. I love my fiancée. I truly do."

"Give me a chance, and you'll learn to love me. No one knows we're here. The room's soundproof. Let your feelings for me blossom."

"I can't."

"Who'll know? And I'll never tell." Her arm went around his neck, and she pulled him down to her again.

Win wrenched back. "God would know, Jesus would know."

"But they love you anyway. Isn't that the way it works?"

"That's why I have to show him I love him back." Win pulled her hand down. "I love Ginger very much. She's my life. I couldn't betray her with you. I'm sorry, but I have to go." He turned and walked toward the closed door. When he reached it a shot rang out, and the soundproofing material a few inches from his head exploded. Shocked, he turned, his face contorted incredulously.

Teri stood there, her expression stone cold. "Sorry—accidents do happen."

CHAPTER 13

Win wasn't sure how to react. He'd been shot at. Missed, undoubtedly on purpose, but still—he'd been shot at. Teri shot quickly without aiming. He could have been hit, no matter how good a shot she was.

Things like that just didn't happen at the seminary.

Of course, there were plenty of professors he thought wanted to shoot him. At one point, Win had been quite thankful for a restraining spirit when Professor Winter's wife found that goat in her bathtub.

So. What should he say? After all, Teri looked like she might be getting ready to fire again.

"You won't shoot again."

Maybe it was the sound of his voice, or just timing, but the moment Win spoke, Teri collapsed in tears. "I can't believe I did that," she stormed. "What have I—"

"It's okay—" Win said in quick consolation.

But Teri had no intention of being consoled. Rifle in hand she burst around him, threw open the door, and ran from the room. Win spun to see her disappear around the corner toward the elevator.

Well, now, thought Win, the shock of the moment giving way to a detective's spirit. *Should I go after her? Or take the opportunity to explore?*

His job ultimately was people, and Teri was definitely one of those. If there was anything to find down there the Lord would let him find it later. He moved quickly to the elevator. She'd already taken it.

He pressed the up button and waited. And while he waited, for reasons he would never know, he decided to transform a nagging suspicion into firm belief. Teri—the bullet in the cow's brain—the scent of wildflowers and the hint of sour smoke he'd noticed on her at their first meeting. She was the marksman who'd fired the bullet into his tire—intending Bray's death in the accident—to drown as Win's '54 Chevy careened into the lake then sank into the lake. Of course, he had no proof, but it was time to rely on instincts.

While he was buried in thought, the elevator door slid open. Phil Sanderson stood there. His eyes widened in surprise. "You lost?"

"I went into the pantry for a snack and found myself down here." There was no need to get Teri in any more trouble. Trying to kill Bray and those bowling pins would be trouble enough.

"Well, allow me to help you find your way back up."

Teri didn't stop running until she reached her house. Closing the door behind her, she relocked it, butt her head against it, and then slid down until locked knees prevented her from slipping any further.

What had she become?

She'd contemplated murder twice now. First for greed. This time for anger. Though she told herself she really hadn't wanted to kill Win, that wasn't entirely true. The angry part of her wanted to put the bullet right between his eyes.

She slammed her fist against the door.

Adrenalin pumped—her veins charged with it. She had to work it off or burst. Within minutes she was down at the cavernous boat dock.

Foster, his overalls smeared with grease, approached as she climbed into Boat Eight. "Not that one, Miss Sanderson."

"Why not?"

"Hank's been working on it. It's broken."

She climb out of Boat Eight and leaped into another. "Anything wrong with this one?"

"Nope. But be careful."

"Fat chance," Teri said, her expression granite.

Seconds later, ignoring the "no wake" rule, Teri gunned the inboard and shot from the cavern onto the lake. Nose high, the boat leaped over the growing chop. When hot fires burned inside, Teri had no clear idea where she was going. But where didn't matter, only *that* she was going. The high-pitched cry of the engine, the blur of the world rifling by, the raw, visceral danger in the speed, all of it worked to tap the energy and dampen the fire, bringing everything down to something emotionally manageable.

A sense of invincibility exploded within as she rifled south down a long stretch of lake between several rocky islands.

"Teri," Ginger said, watching the billowing black hair through binoculars.

Pam brought up her own. "Moving pretty fast."

They watched as the boat blazed over the water, the wake savage-white. Suddenly, nose to the clouds, it spun on its tail, then headed back toward the island, spun again, this time completely around and half around again, finally slamming the water hard and taking off toward a distant island.

"What's she up to?" Ginger asked.

"Just seeing what the boat can do?"

"It might fall apart."

Another boat exploded after her from the island. Win? Were they going to end up on some beach? That *From Here to Eternity* scene with Deborah Kerr played in her head a few times as Ginger focused and refocused the binoculars trying desperately to identify the pilot of the pursuit boat. No. What was left of Win's hair was fuller. This guy's was marine-short.

"He's trying to catch her," Pam observed.

A little more relaxed and far less involved, Ginger observed, "He'll have to go some to do that. She doesn't want to be caught."

Teri moved with thunderous determination, her hand firmly on the throttle, her eyes straight ahead, her nerves taut, ready for anything.

But the energy wasn't dissipating. If anything, it grew. Her instincts told her she had to do something daring, even foolhardy, to lessen the pressure.

But what?

A massive boulder protruded from a nearby island. She screamed within a few feet of it. She could have reached out and touched it. Two outcroppings, the opening between them no more than a few inches wider than the boat. Engine roaring, she negotiated the notch with just a minor scrape. Elated, she gunned the boat again.

That's when she saw an inclining shale shelf jutting into the lake. She'd been around this island a thousand times and had never seen it. Maybe it was created by the recent twister, or maybe she'd never been in the right position to see it, but there it was—a natural ramp. Without hesitation, she aimed the craft at it, gunned the engine and hit it full throttle.

The hull hit hard, the boat's nose reaching for the dying sun. A deafening scrape as the boat leaped into the air. When the boat hit the water instead of catapulting forward like a skipping stone, it stopped dead, burdened by massive drag.

A quick glance down told her everything—a shredded hull and the lake bubbling in. Teri was sinking. Adrenalin still pumping, she prepared to dive overboard before the boat plowed into deeper water.

"Teri!" A man's voice from behind. Turning she saw another boat easing up, Michelson at the controls. "You okay?" he called to her.

Michelson powered down and bobbed about ten yards off.

Feet planted firmly in the center of the boat, Teri cried out to him. "I really don't need you following me around."

"I was concerned."

Water lapped at her laces but she stood defiantly. "This is none of your concern."

"You're sinking."

"So?"

"Is that your plan?"

"If it is or isn't, it's still *my* plan." The water lapped at the tops of her tennies.

"I can help."

"Help someone else," she barked.

"You're the only one here who needs it."

The water was up to her ankles and began coming over the top of the boat.

"You going down with her?"

"If I do, I do," she said, planting hands on hips. "I'm out here to enjoy myself. And that's what I'm doing." A large wave swamped the bow and the nose dipped decidedly. The water was up to her calves. She remain unperturbed.

"Can I make a suggestion?" Michelson asked, gunning the engine to maintain position.

"And that would be?" The hull was now submerged, and Teri appeared to be standing in knee-deep water.

"Come on board. After fifteen minutes, if you don't want to talk to me, I'll throw you overboard again."

"Just like a guy. You want all the control."

"True. But you don't have a whole lot of control where you are. Come on aboard. You can do all the talking."

"All of it?"

"Sure. Why not?"

Teri thought for a moment, the water up to her stomach. She nodded.

A few minutes later, her black hair still dry, she sat on cushions aboard Michelson's boat. A stiff breeze chilled her. She shivered.

Michelson pulled a plastic cover from a hatch and wrapped it around her shoulders. "It's getting a little rough."

"I like it rough," she said.

"There's a cove over there," Michelson pointed. "Let's pull in, and we can relax for a second."

"I don't want to relax. I wasn't driving like that to relax."

"No. You were driving like that to die."

"Could be."

"Then let's relax 'til that feeling passes."

She looked at him with suspicion. "Okay. But why the cove?"

"I don't want to go back just yet. You're my excuse."

That intrigued her. "Let's pull in."

A few minutes later Michelson dragged the boat up on a shale beach. And a few seconds after that they sat together on a tangle of tree roots, the tree offering shade.

"What's your first name?" Teri finally asked.

"Randy. Randy Michelson. Some call me Mike."

"What do you want me to call you?"

"Randy—you'll be unique."

"You want that?"

"Sure. You *are* unique."

"Because I'm a member *of the family*?"

"No," he shook his head. "You're just unique. Real cute, a little crazy—enough to be interesting."

"Interesting? And how would you know that?"

"Just by watching—a lot."

"A lot?" Teri repeated, having difficulty hiding her pleasure.

"I'm always around. You saw that."

"I just thought you were working nearby."

"I could work anywhere."

"You could?" she squealed softly.

"How come you took off like that?"

"I get a little unstable sometimes. I have to work it off."

"Did you?"

"Some of it," she said, as she took an internal inventory. "It's gone now."

"What's gone?"

"The energy—"

"I bore you?"

Teri laughed. "No, let's just say you redirected my attention."

Michelson nodded. "That's a good thing."

"Sure."

They were silent for a moment. Off over Vermont lightning sparked between clouds and earth. Thunder rolled. The sun, made a little dirtier by the ash in the air, rolled toward the horizon. Finally Randy asked, "What was it that got the adrenalin pumping?"

She cleared her throat not sure how to announce it. "I shot at someone," she admitted, clearing her throat again. "Yep—I wanted to kill him."

"Kill him," Michelson echoed. "Did you?"

"I was close. It's that adorably unpredictable part of me." Then she added quickly, "But the obsession's over."

"Was shooting him the only way to dampen that?"

"Don't know," Teri said. "Didn't try anything else. So, why don't you want to go back?"

Randy took a deep breath. Then hesitated. "Moral dilemma," he finally admitted.

"On the island? No one on the island has morals. It's part of the application. Sex: Male or Female; Morals: Yes or No. Anyone who circles yes is *deep-sixed*."

"Mine are a recent acquisition."

"Well, we're going to have to change the application—'Do you have morals or ever plan to have them?' How did you acquire these horrible things? Not mail order. We check all mail."

"A church on the mainland. On one of my afternoons off just after Mr. Sanderson died. I met two guys. A Reverend Flowers did most of the talking. Never saw him again. What he told me has haunted me ever since."

"Haunted?" Teri rolled the word over a couple times. "Apropos. So, what's the dilemma?"

"You really want to hear about this?"

"Why wouldn't I?"

"Because I'm just a hired hand."

At the mention of it, Teri took his hand in hers. After a moment studying its firm texture, feeling its strength, she clasped her hand on top of it. "Since I hired this hand, I should always know where it is."

"So," Randy said haltingly, "I'm really going to tell somebody."

"Sure. Why not? I didn't bring my gun."

"But you're a Sanderson. I'm not sure I can tell you about it."

"Nobody talks to me. Ever. And believe me, I talk to no one."

Randy stopped. He stared off into the yellow sky, put his hand out, and let a film of ash from the distant fire collect on it. "Somewhere things are burning up," he said, the words more breath than sound. "I've been asked to do something that's really wrong."

"You work where?"

"Around the grounds. Sometimes at the dock."

"The cavern dock?"

"Sometimes."

He doesn't know what we do on the little island. "Well, my dad is quick to point out that *wrong* is a relative term."

"*He's* wrong."

"Well—he *is* a relative."

Not acknowledging Teri's little joke, Randy plowed ahead. "There is right and wrong."

"You're certain about this?"

"Very."

Teri sighed and nodded. "You're right. It would be hard for me to call shooting at someone this afternoon right."

"Reverend Flowers gave me a New Testament."

"Like half a Bible?"

"I've been reading it."

"The Bible? I could never get through more than a verse or two."

"I *never* read it before. Never." Michelson's energy level rose. "My dad was a Marine. Away a lot. Even cheated on my mom. I never wanted any part of a God who'd let that happen to her—or me."

"But that's changed?"

Randy nodded emphatically.

"What did that Bible of yours say?"

"Among other things, it said I couldn't do what I've been asked to do. I mean I really can't do it."

"Then don't."

"It said some other things, too."

"What?"

"That whether I do it or not, I'm a sinner. I can't believe I actually said that to you."

"You do scare me—you talk like religious people—they're all a little nuts, you know." But she said it with a hint of humor.

"Well, I'm scared, too. Everything's suddenly changing for me. Just talking like this to you is a change. I never thought I'd ever be talking to you like this." He stood. The dying sun made the sky even yellower than before. More lightning over the Vermont mainland, more thunder rolling toward them. "The twister last night—what'll happen tonight?"

"Whatever it is it won't happen to me."

He didn't hear her. Clouds were building above their heads. Unusual clouds, piles of white with wispy tendrils reaching out. "I don't know what to do."

"Maybe you should talk to that Petunia-guy—"

"Flowers."

"I don't know anything about the organized stuff. I pray, but only in my bathroom with all these candles."

"I've been reading John, Luke, Galatians. The words mean something. I can read for hours. In my room. In the caves. When my roommate's gone. In the john—I read John." He laughed at the pun. But it was an uncomfortable, introverted laugh. "It said I needed to be saved. From hell. It said I had to call on Jesus."

"Now you really do sound like a religious fanatic. The career path on the island is limited for religious people. There is none."

"I don't think much about careers," he said.

"You know, we were having a good time here. Then you started talking about these things."

"I know," he said, turning to her, his expression filled with longing. "I was having a good time, too." He turned back to the lake. Then up at the sky. "But I have to talk about these things. When you were out cold last night, I prayed that if Jesus let you live I would commit my life to him. Asked him into my heart—asked him to save me."

"You brought me around."

"So when I got back to my room last night, I snuck away so my roommate wouldn't see me, read a couple more verses and before I knew it I was on my knees—"

"I don't believe that stuff. I really don't."

"—and I asked Jesus Christ to be my Lord and Savior."

Teri heard a choke in Randy's voice. "You're really a nice guy. How could all this change so fast? Why'd you bring me out here, anyway?"

"Now I have to tell someone something."

Teri stood. "This is too much. Maybe shooting you guys *is* the best thing."

"This is confusing to me too. You're such a neat woman. So beautiful. I wanted to bring you out here and sweep you off your feet. And then we started talking. You have to understand."

"My religion consists of my praying to candles in my bathroom."

"So you're praying not so much to a Mighty God as to a Tidy Bowl."

She laughed softly and slipped an arm in his. "Well. Now I have a dilemma. I can't be mad at someone who can say something like that."

"I think I'm a Christian now, Teri," he said, as if warning her.

"Okay—but why don't we wait awhile and see if it takes. Who do you have to talk to?"

"Bilba."

"What do you have to do with her?"

Lightning flashed a few miles away, thunder growled.

"You think the storm will ever get here?" Teri asked idly.

"We'd better get back."

When Randy started to get up Teri gave his arm a hard tug. When he turned, she planted a kiss on his lips.

To his surprise he pulled back slightly. She didn't notice.

"What do you need to tell Bilba?"

Randy looked at her for a long moment. "It's best I just talk to her."

"She kissed him," Pam said, eyes glued to the binoculars. She'd been watching them since Teri's boat began to sink. Ginger's vigil ended after finding out it wasn't Win in pursuit. Now she just leaned over the side of the boat and watched the rocks and boulders not all that far below the surface.

"Kissed? She's two-timing Win?"

Pam's binoculars came down, and she peered at her friend through narrow eyes. "You've got a definite problem."

Ginger groaned. "I do, don't I?" She stared again at the water. "I can see rocks. They don't seem all that far down. How deep do you think it is right here?"

Pam gave her friend a long look. "There's nothing to be afraid of. Even if we sank we'd make it to shore somewhere."

"I don't swim. Even my dad couldn't teach me to be brave around water."

"Your dad? What did he do?" Pam peered through her binoculars and saw Teri and the guy returning to the island. No hurry this time. Over Vermont several white threads of lightning stitched clouds and earth together. Thunder detonated like artillery shells—a distant cannonade.

"When I was a kid," Ginger began, drawing Pam's attention back, "he tried to show me I had nothing to worry about. I'd be swimming, and he'd sneak up behind me and push my head underwater. He'd keep it under for about an hour. Then let me up. He wanted to teach me how long I could actually hold my breath under there so I wouldn't be afraid."

"So he'd nearly drown you to teach you that you didn't have to worry about drowning?"

"Sure."

"No wonder you're afraid. You probably think someone's about to dunk you right now. And what if his watch stopped? Or he miscounted? Daddy did you no favors."

"Think so?"

"And if he did that, he probably did other things."

"Like taking my favorite toy and burning it so I knew it wasn't important?"

"You're kidding." The binoculars came down again.

"I learned they were just toys."

"And that your favorite stuff was eventually going to combust on you. You're probably waiting for someone to ignite Win."

"She already has," Ginger groaned.

Pam studied her friend with sympathetic eyes, then wrapped caring arms around her.

Ginger appreciated the affection—the warmth. "I guess there's really nothing to worry about," she said, without conviction.

"That's why you've waited to buy the wedding dress, isn't it."

Ginger looked up. "I couldn't bear to fall in love with a dress—something that makes me look so beautiful—something that really says I'm getting married to the most wonderful guy in the whole world—and then never wear it. But that's what would happen. I'd get dunked, or my toy would get burned again."

Pam sighed, then shook her head in frustration. "Just telling you not to worry won't help—just like telling that storm out there to stay put won't help."

"Win got caught in that tornado thing. I'm really not in the mood for a storm. Not out here. Let's find a cellar someplace."

"Lightning, but not many clouds. That fire's made things very strange." Pam flipped the radio on and found the news station. No weather forecast yet, but she kept listening.

Then, changing thoughts seamlessly, Ginger said, "There must be some kind of a dock behind those rocks—the ones just to the east of that little island. That's where Teri and the guy came from, and that's where they're returning."

"A hidden dock," Pam nodded.

"If they're making anything illegal, they have to ship it. It'll probably come out of there. Under cover of night. Probably just after the storm hits." Her energy evaporated, but then returned. She was a cop, and it was about time to start acting like one. "Let's put on our best fisherman's pose and check things out. Then we can hole up in one of these coves and wait."

"Or," Pam said, "we can sneak onto the island, and I can show that therapist what twenty years of hefting twenty-pound doll molds has done for my biceps."

Ginger laughed. Then groaned. "A storm. Lightning. The lake. We need to pray." They did.

In the rec room, Win collapsed wearily in the overstuffed leather chair next to Bray. The big-screen television was turned to baseball, and Bray sat watching it. Or that's what Win thought, until he heard Bray's gentle snore.

Win poked him with a stiff finger.

"Huh?" Bray whimpered, eyes fluttering open, the look of the dead all over him.

"You and Phil give up?"

"Winning made me sleepy." Bray yawned. "Did you wake me?"

"I had to."

"Why?"

"You talk to a sleeping guy and see how far you get."

"How long before I'm in jail for murdering you?"

"Sounds like one of those logic problems you're so good at." Win settled into the chair. There were things to talk to Bray about. If Teri was the one who'd shot at him, she might need watching. She had saved Bray's life by snatching him away from the railing, but maybe that was reflex. Maybe she had to work herself up to earning the million dollars. Or maybe she'd had second thoughts, which meant that she could have third and fourth thoughts, each leading her to opposing decisions. "I need to talk to you about something."

"Now? I really am tired. What with the therapy in the morning and dealing with you all day—a man just gets weary."

"Teri shot at me."

"And I'm supposed to blame her?"

"We were shooting up the bowling alley, and I rejected her advances. She found me irresistible, and when I told her I was in love with Ginger, well—"

He seemed to sink deeper into the chair. "That's a pretty small place to miss you. It's downstairs, isn't it?"

"Phil was a little upset when he saw me down there. But, there's something else." Win stopped, took a deep, fortifying breath, and went on, "I think Teri shot our tire out on the way up here—when I hit the fruit stand."

"That was a blowout."

"All the evidence points to the tire being shot out from under us. And the rest of the evidence points to Teri."

"'Because she likes guns? I like guns, and I didn't shoot the tire out."

"Ginger and I found where the person fired from. The rifle blast started a little fire. When Teri came up to help my arm I got a good whiff of her. Wildflowers and smoke."

"This whole part of the world's being bathed in ash from that fire, and you think—"

"Then she fired at me—not to kill me, just to make a point."

"You're nuts. When you fell down out there, you must have hit your head."

Win could only lean back in frustration. Bray was right, in a sense. What Win was basing his belief on was pretty flimsy, but he knew—he just knew. "Listen, Bray—" Listen Bray, what? Finally he just said, "I'm sure of this. Take care when you're around her."

"She saved me from falling off the balcony, Win."

"I know she did—but I'm sure about this."

Bray just looked at him with disdain. "Well, I'm sure about something, too. My family might be a poster family for dysfunction, but they're my *family*. Whatever they've done or will do, they have my best interests at heart."

At that moment Teri strolled into the room, Michelson with her. She acknowledged neither Win nor Bray but walked to the television and flipped on TNN. They were airing a segment on turkey hunting. As Teri settled into the sofa to watch it, Michelson said, "Well, I have to go talk to you-know-who." He kissed her lightly on the lips before leaving.

Teri smiled at Bray then grinned at Win.

Bray leaned over to Win. "Yeah," he said. "I'd call you irresistible." He laughed. Grabbing his cane, he hoisted himself up. But as he stood, he noticed something that had been wedged between the cushion and the chair's armrest. Maybe put there while he slept.

"What's that?" Win asked.

Bray produced it—flat, wrapped in newspaper, about eighteen-by-six inches. Leaning against the pool table to free up a hand, Bray tore the newspaper off allowing the wrapping to fall to the floor, he held a piece of fiberglass, smudged with charring. Painted on it in lettering obviously done by a nonprofessional was *Contusion*—the name of Henry Sanderson's boat.

The instant Bray saw it, his free hand grabbed it. While studying it, his expression slid from shock, to disbelief, to sadness. "It's genuine," he said, handing it back to Win. "From their boat." Without thinking he took the bear charm from his shirt pocket and rubbed it against his lips.

"You sure?"

Bray nodded, squeezing the charm in the palm of his hand. "I painted this myself. I can remember it as if it were yesterday. So it didn't go down—it didn't go down."

CHAPTER 14

Darkness devoured the light, leaving the stars as a sprinkle of crumbs.

Bilba sat in the butterfly house. Michelson had been watching her for an hour, trying to decide what to do and to summon his nerve to actually do it. He considered escape, but that seemed cowardly, not fitting for someone now trusting God. But if he stayed and told her, wouldn't she just send someone to kill him? Wasn't he supposed to flee from danger? And wasn't asking God to protect him while he was a big fish in a very little barrel testing God? He'd read somewhere he shouldn't do that either. Back and forth he went, and as he did he had the distinct feeling that all the indecision was just a tactic to delay the inevitable—just flat-out telling her and letting God take care of the rest. When he decided to do just that he was surprised at how satisfied and powerful he felt.

Approaching her as she sat on the bench, butterflies dancing about her, he said, "Miss Sanderson."

She looked up just as a butterfly took up residence on her nose. As its wings moved hypnotically up and down, the old woman's eyes followed them. The right eye following the right wing and the left the left. A strange picture.

After a long moment the eyes came back to where they ought to be, and she looked up at him. She did not, however, move either head or body. "He's still alive," she said.

"I know."

"What's your plan?" she asked, eyes following the wings again.

"I need to talk to you about that."

"I'm sure your plan is fine."

"I have no plan."

"Trouble being creative?"

"Trouble being a murderer," he said forthrightly.

"Well," said Bilba, like a mother facing a child in need of guidance, "we all have that problem at one time or another, don't we? We just need to take ourselves by the bootstraps—"

"I can't ever be a murderer. I won't to be able to do what you want."

Bilba suddenly brushed the silly butterfly from her nose and stared at the young man before her. "Not do it? But you must do it."

"I can't."

"And why not? You don't want a bonus or something. More money is simply out of the question. It would have to be budgeted, and I can't go through that process. Not for this. So, why can't you?"

"I became a Christian," he admitted, not with the boldness that he would have liked, but at least he'd said it.

"A what? Like a Methodist or something? There were Methodists in my family. I might even be one—since they were in my family. Perhaps we have things in common. I'm sure we can work this out Methodist to Methodist."

"No. I don't know what I am. Probably nothing right now. I'm just a Christian, and I can't set someone up to be killed."

"Why do you think you have a choice? I asked, and it must be done. If Breck asked someone to do something, they dared not refuse. It's because I'm a woman. You're sexist. Just because I'm a woman."

"It has nothing to do with that."

"Then what then? I belong to the AARP. Are you anti–old people?"

"I'm a *Christian*. I've given my heart and everything else to Christ, and I can't go around killing people."

"Sure you can. As I remember, Christ loves you no matter what. What's a little murder between the two of you?"

"I can't do it, and that's that."

Bilba sat looking up at the lad. She wasn't sure how she should feel about this. She wasn't used to being in command and certainly not used to ordering someone's demise. So, being refused like this wasn't the norm. There was however, something inside her that said she should be angry.

So she became angry. "Look what we've done for you. Everything. Given you a job, given you wonderful clothes to wear, a bed to sleep in. And you won't do a simple murder. You ingrate. You miserable ingrate."

"Then I turn in my resignation."

Now that was a wrinkle she hadn't expected. Quit? Leave the island? Knowing that she wanted Bray Sanderson dead? That's what he wanted—to blackmail her. He wanted to blackmail her. That was it.

"I'll never give you a red cent, not one."

"I don't want a red cent. I just want out of here."

"Well," said Bilba, another butterfly landing on her ear. She brushed it away violently. "You don't have to do that. We'll just forget the whole thing. I'm sure I was only joking, anyway. That's it. I was joking. No. Not joking. I was testing you. And you passed. Yes. You passed. I was just making sure you were trustworthy, and you passed."

"Trustworthy?"

"For a new job that's coming up. That's it. The new job. And I had to make sure you were a moral, upstanding citizen. Now get along. Scoot. And I'll have you contacted about the new job. Go. Leave me to my planning. I have much planning to do. Bushels of it."

Bewildered, Randy Michelson left Bilba studying the floor.

"Have you found anything?" Win asked Bray as he entered his friend's room. On and beside the small table near the balcony window were the three cardboard boxes filled with his parents' things. Each one opened but its contents returned.

Bray pointed at them dismally. "Nothing but stuff nobody wanted."

"No more diary pages, notes on napkins, anything that indicated what Breck might do?"

"I'm a detective, too, and there's nothing in there."

"Can I take a look?"

"Be my guest. Sometimes a fresh eye—"

The fresh eye found nothing. "The ash trays are still dirty."

"Both smoked—evidently a lot that last night."

Win nodded but wasn't sure why.

Bray eyed him incredulously. "You don't really believe Breck killed them all?"

Win took a small notebook from his pocket and tapped it. "From the Sanderson Island Memorial Tree Tour." He read:

"Charlotte, Phil's mom, died July 4, 1942; Shelly, Phil's wife, died, Christmas day, Dec. 25, 1965—the holiday deaths. Madge and Sam Sanderson, Breck's brother were killed in a light plane crash Sept. 10, 1951. Then your parents, Henry and Marsha died June 18, 1970." Win looked up. "Plane crash, boat explosion, an ice-fishing accident—how did Charlotte die?"

A preoccupied Bray shrugged. "Heart attack or something."

"She was twenty-three. I guess it happens. Look at Bobby Darin. Maybe she had a birth defect."

Bray could feel the little stone bear pressing into his palm. He looked up. "Whoever's giving me this information wants me to believe they were all murdered. If Breck did it, why go to all this trouble? Not many corpses are sent to prison."

"Maybe it wasn't Breck. Maybe someone still alive was working for Breck."

"One of the family?"

"Every murderer is a member of somebody's family."

Bray squeezed the bear even harder. "I loved my mom. Like you, I wasn't all that fond of my dad, but Mom was good to me."

"Well, let's just hope there's some more information soon." Thunder growled off somewhere. "I'm not sure I like it out here. I get the feeling things are going on behind the scenes that'll jump up and bite me."

Hank stepped into the cavernous dock carrying the fuel system he'd been working on for Boat Eight. As he walked toward the boat, Foster fell in beside him. The floating dock pitched and yawed, mostly from their weight, some from the growing malevolence outside.

"Weather's coming up," Foster said.

"When will the shipment be ready?"

"In about an hour—about ten."

"That's still early. Weather doesn't bother these boats too much. Make it eleven."

"Done," said Foster.

Boat Eight bobbed a little at its mooring, the hatch to the engine compartment open. Being careful to miss the tools scattered around, Hank stepped down inside the boat. Then, after examining his handiwork one more time in the dim light, he set about reinstalling the mechanism. *Ingenious*, he thought, surveying the small, radio-controlled detonator attached to the fuel filter. When signaled, the detonator would set off a fire that would quickly spread to the gas tank and explode. He'd already weakened the gas tank and the hull of the craft so that the explosion would go up into the main compartment, bathing the pilot and any guest in fire.

Would an investigation find what he'd done?

Not for the kind of money he'd offer.

Tomorrow the waverunners would come for the Brightstars, and Tuesday he'd be a million richer in mainland money.

Then Plan B, which he still had to talk to Tommy about, would go into effect, and he'd take complete control.

The dashboard on the Carver Montego was deep and flat. Though a platform for gauges and controls, there was also room for a picnic. Normally on a boat this size, one ate in the stateroom below where there was a cramped but functional galley and comfortable seating. But Ginger wasn't in the mood. It'd been a long emotional day. She'd faced and ridden out some deep fears. She'd also caught herself whining. She hated whining. But there was a time when whining was her only defense and part of this day had transported her to a place where she needed one. As she said a brief grace before sandwiches on paper plates she thought about these things—but said only thank you.

"I'm not hungry now," Ginger finally said, staring at the tuna sandwich. "I've never eaten at nine. Well, that's not true. I started on a second pizza once."

"Did he really burn your favorite toys?"

"A couple times. I had a little white bunny rabbit with long, floppy ears—soft—a soft you could kill for."

"He burned a little white bunny rabbit?"

"Melted bunny eyes—all that was left."

"You came home from school and found—?"

"I'd wake up in the morning."

"He took the bunny out of your arms?"

Ginger nodded. "He thought he was teaching me a good lesson."

"There had to be another way."

"I started hiding things after a while. Sleeping with my least favorite toy—a scratchy old camel. *I* finally burned that one myself."

"When we get back I want his phone number. Any bozo knows you don't do that to a kid."

"He wouldn't now. Toys are expensive."

"And he knows you'd deck him. Did you know your first husband drank when you married him?"

"I didn't think it mattered much. I really didn't. It was only on the weekends—all weekend."

"So the good stuff gets burned up, and you're left to cherish the ashes. Pretty soon you don't think you deserve the good stuff—feel uncomfortable when you've got it. I know whereof I speak. I've gone through my share of therapy."

Ginger looked up. "It's not quite like that."

The cruiser shuddered as an unusually large wave slapped it. Although slightly sheltered by a cove, they fought to maintain position near its mouth and the lake's turbulence. There they could keep an eye peeled for the island shipment they assumed would come sometime soon.

"We all have to survive our childhoods," Ginger inserted.

"I've heard Win say that God puts us in our particular childhoods so that we'll seek Jesus. I'll tell you this, I've never sought the Lord when things were going good. I'm seeking him like mad right now." She peered through the windshield to a flash of lightning over St. Albans. "It's getting closer," Pam said.

"I wonder how much longer we'll have to wait."

Bilba loved the butterfly house most when it stormed. The butterflies became excited in the electric air—truly magical—clouds of Tinkerbells.

But Tinkerbell wasn't the only thing on her mind. She'd brought two things to the butterfly house for the first time—a small pistol, a .38 she thought, and a shovel.

The .38 belonged to Breck. He'd kept it in the dresser beside his bed, and it had been there when she moved in. She couldn't imagine putting it to use until tonight. The shovel was little more than a garden trowel with a long handle, but it would have to do. She would bury the body below one of the greener, fuller shrubs. No one would ever look there, and the weather would never uncover it.

Of course, Randy Michelson was the body. She couldn't let him leave the island. When Bray did die, even if it was from natural causes, he would undoubtedly accuse her, send her up a very long river.

At Teri's house, Teri and Randy were just finishing microwave popcorn and Cokes—dinner.

When the bag was empty, Teri cooed sexily, "Want some more? I'd pop corn for you all day long."

"Well," he said, crumpling the bag on his way to getting her another Coke, "that's something else you and I have to talk about."

Bilba had called about a half hour before. Sounded conciliatory—actually humble and repentant. Returning with the Coke, he was already preparing emotionally to go see her.

"Why can't you tell me what she's asked you to do?"

"Since I'm not doing it and she might never have it done, it wouldn't be right."

Teri could only nod. "You coming back here?"

"After work."

"Good," Teri said, giving him a lingering kiss.

He wasn't all that sure whether he should be enjoying the kiss as much as he was. Having no conviction either way, he didn't back away this time.

The wind blew, steadily punctuated by strong gusts that whipped thick limbs around. Lightning flashed more regularly, thunder detonated more closely. There was still no rain, and there were places between the clouds where Randy could still see the stars. It was very strange weather. It was even stranger to feel the film of ash when he grabbed the knob and pulled the butterfly house door open. Although tall windows could let the light in, it seemed far darker inside. "Miss Sanderson, you here?"

Bilba called to him, "On the other side of the sculpture."

It was difficult for Randy to see. Not only was it dark, but his eyes hadn't thoroughly adjusted yet. But it wasn't that dark. When he stepped around the sculpture, he could easily make out the gun Bilba pointed at him.

His first inclination was to run. But fear prevented it. Being in the Marines, he'd had guns pointed at him before, he'd even been shot at. But it hadn't prepared him for having a pistol leveled at him and knowing that the trigger could be pulled any second.

"What's the matter, Miss Sanderson?"

"I have to kill you. I hope you understand. I can't allow you to leave the island and tell people about what I wanted you to do."

"I wouldn't tell. Really."

"But you'd have to. When Bray dies, well, you'd have to talk."

Randy sighed. "I guess I would," he said. "I'd have to tell the truth."

"So there you have it. I have no choice. Unless you decided to help me kill Bray again."

"I can't do that."

Outside flashed white as lightning tore at the sky just above them. Butterflies darted about, their wings glistening in the sudden brilliance.

Bilba blinked. And Randy leaped at her. Grabbing her gun hand, that cold, icy hand that seemed poised on the edge of death, he tried to wrench the weapon from her. But she fired.

A searing pain pierced Randy's right thigh. Collapsing onto the floor, he let go of the gun and found himself looking up as Bilba stood over him, the .38 leveled at his head.

"Now this won't hurt, I'm told. The bullet will go into your brain, and all feeling will go away. I hate to do it, but I have no choice. You know that. No choice at all."

Another boiling flash of lightning. The hair on his arms stiffened as electricity danced on his skin. Thunder like bombs going off just outside.

The palm tree leaped in a hail of sparks and fire. Bilba saw it out of the corner of her eye while Randy saw it head on. Randy shouted and in his pain tried desperately to move. Bilba wondered if she could possibly finish what she'd started, but there was no time to make the decision. Breck's palm tree fell against the double-thick glass, shattering it and sending a million razor shards in on them.

If butterflies could scream, their cries would have been deafening.

The shards fell harmlessly around Randy, but a couple of jagged ones struck Bilba's face and arms. Blood oozed from her leathery skin as the tree continued on to strike the sculpture, which it hit with a great force. The sculpture was knocked off its foundation. Yielding to the tree, it tipped and then toppled onto a bench, crushing it. Then, as quickly as the chaos had erupted—falling trees, toppling sculptures, butterflies flitting for dear life, glass shards clattering everywhere—now there was a dead silence save the wind blowing butterflies around. Many huddled on the greenery, undoubtedly terrified.

Blood caking her cheek and arm, Bilba realized it was over. The world had collapsed around her, but she was still standing.

And she still had killing Randy to finish.

As Randy came to realize that he'd been spared one death only to face another, she raised her gun. That's when she saw it—in a shallow cement tub in the base of the sculpture—now exposed.

At first it looked like a pile of bleached twigs and branches, but then, in the dim light, they took shape. And when they did her heart came apart in her breast. She knew instantly what she beheld. As if life were being torn from her very center, she screamed—the scream of the dying and the dead.

CHAPTER 15

Bilba's screams rivaled the thunder, then outlasted it. Horrible screams—screams from the center of her heart, screams propelled by every shattered hope and dream, screams twice the size of the woman making them.

Randy lay there. First terrorized by the bullet, then by the falling tree, then the sculpture, and now even more terrified by the skeletal woman whose contorted face seemed to be tearing itself apart right before him, the gun waving back and forth, perfectly capable of firing another deadly round.

Teri arrived first. She all but fell through the door and slammed head first into the toppled sculpture before calling Randy's name.

"Over here," he responded. "Watch out! She's got a gun."

Bilba no longer screamed. She'd turned away, her body bent as if trying to reform itself into the womb, and as it did, she whimpered.

"Oh my God," Teri cried, seeing Randy. "What have you done to him?"

"She shot me," Randy shouted. "That crazy old woman shot me."

Teri unceremoniously grabbed the gun from Bilba's hand and knelt beside Randy's wound. Taking a knife from her pocket, she folded out a blade and cut the leg of Randy's pants exposing two holes in his thigh—entry and exit wounds. She studied them for a moment. Cutting the rest of the pant leg off, she pushed it against the two holes. "It's bleeding but not badly. That God of yours is taking care of you." Keeping pressure on the wounds, she glanced around toward Bilba, and when she did she saw what lay in the uncovered base of the sculpture. "Bones?" she gasped.

"Yes," cried Bilba, tears storming at the mention of them. "Bones."

Phil was there. He'd run from his house next to Bilba's and had climbed in over the palm tree. Now he stood beside his aunt. He made no attempt to comfort her. However, he did manage to say something soothing about the effects of old age. Then his eyes came in contact with the cement grave. "What—?" he began. "Who?"

"Dad, we need a doctor for Randy," Teri pleaded.

"What happened?"

"She shot him."

Phil turned to Bilba, "You shot someone? Why'd you do that?"

"I *had* to," Bilba said with a tortured voice. "I didn't *want* to."

Win and Bray were there now. Torn between comforting the old woman and investigating what had brought on the outburst, Win chose the woman. Bringing a consoling arm around her, he allowed her head to rest on his shoulders. How stiff she was, how bony, how void of warmth. Age had eaten most of her flesh and blood, and the shock had taken the rest. The instant her head rested on his shoulder, she began to cry freely.

Bray leaned over the bones studying them.

"Who is it?" Phil asked again.

"Her baby and Gordon Fritz, the father," Bray said without hesitation. "He didn't kidnap Erika after all."

"Her baby?" Phil and Teri asked simultaneously.

"Yes," came a cry from Bilba, her body erect again, her eyes narrow slits looking off toward heaven. "My baby—my Erika and my beloved Gordon—oh if only his blue eyes had remained."

"Quite a picture," Teri said, void of feeling. "Blue eyeballs rolling around amongst the bones."

"Shut up, Teri," Phil fired at his daughter. "What's this all about?"

"Bilba had a baby by that man—" Bray said.

"Nearly fifty years ago," Bilba wailed.

"Well, it couldn't have been last week, now could it?" Phil chided coldly.

Sylvia arrived, then Hank.

Bray studied Bilba. Such pain. She'd always appeared as incapable of emotion as barbed wire, but now she was crumbling before his eyes, "She's thought all these years that he had kidnapped her baby. If he did, he didn't make it very far."

Sylvia approached the bones and peered down at them.

"Don't touch anything," Bray warned.

"Glad you said something," she snapped. "I live to touch old bones." Then the large woman peered at them again, and her expression softened. "A baby. I've always wanted a baby. Why couldn't I have had this one?"

"Because it was my baby," Bilba snapped. "I can't look any-more—oh, Erika's little skull."

"Win, why don't you take her up to her room," Bray suggested. "Stay with her while we figure out what to do with all this."

Win nodded and gently escorted Bilba from the structure and across the common area, the wind churning up around them, to the main house.

"What happened to him?" Hank asked, tossing a hand toward Michelson.

"She shot me," Michelson said.

"Nonsense," Phil injected, turning toward Bray. "I suppose we'd better dig a hole and give them a proper burial."

"Not until the cops have a look," Bray said stiffly. "This could be murder."

"Murder? It's just a grave that's been uncovered. They were buried."

Had it all not been so tragic Bray would have laughed. "You're kidding, right?"

"I am not kidding. We don't know anything about these bones. The sculpture was delivered here, the bones could have been in them when it was delivered. All we have are the ravings of a seventy-three-year-old woman."

With great difficulty, Bray bent so he could get a better look at the bones. Scanning them for a second time he noticed something protruding from one of the ribs—something metallic. He knew instantly what it was. "It was murder," he proclaimed, working himself back to an upright position.

"How can you be so sure?"

He pointed. "The knife penetrated the rib and broke off. The point's still there."

"A knife point?" Sylvia repeated and bent low, intent on soaking up as much information as she could.

Teri interrupted. "I need help getting Randy to a doctor. He's been shot."

"No one's been shot," Phil insisted.

"I've been shot. Miss Bilba Sanderson shot me."

Phil's fiery eyes turned on his daughter. "Is the bullet still in him?"

"No. It went through."

"Then he hasn't been shot. Get a couple of the guards to help you—"

Bray placed a firm hand on Phil's shoulder. "A man's been shot, and there is possibly a murder. You have to call the police. They have to come."

Phil stared at his brother for a long, tense moment. "I don't want police on the island."

"They'll come, ask a few questions, then go. Your operation on the little island won't even come up."

Phil took a deep breath and ran his hand through black hair. Then he turned to Michelson. "Why'd she shoot you?"

Eyes on Bray, Michelson just shook his head. "I don't think it's right to say."

"The cops'll love that," Phil said.

Hank eyed Michelson's wound. "It was a cleaning accident."

"Actually," Michelson began, "it was an accident. I fought her for the gun and it went off."

"Good," Phil exclaimed. "An accident. The tree fell and caused a—whatever—and the gun went off."

Before Bray could comment, he heard Win's voice. Bray turned to see his friend on one of the balconies. "Bray, I need to talk to you."

The instant Sylvia confirmed in her own mind that it was the point of a knife sticking in that bone, she had drifted away from the others. When she was sufficiently distant, she'd turned and moved quickly to Hank's house. Entering, she closed the door behind her.

It had been a long time since she'd set foot in his house. Since there'd been a recent move, she expected to see things in disarray, still not put away. As it turned out, everything was tidy.

All of Hank's car models, the paintings of cars, planes, and motorcycles, and the chromed Cadillac engine that sat on the corner pedestal, everything was where it should be—all looked neat. She felt terribly unneeded as she walked stealthily to his bedroom.

There was a time in the early years of their living in separate houses that she still did his laundry. On one of those occasions, when she was putting away his underwear, she'd come upon a long, flat velvet box in the back of one of his drawers, a box she'd never seen while they were living together.

She'd opened it that first time as she did now.

Lying there on a satin bed was the knife she remembered. The tip broken off.

Picking it up, she stood staring at it, transported to the horrible moment when it was being plunged into the side of another human being.

"Put it down," came Hank's voice from behind. "Put it down before I use it on you."

Win stood at the top of the stairs when Bray entered. "Up here. Something you need to hear."

"Bilba?"

"She's talking."

Bilba lay in bed, her head propped on three pillows, her hands by her side. She hardly moved, yet the tension electrifying her was so intense, she seemed animated.

When Bray neared the bed, she began sobbing, "I'm so sorry, Bray, so very sorry. What have I become?" Her bloodless hand took Bray's.

So cold, so deathly cold, was that hand.

"How can you ever forgive me? How?"

"For what? You're the one who's been wronged here."

"I tried to kill you," Bilba said, her voice saturated with tragic admission. "Oh, Bray, if I had succeeded. If either of those bumblers had succeeded—" Then she croaked, "We never could hire good people—did I really say that?" Her head wagged violently from side to side. "What have I become? No, I've always been like this. Always. And now I'm seventy-three and will always be

like this. Just put the pillow over my head and snuff me out."
She squeezed Bray's hand.

"You tried to kill me?" Bray echoed as if just understanding.
"You blamed Teri," Bray fired at Win.

"Well, the railing," Win said, "and that trap at the memorial
trees—when that guy fell."

"That was real?"

"And I actually tried to kill that poor unfortunate lad down
there when he refused to kill you."

"He refused?"

"I tried to kill two people. Where would it have stopped? It
would have never stopped. I would have become the Grandma
Moses of blood." More rapid head movement, her legs kicked
the covers and the bed shook anxiously. "It is I who should have
been in that grave down there." A great wail arose from her thin
body. "My baby—my Erika—what have I done to you? What
have I done?"

Tears stormed from her eyes again and thin, bony arms waved
about. Although she'd lived for her butterflies, now she looked
like a praying mantis.

Win eased Bray out of the way and took hold of her hands.
"Now, now," he soothed. "Rest. Take a moment and breathe
deeply. You're just coming to a place many of us come to in life."

"I am?" came the thin voice.

"And you need to rest a moment. The Lord's given you seventy-three years, filled them with events and emotions and has
brought you here."

"My baby—my beautiful baby. She was only a couple of
months old—she used to hold my fingers and looked up at me
with such love."

"You were planning to leave the island, weren't you?" Win
said, leading her along.

"I couldn't bring up a baby here. The baby needed room. I
needed room. She had my brown eyes and Gordon's roundness.
She was so beautiful. How could anyone kill a baby? What am
I going to do now?" Bilba asked, tearful eyes looking up at Win
as if he, and only he, held the answer.

"You're going to come to the one who truly loves you—who's calling you to call on him for healing. You're going to do what I did when I was lost, when my mother died."

Bray suddenly erupted. Stepping back as if to get a better look at this travesty, he began a volcanic sputtering. "She tried to kill me," he said. "I could be lying in that grave out there, my skull crushed against the rocks. And you're doing this? If you want to do something, thank that kid down there."

Win turned to him with forced calm. Witnessing always brought Win anxious moments, and to be interrupted caused even greater anxiety, but this was Bray and Win needed calm. "She's in terrible turmoil right now, Bray. She did try to kill you, but someday you're going to have to come to grips with the fact that she didn't. That in each case, someone saved you."

"Only once. Teri. No other time."

"Each time it was the same person—the same God."

Bray stopped. But after a moment his head shook, first in slow, broad movements, then in quick, angry twists. "I take care of myself," he said with controlled rage. But then he lost it and shook his cane at Win, the tripod making his point three different ways. "I don't need any crutches. Least of all a bunch of myths." Standing on his one good leg, he lost balance and brought the cane down just in time to save himself from falling.

"A member of my own family wanted to kill me," he muttered as he turned. "For a lousy million bucks. And if it weren't for some no-name guard . . ."

"I never wanted the money," Bilba called after Bray's back. "I was just being loyal."

Bray turned, hate stamped on his face. "I could have understood the money."

He hobbled out.

"Oh, Bray," Bilba groaned. "I always admired Bray. I truly did. He stood up to Breck. I never could. I knew Gordon could never have kidnapped Erika; he loved us both too much. I knew Breck had entrapped me. I knew it all. Breck planned this business when he was in college—no one could ever leave the island once he knew about it. But it wouldn't matter because all your needs would be taken care of here. I knew I couldn't leave. And yet I dreamed. Surely he didn't mean me, his own sister. In my heart

I knew that if I got pregnant, he'd let me go. But when all my reasons for leaving went away, Gordon and little Erika, I knew he'd had something to do with it. I brought my baby into the world to be killed. What kind of a mother does that?"

"We all do horrible things, sinful things. Everyone of us. We're all laden with them. Our hearts are crusted hard with them, dead with them."

"Mine feels so dead now. I've prayed for death so many times. Not because I wanted to die, but because I wanted to catch up to my heart. It's been dead for so long. That's why I love the butterflies. They're so alive. And yet all the butterflies in the world couldn't bring my heart back to life. And I was so close to its grave. All those years I was so close to where my heart lay. And now that it's uncovered, it feels as dead as it always has."

"I know how to bring your heart to life."

"Not after all I've done."

"What think ye of Jesus?" Win asked, bringing to life what the Puritans would ask.

Suddenly her body lifted slightly, and as she took a breath tears rolled down bony cheeks. "I think of my father. When I was a little girl, he spoke to me of Jesus. Why does that name make me *feel* so? I *feel* something."

"You've sinned, Bilba. You've sinned not against Bray, or your baby, or Gordon, or anyone else. You've sinned against God."

"Is there a God? Oh, there is, isn't there? I sense him. I sense him here. Can I be right? Can I? My father said there was a God, but he died so young. Is he with God? With Jesus? I said the name. I said *his* name. I feel. Oh, I *feel*." Both hands reached around and grabbed Win's. They held on as if gripping life itself.

"God's calling you, Bilba. He wants you to call upon Jesus—now. I want you to ask Jesus to recreate that dead heart of yours. I want you to tell Jesus what you like about him right now, Bilba. Right now."

Hands clutching hands, the strength of a thousand emotions, a thousand transgressions, a millennium of hurts—Bilba's lips began to form the words produced by a new, wondrous heart. "Oh, Jesus—Jesus—You are my only hope, you are the only one, Jesus. If there is love in this rag of a body, may it all be yours. Oh, I can hear my father's voice, so sweet was his voice. He left me. Don't ever leave me. Please forgive all I've done to you. What I've done to my baby—to that boy down there—and that young man on the cliff." Then tearful eyes came up to Win's. "He's here. He's in this room. There is peace in this room— for the first time. Oh, that everyone might know the peace of this old woman."

"That's my prayer, too," Win said, tears welling in his own eyes. "That's my prayer."

Sylvia watched her husband move slowly toward her, his eyes never leaving the knife on the satin cradle. "My father's knife," Hank said. He could have lied. Could have said he'd found it somewhere on the property many years ago. Didn't know who owned it. Maybe he could have implicated Phil or a guard who'd long since gone. But he wasn't in the mood to lie. Soon they'd all be working for him anyway. There was no need.

"Your father's?" Sylvia repeated. "He killed Bilba's baby?"

Hank was next to her now. He carefully reached over her arm and took possession of the knife. Snapping the cover down he placed it back in the underwear drawer and slid the drawer closed.

"Answer me," Sylvia insisted. "Did he kill that baby? You couldn't have. You weren't even born yet."

"He must have."

"You don't know?"

"He told me he'd broken the knife playing stretch with it. He and I used to play stretch when I was a kid. Said he'd hit a rock when he threw it."

"So you didn't know he was a murderer?"

"I knew," Hank said.

"You knew?" Sylvia's voice became a gasp.

"He was Breck's enforcer."

"Enforcer? Breck had an enforcer?"

"We're playing for keeps here. If this game ends, you don't just turn in the houses and the hotels. There are no *get out of jail free* cards. It costs to leave."

"But who?"

"Madge and Sam—he rigged their plane. Charlotte—"

"Phil's mother? Oh, no—murdered."

"Breck thought she was going to go to the police."

"Shelly?"

"No. She was an accident."

Breathing heavily, her heart pounding audibly within her massive bosom, her brows suddenly dipped sharply, and her voice became grave. "Are you the enforcer now?"

"Why do you ask?"

"You said we always had to have one. Your father's dead. Are you following in Daddy's footsteps?"

"Only once. I rigged Bray's parents' boat to blow."

Her voice rose. "You were only fourteen—you've said that to me more than once. Fourteen and you were a murderer?"

"Quiet!" Hank growled, actually looking around to see if someone was listening. "We're all in this up to our eyeballs. Survival's the name of this game, and I intend to survive—and when I do, you survive with me."

"I can't be married to a murderer," she whispered, more to herself than to him. "I have to go."

"Where?"

"Anywhere. Off the island."

"Why?"

"You have to ask me that?"

"Sure. What's changed?"

"What's changed?" Sylvia cried, her heart suddenly pounding, her breathing frighteningly erratic, her large breasts heaving like sheets in a wind. "You've murdered people. And you feel nothing for that baby and her father in that grave, so you might as well have murdered them, too."

"And nothing's changed. Nothing. The only thing is that now you know. Nothing's changed."

"Everything's changed *because* I know. I'm not a murderer. If I stay I become one, just by staying." Her head pulsed back and forth. "Breck's still alive, and he's still running things from that pine box."

"Titanium alloy box."

"I wish it were pine. The thought of him being eaten by worms warms my heart somehow."

"Wood or metal—makes no difference. You're not leaving."

"I have to."

As if he could take no more, Hank grabbed her fleshy arm and spun her away from the chest. Pulling out the drawer he retrieved the velvet box. A heartbeat later the knife was in his hand, its broken point a lash from her eye. "You have to stay," he hissed.

Sylvia pushed back, slammed against the chest then the wall, trying to escape the knife. But she was too big and moved without grace or quickness. Hank was on her again. "Get used to it," he said. Then he removed the blade and straightened. A smile whisked all the menace away. "Look at it this way. This is only a place. Anywhere you go is just a place. Get used to *this* place. You're staying." Opening the drawer again he tossed the knife inside. "Anyway, I'm going to run things in a few days. Then you'll have even more money to waste than you do now."

"Run things? Do Phil and Bilba know this?"

"Only you know. If they find out, I'll know how they did. Then we'll resume our little discussion. I'm a mechanic, I'll take you apart."

Hank laughed, a grating sound, glacier cold.

Sylvia staggered to her own house a few minutes later.

Stepping inside the safety of it, she closed the door behind her then fell against it. "Well, my dear husband, *you* won't have to start this conversation up again. No, this conversation's not over."

Bray moved ponderously from the house. Every step was a chore made without thought, for his thoughts were far away. For the past few days he'd been excited about having a family again, excited about connecting and being connected to, excited about roots and planting them deeply in native ground.

Now those roots had been yanked up.

Win was right. Breck had reached from the grave for revenge. Thankfully he'd been thwarted. But not by a family rising up, demanding that he fail, but by a freak of nature, a falling tree and an exposed horror.

He had a bad case of lead-heart. So heavy that it weighed down his steps.

But lead or not, his feet took him back to the battered butterfly house. Phil was the only one who remained. As Bray approached, Phil straightened as if he'd been waiting for him.

"Everyone else gone?" Bray asked.

"I got Michelson to Teri's couch—he'll be okay in a couple of days. Hank and Sylvia went off somewhere. Everyone's trying their best to deal with this."

"Won't be easy."

"You really think Breck did it, don't you?"

"It happened fifty years ago. There are some things you can get from bones. Maybe age, sex, do some DNA tests, figure out whether they had arthritis, maybe their race. Nothing that'll help here. That broken blade would help if we found the match. But in all probability, the murderer looks just like they do right now."

"I didn't have anything to do with this, you know."

"You were five or so when it happened. Don't think so."

"I don't think Breck did it," Phil said firmly.

"We'll probably never know. Families have done horrible things to one another all through history—this is just another one."

"I'd hoped we were different."

Bray looked at his brother for a protracted moment. "We're not. You gonna call the cops or should I?"

Phil eyed the remains. "You'd better. You know them."

Bray nodded. "You said Michelson's with Teri."

"I don't like a man staying at her house, but she insisted, and he's too hurt to do anything."

"Diane and I never did have kids, but I imagine if I had a daughter, I would have put a bullet through a suitor or two to slow 'em down."

A moment later Teri opened her door to Bray's knock.

Seeing him, she threw the door open and fell into her uncle's arm. "Oh, it's so horrible, Uncle Bray. What's our family become?"

"What it's always been, I guess. I need to talk to your buddy."

"Randy?"

"For just a sec."

"I'm in here," came Randy's voice.

Teri stepped out of the way, and Bray hobbled in.

Randy lay on the sofa, his head and back along with his wounded leg propped up on several pillows. He looked surprisingly chipper. "Yes, Mr. Sanderson."

Bray stood for a moment looking down on the young man, then he said, "Thank you."

"You know?" Michelson managed a smile. "I couldn't do it."

"Do what?" Teri asked.

"Nothing," Bray said. "But I won't forget."

"It's okay," Randy affirmed.

"Well, I've got the police to call. What about a doctor for you?"

"I was about to go get one," Teri said, eyes on Randy. "He's so brave, so principled."

"Don't let your principles get in the way of good sense," Bray found himself saying. "When the police ask, stick to the accident story. Bilba's pretty broken up about what she did, and if you can forgive her, putting her in jail won't do either one of you any good. The accident story will do that."

"I forgive her," Randy said, a certain nobility in his tone.

"I haven't yet. But I'm also not sure I want her dying in prison. I'll see you later."

Raif was surprised to hear from Bray. "I haven't been out to that island ever—now I'm thinking about opening a branch office there."

Bray grunted. "I've been a cop for a long time, Raif, and I've learned some things. One is that funny cops die young."

Down in the hidden dock, the night lights glowing a secret red, Foster pulled the boat that would be used for that night's shipment from the secure loading area. Now, with the shipment locked in the waterproof hatch, he turned the boat over to this night's jockey.

"It's just about eleven," Foster said. "You can leave anytime."

The jockey nodded and climbed in. Making sure the few gauges were reading as they should, he eased the boat to the lake entrance, made a last check, and punched it.

Ginger saw the triangular craft first—a fleeting, black shape that emerged from the hidden dock and was silhouetted just for an instant against the boulders. She caught another glimpse of it when the sky ignited and lightning leaped from cloud to cloud. Suddenly the boat was glistening in stark relief, its edges reflecting the fire in the sky.

"It's coming," Ginger said.

Pam was curled up on a comfortable padded bench in the stern, but the moment she heard Ginger's announcement, she was up. Less than a second later she stood on the bridge with Ginger, her binoculars up.

"Coming fast," Pam observed. Taking the controls from Ginger, who'd been keeping the boat positioned at the mouth of the cove, Pam eased the nose of the sleek craft around, preparing to follow. Then she waited for the boat to pass.

Keeping to the middle of the channel and flying at full throttle, the black boat clipped the tips of the chop, and within a minute of Ginger having spotted it, passed the cove. The instant it did, Pam eased forward on the throttle and moved out onto the lake. With a total of eight-hundred-thirty horses chomping at the bit below deck, Pam pushed the throttle forward. The pursuit was on.

CHAPTER 16

The Montego's running lights off, the instruments lit in red, Pam and Ginger stayed on the west side of the channel between the islands, keeping the smaller boat constantly in view. Since the moon appeared and disappeared at the whim of the clouds, keeping the black boat in sight on this black night was no easy trick. There were times when only a fortunate flash of lightning kept them on track. Even though the Montego glistened white and seemed to reflect every conceivable light source from dock lights to stars, their presence remained a secret.

Ginger sat anxiously in the copilot's chair. Although the large craft clipped the surface of the water like it owned it, although it was heavy and powerful enough to obliterate any wave that dared rise against it, although it kept a surprisingly even keel, it was still just a boat. And it was still rocketing along at a speed Ginger preferred only to guess.

Ginger was scared.

But she refused to give way to it. At no time did she even hint to Pam that she wanted to slow down.

"He's moving pretty fast," Pam called to Ginger over the growl of their own engines.

"He's got to know we're back here."

"He hasn't blinked if he does."

"How much more speed do we have?"

"We're not full-throttle yet." Then Pam added, "But I hate going this fast not being able to see anything."

"And we're doing this for men," Ginger said.

"You wanna quit?"

"No way."

The number of islands thinned as they broke onto a long, uninterrupted sprawl of lake. But, although there were no islands, there was an irregular shoreline on either side, Vermont to the east, the Grand Isles to the west. The Vermont side was defined by a ragged line of lights—houses, motels, small hamlets—bright, dim, clustered, solitary, colored, neon. The Grand Isles was not defined. Now and then a house, or a string of houses, showed itself with angular yellow, or a dock reached out into the water with a light planted on the end of it. But no definition. The shoreline came and went in secret gloom. Positioned in the channel a little right of center, Pam felt reasonably safe.

Ginger, sensing an overwhelming need to go to the restroom, spun the chair around, and got to her feet. Now peering into the night over the aft section, she instantly saw they were being followed.

"Pam," she called out apprehensively. "A visitor."

Pam turned, and they both saw it. Employing the meekest running lights, a low, sleek, javelin-shaped craft thundered after them—closing fast.

Hank waited until things had died down around his father's grizzly handiwork before he slipped out the back of his house on his way to Tommy's house. He'd planned on speaking with him tonight anyway, but now that Sylvia was upset, things needed to happen more quickly.

Hank had long ago fashioned keys to all the houses, even the main house. He figured it was just part of his job. Now he used the duplicate to open Tommy's door.

"Tom," he called, just above a whisper.

But there was no reply.

Knowing that Tommy could easily be lost in his computer, Hank headed there.

No Tommy. But there were screen savers. At least four of his larger computers were on, the oversized screens alive with tropical splendor. Hank was about to leave when one of the screens started to talk. The screen saver must have been a digitized video, and it began to play. An olive-skinned fellow in cutoffs and a Jamaican shirt spoke with a Caribbean accent, "Tommy, m'lad, the surf's up, the women are tantalizing, and there's all the electricity Venezuela can give us for those computers of yours. Come on down. Have a great time on me. See you soon, it's Carlos, baby." Then more surf and sun and sand and the video ended with a bikini-clad beauty walking out to this fellow on the beach carrying a tray with a mai tai on it. Hank paid no attention to the drink—or its little umbrella. Another video started talking, with another right after it. He stayed for both bikinis.

Then he left. Not thinking, he headed for the front door. Just as he opened it, he heard Teri's voice from next door.

"I'm going to go get the doctor," Teri was saying.

"I won't be going anywhere," he heard Michelson's muffled response. "I'll be reading the book Flowers gave me."

"If the leg starts hurting again, call Bray—the phone's right there."

Then he heard her footsteps heading for the dock.

When she was safely out of sight, he eased through the door and returned to his place. He never wondered where Tommy was.

Tommy was at the other island, at the storage cave making a few last-minute adjustments, a little rewiring to make the show a little more dramatic for his uncle. He was also gathering a few more "clues" for Bray. His only regret was that he'd never be there when Bray found those clues. He could only imagine the looks of puzzlement or even horror on Bray's face. The great detective detecting something so very personal.

There's no escape, Bray, at least for you.

"He's on our tail," Ginger reported anxiously. She sat facing the stern. She watched the sleek speedboat follow them as they, in turn, camped on the glistening wake of the smaller craft. "I better get my—" she stopped. "I didn't bring my gun. I didn't bring it. I've been on leave too long. I left it at home."

"It may not be the way it looks," Pam said. "He might just be going where we're going. We could change course and see what he does."

"And lose the other guy?" Ginger exclaimed.

Several minutes passed and nothing changed. Ginger finally said, "We can't go on like this. If that guy behind is working with the guy ahead, we're not going to find out anything. We've got to go underground somehow."

"This ain't no submarine."

Ginger sighed. "I can't wait any longer." She stood. "I'm going to the head. Keep doing what you're doing, and I'll be right back."

With the cruiser rocketing along at such a high speed, every step was a balancing act, but, by hanging on to the handrail and planting each step as if it might be her last, Ginger made it to the lower deck.

The cabin was luxurious—appointed in leather and mahogany. But even in dock Ginger would never have enjoyed it. She certainly couldn't now—in pursuit and being pursued. In fact, being in the cabin was actually *more* frightening. At least outside, even in the pervasive darkness, she could see danger coming, inside she was at the mercy of a God she didn't completely trust. But true panic didn't come until she closed the door to the head. While sitting in there all she could do was pray—a desperate prayer to a God she was sure would eventually sneak up behind her and shove her head underwater—and never let her up. To her surprise, though, her prayer ended positively. When the final amen sounded, it was as if the Lord told her, *Never mind the fear, here's an idea.*

On her way back Ginger grabbed some props from the galley.

Pam heard an unexpected clanking behind her. Afraid to lose track of the boat ahead, she didn't turn. "What are you doing?"

Ginger was beside her now, a tequila bottle in one hand, a bottle of white wine in the other. "Which one of us wants to be the hard drunk?" she asked, holding out the tequila.

Knowing instantly what Ginger had in mind, Pam took the clips from her auburn hair, gave it a shake so that it waved full in the wind, and grabbed the wine. "I'm not sure how great we'll look in this fishing gear."

"Not very, I hope."

Pam laughed and slammed the throttle forward.

Its engines screaming below deck, the cruiser leaped forward.

Seemingly unaware that he was being gained upon, the pilot of the smaller craft kept eyes forward, his wake steady.

The boat in back sped up to keep close.

"How crazy do we want to get?" Pam laughed, clearly beginning to enjoy herself.

"Not too. I've got limited courage, and we don't want dates with these guys."

The Montego was about fifty yards back and closing, the speedboat about the same.

Getting into the swing, Ginger lifted the corked bottle to her lips and took a long swig then roared with laughter and waved. To her surprise, the pilot of the speedboat waved back.

"Contact," she said.

"I thought no dates."

Now only about thirty yards back, it was Pam's turn. After her generous drink from the corked bottle, she nearly fell off her chair. "Did he wave at that?"

"No. But he's closing on us. If he asks for a phone number, we'll give him Breed's." Ginger again took a fake drink and did a little jig on the bridge. Just standing up unassisted was a feat, dancing around was a major achievement.

They were only twenty yards back when the pilot of the smaller boat finally turned. After a long, evaluative look, he turned back, his mind back on business.

Ahead lightning flashed. The blast of white illuminated everything for an instant—boats, shoreline, everything. The image remained.

"We're too close to shore," Ginger warned.

Pam eased to port. "He wasn't surprised," Pam said.

"What?"

"The guy we're following, we didn't surprise him. He knew we were back here."

Ginger nodded. "Think he called for the speedboat?"

"Could be."

Back in character, Ginger laughed uncontrollably, took a long pull on the tequila bottle, waved it, then whooped a few times. As she played her part, they closed to within a few feet of the smaller boat. Keeping to the Vermont side, Pam called down, "Wanna race?"

He shook his head unperturbed and waved them on.

"Let's have some fun," Ginger shouted.

Having heard her, the guy shook his head again. This time he appeared anxious and waved them to pass more emphatically.

Pam pulled even. Now the thirty-four-foot cruiser and the dull black Sea-Doo plowed through the waves nose to nose. Pam laughed heartily and faked another long drink. "Want some?" she called, pushing the bottle down toward him. "We got plenty. My boyfriend's boat. He's a lush."

More shaking of his head. He was clearly nervous now, and who could blame him? One erratic move by these two drunken women, and both he and the little boat would be split in two. He applied more muscle to the throttle. The little craft pulled ahead slightly and to starboard, increasing the distance between them.

Ginger looked back. The speedboat, its javelin nose slicing through the darkness, was about thirty feet behind. She could see the guy at the controls—a dark fellow with darker glasses. *How can he see,* she thought. *And they always look like robots. The Stepford Crooks.*

Teri waited anxiously as the doctor examined Randy's wound. He studied both the entry and exit, then, after applying an antiseptic salve, he bandaged the wounds. "How did it happen?" he asked.

"Cleaning accident," Teri said.

He grunted. "I'll have to make a report. You're sure it was an accident?"

"Positive," Teri assured him, the lie easy.

The doctor straightened. "Well, son, how do you feel?"

Randy took hold of Teri's hand. "Really good. Better'n about a hour ago."

The doctor eyed Teri, "You gonna ferry me back?"

Teri nodded. Then she turned to Randy. "I won't be long."

Randy also sat a little straighter. "Send one of the guys to help me back to my room."

"No," Teri protested. "Stay here."

"I'll get a pair of crutches from somewhere—"

The doctor rubbed his chin. "Teri won't molest you, and it would be better if you stayed off that leg for a couple days. It's received quite a trauma, and it needs to heal. Stay on the couch, at least for tonight."

"See," Teri told Randy, "It's official." She kissed him lightly on the lips—kissed him as naturally as a wife might kiss a husband before he leaves for work.

Randy liked the warmth of those lips, and this time kissed her lightly back. When she was gone, he took out his Bible again and began reading.

Hank telephoned Tommy every fifteen minutes, and each time Tommy didn't answer Hank became more frustrated. So, by the time his own phone rang with a message from Foster, Hank was beginning to boil.

"We got a problem, boss. The shipment's being molested. A couple of drunk women."

Hank exploded. "We've never lost a shipment, and I'll be hanged if the first is going to be on my watch. A couple of drunken broads can easily pile up on some rocks someplace. Take 'em out."

"Hey!" Ginger called down to the pilot of the little boat. They'd closed on him again, and she leaned precariously over Pam. "You tryin' to run away from us? We're just havin' fun. Want to have some fun, too?"

The pilot kept his eyes forward, his right hand on the throttle. The little craft skimmed along, its wake a spray of phosphorus white.

If it were possible, the night was growing darker. Perhaps the cloud cover was thickening, growing more compact.

Ginger turned her attention to the speedboat and, for the pilot's benefit, pretended to take another long drink. She could now hear the thunder of his engines over the whine of their own. He had closed another ten feet and was now frighteningly close. She could see flames painted on his hull.

"It's a Scarab," Ginger cried. "How much power?"

Pam glanced back. "About as much as we do, but a lot less weight."

"So he can outrun us?"

"He can blow us away any time he's ready."

He was ready.

With the roar of an angry lion, the Scarab leaped to their Vermont side, the shadowy figure in the dark glasses smiling up, his teeth shark white. He waved.

Wine in hand, Pam grinned and waved back dumbly. "How can you see in those things?" she called, as if to an old friend.

Responding like one, the guy laughed. Unlike an old friend, he eased the power boat to starboard, closing the gap between them to only a few inches.

"He's going to ram us," Ginger cried.

Pam pulled the wheel to the right. The cruiser responded, moving closer to the smaller craft. The smaller craft bolted out of the way, but now threatened by an approaching shoreline, its pilot abruptly pulled back on the throttle and dropped back.

Now nothing lay between the cruiser and the shore.

Keeping an eye on the smaller craft, Ginger called to Pam, her voice sharp, "He's going to the center. The other side of the Scarab."

Pam nodded but didn't answer. No time. Things were unfolding too fast. "He's driving us into the rocks."

Ginger gasped. The Scarab's pilot waved again, then eased his boat up to them. To avoid a collision, Pam pulled right again. "I think they've already seen us," Pam said, and flipped on the running lights. Light flooded the area just ahead of the boat. The rest of the world, that world rushing at them, remained black.

Heart thundering, Ginger all but leaped to the starboard side of the short back deck. This section of the Grand Isles was noted for a severely irregular shoreline—coves, jetties, fallen trees, submerged rocks. There were buoys warning boats all over the place. In the broad daylight moving any closer at this speed would be foolhardy, to do so at night might be deadly. Ginger tried as best she could to see any obstacles, but the lights didn't reach out far enough. They'd only see death when it was too late to avoid it. Ginger couldn't help thinking that dying might be happier with the lights off.

"Whatever you do," Ginger called up, "don't move right again."

"Like I'll have a choice."

Knowing she was of no help down there, Ginger grabbed the handrail and pulled herself up to the bridge. Beside Pam again, she eyed the Scarab, now running parallel to them. "Maybe we should drop back—"

The words were barely out of her mouth when the speedboat closed the gap again. And before Pam could react, it rammed them. The jolt knocked Ginger against Pam's chair.

Pam pulled to the right again, but this time when she did she pulled back sharply on the throttle. The cruiser slowed. The speedboat shot ahead, but only for a heartbeat. It, too, slowed and being lighter and more maneuverable, spun on its aft axis and came back at them. Pam jammed the throttle and the cruiser leaped forward. Then she spun the wheel left to get as far from the rocks as possible, but the Scarab cut them off and instantly began applying pressure again. After pushing them even further starboard than before, the pilot, his dark glasses gone, laughed up at them, and cried, "You're goin' down, ladies. You're goin' down."

"He might be right," Pam groaned.

He certainly appeared to be. The instant he pulled alongside, he closed in on them, forcing them even further toward shore. Pam pulled right to avoid a collision, but there was no avoiding him. Again and again he forced them right. "I don't know what to do," Pam cried out anxiously.

Indecision, however, was not an option. With each intimidation Pam faced a choice. Move right and risk unseen rocks, fall back and try to elude him, or stay on course and risk collision and flames. She never stayed on course, that seemed far too risky. She did try falling back a couple times more, but each attempt ended the same. He never failed to outmaneuver them. In the end there seemed no solution but to keep moving right and hope for a miracle. And, if they were to escape, the miracle had to come soon.

Doing the only thing she could, Ginger suppressed her fear and knelt near the waterline on the starboard side trying to peer beyond what the running lights revealed.

"I can't see a thing—black's black."

The Scarab slammed into them again, then again. The jolt pushed the cruiser over.

"The shore can't be that much further away—it just can't."

Another jolt, this one moved the cruiser over by force alone.

Lightning.

Fingers of it cracked above.

Pam gasped. Ginger screamed.

Burned into their brains was the blazing outline of a natural jetty just ahead. Seeing it now only in the back of the eye, it reached out into the lake, irregular boulders like teeth, ready to rip them apart. They held their breaths as if it mattered, as if it might lift them over it.

Nothing.

They'd survived. The Scarab must have shoved them over just enough for they slipped through a separation.

A sudden scream of tearing metal, a deafening breech. The boulder beside them tore into the Scarab's hull. Bathed in the death of its own light, the Scarab leaped into the air, its hull ripped, shattered, then it slammed down on the rocks, bursting into flame, its fuel spewing on the rocks and over the water. The flames spreading and reaching into the night sky turning black to brilliant fists of reds and yellows.

As fast as the Montego was going, the flames diminished quickly—but grew again with an explosion that tore at the blackness with crimson fingers then died away just as quickly. Finally it became little more than a campfire in the distance. Then the night swallowed it completely.

Raif told Bray he and the St. Albans medical examiner would be at the island in the morning. Satisfied, Bray stopped by to see Win.

Win, propped up on several pillows, looked up from a Far Side book he'd found. "Quite a night," he said.

Hobbling into the room, Bray asked, "What happened with Bilba?"

"She accepted Jesus as her personal Lord and Savior," Win told him. He enjoyed this. It was another opportunity to bring Bray face-to-face with the concept.

Bray wasn't impressed. "So God's going to forgive her for trying to kill me."

"What should he forgive you for, Bray?"

Bray just stared at him. Then he smiled. "I don't need him," he said, dangling his little bear on the end of the chain. "I got this."

Win smiled and shook his head. "I hope you never need it."

"Raif and the medical examiner are coming in the morning."

"So, you're safe," Win pointed out. "All you have to do now is make your decision about the business."

"My luck I'll say no and find out they're selling life insurance. You gonna be leaving?"

"No reason to stay."

"Stick around for a couple days—we'll do some boating."

"No fishing?"

"No fishing."

"Good—terrible things happen when I fish."

A few minutes later, the lights out, Win prayed. He had a number of things for which to thank God, not the least of which was Bilba's salvation. He also missed Ginger terribly and asked the Lord to be reunited with her soon. Maybe one more day for Bray's sake, then he'd leave. After the amen, he slept.

Teri poured a couple of glasses of cream sherry. "Relaxes me," she said, handing Randy one of them.

"I don't drink," he said, handing it back.

"Good," she replied, downing the first glass in a single jolt then, planting herself in the overstuffed chair opposite him, began sipping the second. "You comfortable?"

He lay on the sofa, his injured leg elevated on pillows, his head planted deeply in a couple more. "Fine. Really. Hurts a little, but I'm an ex-Marine, right?"

She nodded, said nothing, and looked off somewhere. Finally she said with a flatness of tone—a resolution to the truth of it, "Uncle Breck was a murderer." She sipped the sherry without tasting it. That would have taken too much brain, and she had no brain left.

"The guy—and a baby."

"Even if he didn't do it, he *had* it done and had the bodies put in there."

After a long moment, she went on. "I'm as bad. Every bit as bad." A tear crept from her eye, a tear that seemed to have no origin. She brushed it from her cheek. "You know why I like guns?"

"The power? The feeling of being somebody? Seeing things explode?"

She smiled feeling safe, connected. "You like the power?"

"I like to see things explode."

"How about tops of bowling pins?" she said, then shook her head to erase all that. "I do *feel* like *somebody* with a gun in my hand, and I have power. But there's something else. I like guns for what they are. They're completely independent. They're what they are—no more, no less, no apologies. They're not connected to anyone or anything. They shoot bullets—one bullet or a hundred bullets. And that's neither good nor bad. They just do it. They're the same hanging on the wall or on a battlefield. No difference."

"And you're like that?"

"I thought I was. I hoped I was. I grew up on an island wanting to *be* an island. It's the best way. At least I thought it was. In the past few days I've flirted with the idea of connecting up with someone. I'm glad I didn't."

"How about with me?"

Her eye came up. "It's best I don't."

"Why best?"

"Just is."

"Why?"

"Do you get the feeling I don't want to talk about this?"

"It's me. I saved your life."

"How often are you going to cash *that* in?"

"Until it doesn't work anymore."

"Well, it doesn't," she affirmed.

"You think you're like him?"

"Who?"

"That uncle of yours—Breck."

"Like him?" Her head cocked questioningly, but she knew what he meant.

"If he could kill someone—even a baby—you could kill some-one."

She looked deeply into Randy's eyes. What color were they? She couldn't tell in these shadows, and she couldn't remember. Was there a God? Had Randy found him—or her? And if he had, was that God now letting him see inside her? "It's like we all killed that baby," she said. "All of us."

"How so?"

"I feel like I'm responsible."

"You're how old?"

"Age doesn't matter. Breck killed them to preserve the busi-ness. That's the only reason he did anything. And all of us have benefited from the business all these years. We've been fed off it. We've been fed because they died—because that baby died. In a way we approved."

"It's a little far-fetched, don't you think?"

"It doesn't matter how far-fetched it is, it's true. I am like him. Very much like him. And under that statue rests what I'm capa-ble of doing."

"You're not capable of that."

"No," she said, her eyes off somewhere again. "I am—I am." She downed the rest of the sherry and went to the kitchen for more. She came back with two more glasses, handed him one, and when he refused again, she downed it as she had the last one. Then she threw back the second one. "I'm just like him. Exactly." Another tear slipped from her eye, and she brushed it away. "I'm tired. You sure you're comfortable?"

"He was a horrible man—and you're a wonderful, sweet woman."

"The only difference between my uncle Breck and me is a fruit stand."

Pam and Ginger were still shaken from the explosion and what it meant. "A guy died back there," Ginger said after the exhila-ration of survival dissolved.

Pam could only look at her. No words.

They continued south. Not only had the Scarab nearly pushed them into the rocks, but it had slowed them down allowing the Sea-Doo to disappear into the darkness. Although they never expected to find the little boat again, they weren't willing to give up.

They couldn't give up. They'd nearly died out there. Had the Lord not been on watch, they would have. So they kept their speed up and headed toward Burlington. They probably would have barreled right by had they had the gas. But about a mile before the New York Ferry dock, the fuel indicator hit empty. "It's nearly 1:30," Ginger said, adrenalin giving way to yawns. "There can't be a marina open."

"Lights," Pam said, pointing toward the Vermont shore.

A cluster of white eyes peeked out on the lake, blinking and flickering with distance.

Flipping off their own, they decided to slow down and approach cautiously. One set of lights was obviously a truck's, the others belonged to a small black boat bobbing at a rotting dock. When they were within a hundred yards, they eased the throttle to trolling speed, then both studied the activities through binoculars.

"I can see the truck pretty well," Pam whispered. "Got most of the license number."

"They're transferring boxes from the boat to the truck. It's almost two in the morning."

"All lit up?"

"So it looks normal."

They watched for another few minutes until it ended. "The guy's firing up the boat again."

Pam grabbed a pen from the dash and scribbled down the truck license on a chart lying there. Then they eased toward the Vermont shoreline as the boat they'd been watching sped by.

"We'll get that number to Breed in the morning," Ginger said, her voice filled with a vengeful triumph, "and see what he has to say."

"Are you okay, Aunt Sylvia?" Tom's voice, always low and deliberate, had just a hint of alarm in it. When returning from the storage island, he'd seen her bulky form standing stiffly on the edge of the cliff looking down to the lake-battered rocks below. Since his aunt lived on the edge of a breakdown, seeing her like this triggered concern. Not particularly for her, but for the business. Having the cops out two times in as many nights was two times too often.

Sylvia's eyes widened. "Tommy, that you down there? I'm fine. Just watching the waves." He was about to crank the motor up and pull around to the dock when she said just loud enough for him to hear, "Shouldn't the waves all be the same?"

"They are."

"Each is a little different."

"Just a little."

"Where you been?"

"Getting some air."

"Why'd you come back?"

Tommy laughed and shook his head. "I'll see you later, Aunt Sylvia."

"You hear about the bones?"

Tommy shook his head, his interest renewed. "Bones?"

"In the butterfly house."

"What bones?"

"Nothing."

"You can't just leave it at that." Tommy stood in the boat, staring up at her.

"I gotta leave it at something," she said, turning and walking away from the cliff.

After calling her name a couple more times, Tommy stood there for several seconds just shaking his head. Finally he fired up the engine and headed for the dock.

A few minutes later he stood over those bones. After studying them for several moments, he rubbed his chin thoughtfully. "I wondered what he'd done with them."

Phil Sanderson stood on his roof patio and studied the lake. The various shades of black. The occasional house. The Grand Isle side looked forever desolate.

He saw a crimson ember glow then fade on Hank's roof. Hank was smoking a cigar.

"You over there?"

"Nope. I'm a ghost. A cigar-smokin' ghost. Can ya see m' lungs fill up?"

"So, I bet *you* think Breck killed those people, too."

"You think he didn't?"

"Tough management is always saddled with legacies like these."

Hank laughed, the cigar gripped tightly in his teeth. "Yer kidding, right?"

"Why would I be kidding?"

"You don't think that those bones are the result of Breck's management technique?"

"Breck was a hard man. But a baby? How could he do that to a baby?"

"Breck did it or ordered it done—the only thing Breck didn't do was knock that big headstone off the grave. And, if you look at where the tree was planted, maybe he did."

"He wasn't that kind of man."

"Sure he was. You know what we do for a living. Not only was he that kind o' man but we are too."

"We don't kill babies."

"Babies are just people. They just can't shoot back—unless you consider projectile vomiting."

"How can you equate what we do with—?"

"You know we might be overheard here—"

"Okay, but how can you?"

"Right's right. Wrong's wrong."

"There are degrees. We're businessmen. We do business. We provide a product that people pay for. That's it. Breck knew that. Toward the end his head got a little warped, but he knew that."

"You're just wondering who else he might have done."

"What's that mean?"

"You're not stupid. If he did a baby in and some innocent clodhopper, he could have done folks a little closer to home."

"I never thought that. Never once."

Hank huffed. "That's all you're thinking about."

"Never once. That can't be true."

"Want to go down the list?"

"I do not."

"I wouldn't either if I had a mother and a wife on the list."

"How dare you even suggest—"

Another laugh. This time the head went back, the cigar still clenched tightly in his teeth. "Ever wonder why both of them were on holidays?"

"You're sick."

Hank turned stone serious. "No. We're in a tough business. If the garden's got weeds—"

"We can't run a business like that—"

"Phil, you act like there are moral absolutes on this side of the fence. We're capable of anything over here."

Phil's brow knit. "What do you mean, over here?"

"On this side of the fence—the bad side."

"What bad side?"

"There's two sides to the fence. There's Bray's side. He's a cop. There's his buddy's side. He's a preacher or somethin'." He made a broad sweep with his hand, the cigar clutched in his fingers painted a flat red arc. "There's most people out there—raising their kids, going to church, workin' from nine to five—all of 'em are on the side of the fence marked *goodness*. Then there's our side of the fence—"

"It's not clear like that," Phil said. "There's no line. It's like a scale that starts at perfect and slips to perverted or something. You choose where you want to be on that line. Then you don't go below that line—never go below it."

Hank laughed again, then took a long draw on his cigar, the crimson glow igniting his meaty features. Phil figured that if the devil had a face, it would look like Hank's did just then—red, deep shadows, snake eyes. "So Breck's line is somewhere below yours."

"I'd never stoop to—" and he stopped, his point made.

Hank shook his head. "When there's no other choice, you'll draw the line as low as you have to."

"I will not," Phil said with deep conviction and a hint of anger.

"Well, maybe we'll see, won't we?"

Phil looked at Hank for a long, penetrating moment, "I'm going to check on Bilba, then go to bed."

"I just hope it's not me that pushes you over the edge," Hank said gravely. Then he laughed. "Please don't let it be me."

After Phil left the roof, Hank leaned back in the lounge chair and drew heavily on his cigar. As the generous smoke trailed from his lips, he saw a light go on next door. Flushed with a sudden excitement, Hank leaped to his feet. Tommy was home, and the time had come to talk.

Tommy sat at one of the computer workstations as Hank stepped in.

"We're supposed to knock," Tommy admonished.

"Knocking's for strangers."

"No. Knocking's for me."

"Then I'll knock on the way out. I got a thought for you that'll make you and me rich."

Tommy spun his chair around and faced Hank. "At least you used the right words."

"You're aware of the bones."

"Your dad was clever."

"You knew it was him?"

"You forget, I have access to all the books. I've learned a lot over the years just reading who got how much money for doing what."

"Then you're aware the family is falling apart."

"Which I predicted when Uncle Breck died."

Hank looked impressed. "You're amazing. Truly amazing. You're quite the brain."

"And I use it," Tommy said.

"That you do." Hank looked around appreciatively at all the equipment. One of the tropical screen savers was still saving a screen. Hank hoped the bikini would pop up soon. "You have to use it to know all this. These computers. I think I'm smart 'cause I can fix a car. But you can sit here and go just about anywhere."

"I *can* go anywhere."

"Really?"

"I was talking to a guy in Bangkok yesterday. He's sending me pictures. This morning I was in Hawaii. A week ago Alaska. I'm working on some virtual reality stuff—tie in sensation things so that when I'm talking to Alaska, I can see Alaskan landscapes and feel the cold—even hear background noises like whale calls, glaciers breaking off, little baby seals being clubbed."

"Inspirational. What about your tropical thing here?" He pointed to the screen saver.

"Aguilar—neat place—in the Caribbean. A friend I met in college—his father runs the place."

Carlos came on again, and they both listened until the bikini came on. When she did, Tommy turned away. "I could sit on the beach all day and work."

"Work? Sure, right. Computers are great. At least you wouldn't have to deal with this crazy family anymore."

"The future is computers. Especially in what we do."

"Graphics."

"You understand!" Tommy exclaimed, taken aback by Hank's knowledge. "I didn't realize."

"I understand. And it's time you and I began to protect ourselves."

"From what?"

"From our dissolving family. Bilba's gone bonkers, your dad's on a power trip, Teri's bringing strangers on the island, and Sylvia's in some kind of twilight zone."

Tommy nodded slowly, wondering what Hank had in mind.

"We're the only ones keeping this place afloat."

"That's true," Tommy said. "What do we do?"

Hank pulled up a rolling chair and sat. "You're the keeper of the electronic vault."

Tommy's eyes narrowed. "And?"

"We need to move our share to Switzerland—a numbered account."

"Our share?"

"All of it."

"Embezzle it?" Tommy said, shocked. He'd been trusted nearly since birth with the finances. Uncle Breck had drilled into him from that moment to his death Tommy's sacred trust—and that if he ever did embezzle anything there were forces in the world that would hunt him down like a dog and destroy him—forces that knew everything or *could* know everything *whenever they darn well pleased.* The very thought of it fired off a chill from the center of his brain to his heart. "Embezzle?"

"Keep the business going. On our terms."

"Our terms?"

"The terms that will keep it going. You doing the business end, me doing operations. You keeping track of the money, me keeping it coming in. The others can't do either."

Tommy's whole expression lit.

"That's not embezzling, that's just reorganization and budgeting."

"And since we don't mind living on the island and being rich, we don't have to worry about restrictions. We can remove 'em."

Now Tommy's expression brightened. "When?"

"As quick as you can. Leave the others a little something."

"A million or two."

"A couple hundred thou would be plenty."

"More than enough."

"Well, why don't you work on it. And remember. I'm in operations, so I know all the people your uncle did—the ones who know things."

"Hank, I'd never even think of going it alone. I'm incapable of it."

Hank smiled then patted him firmly on the shoulder. "This is a new beginning for this little effort your uncle started. He would have wanted it this way. He always wanted to get rid of the deadwood but he never could. Except, of course, when the deadwood left him." Spinning Tommy around and pointing him at the computer, he began massaging his neck and shoulders. "And the way they've treated you over the years, it's time you got a little revenge."

Tommy nodded and punched in a few keys. The screen came alive. "I start tonight."

Hank laughed good-naturedly and patted Tommy paternally on the shoulder. "See you later, partner."

Aglow with success, Hank returned to his house, popped open a beer and, while staring at the architect's drawing of the most advanced auto repair facility in the world, he drank it in two gulps.

About ten minutes later, the glow turned black. A messenger brought Hank word that there'd been a fatal accident on the lake.

Back at his computer, Tommy went to work. Since the business accounts were varied and in several hundred institutions throughout the world, gathering them together was not easy. And while he thought about how he might do it in the fastest, most efficient manner, something happened. He made a leap from one reality to another.

Breck had drilled into him—day after day, even hour after hour—that he was to keep their finances spread out in as many places as possible—distinct and unrelated places. So that if one place was found, the others would still be safe. The thought of betraying that plan was unthinkable. And if he did betray it, death would immediately ensue.

But now Breck was dead, and with just a few strokes on a keyboard he'd vanquished that reality—and if that reality went down in flames, so might another. He began to dream of a time when he might be completely on his own—he and his computers, he and a new reality—a reality where no one could get at him, where no one would ever find him.

That's when the screen saver began to talk. Since he'd heard that voice a thousand times it took a moment for it to break through. But when it did, it completely took over. And when Carlos suggested he come to Aguilar, every element of his concentration was focused.

Could he? Was it possible? What about the forces? Those creatures of the darkness who would know everything and hunt him down? What about them?

No. He could never pull it off.

Or could he?

Sometime later, a breeze billowing the curtains, thunder rolling somewhere off in the distance, Win woke.

He wasn't sure why. Maybe a noise, maybe a chill. But he woke.

Then he heard a voice, soft, a haunting thread. He turned toward it. "Bilba?" he asked in a voice coming from somewhere else.

An ancient face hovered ghost-like over his—Bilba, her face white, more skull than flesh, eyes black holes. She spoke. "Breck would have never done it himself," she whispered. "Never."

"He wouldn't?"

"I told them we had to stop. I told them."

"You did? Who?"

She didn't reply. She turned and floated to the bedroom door, opened it and disappeared beyond. Was she sleepwalking? Dreaming? Was she even there? Had he been dreaming?

To find out, Win rose and ran to the door and peered out into the hallway. The hallway echoed with emptiness.

From the top of the stairs, Phil Sanderson saw him.

After Bilba had told him that they needed to stop the operation because God was watching her, he figured she was going to have to be committed. Declared unbalanced. Obtain her power of attorney and have himself declared her guardian. But when she told him she might have to tell the police—depending on how her conscience dealt with it all—he wasn't sure what he should do.

He'd left her. Actually made it all the way to the bottom of the stairs before he knew what his only course of action could be. Sneaking back upstairs he saw her float into Bray's friend's room. Waiting for a minute or two, he saw her emerge again. After she'd gone into her own room, Win had appeared. Finding the hall empty, he'd returned to his room.

When the hallway was empty again, Phil moved stealthily to Bilba's room and waited outside her door for a few minutes until he heard her snoring.

Slipping inside her room, he closed the door behind him.

He stood by her bed for several minutes wondering if this was his only option. It was.

Slowly slipping the pillow from beneath her head, he gripped it firmly with both hands and pressed it against her face.

There was a brief struggle, but nothing of consequence.

Before he thought possible, it was over.

Bilba lay still—an eternal trip had begun.

CHAPTER 17

In the morning, after getting a couple of hours sleep in the Montego's cabin, the women woke to Larin Breed banging on the door. Breed, Commander of Burlington's Detective Division, was openly disappointed with what he saw as *minor damage*. "Look at it," he demanded. "Only a few scratches. I used to measure a good police effort by how much damage was done. This was not a good police effort."

"But we got that license number for you," Ginger protested, her eyes burning, her hair like a haystack.

"Not much of a number. Believe me."

"No priors?"

"Oh, it's illegal, all right. Stolen from an abandoned car, but they could be just avoiding the fees. The cargo itself could be very legal. I've also done some checking on Bray's family. No priors. Nothing. They pay their taxes, they have all the necessary business licenses. They say they do consulting."

"They must have been shipping secret reports," Ginger quipped sarcastically.

"The guy in the Scarab was killed. We're still picking up those pieces. How'd you get through those rocks anyway?"

"Angels," Pam told him.

Filling the tanks with gas was a traumatic moment to say the least—"Two hundred gallons!" Ginger gasped, handing the guy her Visa and calculating how long it would take her to pay it off. But that was a different problem. Taking on the one at hand, they fired up the engines and headed back.

"Looks like we'll have to intercept the next one." Ginger groaned, contemplating another chase.

"I miss Bray," Pam said, dismally. "I'd be reading the Bible to him right now if we were home. Do you think reading it to him will ever matter?"

"The Word doesn't return void," Ginger quoted. "Incognito sometimes, but never void." Ginger noticed a familiar shoreline. "Stop off at my house. Chad's next door—I want to make sure he's okay." The sense of panic immediately returned as she watched the rocks begin tearing by. They appeared so close— just inches from splintering the Montego's bottom. At least that would make Breed happy, Ginger cringed.

Bray rose at first light having slept fitfully after the disturbing discoveries the night before. Brighter after his shower, he headed down to what was left of the butterfly house and the exposed grave at its center. Nodding to the guard Phil had put in place, he made sure nothing had been disturbed, then hobbled toward the visitor dock to wait for Raif.

He didn't have to wait long. A few minutes after greeting the guard on the dock, he heard the whine of an outboard coming from the St. Albans side of the island. A few minutes later, Raif, a St. Albans detective, a meaty Norwegian with sharp eyes and placid face, stepped onto the dock. After a quick look around, he turned and helped the guy with him. "This is Dr. Hamblin, the medical examiner," he stated. "Someone from the State Attorney's office will probably be here soon. They were interested."

Dr. Hamblin was a young guy with a broad, eager smile and several black trash bags. "I've been looking forward to this since I got the call," he said, eyes searching the ground for what he'd been promised.

"In the commons," Bray pointed with his cane.

"Fifty years old—talk to me, bones," Hamblin chanted, as he and Raif marched toward the open grave.

Shaking his head at the doctor's lack of respect, Bray took a few steps along with them but stopped when he heard Win calling him from his balcony. "Can I see you for a minute?"

"The authorities are here. Can it wait?"

"Don't think so."

Bray sighed dramatically and limped toward the main house. After negotiating the stairs, he joined Win in the hallway.

"What now?"

"After what you found out yesterday, Bilba's probably not one of your favorite people. Right?"

"This isn't a lecture on forgiveness."

"No. But don't forget the concept."

"Well, get this concept. I don't forgive people who try to kill me."

Standing in front of Bilba's door, Win told him, "It's a little more serious than that."

Without knocking, he opened the door.

"She's asleep," Bray said softly.

Both inside, Win closed the door. "Even more serious than *that*."

"Dead?" Bray said, his eyes coming to rest on the ancient face.

"Think so."

Bray made it to the bed and placed a gentle hand on her neck. "A stone."

"Last night was just too much for her," Win said, empathetically. "But at least we know where she's going."

Bray glowered. "Six feet under. At least the coroner will save a trip." A deep sigh. "This is getting embarrassing."

"It must have happened after 2:00 A.M. I saw her about then."

"At two? Why?"

"I woke up, and she was in my room. Telling me something."

"At two?"

"She wanted me to know that Breck never did anything for himself—that someone else must have actually done that deed down there and that she'd told 'them' they had to stop."

"A hit person? It happened fifty years ago. If he's still alive he's probably in a walker. Of course with this," Bray jiggled his cane in the air, "I couldn't catch him anyway. And stop what?"

"What they're doing." Win ventured. "The business."

"Why?"

"Because if it is illegal—"

"Ah—the Jesus factor."

"Right," Win said. "The Jesus factor."

"So you think it *is* illegal, and she, because she caught religion, couldn't abide by it anymore?" Bray rubbed his chin. If there had been any beauty in this morning, it had faded fast. "If that God of yours is a God of peace, why the turmoil when he drops by?"

"That a rhetorical question?"

"You've never *heard* such a rhetorical question." Bray walked over to the balcony window, pulled the curtains, and opened it. The curtains billowed with an early morning breeze—the smell of wood smoke. "I can't believe they haven't put that fire out yet. The feds must be managing the effort personally." The Grand Isles sparkled emerald green and the lake a rich blue, while the sky remained washed in yellow. He saw some new activity near the dock. "They're rebuilding the fruit stand."

"The insurance company must have settled."

Bray turned. "She wanted to kill me out of loyalty. I couldn't sleep thinking about it last night. She even made a point of telling me. I said I understood. Of course, I figured she was talking about kicking you off the island, or something." He shook his head. "She lived seventy-three years for that murderer," Bray finally said. "How can you be fooled for seventy-three years?"

Win didn't reply. Bray, too, was serving a liar and murderer, and Win wondered the same thing about Bray—how blind can someone be and for how long? Of course, it was the Lord who unblinds the eyes and unstops the ears, and until then Bray would never see. Praise the Lord he'd acted in the last hours with Bilba.

"And to find out you're such an idiot just before dying. It would have been better never to know."

"Not this time," Win said.

"I'd better tell the coroner."

"And the others?"

"Sure. But I bet they don't care."

"Guess we'll find out." Win looked down at the eternally sleeping form. "I'll stay up here."

Bray nodded, looked down at Bilba, shook his head with a mix of disgust and sadness, then left.

Alone with her, Win bent down to pray. He'd always wondered what value praying for a dead brother or sister was. God had already taken him or her, and yet there seemed to be something comforting in asking the Lord's blessing on them. Eyes up again, he saw something shiver on the old woman's eyelash—a thread, or a hint of lint, something like that. Curious, he bent close and studied the eyelashes. It was a thread. From the pillow? It certainly was the same color. She could have been sleeping on her side, picked up the thread, turned over on her back and expired.

But if that were true, wouldn't the bedding be in disarray? It wasn't. It was as if the bed had been made around her.

Confirming he wasn't being watched, he slipped the top of the two pillows out from under her head and examined it. Nothing out of the ordinary. He slipped it back beneath her head and took out the bottom pillow. After examining one side he examined the other. In the middle of it was a slight discoloration, like dried saliva. There was also a smudge of something dark. He peered into Bilba's closed eyes, then, when he didn't see what he wanted, he gingerly pressed his thumb to the lid and opened the eye. He hated touching the dead, but he did and when the eye was open, he saw the faint residue of eyeliner—the black smudge. Being the lower one it was unlikely, though not impossible, that she'd smudged it while she slept.

He studied the arrangement of the saliva and smudge.

An impression of her face.

Win sighed, his heart turning to lead.

She'd been murdered—maybe.

Christian courage sure can take you home, he thought with a certain sadness.

Before he could put the pillow back, the coroner, his eyes still bright and eager stepped into the room. "Fluffing the pillow for her? She doesn't need it any softer. Who are you?"

Win introduced himself. "And you?"

"I suppose I could get hard-nosed and have you call me sir, or Mr. Coroner, but, hey, I'm just folks. Dr. Ty Hamblin, boy medical examiner and physician extraordinaire. Treat me with respect, I'll be president one day."

"I should have waited for you—"

"Goes without saying."

"But I started looking around. I found this on the bottom pillow."

After seeing what Win saw, the coroner looked up at the assistant preacher. "And you think this means something—eyeliner on a woman's pillow—and drool. You sure know how to set a case on end."

"So it doesn't mean anything?"

"It could be a murder weapon." Hamblin studied Bilba's lifeless features at close range. "No discoloration. Doesn't look like a struggle. Even old people struggle. If she has been smothered, there are some indicators. But, again, if it happened in ninety seconds or so, usually there's not much. Maybe an autopsy'll tell something." He took a quick glance around the room. Seeing the bathroom door standing ajar, he said, "The medicine cabinet might tell us more, though." Taking a couple quick steps to it, he opened the mirrored cabinet and began fumbling around prescription bottles. After a moment he began producing one bottle after another, "Atenolol, Lanoxin, Adalat, Zestril, and Lasix—she had congestive heart failure." He read the physician's name on the label. "This won't be hard to check."

"So you won't do an autopsy?"

"Oh, we'll do one—on this island even when they fall off cliffs, we do autopsies. This is a spooky place."

"So, when would you know for sure?"

Hamblin shrugged. "Gotta send her to Burlington. Depends on the body stack there. If we're lucky, this afternoon."

"What did you find in the grave?"

"Old, old bones. Tip of a knife buried in a rib. Probably murder, but I think it's safe to say whoever did it got away with it. Even if we had a pretty good idea who did it I doubt if there'd be enough evidence anywhere for a warrant or, after fifty years, anybody to serve it on. You think this might have something to do with that?"

Bray appeared at the door. "The word's getting out."

Dr. Hamblin handed Bray the pillow. "Handle with care. It might be the murder weapon."

"I just have a suspicious mind," Win said.

"You and Elvis," Hamblin quipped.

Bray's brows dipped. "You're kidding, right?"

"I found some stuff on the pillow."

"Eyeliner and drool," Hamblin told Bray, a large portion of "who does he think he's impressing" in his voice. "But she was taking all these for congestive heart failure." He presented a handful of prescription bottles.

Bray eyed the bottles for a moment, then turned accusing eyes on Win. "And you think someone smothered her?" Bray asked, incredulous.

"It was on the bottom of two pillows."

"When were they last washed?" Bray asked, then his hands went into the air, and he backed away from the question. "It doesn't matter. You don't know how she used the pillows. Anyway, this isn't mine. I can't do this. I can't." He turned on his good leg and moved quickly from the room. Win followed. When they were in the hallway he muttered, "It could be that kid she shot— maybe a guard—could be just about anybody." Then he stopped. "She was an old woman with heart problems—that's it."

Win didn't reply. Maybe he had been around criminals too long. It seemed all too easy to take the flimsiest evidence and build a murder out of it. Then, he was disappointed when he wasn't able to make it stick. That's what disturbed him the most. He was becoming ghoulish.

Raif passed them in the hallway heading toward the room they'd just left. He called to them, "I don't want anybody leaving the island."

Bray nodded without turning around. "I'll tell 'em," he said. Then he dropped his head and shook it with deep confusion. "The family's falling apart."

Win placed a firm hand on his friend's shoulder. "Maybe we should get off the island for a while. Let the family find its own way for a while."

"You didn't hear Raif?"

"He couldn't mean us."

"Try him. Anyway, I'm part of this family. Whatever it's going through—"

"It's going through things you know nothing about, Bray."

"I know these people. I'm part of them."

"Uncle Bray?" Teri voice called up to them from the base of the staircase. "Is it true?"

"About Bilba? Yes. Died in her sleep."

Teri stayed at the foot of the stairs as Bray managed them one at a time. She asked, "Was she—murdered?"

Bray gnawed his lower lip for an instant. "She probably died of heart failure. Why would you ask that?"

"With the bones and that knife point—I guess I'm just thinking that way."

"Well, stop it."

"There'll be an autopsy," Win told her.

"So *you* think she was murdered?" Teri's voice sounded more frightened than shocked.

"It's more likely heart failure," Win told her.

"It's not more likely, it *was* heart failure," Bray affirmed, an angry look toward Win.

"She was taking pills for a heart condition."

"She was?" Teri sounded surprised. "I didn't know that." She thought of a moment. "When will they know for sure?"

"They know already," Bray said, his tone dogmatic.

But Teri turned eyes on Win, "But something tells *you*—" Teri pressed.

"Nothing tells him," said Bray. "He's nuts."

"Can I see her?" Teri asked, resigned to knowing no more.

"Sure," Bray said, another grim look at Win. "Come on, we'll both go."

After renegotiating the stairs and hallway, they stepped into Bilba's room. Raif stood on the balcony overlooking the lake, smoking a cigarette while Hamblin was on the phone.

Both turned when they entered. "What's going on?" Raif asked.

"Teri wanted to pay her last respects," Bray offered.

Hamblin pressed the phone to his chest and addressed Teri, "Did you know Miss Sanderson was suffering from congestive heart failure?"

"No," Teri said, her eyes dropping, "but I didn't care. I should have."

Hamblin sucked the back of his teeth and went back to his phone call.

Raif called from the balcony, "Don't touch anything."

"Like I'd want to," Bray said.

Still weighed down, Teri stepped cautiously to the edge of the bed and surveyed the body. From all Win had gathered so far he would have expected a little more coolness. But Teri seemed genuinely touched and finally laid a warm hand on Bilba's cheek. "I'm not sure I said a civil sentence to her while she was alive. Even as kids Tommy and I saw her like a chicken might a chicken hawk. Why do I feel so—? Like someone important to me died?"

"It's family," Bray said. "She was family."

"Maybe it's just the opposite. Maybe I'm mourning because she wasn't family—and I'm not, either." Her eyes came up to Bray's. "None of us are."

"Sure we are," Bray protested. "Some more than others." Then he took Teri's hand. "At least *we're* family."

"Are we, Uncle Bray?"

"I thought we settled that."

"I don't know. I feel so disconnected. I wonder if she felt that same way—alienated. I sure never worked on being close to her."

"Well, I sure got close to that railing," Bray said.

Teri only looked at him, a strange look as if she wanted to blame someone for something but didn't know whom or what. "I need to change Randy's dressing," she finally said, "I'll see you later."

Hamblin replaced the phone on the nightstand.

"What did her doctor say?" Raif asked, the cigarette down to a nub.

"We need to cut her open. But the heart's likely."

Raif flicked the butt over the railing and stepped back inside. "I'll get the bag boys up here to pick her up."

Bray walked Teri from the room, then stood at the doorway until she disappeared down the stairs.

Win joined him. "Lonely girl," he said.

"She's working at it," Bray said. "I guess we all are."

Fifteen minutes before, about the time Teri was walking up the steps to join Bray and pay her last respects to Bilba, Hank was banging on the front door of Phil's house. Still in a green velour robe, Phil opened the door. Having seen Hank through the side window, he merely allowed the door to swing open and returned to the living room. "What do you want, Hank?" he asked, reaching his recliner and planting himself there.

"So you did it," Hank said triumphantly, "you proved me right."

"And how did I do that?"

"Bilba's dead."

Phil's eyes widened. "How?"

"That's good. The reaction. Use it on the police."

"And that means?"

Hank clucked a laugh. "When the reasons are there, you'll drop the line."

"You think I—"

"What else would I think?"

"Bilba was my aunt. My family—"

"And she gave you a reason. What was it? Was she getting too unstable shooting that kid? Afraid she'd snap after last night?"

"No one was more stable than Bilba."

"That's still true." Hank laughed. "But for you she was jumping off the deep end. She shot a guard for no apparent reason. Went nuts because of some old bones. Why did she shoot the guy, anyway? I was so tangled up with the bones I forgot to care." He took a knowing breath. "I bet you found out. And that was your reason."

"I killed no one. Will kill no one. I'm a businessman."

"You smothered her."

"You're sick."

"She was a wiry old broad. She put up a struggle? If she did there'll be clues."

Phil's eyes remained steady, but Hank thought he saw a slight tic at the corner of his mouth.

"Well, clues or not, you did good. After all, how long would she have lived anyway? And if you had a reason, what's a few days on earth versus whatever your reason was." Hank then grinned. "I love to be right. Just love it." He slapped Phil on the knee, laughed out loud, and left his wife's cousin with flint in his eyes.

Win and Bray let the phone system find Hank. "Win and I want a boat for a few hours. We'd like to tool around a little this morning. We need a break."

"What about your massage?" Hank asked, his mind suddenly racing.

"Not this morning. Cancel it for me. Last thing I feel like is a massage."

Hank laughed. "Then I'll use it." A pause. "About the boat? Give me a minute, a little more than a minute, and I'll bring one around for you." Hank couldn't believe what he was hearing. He'd expected to have to coerce them onto the lake tomorrow, and now they wanted to go today—on their own. This was just too perfect. Breck gone, Bilba gone, and Sylvia all but comatose. Now with Bray out of the way, he'd be able to go after Phil, the only pin still standing, with a million in mainland money. He had a hard time containing his excitement. All he had to do was contact the Brightstars and everything would be set. "I'll have it as soon as everything's ready," he told Bray.

CHAPTER 18

After checking that Chad was okay at Mrs. Sherman's next door, both Ginger and Pam decided to shower off the previous night's excitement. For Pam, the shower was especially wonderful. She even took a few extra minutes to luxuriate in the warm water. But when it was over, it was over. Both resolutely donned their baggy fisherman disguises, and on her way out, Ginger grabbed her Glock 20, the extra magazine, and two boxes of 9mm rounds. She wouldn't be caught naked again.

"You know, of course," Ginger pointed out as Pam fired up the engines and Ginger took her place on the copilot's chair, "Win and Bray have probably already found out that everything's on the up and up and they're going to spend the rest of their time on the island lounging by a pool. Teri on Win's arm and the therapist on Bray's."

"Think so?"

"Gotta be—it's the worst possible scenario. Where all roads lead."

"The shower didn't help you at all, did it?"

While they waited for the boat, Win skipped stones off the visitors' dock. He had a skill for it. When he'd first arrived at the lake right out of six years of seminary, he wasn't sure he possessed such potential—those little skills that mean so much. He'd already perfected his "tosser-thing" a small barrel with a hole in the top that hung from a foot-long string attached to a handle. The idea was to flip the barrel and catch it in the hole with the handle. In about a week he was a master. Now skipping stones, something he'd not spent much time on, was becoming a source of blooming pride.

He sent a particularly flat quarter-sized piece of shale out over the lake in a slow arc. It hit and skipped three times before burying itself in the water.

"That goofy part of you is taking over again," Bray warned from the bench at the base of the dock.

"Skills are important," Win responded, tossing out a two-skipper.

"That's no skill—that's a pastime and a darn poor one at that."

"It takes a keen eye and real muscle control."

"Then why can any four-year-old do it?"

"Because they have keen eyes and muscle control. I never met a four-year-old that didn't."

"And you've met a lot of 'em. Go out Saturday night with your four-year-old friends?"

Another three-skipper that nearly became four; maybe it *was* a four with the last skip really short. "You're still ticked 'cause I was right," Win said.

"And I'm so much happier because you were."

"You'd be happier dead?"

"I wouldn't be feelin' like this. And I don't know why you're being so cocky. Your great powers of deduction exposed none of this."

"But I was right." A pitiful one-skipper. Win checked his grip, recalibrated his stance and follow-through.

"You still think Bilba was murdered?"

"Maybe the autopsy will tell."

"And maybe it won't."

"If this is the family you had in mind, we wouldn't be talking about these things."

Bray took a deep breath and shook his head. "But it doesn't matter. It's my family."

"Are they?"

Bray looked at his friend, shook his head incredulously. "And that means what?"

"Sometimes families aren't the people we're born into. Sometimes they're the people we're reborn to."

"Well," said Bray with a sharp edge to his voice. "I was born to this one, and a few days ago I was reborn to it. They're my family. My people."

He flipped a three-skipper. "Think I'll ever get four?"

"Keep talking this way and you'll be tossing them with *two* broken arms."

Win scratched his chin with his cast. Then flipped another stone—this one skipped a sure four times. "Now, if I can do that again." He looked around the ground for just the right stone. "So Phil's really in charge now."

"If you talk to him, he's always been in charge. Tell him and you've told 'em all."

Win was about to flip the stone he spent so long finding when he stopped. His momentum spun him around.

"What's wrong?" Bray asked.

"If the boat comes, hold it," said Win, dropping the stone. "I need to talk to somebody."

Hank expected to make a few phone calls, wait for the Brightstars to appear, bring the modified Boat Eight around for Win and Bray, then just wait for the explosion. But it didn't turn out that way. The instant he returned to the cavernous dock, he could actually see things begin to crumble.

Foster bounded over the bobbing docks to meet him. "They want you to talk to the pilot."

"What pilot?"

"Last night's."

"I thought you already did—"

"They trust you."

Hank shook his head. "It's not trust. They want me to be hangin' on the hook. Waitin' for the butcher." Hank pushed a hand through tar black hair. "Get what's-his-name while I make a couple of phone calls."

As it turned out he had to make only one.

Using the dock's office phone, he called Clancy's Bar, found that the waverunners had just arrived and the Brightstars—Teeter, Skids, Parsnip and Wink—were outside drooling.

Wink came on the line. "Who this?"

"Bonzo."

"They're great, man—I mean, ape. Wow. I never seen anything like 'em. How fast they go, anyway?"

"You're the experts."

"Right. But these are great. You sit on 'em, huh? Like motorcycles? Wow."

"You've ridden a lot?"

"Hours and hours. But you sit right on 'em. That's awesome."

"Well, you experts gotta hurry. The guy I want roughed up will be on the lake in about an hour."

"An hour? Fat chance, your apeness. It'll take a half hour just to get 'em on the lake. How do you start those things?"

"Ask the driver. You still got the instructions I gave you?"

"Sure. Right here. Read 'em a bunch o' times. Sounds like things have changed some."

"Some. Just show up looking like a bunch of hoodlums out harassing people. I want the boat overturned and both of 'em run over by the waverunners, maybe a couple times. You clear on that?"

"Sure, what's not to be clear. You sit on those things. Unbelievable. This is gonna be great, really great."

"Put the driver on."

"Sure—whatever."

Hank heard the sound of the guy being called and a moment later a smoother, more cultured voice spoke. "You trust these guys?" the voice said.

"They don't have to do much. You do the modifications to the waverunners?"

"Sure—piece o' cake. But you do have a mean streak." Then the driver's voice darkened. "Bugs is concerned. He's never lost anyone on this run before. Not in the twenty years you guys been doin' business."

"Then it's about time. But we're taking more precautions from now on."

"I'll tell 'im. He's just worried someone's got your number. Bugs had a lot of confidence in Breck. Now that he's gone—"

"He can have confidence in me."

"Sure," the voice said skeptically. "We'll just see how this little thing you've got planned here works out. Seems a little spacey to me."

"If you did everything I said, it'll work just fine."

"I hope somebody videos it. We need a good laugh."

After they'd hung up, the driver, a husky guy with an iron expression, spoke to the bartender. "Got a question for you."

"Yeah?"

"Have I, or anybody else connected with those machines out there, ever been here?"

"Maybe an ape?"

"Who you calling an ape?" the driver growled, pushing a palm-size pistol in the bartender's neck.

"The guy was dressed in an ape costume."

"You're kidding." The pistol came down. "Maybe I should have come as Daffy Duck."

"Four feet, webbed feet. Don't matter. You was never here."

"Good. You'll reach old age." The driver then counted out five one-hundred-dollar bills. "For retirement." He left.

After Hank hung up he pushed another thick hand through black hair. He hated being watched. It ruined the illusion of independence. And he needed independence.

The pilot of last night's shipment knocked lightly on the office door. After he told Hank everything, he waited for questions. "They were drunk?"

"They acted that way. Came out of nowhere, couple of bottles in each hand, drinking like fish."

"What about what's-his-name—the other guy?"

"Hit a rock. Humongous ol' bang. The women escaped. I didn't see them again."

"The cops pick up the pieces?"

"They were working on it when I went back through."

"They look suspicious of anything?"

"Cops always look suspicious. But they didn't have anything. People hit rocks all the time out there. No reason this was anything but another accident."

Hoping the cops would say the same thing about the explosion coming in about an hour, Hank took a deep, finalizing breath and told the pilot to get some sleep. Before the guy was out of his office, Hank grabbed the phone again and called his customer. He told him everything was fine and that they'd watch things a little more closely for the next week or so. Hank was relieved when he heard a simple grunt. It was followed by a threat, but threats didn't mean anything. They were expected in this business.

He looked at his watch. The Brightstars should be watching the waverunners being lowered into the lake right now.

Foster stuck his head in the door, "Just to let you know, Bilba's body's being taken to the morgue—or wherever they take bodies."

"Probably where they make dog food."

Win strolled into the main house to the dining room. Phil sat alone at the head of the table. On the table was a full spread. Platters of scrambled eggs, bacon, muffins, fruit, pitchers of juice, and thermoses of coffee. It all sat untouched.

"Hi," Win greeted.

Phil looked up from whatever he'd been thinking. "I'm tired. I didn't hear you."

"I said 'hi.'"

"With conviction, I'm sure."

"This is quite a spread."

"I ordered it," Phil said, with just a hint of pride poking through a dispirited tone. "I wanted my first breakfast to be a good one."

"It is. Anybody RSVP?"

"I didn't invite anybody."

"Is this one of those family rituals nobody but an insider would understand?"

"It's mine."

"So I'm crashing."

"That's okay. I've had the time I wanted."

Win pulled a chair out and sat. He took a morsel from the edge of a muffin. "It's a shame your dream is realized over Bilba's death."

"That's the way it works. When I croak Sylvia will order breakfast. She'll order two, three breakfasts. Eat 'em all."

"Bilba sure had one of those days yesterday," Win said, taking another morsel, this one a little larger. "Some real lows, some greater highs."

"I guess you could call it the worst."

Win took the top off the muffin and broke it in a couple pieces. Ate one of them. Apple cinnamon. Good. He ate the other. "She seemed to be weathering things okay. Physically she was a little drained, but spiritually she seemed strong. And she was recovering physically. How was she when you saw her this morning?"

"When?"

"This morning—a little before two."

"What makes you think I saw her?"

"She told me you did."

"This morning?" He looked incredulous.

"She woke me—told me."

"Just to tell you I'd been there?"

"Among other things. She said she told you about some spiritual matters."

"She did?"

"She did."

"What are you talking about?"

"I can be confusing sometimes," Win said. He downed a second muffin and wiped the crumbs from his chin. "She said she told *them* something. She only talked to one person, so the *them* had to be the boss who'd tell everyone else. That would be you. Got any bran muffins? No?" He tore a hunk from another apple cinnamon.

"You base it all on one word. The woman was half out of her mind."

"If the Lord can base some arguments on one word—well—let me see if I can piece things together a little more clearly. You went in to check on her. She told you she knows Jesus now. Has to do the right thing now. Inconvenient, huh? Those Christians can really throw monkey wrenches into the machinery. She told you to stop the business. Hard news, huh?"

"She's done the business for fifty years. Why would she suddenly tell me to stop?"

"Jesus," Win said flatly. "You got any milk back there? These muffins need milk." He ripped the top off a fourth muffin and took a big bite of it. "Did she say something about telling the cops? Coffee would be okay with these, but milk would be best."

"Cops? About what?"

"Now I know what you do on the little island is perfectly legal. But somehow I think you would object to her being so vocal about it."

"You're accusing me of murdering my aunt?"

"Now how could I be doing that? They don't even know if it's murder yet. Of course, they might know by this afternoon. The autopsy." Win leaned back and chewed the last of the muffin. "These are great. But just a little dry. Be right back." Win pushed the chair back. "I gotta get some milk." He pushed through the kitchen door and returned a few seconds later with a glass of milk. "Now that's more like it. I've heard that when someone's been suffocated, that even when it's quick, they can find things."

"I think you'd better leave," Phil said firmly.

Win glanced at his watch. "You're right. Hank's getting Bray and me a boat to power around the lake. If it wasn't for the fire in New York smudging everything with its soot, this would be an incredible day. I want to enjoy a little of it."

"I've certainly enjoyed our little chat," Phil said sarcastically, his eyes narrow with angry loathing.

"Right," Win sparked. "That boat could be waiting. See you later." Win downed his milk, then grabbed two more muffins, poured coffee into a Styrofoam cup, put a top on it, and left.

On the way out of the house, when Phil could no longer see him, he stopped. Took a deep breath and a moment's stock. Was Phil acting like a guilty man? He wasn't sure. He was sure of his logic. Bilba had said she'd told *them*. That terminology is the Chairman to the President, the CEO to the COO. Bilba to Phil. An order from the top. But had there been a murder? That would have to wait until later, after the autopsy. But if there had been, Phil was the guy. He had to be.

Hank called the driver again. The Sea-Doos were in the water. "You should see these clowns," he said, his laughter bitter. "You're quite the recruiter."

"As I said, they don't have to do much."

The driver watched one of the foursome slap into another one's wake and end up straddling the handle bars backwards. "You sure you can't video any of this?"

Hank hung up. It would take them about fifteen minutes to get to the island, assuming they found it. Just about as much time as it took Bray and the other guy to get settled on the lake.

Finishing his coffee, extra strong to keep him awake, he checked the modifications he had made to Boat Eight's fuel system.

All was set.

The fuel line would begin dripping immediately. After only a few minutes, the inner hull would be awash in gas, the trickle would become a pool. When he triggered the spark remotely, the explosion would rupture the weakened flooring and bathe them in flames and molten fiberglass. It would be just like twenty-some-odd years ago when he'd done the same thing to his current victim's parents. *Sweet irony,* he thought. *Did I use that word right? Maybe sweet déjà vu? Whatever it is, it's Sweet Burning Bray.* He laughed. He liked working with his hands—doing a job well.

Win returned to find Bray still sitting on the bench, but this time less combative and a little more pensive. The cane was before him, his hand folded over the top, his chin resting on his hands looking out over the lake toward the Grand Isles. Win pushed the coffee and the muffin on top of the lid in Bray's direction.

"Oh, thanks. Could use it."

Win took a bite out of his.

Bray took a sip and nibbled the muffin.

"No cheese Danishes," Win told him.

"This'll do. Thanks."

"Don't mention it."

There was a long silence now as the two thought about the doughnut shop in Burlington. Talking would have spoiled it. Before either could say a word they heard the whine of an approaching engine, then Boat Eight appeared with Hank at the controls.

"Now we ought to have some fun in that," Win said, excitement renewed.

"Will you stop being so blasted cheerful. People have died."

Win peered back behind a know-it-all smile. "People are in heaven."

Hank made sure they were placed right, Win behind the controls, his cast laying across the wheel, and Bray on the bow. "Otherwise when you gun it the nose'll be so high you won't be able to see. And I want you to see everything."

"That's nice of you, Hank," Win said, his cheerfulness nearly annoying. It wasn't manufactured, either. There was something bubbling up inside him this morning, and he wasn't sure exactly what. But he certainly didn't feel like fighting it. Bubbly mornings don't come along very often, particularly when surrounded by all this dark stuff—death, demons, and too many apple cinnamon muffins.

"It goes about forty miles per hour so be careful. And if you smell a little gas, don't worry about it. There's a chronic leak somewhere we've been fighting for years. Evaporates the moment it's out."

Firing the boat back up, Win eased her from the dock.

The lake was glass, reflecting the world around and above it— a glistening mirror. The New York fire was playing a little havoc with the sun and clouds, even the blue heavens looked smudged, but only a little. When they'd buzzed out a few hundred yards Win looked back on the island and saw Bilba's body being transferred to a boat. It must have arrived as they were leaving. That's when it struck him. The island resembled the world and God at work in it. Satan buried at its center, pulling strings from the grave, people loyal to him and what brings them death, and God working unperturbed to bring his people in and keep his people safe.

Win studied Bray.

His friend's shoulders actually drooped from the world's weight. *Lord*, Win began, *please keep him safe for you.*

Coming to a spot just far enough from the island, Bray came to life. "Remember the speedboat we took out that night to look for Chad?" he asked.

"Quite a night—could hardly see for the rain."

"Forty would have seemed slow. I had a purpose then," Bray said. "Come on, let's see what this thing'll do."

Win pulled the wheel around and pointed the nose toward the fruit stand. "Let's go see how the reconstruction's going. I'm still feeling guilty about that."

"Why?"

"Don't know. But it just seems like the right thing to do."

"You gotta do that now? Okay—whatever."

Hank watched from the dock as the pair headed toward Grand Isles, then he strayed toward the commons. After speaking with the guard in front of the main house, he proceeded toward his own. When inside he ran up the stairs to the rooftop patio. Although he was only a single story off the ground, his view commanded the lake several miles to the south, from the dock on the Grand Isles all the way around to St. Albans. Since there wasn't much north of the island but marsh and shallows, it was likely Win and Bray would putter into view soon.

That's where the Brightstars would meet them.

Hank scanned the horizon. The Brightstars were nowhere to be seen. But they had to be on their way. They just had to be.

Pam had the cruiser plowing along at about half throttle while Ginger sat on the narrow aft section.

Her fear was still there. For a few minutes last night, when they were wildly cutting a phosphorus wake camped on the end of another phosphorous wake, her fear had actually subsided. She thought that a paradox. When she should have been tightly in fear's grip—when her life was actually in danger—she'd felt strong.

But now, as the boat moved with assurance, knifing through a calm surface, she felt sure any moment she would be living with the fishes—she'd be desperately trying to breathe and there would be nothing filling her lungs but water. Just thinking about it made any movement at all heroic achievement.

"You okay down there?" Pam called out.

"Peachy," Ginger called back.

Win's insurance company had come through, at least partially, allowing the farmer to begin reconstruction. So, having salved his conscience, Win pulled the boat from the dock and pointed it north toward the shallows.

"Thought we could putter around a little in there. Talk."

Bray hunched again slightly.

"Talk. My favorite thing."

"We need to talk."

"Whatever," Bray said as the boat grumbled toward a rash of islands that soon changed complexion and became a maze of waterways and marshes.

Hank watched as the small craft left the Grand Isles dock and headed—

North!

They can't head north. Wink and the boys would be useless if Bray and that kid stayed up there.

And that boat couldn't just explode without provocation. The police would be all over it if it just blew up.

Hank's heart sank into his shoes. He was about to lose sight of them. Good grief, what if they got lost up there? Or finally ran out of gas and started poking around and found all his precious little modifications?

"Oh, well," he muttered, pulling out a cigar and lighting it.

At least there was one fire he could light whenever he wanted.

"So," Bray finally said when they'd reached the northern side of the island and Win was preparing to figure out where he would head next, "you think I'm nuts, don't you?"

"You had high hopes." Win sang the last words. Bray groaned. Win had no voice.

"I've been thinking a lot about my mom," Bray said, his eyes idly scanning the nearby reeds for birds.

"Good subject," Win nodded.

"Your mom died when you were young."

"I miss her. Holidays would sure be a lot different."

"Your dad raised you."

"He tried—I guess. Fortunately, Mom had a reasonable shot at me. Ten years."

"My mom had all of me. She says in that diary page that she thought she and I were a lot alike. I'm not so sure. She was loyal. I'm not so sure I am."

Win eased the boat up a canal bordered by thick emerald foliage, probably the mouth of some river. "She was loyal how?"

"Her family—my dad, me, to a certain extent, Phil."

"She was *married* to your dad. She was *your* mom. She *signed on* as Phil's mom. She just honored her obligations. Of course, *loving* you probably had something to do with it."

"We all have obligations to our families."

"When she died she was trying to escape them. I don't see anything in Scripture that says children honor your uncles or aunts. Or aunts, love your nieces or nephews. Or bow down to dead uncles, or plant trees because members of your families have died."

"I'm not talking about the Bible here. I'm talking about truth, the way civilizations have survived. They've survived taking care of family."

"We do have a point of departure here," Win said, pointing the boat at the middle of the narrowing channel. "I know you've always wanted to connect up with someone. Nobody could possibly like being alone as much as you portray."

"I need someone," Bray admitted, a hint of reluctance. "Diane—Pam."

"But there's no need to be loyal to people who might be dangerous—even if there is a common ancestor somewhere."

"Danger? I thought that stuff was over. Bilba's gone, your theory about Teri didn't hold water. Bilba had a bad heart so it's obvious that she died of a heart attack and wasn't knocked off. The danger's gone."

"I wonder how many knew she had a bad heart."

"I doubt if anybody knew much about anybody. Listen, keeper of the tiller, we're about to relive that scene from *The African Queen*. The one where they're trapped in the reeds with the heat and the leeches. Turn this thing around and get me out to the middle of the lake. The danger is you getting us caught in here and us being found in fifty years by an expedition. I want water stretching out in every direction. That's where I'll feel safe."

Hank couldn't believe his eyes. The Brightstars were coming like a flotilla. Four red waverunners, now only slivers on the horizon, but all in a perfect row, all eight noses aligned. And where was Bray? They were coming, and where was the guy they were coming for?

That's when he saw the little Sea-Doo buzzing around the island from the north, Bray still lying unsuspectingly across the bow, the other guy steering as if he had a destination in life.

He does, Hank thought. He, Hank, was going to send him to hell.

Hank laughed.

This was going to be just too easy.

CHAPTER 19

Hank kept a pair of binoculars on the roof patio and grabbed them now.

Focusing, he quickly found Wink at the center of the charge, his massive bulk hanging over the waverunner's seat in folds. Like Wink, the others looked like they had in the bar, except that now the wind plastered their hair back, and their unbuttoned flannel shirts whipped wildly behind them. Luckily Hank had ordered the big Bombardiers, the GTXs, 782 cc displacement, 110-horse-power three-seaters that now seemed hardly big enough for one.

Putting the glasses down to get the panoramic view, Hank grinned. Bray's boat crept along with only a hint of a wake, the two passengers deep in conversation, thinking the day was all theirs. While several hundred yards away a wave of flannel-clad marauders was about to snatch it from them.

Hank took the remote from his pocket and prepared to acti-vate the mechanisms. The waverunners would be in range in just a few minutes.

It was unfolding just as planned. Soon Bray and the Kid would be smothered in bad news.

"How much further, Pam?" Ginger asked.

"That was my favorite back-seat question as a kid."

"Well, I'm an adult, and I deserve to know. I keep seeing those boulders silhouetted in that lightning flash last night."

"God was really on our side."

"He just wanted me to get a taste of what was coming."

"That glass of yours is getting emptier and emptier."

"I feel like Eeyore," she confessed. "Those rocks down there look really close. How deep is it here?"

Pam laughed. "It won't be long. Ten, fifteen minutes."

"That's better," Bray said, the expanse of blue lake refreshing him. "This is one of those times that the lake is really clearing the sewage away. Want me to drive? It can't be easy steering with that cast."

"It's okay. Need the exercise."

"You really think there's a God in control of all this chaos?"

"I do," Win said with deep conviction. But Win knew it was a manufactured conviction. It was the kind of conviction he knew he would have if he never had doubts, never worried about anything, never wondered if God really did have his head screwed on right. But he figured eighty percent of him believed, and he did try to live his life as if the percentage were higher. But there were doubts—planted and nurtured by Satan and his own desire to be top dog at least once in his life.

"There are times I try to believe it," Bray confessed.

"Really?"

"It'd be easier in a way. But I can't. When I learned I had a family again, and thought I could trust them, I found it easier to think there was a God out there I could trust. But then I saw them. They're just people. I'm still the only one I can rely on. Bum leg and all."

"We're all just people. I don't bank on anybody. Everybody lets you down sometime or another. But God won't. Never. Loyalty to God is never misplaced."

"Maybe."

Hank didn't need binoculars now. From the east, Wink and the boys bore down on their prey. Oblivious, the boat grumbled in a small circle in the center of sprawling water—Bray and the other guy locked in conversation. *It's so sweet.*

The time had come. He powered on the remote.

Within the four waverunners and the boat, a current ran through microswitches as Hank leaned against the railing, anxiously waiting for the perfect moment.

Wink and the others saw their target as they thundered around a small island. The straight line was Wink's idea. He'd seen it in battle movies, and it looked awesome. Right now he wanted to look awesome. He wanted the feel of awesome, of real power. His whole life he'd wanted that feeling, and now that some guy in an ape suit had given him the chance, he didn't want to muff it. And he loved the feel of the waverunner. The way it hugged the surface of the water, commanding it—the freedom of a Harley.

Unable to make himself heard over the roar of the engines, Wink pointed to the small boat. The others, their hands tight on the handlebars, feeding their machines level throttle, grinned excitedly and nodded, each feeling his own power in his own way. *What a great day for the Brightstars*, Wink thought.

And, Wink resolved, *it should last awhile.*

They couldn't just go in there, smack that boat around, and leave. No. This adventure had to last. *This chew had flavor and needed some chewin' to get it all out.*

Or—leavin' awesome too quick just wasn't cool.

He recited the concept to himself another couple of ways, but they all added up to the same thing. The fun had to last.

Wink laughed. A throw-yer-head-back kind of laugh that, at the end, became a shriek.

An idea.

He didn't get many ideas, but when they came they were beauts. He turned to his brothers and made a circling motion with his finger. They knew instantly what he meant, and they grinned. Parsnip, named that because he put his whole self into things, bounced repeatedly on his seat until he nearly lost control and was forced to calm down.

Win and Bray heard them first. A dull, steadily growing whine—the approach of a giant mosquito. A moment later Bray saw them and idly commented on how crazy some people were and how some people just didn't care about driving a beautiful morning into the ground and why didn't he have his gun for occasions like this.

Then the whine became a lion's roar as they closed in.

"What're they doing?" Win cried. "They're not slowing down. Good grief! They're speeding up!"

And as they approached he saw the riders lean forward, granite expressions determined, yellow teeth bared like old Buick grills. He wasn't sure the exact instant he knew they were coming after them. But he knew now.

"Get off the bow!" Win cried, as they melted from a charging line into a file.

Shock leaped from Bray's face and, just as the first waverunner blasted by, he rolled off the bow onto the wet floor.

Bray yelled something at them, but it became garbled as the sudden wake slapped against the little craft and tossed him around like so much baggage.

"They're coming back!" Win warned.

The first one had already spun a wide circle and, followed by the others, was charging for a second pass, this time to their rear. The little boat was still reeling from the wake assault in front and was now about to be treated to a battering aft. Bray braced himself while Win draped himself over the steering wheel.

As the first marauder thundered by, Win screamed something unintelligible. Then again at the second. By the time the third blasted by, the little boat was pitching violently. His cast slammed against the wheel, pain rifled up his shoulder. Bray cried out and grabbed his bad knee as it bashed the hull. The fourth roared so close they thought they might capsize.

"At least *they're* having a good time," Win shouted.

"Glad to hear it," Bray shouted back.

The bad guys were having more than a good time, they were having a fantastic time. While regrouping, they laughed, cheered, told each other how it all felt.

Far less enthusiastic about it all, Bray propped himself up as the boat calmed slightly. "They look like they're right out of the woods. I think I see hobnail boots."

"It's gotta be a costume—look for price tags."

"The boat won't stop spinning."

It wouldn't. The artificial current, first in front then in back, was making a top out of them.

"They're coming back," Win groaned.

"Make it hard for them. Get us out of here."

With them spinning like this, Win was afraid of what might happen if he gunned it. "The boat might roll," Win called back.

"And it might not."

"I think we should just ride it out. They're coming back. Hang on."

Bray hated that idea. His leg hurt more with each jolt, and there were plenty of jolts. Glancing over the top he saw Win was right. The four waverunners skimmed toward them. And those idiots were still laughing—heads back, mouths wide. He wanted to bury a cannonball into each of them.

"There's got to be a way of making them regret this," Bray shouted.

Back on his roof, Hank was beside himself. What were those idiots doing? They were supposed to run them down—make contact with the boat—hit it hard. It couldn't just explode on its own. There were too many witnesses out there to have it just explode. *Come on, you jerks, get with the program. It's like you're playing with your food.*

Wink had never had so much fun. Oh, there was that druggie coed in Middlebury, but she was on dry land. This was on the lake. And the boat was actually spinning. He was making it spin. Watching it charged every battery in him. Finally, after thirty-some years, to actually make something spin—to have an effect.

It was time. Win saw the last of the waverunners flash by and the first of them turn, preparing for another go. "Hang on!" he cried. With the boat violently pitching, he jammed the throttle forward. The engine, as if a protesting teenager, gave out a high-pitched whine. The nose climbed high—Win couldn't see beyond it—then the boat leaped forward, slapping at the turbulence. Bray cried out in pain and grabbed his side.

"You okay?" Win yelled.

"Keep going." Lifted higher, facing aft, he could see everything behind them. A part of him wished he couldn't. The marauders didn't wait to regroup. Each spun with various degrees of aptitude and headed back after them. "Just get us out of here!" Bray cried.

"Now I know how John Wayne felt with all those Indians."

"They've made the turn. They're coming back."

"Climb back on the nose. I can't see where I'm going."

"The island's in back of you," Bray pointed toward the oncoming horde. As he did, he worked himself painfully to the front.

Without another thought Win spun the wheel. The boat planted its aft section and turned on it. Had they been alone on the lake this would have been an easy maneuver. But they weren't alone. Two of the waverunners flashed within a foot, the riders' faces whooping and crying out obscenities as they passed. Their wakes beat against the boat, jarring Win from his seat and swamping them with waves. Bray cried out again, now back on the floor lying in a sloshing pool of water.

"My gun. If I only had my gun."

Win didn't listen. He regained his seat in time for the next marauder to storm by. The throttle had backed off so he jammed it forward again, the nose away from the island.

The boat pitched, a cork in a storm, the lake about them churned to boiling as the last waverunner exploded by. The boat spun in the whirlpool and managed to leap forward, but forward was always in a different direction.

Hank watched, his anger rising. They were beginning to draw attention—a couple of fisherman, a guy pleasure sailing. Soon someone would call the police or the lake patrol. Soon, instead of Win and Bray going up in smoke, his plan would.

Wink, though not noted for his quick wit, began realizing what Hank did. They were going to blow the whole thing. Two hundred bucks each rested on success, and success was more than just havin' fun. He motioned his brothers to a quick meeting.

Getting the hang of these new toys, each pulled quickly into a tight circle.

Win couldn't believe they'd been given a reprieve and aimed the nose right toward their island. But they hadn't covered much water when the reprieve ended. Just as suddenly as they'd pulled into their meeting, the four hoodlums pulled out of it.

Pam was the first to see what was going on and she immediately called for Ginger to come to the bridge. Grateful to be pulled away from the rocks below them and the flaming images they seemed to conjure up, Ginger responded. Flopping into the copilot's chair, she grabbed the binoculars. "Someone's in trouble."

Without another word Pam rammed the throttle forward. The twin engines thundered below as the Montego leaped from the water and rocketed forward skimming the surface, the wake a frantic spray.

Win's and Bray's little boat had gained speed, becoming something to be chased.

For Wink, excitement was mounting. It had become a contest, and Wink loved contests.

Parsnip, forever in the thick of it, loved a contest too. He especially loved beating his brothers. There was never a sweeter triumph. For Parsnip, such triumphs were rare.

Skids's face turned hugely determined. He just wanted to nail those two. He'd been hired to do what he loved to do. Make something happen. And if he ended up the last one standing, so be it.

Teeter was scared. He'd been scared since he'd gotten on this thing. He didn't like the speed. He didn't like the stinging spray. He didn't like the idea that any second he could be bucked off into a deep, unforgiving lake and drown. He didn't like any of it. And he just wanted to get it over with. If that meant plowing right over the top of that boat, that's what he wanted to do. He was ready to head for the barn, and anything standing in his way would soon be history. In their little meeting, when Wink had said it was time to get serious, Teeter had cheered. And now that the little boat was trying to escape, he cheered even louder. All he had to do was get ahead of them, push the waverunner's nose under the boat's nose, and over it would go. He'd be on his way home to level ground.

So now the chase was on. Wink's digital readout said thirty-five mph, then thirty-seven. It was so neat. He could feel the waves give way beneath him as he gained. Skids led the way, but Skids had never been the brave one. He'd probably just bump the boat, it would be up to Wink to actually get into it.

Win could see that the waverunners would be overtaking them soon. He could see it because Bray kept telling him. "They're gaining on us. Can't you get any more speed out of this thing? They're gaining."

The island was much too far away.

He did the only thing he could think of.

He jammed the throttle back to nothing.

Suddenly they were all but dead in the water, and the waverunners tore past.

Wink couldn't believe it. He could have easily rammed them, but his instincts for survival were too strong. He veered to the right, roaring past, then couldn't bring himself to turn sharply at that speed. So, when he and his brothers finally realized what they had to do, they were a good distance away.

As the last waverunner passed, Win spun the wheel, turned the boat 180 degrees, and jammed the throttle forward. Again the Sea-Doo's engine whined like an injured animal, but came alive anyway, propelling them away from their adversaries.

His back plastered on the floor, the floor high as the boat sped away, Bray saw the waverunners scramble as they turned, trying desperately to avoid colliding with one another. To his chagrin, they managed to turn themselves without incident. The race was on again.

"There's an island over there," Win cried.

"Get to it. You've bought some time."

But not enough. They'd gone only a few yards when Bray's play-by-play started up again. "They're gaining. Even faster this time. Is there something wrong with this boat?"

There seemed to be. The whine of the engine didn't seem as insistent, the slapping of the waves seemed more pronounced, which meant they weren't planing the tops. "It's losing power!" Win cried.

Ginger and Pam's boat wasn't. Less than a hundred yards away—

"It's Win—and Bray!" Ginger cried, her whole body rigid now. She'd finally been able to get her binoculars trained on the pilot of the little boat, and though she couldn't see every feature with the cruiser shuddering as it did, there was no mistaking him. Her heart climbed into her throat. "And those Neanderthals are gaining on them."

Pam shoved the throttle harder and got a little more horsepower from the engines. It wasn't much, but it was something, and she had the feeling *this* race was going to be won by inches.

"Lord, you know what you have to do," Ginger prayed, eyes open and trained ahead.

Hank saw the cruiser. He'd actually seen it several hundred yards back but hadn't thought much of it. Now, barreling into the fray, most of its hull skimming the surface, it was becoming a player.

Maybe he should just push the button, blow Bray up now. Maybe it would look like the boat had just had enough and burst. But if anything needed to look like an accident, murder did. Although he was sure all mechanisms would burn and leave no trace, he didn't want to take the chance. Some hotshot detective boring in too deeply might just find something. No. He'd wait.

Wink was gaining, his heart thundering in his chest. The fun was gone. It had become something he had to do. And he would do it any second now. He wasn't first. Parsnip was, and Skids after him. But both were timid sometimes. Wink still hoped he'd be the one to actually run over the top of that boat.

Parsnip's two fingers pulled on the throttle lever, pulled for all he was worth. If there was an ounce of power left in that engine, he wanted it. He loved the engine's whine, loved the spray biting at his face, loved it all. But would the boat go dead in the water again? What would he do? He couldn't just ram the back of it. That'd kill him. Oh, but he wanted to ram it. Wanted to split that boat in two. Wanted to see those two guys thrown head over heels into the drink. Parsnip, of course, didn't want that to happen to him. What should he do if it stopped? Could he react fast enough to clip the front? That's what he'd do, just clip the front.

Suddenly Skids was beside him, a triumphant grin as his pulled up. "I'm gonna do it."

"Y'are not!" cried Parsnip.

"Am to."

"Y'are not!"

And Parsnip rammed his brother. It wasn't a hard ram, but it was enough to knock him a little off course.

Wink exploded past while the brothers battled one another. Wink squealed a laugh as he stormed by. The laugh brought them both back to the race.

Teeter hated the rivalry. *Who wants to be first? First home, yes, but this? Last is fine, let's just get out of here.* He passed Skids and Parsnip, too. No laugh. Just grim determination.

Afraid life's chances were passing him by, Parsnips gunned the engine. For the same reason, Skids did too.

From his perch Hank saw what was going to happen long before it did. And it was just what he wanted. All anxiety dissolved as he waited. Any second all would converge—the Sea-Doo would be overtaken by at least two of the waverunners just as the cruiser, coming up faster than any cruiser he'd ever seen, would reach them. There would be so much confusion in such a small area of such a large lake, that it didn't matter if anyone bumped anything. The explosion would obliterate all memory in any witness's mind.

Of course, it happened a little differently.

Traveling so fast, Pam was actually out of control and didn't know it. Thinking she could turn faster than she could, she anticipated reaching the Sea-Doo just a hair before the waverunners, superimposing the cruiser between the waverunners and the

Sea-Doo, and affording Win and Bray some much needed protection. But such precision was too much to ask from such a large craft. Waiting for the exact moment, she adjusted the wheel. The cruiser didn't respond.

Aboard the Sea-Doo, Win suddenly found himself the target of two enemies, the waverunners coming up strong from the rear and, what seemed to him, a huge, white mountain careering at them from the front. Knowing that something had to give, he cried to Bray, "Get up. We might have to abandon."

Now Wink became aware of the cruiser. More maneuverable, he wasn't afraid of hitting it, but he was of losing his prey. And he had no intention of doing that.

From the rooftop, Hank prepared to push the button. He aimed the remote at the converging mayhem and waited. Any second now the explosion would douse Bray and the kid in what could be considered napalm, and the waverunners, responding to his signal, would go berserk.

Pam cried something to Ginger, but Ginger had already seen what was going to happen.

The cruiser clipped the Sea-Doo, and the Sea-Doo jumped into the air throwing Win and Bray unceremoniously into the lake. Pam, in an effort to keep from doing them any more damage, pulled the throttle back, all but killing the engine. The cruiser settled into the lake like a duck.

Hank hadn't seen the Sea-Doo eject its passengers, the cruiser being in the way. All he knew was the convergence had occurred. He pressed the button.

The Sea-Doo exploded.

"Good God," Ginger gasped.

Flames shot several feet in the air. Molten fiberglass, some aflame, some glowing crimson, rained down upon the water. Gas spread on the lake and the flames billowed after it.

Win and Bray struggled to stay afloat. Bray, weighed down by shoes, his bad leg searing with pain, had real trouble kicking. Win, because of his waterlogged cast, was having equal difficulty getting to his friend. And the flames were spreading toward them.

Pam, in control again, eased the throttle forward in an attempt to get between the advancing flames and the two men. As she did, Ginger leaped to the lower deck, leaning as close to the waterline as possible, hoping somehow to make a difference.

Neither woman realized that something else was going on. With their attention glued to Win and Bray, they hadn't noticed that the waverunners, and the men on them, were wildly out of control.

Although Hank couldn't see Win and Bray battle the water, he could see the waverunners and was laughing. Sure that Bray and Win were history, now he could concentrate on his other handiwork. The waverunners had three modifications—the throttles were now stuck in full, the maneuvering mechanisms were ineffective and essentially choosing direction randomly, and the cut-off switches were deactivated. The Brightstars were on the ride of their lives—hopefully their final ride.

Ginger and Pam became aware that something was wrong when one of the waverunners glanced off the cruiser, the rider screaming to be saved. Then another exploded through the flames, its rider terrified.

"They're going nuts," Pam cried.

Ginger didn't care. She had something else on her mind. The flames were still making their way toward the thrashing men, and though Win had made it to Bray, neither man was capable of dragging the other anywhere.

"Hang on, Win," Ginger cried. "We'll get you out."

"Where'd you come from?"

"Tell you later." Then Ginger called up to Pam, "Get closer."

Pam was trying, but the cruiser was very difficult to manage. The churning waves, the flames, and now the mad waverunners made precision maneuvering extremely difficult.

Ginger grabbed a life preserver, aimed, and tossed it. She missed. It landed too far away for Win to get to it. She pulled it back and took aim again. With flames lapping at the side of the cruiser, she tossed it.

It landed inches from Win. He grabbed it. But before Ginger could reel him in, a waverunner, its rider crying frantically, plowed through the flames and cut across the line, severing it.

Splashed up by the sudden intruder, the flames reached toward the guys.

Seeing the danger, Ginger grabbed the boat side of the line and dove into the water. Since she wasn't much of a swimmer, she called upon raw determination to battle the chop. Grabbing and spitting out handfuls of water, she finally reached Win.

"This cast's lead."

"My leg's on fire," Bray gasped.

"I love you," she cried. "And I can't swim."

"Couldn't prove it by me," Win managed.

Fighting to stay afloat, Ginger managed to affix the line to the life preserver. The instant she did, Win and Bray grabbed hold and Pam eased the cruiser away from the flames, pulling the three of them along. When they were safely away, she reeled them in.

"Hang on, Bray," she called.

"Pam? Oh, thank God."

"That's progress," Win laughed.

A few moments later each climbed aboard via the water-level steps aft. Immediately, Win grabbed Ginger and gave her a deep, lingering kiss. So hard that the waterlogged cast hurt her back.

She didn't care. She kissed him back.

Pam and Bray didn't notice any of it. They embraced as well, then finally kissed.

The two women, a little starry-eyed, pulled back only when they had to. And they had to when reality struck. One of the waverunners hit the same shale ramp that Teri once had, took flight, and plowed, point first, through the cruiser's forward windows. To the sound of shattering glass and tearing metal reinforced with fiberglass, it buried itself in the cruiser's cabin up to the seat.

Its rider, Teeter, kept going. He cannoned over the top, struck his head on the cruiser's radar unit, then continued to the lake beyond. Fortunately the flames in that area had died. Unfortunately, so had Teeter. He had finally gotten it over with. A few moments after disappearing below the surface, his lifeless body reappeared, bobbing on the waves.

Hank also saw the waverunner bury itself in the cruiser. It would have been a source of grand amusement had he not also seen Win and Bray being hauled on deck just before.

He swore, threw the remote to the floor, slammed his fists on the railing, and shook his head in defeat. Taking phone in hand, he punched in three digits and pressed it to his ear. "Foster, send a couple boats out there, and show 'em we care."

Angry, he tossed the phone onto a nearby table and was thinking that things couldn't get any worse when he heard a voice from behind. "Hank?" Teri stood there. "You tried to kill them. I can't believe you tried to kill them."

Hank turned and with eyes blazing like the lake below, beheld his niece with a towering, deadly rage. Meaty fists clenched, he stepped toward her.

CHAPTER 20

Hank slapped a fist in his hand and peered through narrow eyes at Teri. "What do you think you saw?"

"You rigged it. You were trying to kill Bray."

Hank needed to hear no more. With quick, deliberate steps he launched himself at her. She spun and ran for the stairs. Taking two at a time she ran to the bottom and tore from his house to her own. Hank right behind her, she fell through the door and grabbed for the nearest gun. Unfortunately it was an ancient flintlock. She was about to toss it down and grab for another, when Hank burst through the door.

"What's going on?" Randy called from the living room.

Teri had no time to answer. She had to protect herself. She raised the rifle like a club and swung it at her uncle. Hank caught it in his left hand, then grabbed her arm with his right. In a single, violent movement, he threw her back.

She fell onto the living room floor.

"Teri, what's going—"

Hank entered like an angry bear. Lifting her by her arm, he slapped her viciously across the face.

Randy tried desperately to get to his feet, but his leg cried with pain. He fell backward, then rolled from the sofa, and tried to drag himself to a gun.

Seeing him, Hank broke away from Teri, took two quick steps and kicked Randy right in his wound. The pain clawed at his heart. He screamed and grabbed his leg. The dressing was immediately soaked with blood.

Seeing her chance, Teri dove for a pistol nearby, grabbed it, and leveled it at Hank. But before she could pull the trigger, Hank wrenched the piece away then backhanded her. She spun completely around, cutting her lip against her teeth, and fell against the dining room table.

Afraid of what might be coming up behind her, she turned to face Hank again.

Hank was right in front of her and would have struck her again had not the front door flown open and her father stepped in.

"Hank, what in heaven's name are you doing?" Phil exclaimed.

"Dad!" Teri cried. "He beat me up—he tried to kill Uncle Bray."

"He couldn't have. Bray was on the lake."

"He did it by remote control."

"Remote—is this true, Hank?"

Hank said nothing.

"And what's happened to Randy?" Phil asked.

Teri pushed past Hank and knelt beside Randy, trying desperately to comfort him. But his leg ached with the very definition of pain, and his face twisted cruelly in an attempt to endure it.

"Well. Answer me, Hank."

Hank's eyes blazed. If he'd ever been a jovial member of the family, there was no evidence of it now. He stood like an enraged bull calculating his next move, sizing up the matador, picking the most vulnerable spot to sink his horns. Finding it, he said, "I'm taking over."

Phil's head cocked. "You're what?"

"I'm taking over."

Phil laughed. It was an airy, incredulous laugh, but one that realized he might be in serious trouble. "How you gonna do that?"

"I have all the money."

"All? But Tommy's—"

"Tommy and I have agreed that we're the only ones capable of continuing the business."

"Tommy?"

"He's finance, and I'm operations. The rest of you are out."

Phil puffed up his chest. "But you can't do that."

"I have."

"But you can't. I'm the next in line now that Bilba's dead."

"There is no more line."

"But there is. Breck set it up. The family's the family."

"Dad," Teri injected, her voice charged with rage and confusion. "He beat me up. Are you going to let him beat me up?"

Randy whimpered. A pain must have seared a path from his leg directly to his brain.

"You can't just come in here and take over. You can't."

"I have. You, Sylvia, and Teri will be paid off. But the business is mine."

Phil stood there for a very long time just breathing, as if he expected each breath to bring a fresh insight. Then, as if deciding there was no other alternative, he grabbed for a pistol on a nearby wall. Taking it in hand, he quickly aimed. But Hank was on him, and the mechanic's hands were suddenly around Phil's throat. They slammed him against the wall. The guns hanging there shuddered, some falling to the floor. Holding him there by his neck, Hank said, "If you want to work for me, you can. There'll be things to do and a good salary. But I'm boss. This place is mine."

"Dad," Teri cried, the metallic taste of blood in her mouth. "You can't work for him. He beat me up. I'm your daughter, Dad. I'm your daughter."

Hank's hand still around his throat, Phil managed to turn toward Teri. "This is business. Don't interrupt." Then Phil's eyes came back to Hank's. "What kind of salary?"

The state troopers working with the lake patrol spent about an hour determining that the attack was the work of four hoodlums out looking for a good time. Two had died, and the other two were babbling about a guy in an ape suit. When a state trooper arrived telling everyone that the bartender who was supposed to corroborate their story didn't know anything about a guy in an ape suit, they dragged Wink and Parsnips off to jail. Since people had died in the attack, the charges were serious.

The only incident of note occurred just after Win and Bray were pulled aboard the cruiser. Two shotgun blasts rang out. Wink's waverunner had ended up flying up the shale beach and knocking down the fruit stand's new center pole. The farmer had made sure the waverunner would never run another wave.

Ginger kept an arm wrapped around Win. Win, in turn, kept one wrapped around her. They sat on the injured cruiser's lower deck benches.

"You're quite the aquatic hero," Win pointed out, kissing her hair.

"I am, aren't I?" she admitted. "I don't get it. I'm scared of my own shadow out here, yet I'll do something like that."

"It's love," Win said. "You're crazy about me."

She jabbed him in the side, then laughed.

"And you're brave," Win said seriously. "Everyone's afraid of something. Brave people face their fears. Rise above them. Do what needs to be done. You're just plain brave."

Pam and Bray sat on the bridge.

"Breed's gonna love the modifications to his little boat here," Bray said.

"He'll love the insurance money more," Pam said. "There's a little larceny in Breed's wrinkled little heart."

"We should get back to the island," Bray said. "You coming?" he asked Pam.

Pam eyed him with a subdued resolve. "Nothing's changed," she said.

"A lot's changed," Bray affirmed. "You're here."

Neither Teri nor Randy had moved for nearly an hour. Randy's head rested in Teri's lap as she leaned against the sofa staring off somewhere.

Randy remained quiet. Not only because Teri was deeply troubled, but because even moving his lips caused his leg to catch fire. He'd never known such pain. Hank's kicking him hurt more than the bullet had in the first place. He wanted to hurt Hank back. Not because he'd kicked him, though in the old days that would have been enough, but because he'd struck the woman he cared for.

When Teri began crying, Randy spoke. "Talk to me," he urged. "Tell me what you're feeling."

More sobbing—no reply.

"Teri, I felt so helpless watching him hurt you. Maybe I can help with this."

Teri's sobs subsided, but only for a moment. They started up again.

"Teri, please."

She made a valiant effort to choke back the tears. "There's nowhere to turn. There's no one to turn to. There's no help anywhere. I'm no good, and God's never going to let me be anything but no good."

"We're all no good," Randy heard himself say. "We're all down there. I am anyway."

"You just trying to cheer me up?" she said sarcastically.

"In a way, yeah. The Bible says we're all sinners."

"And God's nailing me for it." She rubbed her cheek, still raw from Hank's blow.

"I'll get that guy—I really will. But that's not important now. You are, and there is someplace to go. Someone you can trust. Jesus."

"We've gone over this. I'm what I am. I'm every bit as bad as Hank. He's done nothing I didn't try to do."

"He hasn't called on Jesus for forgiveness. Hasn't called on Jesus to come into his heart and be his Lord and Savior. The Bible says that those who do will be forgiven and saved and live with him forever. And God loves his people, and he makes everything work out for good."

"Like your leg?"

"If I didn't have this leg, I wouldn't be talking to you like this."

"And I wouldn't be listening."

"See. Jesus is real, Teri. So very real. Since I've been hurt, he's never been so real to me. I know I'll be okay."

"Hank kicked you in your wound. You started bleeding again."

"And it stopped, and it's only pain. And you're here with me, and I love you."

Teri's eyes brightened. "You do? But you've only known me for a few days."

"Much longer. That's one of the reasons I want you to know Jesus. He's your father, not Mr. Money there. Jesus is; he'll take care of you."

Teri leaned her head back and allowed it to sink into the soft sofa cushion. "I'm so tired. I've never felt so far down in all my life. So abandoned and far down."

"Then call upon Jesus."

All Randy could hear was her breathing. Deep. As deep as the feelings that pulled the air in and blew it out.

"I can't. I can't forgive myself. I can't ask anyone else to forgive me. You have no idea what I've done. No idea."

"It doesn't matter what you've done. Not at all."

"It does to me. It does to me."

Hank found Sylvia sitting on the end of her bed watching the television on her dresser. Her eyes were large and vacant, and she looked like she'd been sitting there for days. She hardly moved when Hank stepped in.

"I came to tell you it's official. I'm taking over," he said.

Her head cocked and turned slightly, the effort colossal. She said nothing.

"Tommy and I are joining forces to keep the business going."

Sylvia looked at him for a long time. Then uncocked her head and returned to the television.

Completely ignored, Hank shrugged and left.

Without moving her eyes to follow him, she muttered, "And we'll see how much of your precious business is left—you miserable pig."

With the waverunner's rear still protruding from the cabin's bow windows, the cruiser glided to the visitor dock. Two guards, both suppressing laughter, tied the large craft up and assisted the two ladies onto the dock. Win and Bray followed, Bray substituting Win for his lost cane.

After a minute or two surveying for other damage and finding just a scratch or two, all four made their way toward the main house. Before they reached it, though, Bray, who'd been clinging to Win's shoulder for support, stopped. "It was a close call out there."

"Looks like they haven't ended."

"So you think—"

Pam placed a warm hand on Bray's arm and brought her eyes close to his. "Come home, sweetie. This just isn't working out for you."

Bray swallowed very hard. "You think that was planned out there?"

"I don't think anything," Pam said, her palms rubbing up and down his arms. "Even if there's nothing going on, it's time to come home and be with the people you know care about you."

"Bray," came a woman's voice from the side of the main house.

Obviously interrupted, they all turned to see the dramatically endowed Brandiwyne Hortentia strolling down the embankment toward them.

"The therapist," Bray told Pam, softly. Then he turned his attention to Brandi. "There's someone here I'd like you to meet."

"Wonderful, Bray," Brandi cooed. "But I did miss you today."

Pam stared as the buxom woman walked up and pushed out a stiff hand. Pam took it. "Pam Wisdom. Bray's friend."

"Oh, my, my, so many friends," Brandi said, taking the hand. "And it's no wonder. He's such a little sweetie."

"He's certainly a little something," Pam cooed back.

"But I have to go, Bray, dear. I've waited as long as I could and now must go to my next appointment. Shall I see you tomorrow?"

Pam took a breath to speak, but Ginger jabbed her.

Bray shook his head. "I think my visit's over."

Pam looked at Bray with deeply thankful eyes.

"Then I shall miss you," Brandi said, kissing Bray on the cheek before she made it to a small shuttle tied up near the cruiser. Looking up at the waverunner protruding from the cruiser, she smiled, "Entertaining callers?"

"It was quite a party," Bray said.

"Sorry I wasn't invited," she quipped, as her ride to the Grand Isles pulled onto the lake.

"Your therapist?" Pam exclaimed, the fire returning to her eyes.

"Great hands," Bray said.

"Mine are great, too," Pam said, forming a tight fist and driving it deeply into his side. "Want to see my other one?"

"Okay, you two," Win said.

"Me?" Bray groaned. "I'm getting abused, and you're accusing me."

They resumed their walk to the main house, Pam taking Win's place as cane and Win wrapping an arm around Ginger. "Boy, you feel good," he said.

"I want to say good-bye to Teri," Bray mentioned as they reached the commons.

"Did you say something about good-bye?" Hank said, appearing seemingly from nowhere. "You leaving? Can't blame you with what happened out there."

"It's time," Bray told him.

"You saw what happened?" Win asked.

"Just the end. I climbed up to the patio and saw the waverunner hit your boat there." He laughed. "Somethin' to see." He took a few steps toward the dock to get a better look at the waverunner protruding from the cruiser. "That's one of those new ones. Mucho power. Expensive. How much?" Then he stopped. "I want that thing. You want to sell it?"

"I'm not sure it's ours," Win said.

"Sure it is," Ginger said. "A guy gave it to me. Forced it on me. And the cops didn't want it. And I'm a cop, and I want to sell it."

"You sure?"

Hank reached into his back pocket and pulled out his checkbook. "I'll write you a check, and you tell me if it's enough."

Using a dock piling as a desk, he wrote it out.

"That could be evidence," Bray injected.

"Not anymore."

"Name?" Hank asked.

"Ginger Glasgow."

A second later Ginger was looking at a figure she couldn't believe. She handed it to Win who couldn't believe it either. "Ten thousand?"

"With the insurance and this," Ginger said, "Breed can get that bigger boat. I'll be a detective before you know it."

Hank studied it proudly. "I've tried to order one, and there weren't any available."

Hank turned to the guards and with a couple finger snaps told them what he wanted done. They hopped onto the cruiser and began figuring out how to extract Hank's new waverunner.

"Teri in her house?" Bray asked Hank.

"She left—she and Phil. They had things to do on the mainland."

"They did?"

"The doctor prescribed something for that guard of hers."

Bray studied Hank's face for a moment. There was something different about him. Normally his eyes danced with a certain rakishness. Not now. Although he was trying hard to maintain what used to be, he was failing. Anxiety had crept in. He was lying.

But Bray found he didn't care.

This particular family of his hadn't measured up.

"It'll take me a few minutes to gather my things. Pam, give me a hand."

Win and Ginger watched Bray hobble up the incline on Pam's arm. Then he turned to Hank, "I don't think that boat you lent us will be coming back."

"I saw the fire. Must o' been a little hairy there."

"Definitely hairy."

"Must o' been that gas leak. Anybody singed?"

"Just wet. Got thrown out just as it went up."

"That was lucky." Hank smiled and turned his complete attention to the extraction of the waverunner.

"Sure luckier than Bray's parents," Win said, his tone needle-like.

"Huh?"

"Their boat exploded, too, didn't it?"

Hank nodded as if he'd just become aware of the coincidence. "I was fourteen. Terrible. Didn't see it. Only heard about it."

Win wanted a different reaction. He wanted Hank to look guilty—he hadn't.

Bray stuffed underwear, socks, shirts, and the rest of his things in his duffel while Pam sat at the table near the balcony window.

"Nice room," she said, glancing around.

He didn't reply but just let his eyes feast on her. "It's been so long," he said.

"You know I love you, Bray."

Bray couldn't believe his ears. "I didn't know that. Not anymore, anyway."

"I do love you. I can't have you right now. But I love you. I pray for you every night, every morning. Just about every time I draw a breath."

"You're still hung up on that religious thing."

"God loves me too. And he wouldn't have me love you so much without something happening. I'm sure of that."

Bray didn't say anything for a long moment. "But I don't believe what you believe."

"And it's driving me nuts, I have to admit. Being in this room with you is driving me nuts."

Bray nodded and took an uncertain step toward her. He would have taken another but Pam's hand went up. "No. But I do love you."

They both heard a phone ring downstairs—twice. Someone answered. A moment later Win stuck his head in. "It was a heart attack. Bilba died of a heart attack."

"So you were wrong again?"

"And it won't be the last time," Win said, starting to leave. "Unless her heart failed while she was being—but," he continued with a renewed energy, "I guess we'll never know, will we?" Win returned to Ginger who waited for him downstairs.

Alone again, Bray eyed Pam longingly, then, when she remained firm, he shook his head with grim resolve and stuffed a few more things into the duffel. Grabbing the *Contusion*'s nameplate, he studied it for a moment.

"What's that?" Pam asked.

"It was cut from my folk's boat. The *Contusion*."

"Why do you have it?"

"Someone's playing games with me. Suggesting my folks were murdered."

"Murder seems to be a recurring theme around here."

"After today it's easier to believe. Harder to accept. My mom was a beautiful woman—a Latin look—dark, almond eyes. It's hard imagining her burning to death."

"Oh, Bray—" Pam winced. "Aren't there fond memories to replace those?"

He looked up from the nameplate. "Maybe some'll come to me later." But then he added, his eyes granite, "If it was murder, and if the murderer's still walking around, I can't stand the idea of him thinking he got away with it. I want no peace for that guy. None."

"But you'll never know. It's not worth dwelling on."

Slipping the name plate into his duffel, he said enigmatically, "We'll see."

When they joined Win and Ginger on the dock, Hank was watching four of his guys lower the waverunner to the water. "She's a beaut," he said to whoever was listening. "I love just riding around the lake on these things." A few minutes later, Pam and Bray on the bridge, Ginger and Win sitting among the debris in the cabin, the cruiser slid from dock and headed toward home.

As it broke onto the open lake, Teri saw it through the kitchen window. She'd seen Bray leaving the main house with his duffel, so she'd been prepared. An important part of her was leaving. A part that believed in her and truly cared for her. But it was right for him to leave. Her life was here. On the island. Doing what her family wanted her to do. She had been foolish thinking otherwise.

"What's going on?" Randy called from the sofa.

"Nothing," she replied. A few minutes later she joined Randy. She sat on the floor and held his hand while he rested.

Tommy leaned back in his chair and took a break from what he'd been doing. It wouldn't be long now before all the family money was brought together into one safe place. There were only a few more investments to liquefy. As he sat there thinking, the screen saver appeared, the tropical island, the breeze rustling through palm trees. Then Carlos appeared inviting him to Aguilar. He longed for that island, now more than ever.

Something caught his eye out the window—a cruiser easing south. *Nice boat,* he thought, and then realized who it was on the bridge. "Bray's leaving?" he said to himself. "No. Not now."

Then he stopped to think. "He'll come back," Tommy said. "Give him something dramatic enough, and he'll come back."

No matter how much money he'd been able to accumulate, he wasn't about to give up another million. People don't get and remain rich by ignoring the odd million.

As the island grew darker and smaller, Win and Ginger ventured from the cabin to the shallow rear deck. Sitting on the cushioned bench, they watched it slowly disappear.

"Not my vacation ideal," Win finally said.

"I'm just glad you got Bray off of it."

Win gave her a shallow nod and was about to slip his arm over Ginger's shoulder, when he froze.

"You okay?" Ginger asked. "It happened again, didn't it?"

Win looked at her for a long moment, then nodded. "I'm not sure where that one came from. It wasn't that spooky sense of dread I get, but it wasn't peace either." He sighed. "I hate this. I'm just not the right guy for it."

"What did it leave you with?"

Win gnawed on his lip. "That it's not over yet. We may be leaving, but it's not over yet."

Ginger didn't reply. Her breath caught in her throat, as she watched the island grow black on the horizon.

CHAPTER 21

I think you guys stepped off the end of the dock or something," Chad laughed as he overheard Win and Ginger recounting what they'd been through. "Devils in graves and you blasting through rocks. Wow! You guys had a wild time. Of course, not as wild as mine. I went to Ben and Jerry's Ice Cream Factory. Now *that's* fun."

Win laughed with him, finally feeling a sense of calm break over him. It seemed like forever since things had been "normal," and now they were again. His family-to-be sitting around the wrought-iron patio table, the adults sipping coffee and tea, and Chad drinking a soda.

A while later, with Chad off to a friend's to spend the night, Win and Ginger settled into an evening of mindless television. Both were emotionally drained and physically beaten up. Win's arm was hurting more than it had since the accident.

Ginger piped up during one of the commercials. "I still think we ought to see what they're doing out there."

"Intercept another one?" Win said unenthusiastically. "Tomorrow night. We'll do it tomorrow night."

"Fine. No. I've got the outreach committee at church tomorrow night. The night after. We'll do it then."

"It's all in one pile?" Hank exclaimed excitedly as he stood in Tommy's computer room.

"Accessible only by me."

Hank stiffened. "Only?"

"My insurance. That way we can't live without one another."

Hank nodded, still a long way from satisfied. "And what keeps you from taking off?"

"Honor. And I want to make more money. Actually nothing's changed. I could have taken off with it before and I didn't."

"Because you knew Breck would hunt you down like a dog."

"And you would, too. I know who you are—who your dad was. I have all the payment histories. You haven't had to do much enforcing lately, but you're capable of it. And then there's our customer. He isn't worried about the money so much as me being loose. No. I'm not going anywhere."

One of the screen savers came alive with Carlos' image again. Hank turned to get a peek at the bikini. When she gyrated on screen and the video ended, he returned to business. "You know about all the people we've done?" Hank looked coldly concerned.

"All. Don't worry. Mom was losing control of me. I needed to be controlled. Breck was the only one who could have done it. He told me that every day of my life. He was right, of course."

Hank nodded, not sure he believed him. "Okay. I guess I'll just have to treat you with more respect."

Tommy smiled coldly. "I'm sure we'll work well together."

Hank also smiled.

For Randy the real pain lasted only a day, then, to his surprise, he began to heal quickly. Before he knew it he was asking for the pair of crutches Teri had said she knew about.

As it turned out, she never would forget those crutches.

She'd seen them in the attic while looking for Bray's old things. When Randy asked for them, she'd wasted no time climbing up there. In this time of depression, in deep self-recrimination, Randy had become her only link to a happier, more fulfilling world, and she would do anything to maintain that link, even ferret through a dismal attic.

In the light from a naked, low-watt bulb, she found them quickly. Pushing an ancient box of shoes aside, she grabbed one of the crutches. The instant her hand touched the varnished wood, she was overcome by a tidal surge of what could only be *reality*. She began to cry. At first she didn't know why, but after a few seconds of uncontrolled sobbing, the *why* of it all bloomed all around her. She needed crutches too. Emotional crutches, spiritual crutches, something to hold her up, more than hold her up, carry her and nurture her and love her. Randy's words blossomed inside. Jesus. He would carry her. He would buoy her up and be with her through the storm she knew boiled on an approaching horizon.

A few minutes later, her eyes still red, she appeared before Randy, the crutches clutched firmly in her hand, her loving crutch, her cherished crutch held even more firmly in her heart.

"Randy, I've got something to tell you."

Working his way to his feet, Randy limped to her. Knowing instinctively what she was going to say, he wrapped strong arms around her. "Jesus is with you, isn't he?"

"I prayed myself. I couldn't wait. I wanted you there, but I couldn't wait."

He kissed her and hugged her and cried with her.

Then she pulled away. "There's something I have to do. We have to prepare for it. But it's got to be today. I've waited too long. It's got to be today."

Randy eyed her gravely. "I'm ready. Whatever it is, I'm ready."

Tommy watched the screen saver for the fourth time in as many minutes. Freedom. It was a new concept for him. All his life Breck and the others had drilled into him the notions of loyalty and commitment and obligation. But as he was gathering the money together, which Breck had always forbidden, something strange happened. Nothing. He had gone against Breck's training and nothing had happened.

It was a curious moment when he realized the only thing tying him to his past—to Breck, to Hank, to the island—were words. Only words. These shackles around his will—only words. And words wouldn't hold him.

Amazed, he replaced them with a new set of words. "You have millions, you can go anywhere you want, and if you choose where you go wisely, they'll never be able to get to you. Even if they find you, they'll never get to you." It became a mantra. "They'll never get to you." He repeated it again and again as he worked at the computer.

And as he worked to gather money, he worked on something else. He bought a whole new set of computers—ones more powerful than the ones he had. And he had them shipped to Aquilar, c/o Carlos, Governor's Palace.

That morning, the morning Teri found her eternal crutch, Tommy boated to the storage cave. Slipping as often as he stepped, he made it down the steep incline to the *Contusion*. He'd avoided having anything to do with the bones that lay there until he could avoid it no longer. Holding his breath he did what he had to do then climbed back up to the cave's entrance. With each step up the incline, his spirits rose. The steep incline, he began to believe, was a metaphor for the struggle of his life, and the exit, that moment when the sun shone on him again, was a symbol for what his life would be from that moment on.

When he returned to his office he wrapped up what he'd gotten in a box and charged a guard to deliver it to Bray's house. "Don't be seen," he'd ordered. Then, when alone again, he confirmed the seaplane he'd chartered a day before. All that done, he leaned back in his chair. Bray would get the package in about an hour. He'd reach the island a couple hours after that—about lunchtime.

Bray found the parcel when he returned from his morning therapy session at the Med Center. A box about the size that checks come in sat in his mailbox.

No markings—left by hand—a bomb?

With railings falling out from under him and waverunners trying to run him down, it sure could be.

Moving unsteadily, his leg having been reinjured in the waverunner wars, he headed for the Burlington Airport. Using his new cane, he hobbled to the baggage X-ray equipment, and, after showing his badge, he placed the box on the conveyor.

The technician, Bray beside her, gaped, then stopped the conveyor so she could make certain of what she'd seen. Bray felt a tear, and for an instant, turned away.

"A finger?" the technician exclaimed. "That a ring? Some paper—"

The technician didn't finish. Bray reached under and grabbed the box and tore it open. Seconds later he held something grotesquely familiar in his hand—the skeletal remains of a ring finger, the ring on it. He recognized the ring immediately. His mother's wedding ring—quite distinctive, two entwined hearts—and her finger. She'd broken it when he was a teen in a skiing accident and, having hated doctors, had treated it herself. Though it healed, it had healed imperfectly.

He read the note.

Who's responsible? Find out here.

There was a map. Clearly of Sanderson Island and a few others in the area. One about a mile from it toward St. Albans was marked with an arrow pointing to a prominent feature of some kind. The word *cave* scrawled at the top of the arrow.

Bray place the bone and ring gently back in the box, then closed it reverently as one might close a casket. Making it to a phone, he was about to punch in the number to Win's office at the Sorrell Inn when he stopped. Win would try to talk him out of going—or at least talk him into letting him go along—and Bray didn't want company. It could be, when he found out what he wanted to find out, that he'd have some business to take care of. And he wouldn't want a preacher along.

Instead, he called Win's home, got his answering machine, and left a quick message about the island, the markings on the map, and the cave. If something did happen to him, at least someone would know where to start looking. Then he drove as fast as he could to St. Albans.

Several things dampened Win's morning. He woke with a splitting headache, one of the first times he could remember. His broken arm hurt more than ever, and when he went out to get in his car to head for work, there was no car. Ginger had dropped him off the night before, and upon stepping outside that morning, he'd completely forgotten that his little Chevy was laying bent and blistered in a St. Albans' wrecking yard. His headache instantly got worse. As troubles often do, many distilled down to one: this morning's distilled to his car. He missed it. But more than missed it. That '54 Chevy had always meant independence for Win, and, in spite of reality, Win wanted to believe he was independent. And, since it was a fully restored '54 Chevy, it was unique—another desire of Win's.

But there was no bringing it back. A letter waiting for him from the insurance company said they were totaling it. Enclosed was a check for a thousand bucks—after his deductible, what they figured an old junk like that was worth. They called the settlement generous. Maybe that's where the headache came from.

Mel picked him up, but Win lasted only an hour at work. Since the Inn only had aspirin, he returned home for some Extra Strength Tylenol. So, as it turned out, Win got Bray's message about fifteen minutes after Bray left it.

Teri wrapped her arms around Randy and held him more tightly than ever before. The time had come. She'd known the Lord less than four hours, and she was about to change her life physically as irrevocably as the Lord had changed it spiritually. To prepare, she and Randy had spent those four hours in the Word. About an hour of it in the Twenty-third Psalm.

"Randy," she finally said about 11:45 A.M., "we're going to escape."

"I'm for it," he said.

"In five minutes I want you to meet me at the visitor dock. Ten minutes after that we're out of here."

Five minutes later she pulled up to the dock piloting one of the dull black, souped-up Sea-Doos. After helping Randy on board she planted him at the controls, then pointed toward the little island. "Wait for me at that cove," she said. "Be ready to go full throttle the moment I'm back."

Lunchtime.

There were several reasons to do it during lunch. First was *no security*. Workers and guards came and went as they pleased with no security system to stop them. At night the little island became a fortress.

Second, during lunch all the workman would be in the underground lunchroom away from the equipment. They left it all completely unguarded. She could easily get inside the operations room, do what she needed to do, then escape to the surface of the little island in the confusion.

At ten to twelve, Teri headed to the main house and the pantry elevator.

Bray made it to St. Albans and rented a small outboard at the pier. Climbing in, cane and all, he fired up the little fifteen-horsepower motor and pointed it toward the island indicated on the map.

Teri reached the lunchroom and immediately had to avoid Hank. He appeared more anxious than she'd ever seen him. His eyes looked tired, and bags hung below them like satchels. Had he seen her he would have undoubtedly nailed her with a string of unanswerable questions, but he was so preoccupied that when he passed, she ducked into the operations room, and he missed her completely.

Turning from the door, Teri was surprised to find that she wasn't alone. Sylvia was there scurrying from this machine to that, from this storage compartment to the next.

"Sylvia?"

The large woman stopped. "What are you doing here?"

"Uh—"

"Well, you better get out of here right now. This place is going up."

"Going up?"

"Get out!" Sylvia cried.

"You're blowing it up? Me too."

Now Sylvia laughed. "You? Why?"

"Our business—it's just plain wrong."

"Wrong. Who cares? That stinkbomb of a husband's not getting it. This is hate and revenge—and I'm loving every minute of it." Then Sylvia lit a Bic lighter. "Now get out, right now."

Teri bolted from the room and slammed the steel door behind her just as the door shuddered. A horrendous explosion. First everyone heard the blast, then they felt the quake. The door blew open, flames spewing into the hallway.

Confusion was everywhere. Men shouted orders to one another, others grabbed a couple of fire extinguishers, still others just ran about. All in one another's way.

Teri bounded from man to man, wall to wall, the confusion boiling all around her. Now there was fire. Acrid black smoke billowed from the ops room filling the passages with something she couldn't breathe. Bending low to find air, she continued her frantic flight.

Every turn must have been the right one, for Teri bubbled to the surface before she knew it. A good thing, too, for only after she took her first gulp of the fresh air, did she realize how close she was to being overcome by the smoke. Bursting from the camouflaged door, she took only a moment to recover, then ran to the prearranged point. With Randy waiting, she bolted down the embankment and literally dove into the Sea-Doo.

"Boy, you did a job on them," Randy exclaimed.

"I didn't do anything," Teri told him. "But punch it. We gotta get out of here."

Without another thought, Randy rammed the throttle forward. The supercharged engine screamed and the boat all but leaped from the water. But before they'd gone thirty feet, he pulled it back. Teri had spotted someone thrashing in the lake. "Pull over," she told Randy. A few seconds later, both of them pulled Sylvia on board. Although she'd displayed strength in the water, when she lay on the floor of the little boat, she looked pretty grim. Most of her clothing had been burned away, and her hands and face had been severely scarred by flames.

"I need help," she whispered through a smoke-damaged throat. "Help."

Randy punched the throttle and headed for St. Albans.

Bray circled the island twice before he found the cave. It lay beneath a large granite monolith, the prominent feature depicted on the map, its entrance protected by boulders.

With a throbbing leg, it was no picnic getting from the boat to the cave entrance, but after several false starts he finally made it. Leaning against a boulder, waiting for his strength to return, he peered into the dark cave and mentally prepared himself to enter.

The cave was little more than a black hole, the first few steps, the only ones he could see, falling away at a steep angle. With the darkness and the catacomb of silence, it was like standing at the entrance to a huge conch shell.

"What am I getting into here?" he muttered, standing with the aid of the cane on the brink. "Well, no mouse ever got the cheese standing outside the trap." Planting the tripod cane on the first step, he crossed the stone threshold. The instant he did a light came on, washing the cave in anemic yellow.

Amid musky smells of moss and mold were stacks and stacks of stuff—boxes, machines, lumber, chairs, what looked like a piano. Obviously a storage bin. A deep, stone storage bin. And somewhere down there was what *whoever* wanted him to find. Was it a trap? It didn't matter. Trap or not he was going down. Would he find his mother and father? If he did he vowed to give them a proper burial just before he found the guy who'd left them there.

He began his trek.

Step by step, breath by breath.

About twenty feet down he came upon something that told him what they'd been doing on the little island. His heart went sick. Sitting on a wooden bench, probably stacked there by some workman, were several oblong metal plates, each about a foot long and six-inches wide. He pulled one off the top and held it to the light. Plates for the printing of money. This one contained the image of what looked like the Queen of England—pound notes. Another looked like an Italian lira. Counterfeiting. A deep breath to fight back the rage. Did Phil truly believe he would become partners in a counterfeiting ring?

Setting the plate back on top of the pile, he vowed to have all this stuff picked up later. Although he had no idea what he'd do after that.

Another couple steps and his cane slipped, and he had to steady himself against a box. It gave way, and he sat on it. The box split and clothing spilled out. He recognized a dress his mother wore. "Tommy was right—they don't throw anything away."

On his feet again, the ache in his leg renewed, he hobbled another ten yards. That was when he spied the boat's charred remains. Without thought for safety, he scrambled to it.

"Oh, God," he whispered. There they were. Lying exposed on the bottom of the boat—just like in the grave at the butterfly house—bones. Charred and disconnected, loose—ribs, legs, two skulls—his parents—defiled by the rawest indifference.

Rage billowed inside him. He couldn't take his eyes off them, and then, after several seconds, he could look no more. His guilt was so great. Heavy, pervasive. He'd left them. He had severed the cord, which in itself wasn't wrong, but deep inside he had known the danger they were in. And if he didn't, he should have. *He should have.* Now he was alive, and they lay in what was no more than a pile of garbage.

Something broke through his thoughts. He would never know what it was, a sound, an echo, just a sense. It didn't matter. He looked up. A black silhouette against the cave's brilliant mouth. "Who's there?" Bray called.

"G'bye Bray," the silhouette said in a voice whose identifying characteristics were lost in echo—but there was no mistaking the threat. The shadow disappeared.

"I got a problem," Bray muttered. He wasn't sure exactly what it was, but he did know the solution lay outside—in the safety of the lake. His injured leg screaming from his first step, he began scrambling up the slimy surface.

After only a couple feet, a violent explosion rocked the mouth of the cave. A cloud of rubble erupted and at least two of the boulders were torn off their foundations. Instantly, the lake, great, frothy waves of it, thundered in! Slamming against the things stacked on the incline, great fists jarred and rattled them, dislodging most, carrying some along toward Bray.

Speeding away, Tommy thrilled at the sight of the explosion. It didn't seem loud enough, but that didn't matter, it was over now. The ceiling had come down burying Bray, and water was filling in the cracks. Perfect.

Pulling *Savage*, his boat, around, he headed toward the seaplane that was already revving its engine. There was something romantic about a seaplane—so Indiana Jones. His tropical destination fit quite well.

Acting on instinct, Bray managed to ignore the pain and leaped atop the *stuff* and scrambled as best he could toward the cave entrance. The water rushed by like a mad torrent hugging the steep floor. Fortunately, it wasn't deep enough to cause him too much grief yet, but if the cave had an end, the water would quickly begin rising.

Leg crying for relief, he climbed over this box and that, finding a foothold here, another there. He was actually making progress when he noticed, just above his head, out of reach, electric wiring tying together several nodes—each node looking very much like more explosives.

They were supposed to have gone off, too, he thought, but they hadn't. A malfunction. One that could right itself any second. Fighting for more strength, he continued to climb, the water churning below, the explosives just above.

The boxes below him gave way, throwing him into the cascading river. He slid back at least ten feet before he found a handhold. Unable to ignore the pain, he managed to get on top again. He took a second to catch his breath before starting the climb again. This time he chose his footholds more carefully.

He remembered the Navajo bear in his breast pocket—his good luck charm. If there was ever a time he needed good luck, this was it. He took it out and held it in his right hand, his non-cane hand, and continued climbing.

He saw a spark—something ahead—something near the mouth of the cave in the shadows—something sparking, and sparking again. He squinted, forcing his eyes to see what it might be.

Although he couldn't see it clearly, he saw it plainly enough. A wire hung loose, and it was brushing against something metal. To his horror, the network of wires strung above his head terminated in the area of those sparks. That's probably why they hadn't gone off—but, if that wire made contact with the wires above his head, they probably would.

Bray kept his legs churning. Climbing from this thing to that.

A new sound: Gurgling, rushing thunder, from far down in the cave. Had the river hit bottom? Bray spun around. Far beyond the light something was happening. At the rate water was falling, if it had hit bottom, it wouldn't take long to fill this hole. With no time to waste, Bray planted a foot on what turned out to be the counterfeit plates and pushed off.

The stack gave way. Arms and cane flailing, Bray toppled backwards, and when he did, several hundred pounds of steel pinned his good leg to the stone floor.

Recovering from the initial shock, he worked like a demon, pushing the plates frantically aside, the good-luck charm slapping each plate as he moved it.

The gurgling became a muffled roar. The water *was* on its way up.

With the last of the plates off of him, he got to his feet and pushed off with his good leg. A stiletto pain exploded below the skin. "Good God," he cried. "I've broken it!"

But pain only matters if you let it matter. Right? He decided not to let it matter. He pushed off again.

It mattered.

The pain was volcanic.

His bad leg was now his good leg, and his only hope was to launch himself with it.

Dragging the broken one behind like so much baggage, he pushed himself from box to machine, from machine to junk, the pain in the broken leg excruciating.

But he kept going. Inch by inch.

He turned, more to give himself a rest than to see what was coming, and instantly he wished he hadn't. The water was coming—way down the cave, but it was coming very fast. It would engulf him soon.

He pushed off with his better leg, again and again. But each time he did, the pain increased and the distance he covered decreased.

"It's time to start producing!" he cried to the charm.

That instant he placed his weight on what looked like an iron printing press. It gave way, and when it settled, his broken leg was pinned to the stone floor again.

Raging against his death, he threw the charm against the cavern wall then tried desperately to push the press aside. But not only was the press incredibly heavy, but the better leg fired salvo after salvo of pain at his heart, ricocheting and hitting his will. After the next try, he found it increasingly difficult to keep fighting.

"Win!" he cried to the stone. "Where are you?"

Any echoes were swallowed by the approaching water. He tried to dislodge the press again, but it didn't budge.

"You're up there, aren't you, God?" he cried. "You gonna just watch me die? If it were Win down here, you'd save him—but me—" Then he muttered, "I'm not worth saving, am I." Muttered it because he believed it. For the first time in his life he believed that. He'd deserted his mom. She'd needed him, and he'd deserted her. Left her with hungry lions. "God, you know I'm a cynical old goat. Win's not delusional. You're real. And I've let you down in a million ways. I deserve what you've got waiting for me. Hell, death—whatever. I deserve it."

He looked down. The water was bubbling toward him. As it touched a light, the bulb popped. Would the lights be going out soon? Would he die in the dark? A jolt of pain slammed into his heart. He took another shot at the press. It didn't move. He kicked it again and again. The rage growing, exploding in his breast. "God—is this the end? Will I never know you in this world? Jesus—are you there Jesus? Will I never know you like Win does? Will I ever?"

Bray seldom cried. There was an iron core within him that refused to be touched—only a handful of people had ever or could ever touch him. Now the iron core was crumbling, and with it came tears. And so, when he noticed the figure before him he saw it through tears—silver tears—a hand reaching out to him, a vision? Jesus? It had to be. He'd come. "Oh, Jesus—it's you!"

Suddenly the printing press was thrown off his leg. Strong arms scooped him up. One of them stiff, bulbous—a cast.

"Win? What—"

But he never got it out of his mouth. The water was on them, bubbling up around their ankles, their knees.

"I was too late," Win cried, his expression bearing its own pain, probably from his arm. Even as he said it, though, he kept his legs churning. But the water was to their waists, then their chests.

What happened next never could be completely understood. They could see it happening afterwards, could explain it and people would nod like they understood, but Win and Bray never truly understood. The fist of water had passed it sometime before, but Bray's parents' boat, the bones having been washed away, suddenly burst from the rising fountain. As if it were the palm of a hand, it scooped the two of them up. Cradled there, they rode the crest of the fountain to the mouth of the cave. When there, the boat slapped against the "teeth," catapulting both of them into the lake.

The boat must have touched the dangling wire, for the instant they hit the water there was another deafening explosion. Dust, rock, and assorted debris blew from the cave, a few of the larger pieces struck the water near them. It was all followed by a tremendous growl from deep within the earth. As the cavern roof gave way, a massive wave of displaced water spewed out in a bursting plume. It hit the lake, pushing them even further from the island. It also pushed the boat.

"Can you hang on while I get the boat?" Win asked.

"Leg hurts like mad, but all that means is I'm alive. You'll never guess who I thought you were." Then he paddled for a moment. "You know," he said, the realization taking a deep root, "in a real sense, you were."

Teri and Randy sat in the Northwest Medical Center's waiting room. They'd been there over three hours when a doctor came to them. "You family?" he asked.

"She's my father's cousin," Teri said.

"Then I'm sorry. She died—shock. We could never revive her."

Teri's eyes closed involuntarily. When they opened, she walked to a nearby pay phone, dropped a quarter in the slot, and punched in the number. "Hank there?"

A moment later Hank answered. "Yeah."

"How's the fire?"

"Teri? Everything's gone. It'll take millions—"

"Aunt Sylvia's dead—your wife is dead."

There was silence. "Dead? How?"

"She did it. She was severely burned."

More silence. "*She* did it?" Even longer silence. "She's dead?" There was a long silence, then he hung up.

Teri returned to the doctor. "I've told her husband."

They left and when they got into Teri's car, Randy turned to her. "I'm not sure what we should pray for, but I'm feeling the overwhelming need to bring the Lord into this thing."

"Randy. I don't know how to tell you this. But I think we ought to pray for us. I think we're an *us* now. I'm not going back to that place. I want to read the Bible and pray all the time—Randy, we're an *us*. And what's more, I think I love you. Aunt Sylvia just died. How can I be telling you something so wonderful when Aunt Sylvia just died?"

"Maybe because the future belongs to us now."

"Us and the Lord—that's the way it'll be. I want to go someplace where there's space—lots of space—Kansas, maybe, or Wyoming. And no islands to live on. And I want to be there with you and the Lord."

Randy pointed the car south, and, after several hours, west.

Bray hadn't spoken since Win pulled him as gently as he could into the boat. Now they were only a few yards from docking. Bray looked up at his friend. "I thought you were Jesus."

"I heard you say something like that."

"I thought you were him because I know him."

Win tried not to leap up and cry wondrous praises to heaven. "You know him."

"He's real. You're right. I've been very wrong. I'm still what I am. Every bit of what I am. But I know Jesus now."

"You've taken him as your Lord and Savior."

"He brought you a while ago. He's shown himself to be both."

Without another word, Win brought the boat in and tied it off. Finding a couple of old oars, he made a splint for Bray's leg as Teri had done for his arm what seemed like centuries ago.

With the help of bystanders, he got Bray into the back of Mel's Taurus wagon. "Next stop the med center."

"Good—I need it—I been wondering if there will ever come a day when I won't."

Win looked at his friend for a lingering moment. "I love you, Bray," he said and had meant nothing more deeply.

"Kiss me, and you're dead."

CHAPTER 22

The Grand Isles Community Church, the church Win and Mel Flowers pastored, met at Martin Sorrell's Inn, a large, white structure that seemed to glisten even more brightly since Win and Ginger had helped Martin rid himself of some unwanted guests a month or so before. Situated on the shore, the large, green lawn gave way to a small guest beach and was punctuated by the most spectacular rose garden on the isles. And now that the New York forest fire had been beaten into submission, the colors were even more spectacular. Martin Sorrell loved his roses. He also loved Mary Seymour, and they planned to marry the week before Christmas. When Mary had met Martin, she was in a difficult situation, which was cleared up at the same time and for the same reason that Martin's Inn was returned to him. Mary was now the picture of cheer, her nut-brown hair short and pert, her moss green eyes sparkling. And since Martin was very rich, and because he wanted to please her whenever he could, Mary was in a position to do something special for Ginger.

"You're kidding," Ginger gasped when Mary told her what she had planned. "In the rose garden?"

"I've invited the other women in the church, but it's especially for you. We just want to be a part of it."

"Really?"

"You bet. All of us want to see you choose your wedding dress. And since I'm getting married, I really want to see them too. But it's your day. I'll have the bridal shops in town put on a fashion show for you. Then, when you see the one you like—"

"But we're really on a budget—"

"Not any more. Martin's worked it out with Mel that Win's to get a bonus equal to the price of the dress, then Martin's going to donate the money."

"You're kidding—I can't—"

"Sure you can. You and Win have been so incredibly special to us. There wouldn't even be an us without you two. This is the least—and I mean the very least—we can do."

Ginger couldn't believe her ears. She immediately gave Mary a huge hug. "You're so wonderful, thank you."

"Then this coming Saturday afternoon at two, you'll be here?"

"You couldn't keep me away."

Phil Sanderson stood at the center of the commons, perhaps over Uncle Breck's grave, though he wasn't sure. The fire had destroyed most of the island's buildings, the soot and debris falling thick everywhere.

The fire had started with a mysterious explosion on the little island. It had spread quickly through the tunnel to the large island. Climbing the pantry elevator it had rooted itself in the main house's ancient wood. Before anyone could react, the flames had devoured each house in turn. Miraculously Phil's had been spared. Oh, there'd been some singed edges, but the fire had never taken hold.

Hank stuck around after the blaze. Even with all the damage, he still blustered about pushing his kingship on everyone left. He talked incessantly about rebuilding and retooling and how this was an opportunity to make the operation even better. That ended that morning when he and Phil discovered, through contact with their customer, that Tommy had absconded with everything. And not only absconded with everything, but had probably gotten away with it.

"He's at that island?" Phil exclaimed into one of two phones that survived the fire.

"Drag him off," Hank cried on the extension.

"Can't," came the reply. "We've got the place surrounded. I got an army on the Venezuelan docks waiting for him—meeting every ship. I've got boats surrounding the place. There's no way off. But they won't let us on, either. And even if we could get on, he's holed up in the palace. He thought it through."

There was a long silence. Then Hank said, "Easy come, easy go—too blasted easy. You willing to advance us enough money to rebuild?" Hank asked his customer.

"You're kidding, right? Breck we trusted; you just burn things down."

Gnawing his lower lip for a moment, Hank finally hung up. "Well, I guess I'll go fix cars again."

Not long thereafter, Hank was gone.

Phil was the family head again. And since Teri had disappeared and Sylvia was dead, he was the executive in charge of a million pounds of ugly, black charcoal.

With no money to rebuild—because he didn't want insurance adjusters on his island, Uncle Breck had insisted on being self-insured—and no money for employees, Phil was alone. Maybe if he started his own vegetable garden, maybe got a job on the mainland, he'd at least be able to keep the island from takeover by the tax collectors.

"Think she's really going to pick a dress this time?" Bray asked as Win launched Chad's aluminum boat from the small trailer. They were a little south of the fruit stand.

"She's just particular," he said. "She's only getting married once—more."

Getting into the boat was no easy task. Bray's leg, like Win's arm, was wrapped in a thick cast, and his better leg was seriously sprained. Yet, to everyone's surprise, he was able to get around remarkably well on crutches. He sat in the boat waiting for Win. "It's hard to see the damage from here."

"Maybe it's not as bad as the guy said," Win suggested.

It was. Every bit as bad.

Win helped Bray onto the partially burned visitors' dock.

When on the commons, they stood before the ruins awestruck.

Each had his reason for coming. Bray's required the head of the family, whomever that happened to be. And, since the island appeared deserted, Win decided to satisfy his desire first. Someone or something had humiliated him at Breck's grave—had driven him to his knees—planted a dark fear in his heart. Walking boldly toward the grave, he had but one objective—a single act of defiance that would somehow even things up. He'd thought about it for quite a while the night before. It was the perfect statement of contempt, fearlessness, indifference.

He planned to stand at the foot of the grave and spit on its head. However, as he approached that horrible sense of dread took root again—a tightness in his heart, the sense of being hunted by evil.

Win stopped. "Flee from danger," he heard himself quote from Scripture. He stood there only a moment longer, the feeling of intense dread continuing to grow. No. This was not the place for him. His act of defiance had nothing to do with the grave—instead, it had everything to do with living a godly life for Christ.

While he still could, he turned, and with head held high, returned to Bray's side.

Standing there, they both heard the thin whine of an outboard approaching the dock.

A few minutes later Phil appeared carrying a couple of plastic grocery bags. Seeing the two men, he stopped. "You guys come to gloat?"

"To talk. Everybody else gone?" Bray asked.

"Hank, Teri, and Tommy are gone. No money to pay guards. Don't need 'em anyway. Sylvia's dead—you knew that, right?"

"No," Bray said with a sense of loss. "How?"

"As a result of the fire. We buried her next to Breck. Fire took it all. You should have seen Teri's place go up. All that ammunition. A morbid Fourth of July." Phil turned. "Come to my place—we'll have a beer."

"No. I just came to ask you something."

Phil nodded unaffectedly.

"Did you know my mom and our dad were murdered? Did you know that Warlock Breck had them stored in that cave?"

Phil's eyes widened. "No. But I've found out a lot in the last few days."

Bray stood staring at him for a long, tense moment. "Believing you is hard. Very hard. I know what you were doing on the little island."

"You do? How?"

"I found evidence. Where I found Mom and Dad." Another long, horrific pause. "What you were doing here killed them. Whenever you do something like that, people are going to get hurt—die in this case—even babies—" Bray saw in the back of his head the tiny bones in that hollowed-out grave. "If there was any proof left, I'd see you hanged. But there's nothing. And now I'm supposed to forgive you. My savior says so. He and I are going to have long talks about that because right now I want to rip your heart out." Bray brought a trembling finger up, and his words were launched with a great force of angry passion. "Don't ever, ever, even think about doing it again. Never."

"Can't. Can't even afford the ink."

"And you wanted to recruit me for this. You're a sick man. Sick."

"I couldn't bring myself to kill you. Breck would have paid me a million dollars to do that. But you're my brother. So I thought I should do the next best thing—bring you into this thing."

"I'll have the locals watching you every minute."

"I believe you will."

Bray and Win left him there.

Phil didn't wave. Feeling an overwhelming sense of emptiness, he walked to the commons and was continuing on toward his house when he noticed two men. One sat on the fallen palm tree while the other stood several steps back. While the sitting guy looked at Phil with granite eyes, the one further back grinned, and when he did, his right arm cocked back and he launched something toward Phil. Dumbstruck, Phil watched the thing spin and repeatedly glint off the bright afternoon sun. When it was obvious that it was heading near him, he spun out of the way. It struck and stuck in a foot-square hunk of debris near his foot. A stiletto.

"I didn't think they would ever leave," the sitting man said as he got to his feet.

"Who are you?" Phil asked them. "And why the knife?"

"Got some good news and some bad news."

They walked steadily toward him. The grin had returned to the knife thrower.

Phil had trouble breathing. "Who are you?"

"First the good news. We're going to pay your taxes on the island—in your name—so the Sandersons will always own it."

"You are? Then thank you." His head cocked. "But why?"

"That's part of the bad news. We've been sent by your former customer. This, here, is Charlie. Shake the man's hand, Charlie."

The grin unchanged, Charlie pushed out a hand. Phil, knowing what was good for him, reluctantly shook it. "Now for the bad news. Charlie's my best guy. Works hard. Kills people."

Phil swallowed a dry lump.

"The bad news is, you ain't never gonna leave this island. We just don't trust you. Now Charlie here needs a vacation."

"Vacation," Charlie repeated, reaching down to retrieve the knife.

"He's gonna come live with you for as long as you live."

Another hard swallow.

"And we're payin' Charlie a hundred grand to keep you alive."

Phil felt a wave of relief crash over him.

"Now, you're what? Fifty-something? Your life expectancy's about twenty more years? Now if you die of natural causes— old age, heart attack—Charlie gets the money. If he puts a shiv in your gut, he gets nothing. How long will it take, do you think, for Charlie to just get tired of waiting for you to die? How long to do you think, Charlie?"

"How 'bout an accident," Charlie asked.

"That's natural causes sure enough."

"Then it might not take long at all," Charlie laughed surveying the fire's handiwork. "Does feel a little like the old neighborhood—might lounge around a little while." And Charlie grinned at Phil again.

"Why don't you just shoot me. Why this?"

Now it was the spokesman's turn to grin. "It's just me. When I was growin' up my mom used to scream at me every night. 'Lids,' she'd say, 'don't play with your food.' And I used to keep hamsters and those tunnels and things. Set rat traps for 'em in there. They come out of one of them tunnels and *snap!* Just my little way of havin' fun."

Phil's relief was replaced by a thundering breath. "What about Hank? What about him?"

"He ain't sayin' nothing. He let us down, but it wasn't his fault. He's okay. We'll let him be. Gotta go. Take good care of him, Charlie. At least for a while," Lids laughed.

Moments later Phil watched him disappear toward the lower, hidden dock. Looking up at Charlie, he could only groan. *The wheel of life turns real fast sometimes*, he thought. Then he back-stepped toward the house, his eyes glued on Charlie and the knife he used to clean his fingernails.

Ginger dangled bare feet off the dock that bordered the Sorrell's boathouse. She sat there alone having gone there when the others had left. Mary Seymour, a far more gracious hostess than Ginger could ever be, had ushered her guests out at the end of the fashion show, leaving Ginger to think.

She and the others had been shown at least thirty wedding gowns. All types, all designs, each with a beauty of its own. It was the twenty-first that Ginger had fallen in love with. A snow white wonder, delicately beaded and laced. It was magnificent.

The instant she'd seen it she felt tears working themselves to the surface. She'd fought most of them back, having shed only a couple of secret ones. But when it was over, and she'd been asked which she liked best, she had said, "They're all so beautiful. I don't think I can make up my mind."

Some of the ladies pressed her a little, wanting an answer even if there wasn't one. Finally Pam, her eyes calm, told the others to leave dear Ginger alone, "She knows what she's doing—don't you, Sweetie."

Pam was right. Ginger did know what she was doing. And why? Seeing that dress, that wonderful dress, that magnificent, everything-she-ever-wanted dress terrified her more than those rocks on the lake—those toothy devils the cruiser had squeezed through. If she bought that dress, if she invested all her hopes for the future in that dress, when the wedding failed to occur she would be totally, irrevocably crushed.

Alone, her toes kicking at the water, she decided that it would be best to get married in a flower sack.

Then, when the wedding didn't happen, she could store manure in it or something.

"What happened?" Tommy shouted to anyone who could hear him. He sat in his small room in the governor's palace. His room essentially had two things—his bed and his computers. Suddenly his computers—his lights, his monitors, everything—died. Like someone had pulled the plug.

Running from the room, he found his friend, Carlos, standing before an open cabana door. "Carlos, what happened?"

Carlos sighed. "It's just Venezuela flexing its muscles."

"What's that mean? My computers went off."

"They've voted to annex our little island country."

"Annex?"

"They've been trying to get the votes for years. My father wasn't able to stop them this time. But we will defy them. We are a sovereign nation. They cannot push us around. Our resolve is like iron."

"But what about the electricity?"

"We, of course, have refused to cooperate. We get electricity, oil—all energies from them. They've cut us off. But don't worry, they won't invade. They just want to make it hard on us."

"They cut off the electricity?"

"But we don't need it. We have emergency generators and enough gas for them—for the time being—and we have all the food and water we could ever use. We pick our meals right from the trees or pull them right from the sea. We don't need their electricity."

"But I do."

"Computers? With all this sunshine?"

"I need computers. I need them."

Carlos laughed. "You *need* food and water, and we have both in abundance. And we, as a nation, need our freedom."

Tommy all but fell into a nearby chair. "But I need them. To get at my money. How can I access my life without my computers?"

"Well," said Carlos, "while my father and I are alive, you won't have them. But you are safe. We know they're waiting for you if you leave, so you may stay here rent free."

I can't leave, he thought. *This is my only sanctuary. I'm a sitting duck out there.*

Tommy groaned deeply, the tropical air all but gone from his lungs.

"You couldn't find one?" Win asked, incredulously.

"They were all so beautiful," Mel Flowers inserted, being the only man invited. It was a pastor's privilege. Even Martin Sorrell had been banished to his basement greenhouse.

"I'm sure there's a wedding dress out there somewhere," Ginger said, her voice betraying a sadness.

They were at Ginger's, Mel having dropped Win off after he and Bray had returned to Sorrell's Inn. Ginger's jazz station played sweetly in the background. Mel sorted through some of Ginger's CDs while she and Win put a light salad together in the kitchen. Mel was staying for dinner.

"I need a car," Win said. "I guess I'll go looking for a used one tomorrow. I sure do miss the Chevy."

"I'll help you look," Ginger offered.

"You really do need one," Mel advised from the living room.

"I keep telling myself it was just a car—," Win said. "But it's my '54 Blue Chevy. I'm gonna end up driving a Hyundai or something. That's not me. Teri Sanderson owes me a car. Think I'll ever collect?"

"Who's he, and how does he owe you a car?" Mel asked.

"He's a she. And I'll give you the whole story at dinner," Ginger told him.

Mel nodded and went back to the CDs.

A knock on the door.

Win opened it and found Bray and Pam there.

As they entered, Pam said in an irritated tone, "He's asked me to marry him."

"It made her mad," Bray confirmed, right behind her on his crutches. "Hi, Mel." Then as he closed the door, "It's a real parking lot out there."

"It's too soon," Pam protested.

"It's not too soon."

"We've only known each other—well, dated—we've only cared for each other a few months. It's too soon."

"We've known each other almost ten years."

"You're not counting the Diane years?"

"We *knew* each other."

Mel piped up but managed a pastoral tone. "It's too soon."

Bray stopped short. "Oh," he said.

Win thought. "Why don't you be engaged to be engaged?"

"I've heard of that," Ginger acknowledged.

"Okay, we're that."

"I haven't said yes yet," Pam told him, a proud edge to her voice.

"You'll think about it, right?"

"Sure. Thinking's free."

Satisfied, Bray wielded his crutches around to face Ginger. "This came for you," Bray said, handing Ginger a letter-sized envelope.

"Who sent this?"

"There's no return address. Someone who knows my address but not yours."

Without hesitating Ginger tore the envelope open and pulled a single sheet from it. While she drifted away reading, Bray turned to Win, "When did you get your car back?"

"What?"

"Your car's out there. When did you get it back? I thought they were going to sell it for parts."

Win's expression turned to a question mark as he ran out front. There it sat. His blue '54 Chevy. Not a scratch on it, shining brilliantly in the afternoon sun. Except for Ginger, Win could imagine nothing more beautiful. Drinking in every element, Win circled it once, then circled it again. The others just watched.

"You didn't know about this?" Bray asked, leaning deeply on his crutches.

Mel pointed to the ignition. "The keys are in it."

Pam pointed toward the passenger seat. "A note."

Now it was Win's turn to grab an envelope. Win read the note inside. *I thought you'd want this back. Love, Dad.* Win's eyes suddenly went up and he looked around, up and down the street, at every tree and house. "He'd want to see my reaction. He's around here somewhere." Standing in the middle of the street, Win called out, "Dad, I know you're around here somewhere. Thank you." Win suddenly felt something he'd never felt before, a desire to give his father a huge hug. "You understand. He truly understands."

But his father didn't appear. And a few moments later, the finished letter still in hand, Ginger, who had been watching from the walkway, stepped forward. "He loves you, Win. Always has. Just didn't know how to say it."

"I can't believe he did this." Again Win turned, studying every potential hiding place.

"I can't believe it took him so long," Ginger said pulling his attention back to her. She accomplished this by slipping gentle arms around his neck and bathing in his eyes. "I want to say something," she whispered.

Unwilling to break this wonderful connection with words of his own, he only nodded.

"I love you, Win Brady, and I know you love me. Marrying you, spending the rest of my life with you, will be the greatest, most fulfilling adventure of my life. And, as a first step on the road to that adventure, we're going to take this sort of new car of yours and go someplace."

"Where?"

"There's this wedding dress I want to buy."

"There is?" Pam sparkled, her eyes filled with questions.

Ginger handed her the letter she'd gotten as she slipped an arm into Win's. "That was a neat thing your dad did," she said.

"Exceptionally." Again his eyes looked around. "I know he's around here somewhere."

"You'll have to call him. But before you do, let's get that dress."

"You're anxious."

"Very. Come on." Ginger turned to Pam and Bray. "There's salad fixings in the kitchen. We'll put something together when we get back. Chad's at a friend's—we'll pick him up on the way home. We'll be an hour or so." Then she turned to Win. "You'll have to stay outside in the car. But that'll give you just that much more time to admire it."

Mel, Pam, and Bray watched the Chevy disappear down the road.

"What's in the letter?" Mel asked, his tone curious and hopeful.

"I'd like to know, too," came another voice, one none of them had ever heard before. They all turned to see a large, muscularly built man in his fifties standing just outside their group.

"Who are you?" Bray asked.

"You're Walter Brady," Mel said, his brows at a perceptive slant.

"I was just in the neighborhood—"

"Why didn't you come out when Win called you?" Pam asked pointedly.

"I've got my reasons. Most of them have to do with fear. I didn't want to mess up a good thing, and Win and I have a way of doing that sometimes. What's in the letter?"

"Oh, sure," Pam said, scanning the page. "It's from your niece, Bray—Teri."

"Why's she writing Ginger?" Mel asked.

Pam read: "Dear Ginger, I need to apologize to you. I need to apologize for a lot of things, but for right now I'm working on the ones that won't send me to jail. I tried to steal your fiancée. It's been heavy on my conscience. I know you were jealous. I wanted you to be, and I hate myself for it now. Women not only shouldn't do that to other women, but it was just plain wrong. But Win never once gave me the time of day. When I made a play for him, he told me how much he loved you and how he could never betray you. I know he meant it because at the time I had a gun. He loves you very much. I wanted you to know that. God bless you, and I hope we meet again someday. Teri Michelson (Sanderson)."

"She got married?" Pam exclaimed.

"If it's who I think it is, the guy saved my life," Bray added.

"Well," said Walter Brady, "At least Win's got his head screwed on right in that department."

"In many departments," Mel affirmed.

Walter smiled as if he really knew the truth. "Gotta be going. Say 'hi' to Win for me." He turned toward the road and gave a quick wave.

A moment later a chauffeured Cadillac pulled up. A few seconds after that with Walter Brady in the back seat, the Cadillac sped off toward Burlington.

"Strange duck," Mel said. But then he eyed the letter for a moment. "You know. I really feel left out. Usually I'm right in there pitchin' with you folks, but not this time. Here Bray comes to know the Lord, and these neat things are happening—" he indicated the letter—"and I had nothing to do with them. Absolutely nothing."

"Being Win's best buddy, I can see how you'd feel that way," Bray said with a certain condescension. "Come on, we'll go in and wait and fill you in on everything. Then at least you'll live an exciting life vicariously."

Mel turned to Pam. "Is he always like this?"

"Even more so," Pam admitted.

Mel pursed his lips with concern. "Then we'll have to remind him who's really in charge here. For Sunday service, until your legs heal up—you're an usher."

"This Christianity has a pretty steep downside to it," Bray sighed. "Real steep."

"It's a joke," Mel laughed, throwing a warm arm over his shoulder. "We'll go easy on you—this time."

News story appearing in the *St. Albans Independent*:

Clerical Error Sets Felon Free

ST. ALBANS—Warren "Wink" Brightstar, awaiting trial on suspicion of felony assault charges, was released yesterday from the county jail. Considered dangerous, Brightstar was supposed to have been kept in a security wing of the jail, but instead was called for a minimum security work detail—road cleanup. When last seen, Brightstar was wearing blue prison garb. If anyone has any information on his whereabouts, please contact the St. Albans police.

News story appearing in the *St. Albans Independent*:

Local Man Slain

ST. ALBANS—The body of Hank Petrelli, a mechanic at the service station on Hill and Brass, was discovered by Cameron Swiss when he came to open the station at 5:00 A.M. yesterday. It is conjectured that an assailant entered the garage and struck Petrelli with a blunt instrument, possibly a heavy wrench found at the scene. Petrelli died instantly. Petrelli leaves no family behind, his wife, Sylvia Petrelli, having died last month. Petrelli will be buried by the city, and no services will be held.

News story appearing the in the *St. Albans Independent*:

Brightstar Not So Bright

ST. ALBANS—Warren "Wink" Brightstar, escapee from the county jail, was apprehended last night and, without being asked, confessed to the slaying of Hank Petrelli last week. Although it's difficult to piece together the exact circumstances, it appears that Petrelli had recruited Brightstar and his brothers to commit the assault for which Brightstar and one of his brothers are currently being held. Even though Petrelli wore an ape suit when he originally spoke to the Brightstar brothers and was, thus, unrecognizable, Brightstar, when stopping for gas while a fugitive, recognized Petrelli's voice. Since two of his brothers died in the assault, Brightstar said he "wanted to even the score. Which I did—with a heavy wrench—to [Petrelli's] skull." Brightstar's attorney is already beginning to blame Brightstar's behavior on an alcoholic father who abused him before deserting the family when Brightstar was a year-and-a-half old.

ABOUT THE AUTHOR

Bill Kritlow was born in Gary, Indiana, and moved to northern California when he was nine. He now resides in southern California with his wife, Patricia. They have three daughters and five grandchildren. Bill is also a deacon at his church.

After spending twenty years in large-scale computing, Bill recently changed occupations so that he could spend most of his day writing—his first love. His hobbies include writing, golf, writing, traveling, and taking long walks to think about writing. *Blood Money* is the sequel to *Crimson Snow* and *Fire on the Lake*. Bill has also written *Driving Lessons* and the three-book Virtual Reality series: *A Race Against Time*, *The Deadly Maze*, and *Backfire*.